To Future

With m

Jemma

x

WHEN I CLOSE MY EYES

JEMMA WAYNE

lp

Legend Press Ltd, 51 Gower Street, London, WC1E 6HJ
info@legendpress.co.uk | www.legendpress.co.uk

 British Library Cataloguing in Publication Data available.

Print ISBN 978-1-80031-0-148
Ebook ISBN 978-1-80031-0-155
Set in Times. Printed by CPI Group (UK) Ltd, Croydon CR0 4YY

Jemma Wayne is the author of *After Before*, *Chains of Sand* and *To Dare*. She has been longlisted for the Women's Prize for Fiction and shortlisted for both *The Guardian*'s Not the Booker Prize and the Waverton Good Read Award.

Jemma's journalism has appeared in *The Spectator*, *The Telegraph*, *National Geographic*, *The Huffington Post*, *The Evening Standard*, *The Independent on Sunday*, *Red Magazine*, *The Jewish Chronicle* and *The Jewish News*, among others.

Born to an American musician father and English mother, Jemma grew up in Hertfordshire and lives in North London.

For my baby brother Joab, who is no longer a baby.

And Zubey, who knows why.

'Half of me is beautiful
but you were never sure which half.'

RUTH FELDMAN, 'LILITH'

PROLOGUE

And she is gone.

Into the waves, maybe.

Into the darkness, of course.

Into the recesses of the mind.

Yet. No sirens are blazing. No voices are being raised by willing volunteers, arms linked and flashlights waving, scouring ditches and alleys. And beaches. No friends, stricken-faced, clutching photographs to plaster onto lamp posts. No handing over of footage from security cameras that might have seen. No media analysis of glimpses and possibilities, or of loved ones left behind. No examination of conversations. No combing of notepads or receipts or scraps that might hint at something. Something. Anything.

Only. The sound of icy water lapping and crashing, pulling at the sand. Sent, as always, from the sky, from the wind, from the gods. Forced across the fortress depths. See the sea, they say. See the sea. But the sea sees nothing. It tells nothing. A dark, cold-hearted mass, spitting shadows onto the shore. Moving but silent – asleep. Oh yes, sparkling blue in the sunshine, pretending. Pretending pleasure, openness, freedom. But revealing nothing, really. Swallowing light beneath its surface. Hiding its demonic duplicity. Hiding her.

Because. She is gone.

As she was always going to be.

CHAPTER 1

There's a certain glow to the sand at this time of the morning. It's as though the ocean is waking it up, slowly teasing it into the day. Most of the time I stick to the cement path, but now and then a cyclist or roller skater appears in my way, and I weave onto the beach. My footprints tell me how fast I am going. If they are small, toe-tipped, then I am in good shape. If they sink into heavier folds, they are testament to a late night, or too large a dinner. The pier is my end point. From there it is still a 15-minute walk to my house, but I like the way that the lights, not yet flashing, and the signs, not yet singing, and the boards, not yet trodden, mark for me an ending. And a beginning too. Before they have begun. In a few hours, the pier will be packed with tourists. But for now, there is only me, here in my body, panting on empty, peeling wood, mind clear, looking out on paradise.

There is nowhere else like California. When I was a teen, there was a song that used the lyrics from a college commencement ceremony and one summer engulfed every radio station: it advised everybody to live in California once, but to leave before it made them soft. I loved that song, but I won't heed its advice. I don't plan on leaving LA ever. There are great benefits to a soft landing.

On the way up to my house, there is an alley I like to cut through, paved white and bordered by two expensive avenues. Often, lining the luxury, are the crumpled forms of men and women who find themselves outside it. Even more so than I once was. There are so many homeless people in LA that it is easy to grow desensitised, to stop noticing, or to perceive a 'problem' instead of a person. But there is one person I always see. Madge sits in front of her shopping trolley. It is adorned with an array of bin bags tied with coloured ribbon. Despite the shabbiness of black plastic, there is an air of organisation to her colour-coding, an impression of beauty from the bows. The first time we spoke, she told me about the Libbers movement in the 70s, the great fight of it, the unstoppable spirit of action. Now, at this time in the morning she is usually still tucked inside a tattered sleeping bag, her hair folded beneath a wool beanie with the arching logo of the Hollywood Bowl. She wears bright pink lipstick. Over the years, Madge has refused my attempts to help her find a shelter, or to give her a wad of cash big enough to matter, but she will accept a few bills here and there. I try to remember to run with them. Either way, she is always awake when I pass, even this early. She informs me if I myself am early, or late, and what the weather will be. There is a sense as she makes this pronouncement that she is the purveyor of a crystal ball, but there is no real skill to it; the weather will be fabulous.

I have written Madge many times into my notepad. She has a daughter somewhere, but I have been unable to prise from her the details of their parting, the path that led her to this. Still, I have imagined. In my invented guise, she will appear on the small screen in next week's episode of *Moles*.

Moles is my show. It still tickles me to describe it this way. When I am accepting prizes on stage, or talking to *Variety*, then it is business, and I operate without deeper implication. But when I say it inside my own head, that is when the shivers reach my soul, as though a wave has begun on the Thames in Marlow, built towards the estuary, and then surged forth across the Atlantic, all the way to these shores. Just as I have.

As a child, my family didn't do summer holidays abroad, so Octobers must have been when I got a taste for foreign places. Like that October, when I was 11, legs shooting upwards, skin luminously pale since England had been overcast since July. Money wasn't exactly an issue for us back then, but we weren't rolling in it, as my father would say, so English summers would do. Sometimes they were glorious, driven in my father's cab down to Brighton or Land's End, as good as the most exotic of beaches, save for the crowds and the gulls. In rain, we would stay in Marlow – a then-quaint town 30-odd miles from London, famous for rowing, and the regatta, and, according to my father, being the home of T. S. Eliot during the war. We would hibernate there with board games and hot chocolate, or drag on wellies to pull tomatoes at the allotment – glorious too. But pennies were saved for our annual October trip, our out-of-season sun, one last blast before the six-month chill. My parents were ahead of their time that way. Already conscientious global citizens, they recycled, and composted, and ate veggie, and invested in experiences, not stuff. Although we flew to Cyprus.

By then it had already been three years since the first incident. This time, it was sand, not glass, between my toes, but the grains felt like shards, piercing my skin with fear, and blackness, and hard, cold wind.

Even now, I do not like to display my wealth. After *Touching Heaven*, I could have moved up to the Hills, or into Malibu. I could have been neighbours with some of the faces that grace the covers of magazines. But Santa Monica suits me. Besides, compared to Marlow, I have already upgraded. I mean, none of the bathrooms in *this* house are located in an unheated, semi-attached shed that can only be reached from outside.

This kind of observation is apparently called 'acerbic wit', so says *The Hollywood Reporter*. Supposedly, it makes my writing 'acutely English, in a translatable, relatable way'; but it is only the truth. Who knew that to write it was some kind of genre? The truth is, my place now is at least five times the size of my parents' ex-council house, and I do not need more. In any case, in California, everything feels expansive. It is as though the soil knows that people here have come to dream life as far as possible, and the landscape is compelled to reflect that. There are vast valleys and immense hills and immeasurable stretches of ocean. Even my own front garden is bigger than our old patch of allotment. I do not, however, plant vegetables. Instead, there are fruit trees, and flowers in exotic flush, and most importantly, my ramp. To avoid annoying the neighbours, mostly I take my board to the skatepark, where there are tunnels, and proper halfpipes at the top of which I can trial my latest tricks, but I cherish this small offering on my lawn. It is a daily testament to who I am, now, to how brave I have become.

There is no point in wishing I had figured it out sooner. As a child, I could never have left home, even if it was to protect him. Or stopped myself doing what I did. So I couldn't have actually altered things, not then. But when I look back on that time, my stomach contracts with a darkness that is no longer with me. For so many years it haunted. And in the end, all it took was a decision. One decision.

Jade still visits me. Once a year, usually in the winter, she flies out from London where she now lives with her partner, and over Chinese food we reminisce about our university days at Sussex. Jade works for the Civil Service, helping make policy for the Department for Digital, Culture, Media and Sport. One year, I flew back over for a conference she had organised, gracing the stage as a guest speaker. We found it hard not to giggle when she introduced me. We giggle a lot together. Always did. In our final year, we shared a house along with three others, who we would generally hide from, squeezing into her bed on the top floor and passing popcorn while we watched the latest episode of *Big Brother*, claiming that we weren't addicted but interested in it for its anthropological merits. Sometimes, hands would explore beneath sheets, and tongues would follow. All sorts of things open up once convention is cast aside. I had always found Jade beautiful, and amazing. I still do.

Outside of my family, she is the only person who has made the leap with me, traversing from before, to now. At the beginning of our second year at Sussex, I switched from philosophy to English and cut ties with almost everyone who I'd known previously. And after my mother had left that awful, wonderful day, Jade was the only person I told what I'd decided: that I would never marry; never live with a partner; never, never have a child. From that day forth I would never spend the night in the same room as another soul. Instead, I would make sure I was alone, always, and locked in.

If I'd been locked in before that very first incident, aged eight, maybe everything would have been different from the start, less primed, perhaps, for disaster. Because the shredded glass was proof – evidence of a jagged edge slicing something undefinable within me. Not fatally, not dramatically, it was a slow puncture. But it was there. I had been in danger, and the stark physicality of it terrified me. The being there, the being present, in my skin, alone.

Although the second time, in Cyprus, I wasn't alone. There was Cassius.

* * *

We'd only known each other for a term, and barely. At the new high school, he wasn't even in my class, but I recognised him from corridors and the lunch hall. I've often wondered if we expressly notice the people we're supposed to bond with, pick them inexplicably from a crowd; or if the reverse is true, if we force connections with the people who exert intangible magnetic vigour. At the airport, we smiled at each other shyly. His father was lifting a matching set of hard suitcases from the conveyer belt, waving away Cassius's attempts to help. I had been allowed by mine to grab our ragtag collection of holdalls. I was thin, gangly – an impression that was exacerbated by the forever insulting bushiness of my hair – but still, I liked to believe I was strong. So, apparently, did my father. He stood back and let me haul our luggage onto a trolley manned by my mother. She was smiling at the adventure of it all, I remember this vividly – a lipsticked eagerness splashing itself across her face – but all three of us had already declared Paphos 'interesting'. While the airport itself was small and parochial, the military presence suggested inklings of worldly happenings I wasn't yet privy to. On the plane, my parents had given me a potted summary of the island's history, and now, politics rustled itself beneath my fingers, still grasping at too-big bags.

Cassius didn't look at me again after his father relegated him to hand luggage. They trundled through the arrivals hall and straight into a waiting car. We stood in the queue for taxis.

Our rental was on the beach, my father assured us as the taxi swerved onto another mountainous road. Small, run by the aunt of an old friend of his cousin, not fancy, but definitely on the beach. My mother and I peered dubiously out of the taxi window as our first hour of potential sun slipped by, but in the end he was right. The house was directly on the beach, a pretty garden giving way to a short row of steps leading down a rocky bank onto the shore. Not that we were allowed to laze in the sand all day. Mornings were for exploring. Up early, my father folded and unfolded his map, dragging us through markets and ruins and cliff walks. On the way back, we took to stopping at a stall teeming with vegetables, and we'd select tomatoes or cucumbers or olives, and pack these up with bread and halloumi cheese, then migrate down the steps of the old, crumbling house to the beach below. A little further up the strip there were sunbeds and parasols, but we lay on towels, welcoming the October sun, and set up camp for the afternoon. By four or five, a faint chill would lace the air, and the creep of autumn would bring in early night, but by then we were ready for showers and card games, and walks back out to the restaurants my father had worked hard on procuring recommendations to by locals who knew. Those meals remain etched in my memory. We slathered moisturiser onto burnt shoulders, and doused ourselves in citronella, and dressed up. My parents talked about books they'd read and films they wanted to see and events going on in the world, and asked for my opinion. My head felt full, my stomach too, my legs happily exhausted. I'm not sure why it happened again then. Contentment is not supposed to be a trigger.

"What are you doing?"

His voice cut through my confusion, though I remained disoriented, gasping, unable to catch a breath. Icy water whipped almost to my knees. The wind felt like knives against my cheeks.

His hand touched my arm.

* * *

Jade kept up her duty with locks for many months after my decision. Every night, just as she had done since I first begged her to, I would surrender the key to my room, and she'd lock it from the outside, returning only with the safety of morning light. But it wasn't long before we understood the unexpected miracle: as soon as I had decided properly, resolved to isolate myself long-term, found a way to make it work, then I stopped worrying. And as soon as I stopped worrying, it all stopped. The compulsions. The rituals... Everything. Almost completely. It all simply fell away. I had never imagined such a thing to be possible. It was unbelievable. Breathtaking. Breath-making. At last, I could breathe. One rule, fixing it all.

That summer, I went Interrailing with Jade around Europe, staying of course in separate rooms. We did a skydive in Portugal. In August, I went home for a month, and spent every day with my family, laughing and talking in a way we hadn't done in years. But I gave up my house key and stayed in a motel, paid for by a part-time job in a shop I had once stolen from. Although Cassius and I tried to meet, he spent most of the summer with a new girlfriend in Italy, and I think both of us were relieved by that. While I still daydreamed sometimes of his arms around me, in my veins I knew that he had been too close. He had seen too much. I didn't want his knowing text messages. I didn't want his watchful looks. Just thinking of him reminded me of all the things I had done, of all the lies and sins I had committed, of all the ways I had lived up to the demonic name of Lilith. It was easier to cut the cord. To release him. To release myself.

I haven't spoken to Cassius now in over ten years. Whenever my mind wanders towards this, I feel a deep pang of guilt. Because I may have been screwed up back then, but so was he. He had told me as much that night when I visited him in Bristol, he had laid it out straight – how tough things were. A plea. *Spiralling* is what he'd emoted. And I was supposed to support him. *Tease. Goad. Challenge. Confess.* I was supposed to shore him up. Instead, I'd disappeared.

For a few years after university there were emails, but we never really said anything in them. There were sentences full of unasked questions, and gaps where truth should have been. I left him with memories only, to hold as he always had. While I, in my new skin, took my presence elsewhere.

My mother ran into his mother a few Christmases ago on a shopping trip in London, and reported back that she looked well, and that she'd said Cassius was too, but Marianne had never really known anything about her son. That afternoon, I'd opened my laptop and set about to google him, but in the end I stopped myself. Instead, I grabbed my trainers, and my skateboard, and strode outside into the California air.

The weather today is conventionally warm. There is a table read on the lot, so after my shower, I slip into a silk cami and a pair of tailored shorts. My legs still won't tan, but I have learnt to embrace their paleness. I leave my hair loose, emboldening the red with a curl-specific mousse and selecting a lipstick to match. A strong lip is what they call it. My complexion doesn't need much cover – these days I like the freckles to show through – and I can never be fussed with anything heavy around the eye, but I enjoy a strong lip. Especially when I am the person who will be leading the talking. On my first show, I wrote only, but on the next I assistant directed too. Now I hold the director's credit on my own and am also a producer. I do not wear a bra. There isn't time for breakfast, but a runner will fetch my usual superfood smoothie.

At the studio, Patrick is waiting for me. He isn't a part of *Moles* but has a show on the other side of the lot. Patrick doesn't write – he is the money, the team, the behind-the-scenes, but hands-on. He loves to be hands-on. He told me this with a smile the night he first put his hands on me.

"You're early," I say, kissing him on the lips and leaving a streak of red.

"You're late."

I nod. "Madge told me that already."

He hands me a paper bag containing a smoked salmon and avocado bagel, toasted – my favourite. Then slides his aviators back onto his nose. His hair is dark and softly waved. There is a slight dent from where the glasses have been sitting.

"You're going to put the runner out of a job."

"I left him the smoothie." Patrick grins. "Tell him to remember the chia seeds this time."

"You think you know me so well," I say, smirking.

Patrick begins to walk backwards towards his golf buggy. "Still on for lunch today?"

"Yep. So long as this read doesn't go over."

"Usual place?"

"Usual place."

He clicks his fingers in a jokey 'see ya there' kind of gesture, then swings himself into his buggy. A number of the execs drive buggies around the lot, or are driven, but Patrick takes the wheel with an air of comedy. Really, he's too tall for it and has to curl himself over so as not to hit his head, his knees bunched up in front of the steering wheel. He refuses, however, to resort to the car. Even though it's electric, it doesn't feel environmentally conscious, he says. And the lot is too big for walking. He has decorated the inside of his buggy with graffiti, not his own. They are stickers he's had made up from work he's collected. We spent a week the previous autumn in Tel Aviv, and Patrick was in heaven for street art. I was in heaven for the domes, and the cobbled streets, and the weathered faces, and the beautiful, uniformed teenagers slinging rifles, and the feeling inside me that this was a place of urgency and passion and tragedy and conflict, and made me want to write. Which I did. I used some of those notes for a scene in *Moles*.

The whole cast is waiting for me when I stride in, placing the bagel next to my pad, signalling to the runner. There are two A-list women fronting the on-screen line-up, plus an array of female production staff. We were written up in *Variety* last season as a model of post #MeToo progress, but we have worked together on various projects for years. I decided almost a decade ago to go back to my parents' feminist accounting of my name, and its destiny: powerful woman; not demon.

"Lilith, wonderful, are we ready everyone?" the production manager begins. "Lilith, any notes before we start?"

"A few." I nod and open my laptop.

Faces turn towards me. Pens lift to annotate scripts that I have written. My neck straightens and red curls tumble forwards. I smile.

I never grow weary of or used to this feeling: the magnificence of confidence, the freedom, the control. There were so many years, I suppose, of the opposite.

When I allow myself, which is rarely, I can still feel the contours of the girl that I was. I remember one particular Christmas, in our final year of school, sitting with Cassius and some friends in a pub somewhere. A shapeless jumper swamped my maturing frame, my face was smothered in foundation, my hair scratched into a bun. Most of us were still 17 then, but there were a few 18-year-olds who bought alcohol for the rest. By midway through the evening, the usual gaggle of blow-dried, tiny-skirted girls were tipsy on Baileys and fruit schnapps. From the corner, I sipped at lemonade. Until one of the girls, Jenny, turned to me.

"What's your problem with drinking?" she laughed loudly. Loudly enough to commandeer the attention of the group.

I shrugged. "I don't have a problem with it. I just don't like it."

"But what do you think's going to happen?" she pressed. "You're not going to suddenly become a wild child, you know. You can stay… you."

The disdain with which she pronounced this final word was not missed by anyone. Across the table, Cassius was looking at me intently. He knew exactly why I didn't drink. Because I'd read that alcohol could be a trigger.

"Thanks for the permission," I'd attempted to joke – an image of blood, and a knife, rushing through my head – but Jenny didn't appreciate the humour.

"You're so weird," she shot. Not quite in anger, not quite with malice, we were friends, after all, but with enough contempt to create a few nervous laughs, an awkward hush.

"Kinda weird you caring what Lil does," Cassius piped up suddenly. "Why is that?"

Now, all eyes turned to Jenny. "I don't care."

"You seem to."

"No, I don't. She can do whatever the hell she wants."

"Good to hear." Cassius nodded pointedly.

"Thanks for the permission, again," I told her. And safe within Cassius's popularity, this time, she pretended to find humour in my sarcasm. And everybody else left me alone.

Patrick does not like time alone, but he refuses to surf with me. He is athletic – in his garden is a tennis court and a basketball net, at the weekends he abseils and rides motorbikes, in college he played American football and now coaches a team of disadvantaged kids – but he has a phobia about the ocean. When he was a child, he almost drowned once, caught in a rip tide that yanked him beneath waves. The night that he told me about this was one of the first times I felt myself falling for him seriously, but in typical fashion, Patrick does not like to dwell on it, and pretends it is not a big thing. I prod him to the contrary, but not too hard. I know the value of protecting closed wounds. Besides, he evidences his alright-ness by regularly showing off his prowess in a swimming pool, even tolerating boat rides if they can be accessed from paving or wood; it is only the beach he shies away from, he will simply not step onto the sand. It is a shame in LA. I plan to go to the beach after lunch.

"Come back to mine after then," he says.

The waiter leans across us to fill our water glasses. It took me a long time to learn how to order water in America. If you say 'war-ter' with an English pronunciation, you are not understood. If you ask with a Californian drawl, 'wadder', they'll bring you an expensive bottle. If you want a jug of tap water, you have to ask for 'iced wadder'. If you don't want it to freeze your throat, you have to ask for 'iced wadder, no ice'. I take a sip. "Come with me. I'll lend you a board."

The waiter places our salads before us. They are gigantic and impossible to finish, but insanely good. People queue for hours to get a table here. Patrick phoned ahead.

"I'll take a board… game. What's that one you like?"

"Boggle."

"We can play *Boggle*." He says 'Boggle' with an attempt at an English accent and takes a forkful of salad. My accent has relaxed over the years, peppered now with uncertain vowels that sometimes stretch and sometimes contract abruptly, often within the same word; but like all Americans, Patrick enjoys this imitation. "Then we can sushi it up, and you can stay over."

I raise my eyebrows. Patrick knows that I will not stay over. And that he cannot stay at mine. My rule remains. It has been 17 years and there have been many times now that I've wanted to bin it. Years ago, in Turkey, with Emir. Last Christmas back in Marlow. Often with Patrick. I genuinely don't believe there to be a danger any more. It doesn't worry me. But there is always that niggle, that small question, that perhaps it is this rule that keeps me free.

"I'll come for a bit," I promise him.

"Oh, 'a bit'," he teases, English again.

Under the table, he strokes my leg with his foot. I know that beneath his jeans there will be a brightly coloured pair of socks that do not match. It is not a mistake; he separates matching pairs and balls them up this way. Patrick is not my boyfriend, officially. I won't call him that. But we have been together for almost four years. He makes me laugh, often. He is kind. He is adventurous. He is interesting. The sex is fabulous.

After lunch, after more rehearsals at the studio, after the beach, after dinner, after Patrick, I finally return home. I am wiped. It is only 10 p.m., but my day started at five. I leave my board in the back of my truck and trudge heavily up the pathway.

The street is gated, but I still keep my keys at the ready, especially at night. Two years living Downtown will do that to you. On the news, there are stories every day about gang warfare gone wrong, normal civilians caught in the crossfire. Or burglaries. Or stalkings, particularly here where there are so many celebrities to stalk. I am not a celebrity, not by face, and I try not to give these reports much sway, but you can't help hearing them. When a figure moves out of the shadows on my porch, therefore, I jump.

"No, wait. It's me," the man says, stepping further into the light.

I examine the face, foreign but familiar.

I recognise the posture.

The man runs his hand through his hair.

"Oh my God," I breathe. "Cassius."

CHAPTER 2

Cassius passed me the sweets. They were in a bag with scrawling Greek script, a colourful mix, almost like Fruit Pastilles but harder, the kind my mother would tell me would rot my teeth. We were halfway between my beach and his posh-parasolled section of it, perched together on his jacket to avoid the burn of heated sand.

"You don't have to answer," he said, brushing his floppy fringe off his forehead. I liked this look – 'curtains' we called it then, long hair drawn either side of the eyes, windows, as they were, to the soul. The back of his head was shaved. He was already tanned, making his green eyes seem brighter, the blonde an added brushstroke as if to demonstrate the abundance of his beauty. He was shorter than me then, but I was tall. We wouldn't be able to dance together.

"It's OK, I don't mind." I took another cherry-flavoured sweet and leant back on my elbows. I had worn a T-shirt on top of my bikini to meet him. It didn't bother me, but I wasn't yet what you would call 'developed', and I never tanned anyway. My curls were constricted in a bun on top of my head. "It's no big deal. So no, not really."

"Seriously? You weren't scared at all?" He peered out at me from behind his blinds. "I would have been. It's pretty intense."

I shrugged.

"Oh, come on. You're not one of those people who can't admit they have feelings, are you?" he jibed.

"Um, no. My mother's a relationship counsellor."

"Oh, OK, you're just the type who cares if people think you're cool then? Didn't realise. You seem pretty confident at school. But that's fine. So long as I know."

I took my time sucking on my sweet. It was a trick I'd learnt from my mother – that sometimes silence was the best response, the fastest way to exact more from others. Although, Cassius was the kind of guy who didn't need to be guarded anyway, who could afford frankness. I'd seen him at school, gliding effortlessly from group to group, like a bee pollinating. Everybody liked him. Which was fascinating to me, because I never felt like that. Despite having friends, I always felt on the periphery. Despite knowing my mind, in groups I didn't like to express it. Because I was shy, people found me stand-offish. I wasn't disliked, but never quite at the centre of things.

"Well, *I* was scared. You know, to be on the beach that late in the dark. And I had a torch. I think I wanted to scare my parents actually, that's why I went out. But they still weren't back when I got to the room. Theirs interconnects with mine, so I heard them come in around three. They're not even up yet."

He didn't need to be guarded, but this was more rawness than I'd been expecting. "That's a bit lonely for you," I said softly.

He shrugged. "It's fine. I'm meant to be in the kids' club. There's kayaking today."

"Oh. Sorry you're missing it."

"Lily, do I seem like somebody who likes kayaking?"

I looked now straight at his bare chest. He wasn't scrawny like me, but certainly not as muscular as some of the boys on the sports teams.

"It's not Lily actually, really," I stated.

"What?"

"I just don't like Lilith."

He laughed and sat forward. "Lilith? Like the one on *Cheers*?"

"Supposedly it's a strong-woman, feminist thing," I

reproached, turning sideways a little to emphasise my Streisand-esque profile. “Apparently it’s empowering. The unwritten temptress of the bible, or something. But I think it sounds like some kind of vampire, or a 90-year-old woman.”

“You are definitely not a 90-year-old woman,” he pronounced, and though he didn’t move his eyes from my face, I had the sensation of him taking in the rest of me. Redness and whiteness and bones jutting everywhere.

“Don’t tell anyone at school,” I instructed.

He laughed again and lay down, running sand between his fingers. “I won’t.”

There was a lull then in the conversation, and we watched the waves lap against the sand. Land’s End had never felt quite like this.

“Do you want to go in the water?” he asked eventually.

I shook my head. “I’m only meant to be half an hour.”

“Oh. OK, cool.”

“You can hang out with us though, if you want. I mean, if your parents won’t mind.”

“I doubt that my parents would mind,” he laughed. “Or maybe even notice.” He ran his hand again through his hair, a gesture he seemed to employ frequently, like an unconscious habit, or an intentional full stop. Then, laying his cheek against the sand, he covered his eyes as though to shield them from the sun. Or from his own vulnerability. I didn’t know any other boys my age who spoke like this, without that infuriating façade of machismo. He was beautiful, I noticed then.

For a few seconds, I let him lie there, both of us, I imagined, drinking in the openness we had so casually shared, unprecedented at least for me. But soon I shook myself. “Don’t go to sleep then,” I teased him.

Now Cassius grinned, rolling over with boyish vim, and together we jumped up, shaking out his jacket between us. I nodded in the direction of my parents. In the distance, I could make out my father’s bright red swim trunks. He was standing in the sea, face turned towards us. He had probably been watching me the whole time. Cassius linked his arm through mine. I wasn't sure what to do with my dangling hand, or with this boy, this new appendage, but I left our arms connected.

As we kicked through the sand towards my father, who would later ask me myriad questions about Cassius, it occurred to me that although I would tell him a lot, and although until now we had shared almost everything, there was all of a sudden something my father didn't know about me: the strange sensation I felt when Cassius's hand touched mine. He didn't know either that Cassius had been out wandering in the middle of the night, and he didn't know about my own nocturnal trip to the sea. And, I realised, I wouldn't reveal those things. But Cassius, who knew barely anything, knew them already.

* * *

When I properly got to know Cassius in the months that followed, it turned out that he was an ingénu. Not in the way I heard my parents talk about preyed-upon young actresses, because Cassius was anything but guileless. But in the sense that he seemed so vulnerable, so willing to be exposed, and this had the effect of drawing people towards him. Just to watch, to look at his unsullied virility.

Almost nine months since Cyprus, we had both been cast in our year's summer production of *Wind in the Willows*. Of course he was Toad. My part amounted to three lines and a great deal of walking around the stage in various animal get-ups, but to me, this was still a triumph. On stage, I felt free in a way that I didn't in normal life – free to exist outside of myself. Present but absent. A delicious out-of-body experience, wrapped in face paint and costume. Although, without Cassius, I wouldn't have auditioned at all. The theatre had always captured something inside me – not just theatre, but films, TV, poetry, novels, anything that told a story and made me feel. A *vivid imagination* is what countless report cards had informed my parents, who didn't need informing, frequent recipients as they were of stapled-together 'books' or impromptu one-woman productions staged on the living-room floor. For them I would dance, face full of music, legs and arms and torso bending and stretching in their mission to emote. For them I would sing, with belt and twang, horrendously off-pitch, but it didn't matter because, oh, how I felt. But at school, I had never auditioned for choir, or joined the dance club, or put myself forward for a play, until that one. Cassius was the opposite. He lived for performance. Sometimes, even when we were alone, I felt he was performing. Although at the same time, it didn't feel like performance, it felt true. He dragged me along with him.

Afterwards, the school magazine had written about the bravery of his Toad, courageous in its vulnerability. The other lead was Sasha, playing Badger. The term before, she'd been Titania in the whole-school Shakespeare production, an unheard-of feat for a first year; but the magazine hadn't said anything like that about her. She had cried on stage as Titania. I could never imagine crying on stage, in public. Even in costume. But apparently it was only brave when a boy showed feeling.

"You have been so brainwashed by your parents," laughed Cassius, the day after the show had ended, throwing a pillow at me across the bed on which we were sprawled. "Maybe I'm just better than Sasha."

"Incorrect. It's a gender thing," I maintained, tossing the pillow back and moving to the floor. "Definitely." It was a Friday afternoon, the last day of term. We were in my bedroom and had the magazine open between us. My mother was due to give birth in two weeks.

"I cried on stage too, you know."

"I know."

"So you think she cried better?"

I mulled this. "I think you cried equally well. The point is that nobody thought it a big deal for her to do it."

"Equally well." He turned the words over in his mouth, and his shoulders sank a little. There it was – the sudden openness, the crowd-pleasing vulnerability, the raw edge of his emerging masculinity. All the more unguarded when with me. But this was our shtick: tease; goad; challenge; coax; confess. Know when to pull apart or shore up. Do both with honesty.

"You were really good." I softened. "Everybody thought so."

"You know, Lil, I think this is what I want to do."

He swung his legs over the bed and joined me on the floor, flipping through CDs.

"What?" I asked. "Act?"

"Yeah. Do you think I could? Like, really?"

Cassius had only fully committed himself to drama that term. Before that, I'd watched as he floated from the debate team to the entrepreneurs' club, to badminton squad, and to the group of stand-arounds who literally stood around, not joining in anything. He made it seem easy, this flitting, this mesmerising of the masses; whereas it took me years to feel properly comfortable with anyone. Except with Cassius of course, with whom, having started from such a state of exposure, everything had spilled out in an instant. Or maybe Cassius would always have drawn it out of me.

I put my hand on his arm, used now to such things as the touch of his skin. "I do think you could."

He smiled. "Really?"

"Really."

"And you can write me a script. I'll be your muse."

"You can be my a-muse," I teased. "You can entertain me. Distract me. You can be my court jester."

"Why do you need distraction?"

Of course, I'd wanted him to notice, that's why I'd said it. Confessed. But I was always struck by how perceptive he was.

"It happened again, didn't it?"

I nodded.

"Where?"

"In the kitchen."

"Doing what?"

"Nothing. Nothing bad anyway. Just standing there. In the middle of the room." I picked a CD from its case and avoided his eyes. "Holding a strawberry."

He laughed. "What?"

"I know. Just a single strawberry."

He laughed again, stood and pulled me up by my arm. "Got any strawberries now?" he asked. Distracting. Jesting. "I'm starving. Can I stay for dinner?"

Now I looked at him. This is why I'd wanted to tell him. For him to make it light-licked, and not seeped in darkness.

CHAPTER 3

It is as though I am standing again in icy water. Frozen in body, frozen in time. Nothing about him has changed. He is older, of course. A fine whisper of grey speckles the front of his hair, grown now to a sensible, adult length. There are the first signs of tracks around his eyes, where he has laughed, or cried, or acted either. The last time I saw his face was on the flyer for a fringe production of a new comedy. I was in Vietnam by the time it opened, and didn't go, but I read an online review from a local paper. The show was a flop, but they said Cassius was the best thing in it. He has been the best thing in a lot of things. For a long time, he was the best thing for me.

"Cassius," I declare, as though he might also need confirmation of it – his presence, his being. Here on my porch.

"Lilith Fidel," he says softly.

In the depths of my stomach, there is an old high-school sensation of having been caught doing something wrong, found in a place I shouldn't be. But I am allowed here. And so is he. I move to hug him. Before I can, however, he puts out his arm, and a small child creeps out from behind the porch swing into it. He lifts her up onto his hip.

"My daughter," Cassius tells me. "Lilith, meet Jessie."

Jessie looks impossibly similar to her father. She is all blondeness and brightness, with eyes that see everything. But in this first instance, she is not what I am seeing at all. Not at all. As the child turns her face towards me, in a flash, all I can see is Dylan.

* * *

I knew exactly when my baby brother had been conceived. I had counted backwards: in Cyprus. In the master bed of the beautiful, crumbling rental, right on the beach. In the moments when I was alone and frozen and frightened, or maybe when I was with Cassius, or after that, after I had stood nearby, but not woken my parents, not crawled between their chests.

In the first weeks after Dylan was born, however, there were no incidents. And I didn't see Cassius. In the evenings now, I stayed awake to stare at my brother. Cassius was abroad for most of July and August, and he asked me over the phone if it wasn't boring sitting there with a baby all day, but I could have gazed at Dylan for months without moving. I liked to watch his tiny fingers clasp and release and instinctively wrap themselves around things. I liked to watch his miniature nostrils flare, and his chest move almost imperceptibly up and down. I liked the smell of his skin and the sticking-up tufts of brown hair, not red like mine, and the way that it looked like he was smiling when he farted. Nobody had prepared me for this, for the elemental intensity of this bond of blood. Words I'd never properly understood before tumbled through my head. Here my brother was: flesh of my flesh.

At his circumcision, which was late because of his jaundice, I stood with my mother outside the door to our lounge, unable to witness the dreaded moment when harm would be done to my brother's perfect form. I had expected my progressive parents to shun this medieval ritual, but they clung to it. "Find me a Jewish man who wishes he wasn't circumcised," my father instructed me. And – to no avail – I tried, interviewing all the friends who had driven up from London for the occasion, since nobody Jewish lived in Marlow. "Just like a Lilith," one somehow-related relative commented. "Always trying to make men deviate from the proscribed way." I didn't understand this reference but, even amid my anxiety, took some pride in it.

I couldn't watch. I couldn't listen uselessly to Dylan's cries either, and in the end, with his screams full in my ears, I pushed past the room of praying, circumcised men, with the resolution to scoop him up and away, or, at least, to somehow bear witness. But when I reached the front, it hadn't even begun. Taking in my furious face, my father ushered me towards him, and I stood behind his shoulder while his own father held Dylan still on a pillow on his lap and I slipped my finger into my brother's clasping hand. The mohel told me to take my finger, dip it into the outstretched cup, and give Dylan a drop of wine. While he sucked on my alcohol-coated skin, the mohel's practised knife came out, and Dylan barely made a sound.

Nestled a few minutes later against my mother's breast, double-nappied for extra padding, clothes returned, blanket wrapped, Dylan was perfect again. I lay upstairs with him and my mother while the celebrations continued below. Occasionally, my mother would send me downstairs for a plate of bagels and fish balls, and through the air would waft salmon strips of conversation. Sometimes I would be stopped and enquired after: how was school, what was I interested in these days, where on earth did I get my hair and my height? I answered politely, but nevertheless returned to Dylan as fast as I could. I sensed that day that, as well as my mother's milk, he needed my hand on his foot, my breath on his back.

One lunchtime, a week before the new school year began, Cassius finally returned from Italy and turned up with a present that he said was from his mother.

"Thank you, Cassius," said my own mother. "That was very thoughtful. Come, do you want a hold?" Without waiting for a response, she placed Dylan into his arms and gave his shoulders a squeeze.

For a moment, Cassius simply held tight, a stunned expression spreading across his face as though an unfathomable creature had been thrust upon him. Something alien and alarming. I sensed his unease, and apologetic on my mother's behalf, I began to lean forward to lift Dylan away, but Cassius clung on. And then suddenly, he laughed. He looked at me with a manic glee in his eyes, and then he looked at my mother, and he laughed.

"We've missed you round here," Mum told him.

* * *

"Come in," I tell them now.

Jet-lagged, Jessie settles quickly into cartoons on the couch. I say couch these days, not sofa. Though in front of Cassius I get suddenly confused. He and I sit at the island in my kitchen and, despite the hour, drink coffee, strong. Neither of us knows quite where to begin, or how to be. The last time I saw him in person was in Bristol. After that, I went straight from Sussex to a gap year travelling, paid for with the prize money from my Edinburgh play, and then headed to LA to start film school. He'd sent congratulations by email, and I had replied. But when I'd gone home for Christmas, and then in Easter for a relative's wedding, and the following year for my parents' 25th wedding anniversary, I hadn't got in touch. Now he is here, with a child.

"She's three," he tells me.

"She's lovely."

He nods. "She is. Jessie's amazing."

We both sip our coffee, stepping carefully. On my part, glee and astonishment mingle with guilt.

"So are you here on holiday?" I inquire, feeling immediately silly, as though I am in a salon making chit-chat with a new hairdresser and not somebody who once understood the innermost nuances of my soul.

"Yes. Sort of," he says. "We're on a bit of a trip, Jessie and I."

"Oh?"

"Yeah, you see, her mother, my wife… well, she passed away a few months ago. We're having an escape."

"Oh my God," I say. "Cassius, no. I'm so sorry. I had no idea. I mean, obviously. Sorry. I mean I had no idea that you were even married or had a… For Jessie too, that's awful. She's three?"

"Cancer," he says.

"Cassius." I place my hand on his arm. Despite everything, it feels natural. "I'm just so sorry," I say again. "Sorry, that's useless. I don't know what to say. How long did she have it?"

"It was quick," he nods, "at least. Or I don't know if I should say 'at least'. Less suffering. More shock and awe. Bowel."

"Like your mother," I say.

He lifts his eyebrows at me. "You remember that?"

"Of course."

"Of course. Yes. Same. But with my wife it had spread."

"What was her name?" I ask him. "Your wife?"

"Serena."

"Serena. What was she like?"

"She was… She…" He pauses and runs a hand through his hair. The gesture sends a million moments rushing through me. "Sorry. You know, I'm not sure I can talk about her actually. Not yet."

"No. Of course." Awkwardly, I remove my hand from his arm and look over to the couch in the adjoining room. "What about Jessie? How's she coping?"

"It's all a bit surreal still, I think," Cassius answers. "She misses her of course. But she talks about her as if she's still here, just on holiday or something. Or like she only saw her last week. It's been three months now. So."

I give him a look of sympathy.

"The therapist said not to correct her. Let her have her process. But. I don't know. I thought maybe if we went away, had a holiday, it would change things up for her, you know? Reset to a new normal. It's stupid probably. I mean I know that a holiday won't fix things."

"It's not stupid. Quality time with her dad. Some fun. Some sun. Change of scene. A new beginning. Sounds exactly right to me," I say. "And for you too. You must need a break. You always did love LA."

"Yes." He pauses. "Well. And I knew you were here."

He says this pointedly. For a moment we look at each other and don't speak.

"I'm sorry," I say finally. "For back then. I didn't mean to disappear on you. I mean, I did. For me. I planned it for me. I had to. But I didn't mean to abandon you."

Suddenly, Cassius gets up and shrugs. "Water under the bridge." And despite the passing of time, there is the old light in his eyes, the old magnetism. "I should get Jessie back to the hotel. I didn't mean to come here so late. We just arrived this evening. But it felt… I don't know, this is where I wanted to come. This is where I was flying to, I think, if I'm honest."

"Cassius," I say, touching his arm again.

"Silly, isn't it?" he laughs.

"No."

We stand in silence for another moment. In the next room, Jessie laughs at something on the screen.

"Come on, Jessie," Cassius calls, and fishes into his pocket for his phone. "Thank goodness for Uber." He pauses. "Not that your dad agrees, probably. Nightmare getting around otherwise."

"I can drive you," I offer. "Where's your hotel?"

He shakes his head and holds up his phone. "It's booked. It's late. I shouldn't have come so late. You probably have a million things to do. Or want to go to bed. Or…"

"What?"

"Are you married?" he asks suddenly. "Your mum gave me your address, but she didn't say."

"My mother knew you were coming and didn't tell me?"

"She was excited for the surprise. You'd better call her." He winks. "Come on, Lil, you know she always loved me."

"She did," I laugh.

"So?"

"So what?"

He rolls his eyes. "So?"

"Oh." I catch on a little slowly. "Oh, no, I'm not married."

He nods, taking this in. "Boyfriend?"

I hesitate. Patrick is not my boyfriend, but… "Kind of."

He nods again. Not in flirtation, not in satisfaction, but as if…

"Jessie," he calls again into the next room.

Reluctantly, Jessie trudges into the kitchen. "Can't we stay here?" she asks him.

"No, sweetheart." He hangs his arm heavily around her shoulders and she nestles her head into his leg. Cassius's father never draped his arm around Cassius. Nobody ever called him sweetheart. Outside, there is a beep of a car horn. Cassius looks at his phone. "Amir is ready for us," he pronounces to his daughter.

Grudgingly, Jessie rolls her head backwards and stamps towards the door. As Cassius opens it, hand in hand, they turn simultaneously back to me. I never knew Cassius at Jessie's age, but her aura feels like him. On the tips of their tongues, they each seem to have a question.

"Can I come back?" Jessie asks first. "I like your house."

"Of course." I smile at her. Then I look to Cassius. "You can come back too. Or maybe we can meet somewhere? Tomorrow? How about Santa Monica Pier?"

"You're not working?" he worries.

"I can take the afternoon off. I'm kind of the boss there."

He beams. "Just as I would have expected."

"It's good to see you, Cass," I say, and I lean forward to kiss his cheek. When I do, the scent of him grips my stomach.

* * *

We hadn't seen each other for almost two months. When he finally handed Dylan back to my mother, the two of us went up to my room, and before anything else, Cassius told me how lucky I was to have a brother. Readily, I agreed. I was eager to describe it for him – just how lucky it made me – and detail all the other life-changing feelings and practicalities that Dylan's arrival had spawned. I felt worldly-wise that summer and had been storing up anecdotes to tell him. After a while, however – when, for example, I tried to show him the poem I'd written about Dylan – Cassius seemed suddenly to grow disinterested, resentful even. "He's a baby, Lil," he told me. "How much poetry can that inspire? Today, today there was a burp. Total Shakespeare."

Cassius had grown over the summer and was finally taller than I was. The oldest in the year, he was turning 13 the following week. Tanned again, he wore long-sleeved linen rolled up to the elbow, conjuring his time on the Riviera, and flicked distractedly through the novel on my bedside table.

"So… how was Italy?" I asked him, returning my Dylan poem to my desk.

"I dunno. Fabulous," he said.

"Was it like *A Room with a View*?" This was a book of my mother's, too grown-up for me, but which I'd read, and not understood, and then insisted Cassius and I watch the film of.

"Hmm, well, let's see," he began, running a hand through sun-streaked hair, still, I could tell, a little offish, but relenting. "My dad played golf, and Mum sunbathed and drank cocktails, and they pretended to be on honeymoon to get their room upgraded. Then they checked me in separately, so my room ended up being on another floor."

"Oh," I said, sympathy rising as it always did when Cassius talked about his family.

He shrugged. "One lunchtime a waiter was a bit rude to my dad, so he dropped a piece of glass into his meal and got the waiter fired. That was fun. Oh, and they both preferred the adult-only pool, so usually we just met for dinner."

"Cass…" I said, reaching for his arm, but he shrugged

again. I would have to coax it out of him – his obvious hurt, the wounds he was laying out for me to heal.

"No biggie," he said. "Mainly I read by the family pool. It was really hot though. Oh, and I kissed a girl."

"What?" Abruptly, my stomach contracted. I should of course have asked about his parents, I should have done my job as a friend – shore up, support – but I couldn't. Not in that moment. In that moment I could barely even breathe. "What girl?" I stumbled.

"She was from Morocco. She's older than us."

"Oh yeah?"

Neither of us had kissed anybody before that. We'd talked about it. And there'd been opportunities. But we'd agreed that the parties where some of our friends pulled five different people in a night were disgusting, and immature. Instead, we'd watched movies, and read aloud poems that we'd written in private journals, and told each other things that nobody else knew. More intimate than kissing.

"Is she your girlfriend now then?" I asked him awkwardly, a gulf suddenly between us.

Cassius guffawed. "She lives in Morocco."

"Well, I don't know." Uneasily, I sat on the bed next to him. He'd put down the novel but was fiddling with my lava lamp and wouldn't turn to face me. "What's her name?" I cajoled.

"Carmella."

"How old is she?"

"Fourteen."

"How old did she think you were?"

Cassius turned now, and grinned. "Fourteen too."

I whacked him on the arm. "Cassius."

"Lilith," he mimicked, in the same scalding tone. And then, "I'd rather have kissed you."

It was the obvious thing. Of course it was the obvious thing. We'd been building up to it for almost a year and there'd been something between us right from the beginning. Something. A spark. A lightning bolt, separate from wind and waves. Yet it took me off guard. I wasn't ready. He'd said it, he'd hoisted it between us, and I wasn't ready.

It's possible that if it wasn't for Dylan, I might have been. I might have been looking out, looking ahead, feeling the right things. But these were Dylan days. They were wrapped in cellular blankets and vests over heads, cries and hiccups. They drew me in, and backwards. I had no interest that summer in friends or parties or other things on the cusp. I had returned to activities like colouring in. And my ragged stuffed toys. I had even stopped swearing. It was only that year that I had begun to try out such words, scrawling them daringly into my journal, but now I discarded them. I wanted everything around Dylan to be unsullied, wholesome. And I wanted to be innocent again too, pure, young. Like him. For him.

"So? Shall we try it?" Cassius smiled.

"Try what?"

"Shall we kiss?"

There wasn't a way to move away. Not without embarrassing him. Not without hurting his pride. My body was there, present. And his body moved closer.

His lips pressed against mine. His tongue tried to push inside my mouth. I resisted an urge to vomit. Outside of my body, my mind floated, perceiving the two of us as if from far away, observing, racing.

This is Cassius, I told myself. *This is Cassius*. Hadn't I imagined this? Hadn't I wanted this one day?

How awkward my arms looked. How hot his tongue was. How uncomfortable the angle of my neck.

Cassius pulled back and looked at me thoughtfully. "Interesting," he said.

"What?"

"Nothing."

"What?"

He shook his head. Then kissed me again. His hair was longer at the back now to match the floppy front, and reaching for my hand, he placed my palm within it. Awkwardly, I left it there. The strands felt slightly crispy, the result of too much gel. I wondered if I was supposed to run my fingers through it, like he always did, or stroke his scalp, but I didn't ask him. I should have. I should have made a joke about it, or confessed to him the truth – that I didn't want to kiss him. But I said nothing. And then I said almost nothing for another half an hour as we sat clumsily. Uncomfortably present. My body. And his. He smelled of fresh laundry, and something new, sharper. He didn't ask to stay for dinner.

Dylan smelled of purity.

Scooped into my neck, I breathed him in.

* * *

Cassius eyes me now curiously. "It's good to see you too, Lilith Fidel," he says. "You are a good person."

CHAPTER 4

Cassius lived in the pink house. Everybody knew it. Not specifically that Cassius lived there, of course, but the house. It sat alone at the crest of the hill in the middle of a ten-acre plot, and if you walked through the woods at bluebell time, or lay flat amidst the cobalt shroud, it rose up like a distant beacon. Even from the main road many metres below, it could be glimpsed through the trees, and like everybody else, we glimpsed it. We used to speak of it as though it must be occupied by a lord or a lady, or a celebrity at least. But Cassius's parents turned out to be bankers who spent most of their time not in their palace atop a hill, but either in London or New York, and Cassius was enrolled in the normal state secondary, with me.

My mother didn't like me going to Cassius's when his parents were away, which they were often, and she didn't like him being there with only the cleaner either – although she lived in, she didn't speak English, and was barely 19 herself. So he'd become a regular fixture at our dinner table. My mother probed him with what I considered to be a mixture of projected maternal feeling, and the desire to protect me. She had looked ahead perhaps, before either of us had considered it. But we hadn't kissed again. A few awkward weeks had dissolved into easier months, and now, a week after Christmas, we acted as though pressed lips had never passed between us.

My father drove me to the pink house in his cab. From there, it wasn't possible to nip into the village on foot like you could from mine, or wheelbarrow each other to the allotments, or take bikes and cycle all the way down to the boats. Once you were there, you had to stay there – more fortress, in the end, than palace. Still, we could have sprawled. When his parents were home, like his mother was then, they stayed mainly in their separate offices. I'm not sure why we only occasionally ventured down the wide, majestic staircase to retrieve a bag of crisps or can of Coke from the granite-polished kitchen.

In his room, Cassius decided that we should drink eggnog. There were non-alcoholic sachets in the fridge, and he sent me down for them while he sifted through his collection of vinyls. For the last month he had been learning how to DJ – 'Another string to my bow', 'Good for my acting CV' – and now he had a proper set of decks. I had agreed to listen to his attempts at scratching, but first the eggnog. I liked to take my time in his kitchen – there was a real, working jukebox, and a coffee machine, and all sorts of interesting art – but I was just about to return upstairs, when I heard his mother's voice calling out.

Marianne, as she instructed me to address her, had the gravelly sort of tone that indicated a lifetime of smoking, and also conjured for me notions of old-time glamour. I imagined her with one of those long smoking sticks, and she sounded a lot like the guests sometimes interviewed on the jazz station my father listened to, though Cassius assured me that his mother had nothing to do with the entertainment industry and would be horrified to learn that her son's interest in acting was anything more than a fleeting fad.

We were not supposed to disturb Marianne when she was working. But perhaps she wanted a drink too, I reasoned. Or, possibly, a word. Cassius had already mentioned a falling out between them the night before. His father was away, and without him there to buffer things, Cassius and Marianne were often at odds. On the times I'd witnessed it, the conversation seemed to start out amicably enough, but it was as if there were trigger words I wasn't aware of, shortcuts to arguments past, and it would take only one misplaced inquiry or response for either one of them to erupt. Of course, we argued in my family too, but we always made up, and my parents were never cruel, never cutting. Moving slowly down the marbled corridor, I felt that, in loyalty to Cassius, I shouldn't be too friendly to his mother. Yet at the same time I was a guest in her house, and a child, and I had been summoned, and really it was nothing to do with me.

The office door was closed, and I stood there for a moment deciding whether or not to knock, before finally, figuring that she might be on a work call, nudging it quietly open.

Marianne was not working.

Sat behind her desk, she was straddled atop the lap of a man who was not Cassius's father. Her breasts bounced enthusiastically, and I remember in that moment having the ridiculous thought that my own mother's breasts, so heavily veined with milk, were a good deal larger but far less animated.

"Oh my God," I muttered, hiding my eyes with my hand, paralysed to the spot.

"Lily, what the hell?"

Marianne didn't immediately move to stop. This was a detail I later found troublesome. She did, however, eventually right herself, and when she did, the man stood up too, turning towards me. Frantically, I tried to avert my eyes, but as he zipped up his trousers, I saw his penis. I had never seen a penis before, except for Dylan's. The swollenness was disturbing, and it projected in front of him. Not circumcised.

"Sorry," I mumbled quickly, finally finding the faculty to turn away, and trying desperately to rid the vision from my head. "I thought you called me. I thought I heard… Sorry…" And then I stopped, trailing off even inside my head, because here I was apologising, and there she was, having sex with a strange man, while her husband was away and her son was oblivious upstairs.

I ran out of the room. But then didn't know where to run to. I couldn't get home without a lift. Yet if I ran upstairs to Cassius, what would I tell him? What should I tell him? We had never lied to each other; if I spilled out what I had just seen, it would crush him. Standing deer-like in the hallway, the high ceilings felt suddenly suffocating. The marbled floor felt cold and dangerous. From inside Marianne's office, there were footsteps. Panic gripped me. I needed to get out. I needed to get away. My feet started to scramble, and a few moments later, somehow finding myself back in the kitchen, I saw the phone. Lurching for it, I began to dial my mother, the only person I could think of who might be able to tell me what to do; but before I could finish, the receiver was lifted out of my hand. A sharp edge of nail clipped my ear, and I spun around to see Marianne, dressed now, but emitting a musty odour that disgusted me. Her eyes looked red and wired in a way I couldn't then interpret. Fear crept through my skin.

"Don't," Marianne said calmly.

My own voice faltered. "I was just, just calling my mother to pick me up."

She smiled, wide at the corners. "You don't need to go, Lily, not on account of me. You'll upset Cassius." Marianne rested the receiver back in its place.

"*I'll* upset Cassius?" I dared.

She eyed me curiously then. I was as surprised as she by my audacity. But, "Yes. If you just bolt off," she insisted. "Or if you do something, unconsidered. He would be upset. So would I."

Now I stayed silent. Although I was tall, I felt slight standing next to Marianne. She was wearing heels, as always. And bold lipstick. And a sharp-cut fringe.

"There's no need to upset anyone."

Down the corridor, I heard the front door open and shut, a car pulling away. Surely Cassius had heard it too. Or perhaps his DJ earphones had masked it. Perhaps that was the reason for the earphones.

"Does he know?" I whispered.

Marianne smiled again. She reached out and touched a loose bit of hair that had escaped my ponytail. "Such beautiful red," she said. "And so clever too. You're a good influence on Cassius. I hope... Well, I hope you two will *stay* friends. I hope nothing will get in the way of that. Things can, you know."

Still silent, my scratched ear stung. "I really need to go," I mumbled.

But Marianne laughed, gently, and unplugged the phone from the wall. She placed it into a drawer in one of the cupboards and then leant casually against it. "Don't be silly. Stay for dinner. I'll order pizza."

I glanced at the drawer behind her, but even if I managed to get to it, even if I managed to reach my mother, my father was out on an airport run, and we only had one car, so nobody would be able to collect me. Still – if I could just speak to my mother, if I could just tell her what I'd seen, she'd know what to do. She'd tell me – what to do.

"What are you going to do then?" Marianne prompted. "Stay. What do you like, margherita?"

For a moment, I closed my eyes and my mother flashed achingly before them. But she wasn't touchable. Without her wisdom, in any other circumstance, I'd ask Cassius what to do. But he was the one person I couldn't consult.

"Well?" Marianne pressed, her smile faltering.

I had to decide for myself. Quickly. Without my mother, without Cassius. Quickly.

I nodded.

"Great." Now Marianne sat confidently again, picking up a file from the kitchen counter and flipping through it for a pizza menu. I hovered nervously. "Is that for you and Cassius?" she asked, gesturing at the waiting glasses of eggnog.

I nodded again and picked them up.

"Delicious, aren't they? Take some for your parents. Oh, and don't forget to tell Cassius – pizza in an hour."

She turned then, with complete nonchalance, her eyes on the menu, as though she had already forgotten me, or what I knew, or what I might do with that knowing. Or what she had done. It was hard to imagine that just a few minutes earlier she had been so discomposed and compromised. Nobody would believe it.

Would Cassius?

I still had no idea whether or not I should tell him, but the threat concealed within Marianne's friendliness was clear. My hands shook. The eggnog wobbled. Carefully, I began to carry it towards the door.

"Oh Lily," Marianne called after me.

I stopped.

"I know that Cassius hides it well, but do bear in mind, he's quite a fragile boy. Sensitive. Certain 'misunderstandings' might hurt him badly."

I nodded again. This time, because she was right – he was sensitive, and hurt; but she was also utterly wrong. With me, Cassius hid nothing at all.

Yet, I did.

I hid the truth. From him.

First, when he saw my white face returning with the drinks and asked me straight out: "Everything OK?"

Again, while he scratched at his vinyls, and we waited for pizza and then sat silent while his mother reigned over the feast.

It was just for now, I told myself. Just until I consulted my parents. But all evening, the ferocity of my indecision twisted, and twisted.

By the time my father arrived to collect me, my insides felt like a cloth that had been wrung tight and then pegged out on the line to dry, exposed for all to see. Except that, unusually, he didn't notice. Tired after his long drive, he switched on the radio, forsaking his normal string of questions for the quiet strumming of fingers against wheel. And I didn't volunteer anything. Not during that first minute. Not throughout the drive that followed.

Already, I could feel the speed of it like a passing train

– there were opportunities to board or dismount, there were platforms to get out on, but you couldn't jump once the thing was in motion. And the secret was flying fast down the tracks, the chance to tell it streaking by. Meanwhile, I was left with the baggage. The sensation of carrying it was almost physical for me – heavy and repulsive. Images of a bouncing Marianne invaded my mind, visuals of bloated flesh. I couldn't stop replaying it. I needed to tell it, to unload it from my mind.

But if I did, I might destroy everything.

For his family. For him. For me too. For us together.

Dylan had already been put to bed when I pushed quietly into my parents' room. My mother was still dressed, but asleep with a book on her chest.

I couldn't wake her.

I couldn't wake him.

I couldn't tell Cassius.

Could I?

I stood close to my mother, but she didn't stir. Desperately, I wished that I didn't know anything, that I didn't have to decide.

Perhaps it had been a one-off mistake. Perhaps my telling wouldn't make a difference. Perhaps, having been discovered, Marianne would regret it, and stop.

Her smile hadn't seemed remorseful though. More… dangerous, choking the air in my throat, spoiling the taste of pizza, snatching the soft foam of childhood.

My mother sighed, and turned over, leaving space for me to slip, silent, next to her and perch on the edge of her bed, resting my cheek on her back. Her body was warm and as the minutes passed, our breath fell into pattern. In. Out. In. Out. All I wanted was for the knowledge to be out. For me to be oblivious again, free, like I had been a day earlier, like Eve before the apple. Or like my baby brother who, if only I could scoop him up, scoop him up and breathe him in, and feel his newness, would surely return innocence to my arms.

CHAPTER 5

I dream like I haven't dreamt in years. The kind that feels so real that when you wake you are not sure where the dream ends and reality begins. It leaves me contemplating it for hours after. I am at a table read. It is at the studio, exactly as in life, except that Cassius is there. He is one of the actors and we are preparing not for *Moles* but for a school play. Suddenly, the stage of our childhood exploits is conjured in its full wooden glory, the narrow wings, the rickety lights. I am supposed to be directing people on it but am distracted by watching Cassius smoke a joint. "You're not allowed that in here," I tell him. He smirks, and his hair falls out. His head is almost shaved, like it was one summer. Stubbing out the joint, he reaches down to the floor, and out of his bag he pulls a little girl. Jessie giggles and runs across the stage, scattering scripts with her feet. Everybody turns to look at me, to know how they should respond.

CHAPTER 6

On Tuesdays and Thursdays, instead of circling round to the pier, I start there, then run in the opposite direction to a dance studio where I take advanced yoga. This morning, however, I have come by bike. The lateness, and then wakefulness, of the night before has pushed lethargy through my legs, but I would not miss this class. Both my yoga and my run are things I must do. Must. Not quite a compulsion. Not quite mantra-like, but rituals nonetheless. My mind runs through a series of affirmations as I undertake them, and then, endorphin-armed, cleans itself of its darker recesses. This does not seem strange to anyone here; it is modern wellness. Besides, even if I didn't feel coerced, I would choose to exercise. Despite a desire that did not exist when I was a teen, I like to imagine myself now as an athlete. I know that I still wouldn't make a netball team, or, now that I am in the States, a cheer squad. But no longer afraid of my body, I have taken pleasure in training it. I like things that require balance. Surfing. Skateboarding. Standing on my head. It took me five years to work up from the beginners' class to this one. Ria climbed the ladder with me. She is an actor, half Filipina, half German, born and bred in California, with the kind of luscious hair and beautiful deep-olive skin that, if you didn't know, makes her ethnicity impossible to place. It is a helpful versatility, though her career has not yet rocketed as high as she would like it. I try to help and have called her into the studio a number of times, but so far she hasn't been quite right for anything. Often, I feel that she is lobbying me for another audition, but she is a fun yoga partner, and a good friend. Today she is talking to a woman I haven't seen before. I notice the woman immediately because her hair, although sleek and straight like Ria's, is as red as mine. Unlike me, she is petite, neat, as though her entire construction is perfectly packaged and pre-planned. I approach the two of them and Ria makes space for my mat.

"Lil, hey. How are you doing? Love your sweats. Where are they from? Did you get my text about that superfood list you were asking me about? Oh, this is Nola."

I am used to Ria's speed of conversation, and endless energy. She took me once to a workshop all about energy and auras. Hers was apparently yellow-coloured. Mine was red, like my hair, which was supposed to mean something, but I had to leave the workshop for a meeting back on the lot before I had time to find out. In any case, I find that Ria's energy elevates my own. This time, however, before I am able to answer any of her queries, the redhead swivels towards me and waves from her mat. Her energy isn't as abundant as Ria's but there is a vitality to it. "Hello," she sings. "Lil, was it?"

"Lilith."

"Nola. Very good to meet you."

Nola has an accent I can't quite place.

"You too."

"This is my first class," Nola says. "Ria was kindly giving me an idea of what to expect. The low-down."

"I was telling her about Kate's body odour issue," Ria stage-whispers. "And Jonny's enthusiasm for downward-facing dog."

"Those are definitely the two most important pieces of information," I confirm, reaching for a couple of yoga belts.

"I'm more of a dancer really," Nola explains, following me in taking a belt. Her accent adds exoticism, and there is an intangible sexual quality to the way she moves, the belt gliding somehow into her hands. It doesn't quite marry with her physique though. Despite abundant curves, Nola seems so self-contained, so well-wrapped. She sees me examining her. "I have done quite a lot of yoga too," she says, as though in justification. "So they advised this was the correct class for me."

"Sorry." I smile. "I was daydreaming. I'm sure you'll put the rest of us to shame. Have you just moved here? Where are you from?"

"Spain originally," says Nola. "But all over. I have danced with a lot of different companies."

"Lilith's in film," Ria volunteers.

"Oh?"

But we have no time to speak further. The instructor arrives and the class begins. First with gentle meditation, then quickly with challenging active poses. By the time I am standing on my head, I have almost forgotten Nola, and Ria, and the notes I have made for today's rehearsals, and the mammoth shock of seeing Cassius the previous night, and the strangeness of my dream. This is why I love yoga. Balance has mimicked Pacific waves and swept my mind free.

Usually, afterwards, I would stay for a quick breakfast and chinwag with Ria before heading into the studio, but today I want to start early so that I can leave early too. Cassius and I have arranged to meet this afternoon.

"Oh wait, Lil, are you around this evening?" Ria says, grabbing me moments before I dash out. "I told Nola I'd take her out somewhere, show her the hood."

Nola hovers behind Ria. There is something about her I am drawn to and feels familiar. Perhaps the red. It makes me think of a dystopian short in which people cluster in communes according to random genetic disposition. It could be both comic and political. I could write it for one of the newer mediums, maybe Netflix.

"Lil?" prompts Ria.

She is used to my frequent meanderings of the mind, but Nola studies me. I shake my head apologetically. Tonight.

Tonight… I should go. Ria is always showing up for me – at openings, at oddball classes I want to try, when I'm desperate for a carpool. But I am supposed to be seeing Patrick. We have dinner reservations at a new dumpling restaurant in the Arts District.

"Bring Patrick," Ria pre-empts. "Bring anyone. Just something casual. Drinks somewhere. I'll message you."

I laugh. "Sure," I agree. "OK, sure."

Far from radiating yogic serenity, at the studio I find myself rushing through rehearsals. The actors notice and are agitated; it isn't my style. One of them who has known me for years asks if everything's OK, and I nod truthfully. Everything *is* fine. I am not anxious about seeing Cassius, or desperate to do so. Years have passed in which I could have seen him if I had chosen, countless times that I was in England and could have phoned. There is even a kernel of something that tells me to avoid him still, to leave the past in the past, to keep ploughing forward. But – he is here. And as always, I am drawn to him.

As the afternoon approaches, I increasingly hurry. I have a meeting with the network heads to talk about a new idea, and for that I manage to muster focus. They are trying to entice me to adapt a book they've optioned, but I am countering with a new pitch of my own and, to my excitement, they love it. When we part, it is with plans and requests and deadlines. On the way back to the studio, I scribble without pause in my pad – still, apparently, as solid a distraction as it was when I was a teen, because it is only when I am looking up again, looking up from words, at my cast, that the feeling of haste returns. Fortunately, the cast are spectacular, and know me well enough to predict which way I want a scene to go. My reputation is as a fairly prescriptive director. Not to say that I am not open to surprises – I would be hated in this town if I didn't allow actors the freedom to interpret at least a little – but I know what I'm after. It is because of the crossover, I suppose, the amalgamation of writing and directing and producing all at once. When a line needs interpretation, I know exactly what that interpretation should be, because it was me who intended it, it was me who conjured it, extracted it, with purpose, from head onto page. We don't, however, film until Thursday, so there is time. I leave the afternoon in the hands of my assistant director, Will.

Cassius and Jessie can be spotted from many metres away. They are two bubbles of blondeness, the smaller one held in arms. Together they are leaning over the pier and examining crabs on the rocks. I am still wearing the dress I had on for work, overdressed for the beach, but I have changed from heels into trainers, and walk quickly.

"Hi there."

It is Jessie that I decide to tap on the shoulder. I have bought her something from the shop on the lot – a baseball cap bearing the animated face of one of the studio's most famous characters. I hold it out to her.

"Wow!" she exclaims, putting it immediately on top of her head, backwards. "Thank you."

"You didn't have to bring her anything," says Cassius, leaning in to kiss me hello. Again, as we brush cheeks, my skin tingles.

"It's nothing," I say. And then to Jessie, "But I thought you might like it. Colour OK?"

It's turquoise. I noticed the evening before that her trainers were turquoise, and so was her T-shirt. And so were her socks.

"That's my favourite colour." She smiles. It is a beautiful smile. Magnetic, like her father.

"It's your favourite colour this week," warns Cassius.

"No. For at least a thousand weeks."

"How long is a thousand weeks?" Cassius asks her.

"Seventy-two years."

"Hmm. And how old are you?"

"Three."

"Exactly."

"Exactly."

I laugh. "I think your dad is trying to suggest that you haven't been alive for as long as that," I say to Jessie. "But clearly, you had chosen turquoise even before you were born. Right?"

"Right," Jessie agrees. "See, Daddy?"

He frowns down at her with mock seriousness. "Oh, of course. So sorry. My mistake."

Jessie is small for her age. It reminds me of when Cassius and I first met, and I towered above him. Cassius interacts with her in a playful way that makes me think of my own father; he entices her into deep conversation, takes her seriously, and when she responds, her littleness renders her vocabulary incredible. Dylan was like this too, gabbling away when still pint-sized.

I try not to think of Dylan at this age. It sows inside me something un-harvestable. Because my decision has been made. My decision is what keeps me free. I should be thankful for that. And I am. I am. There are plenty of upsides to childlessness. Yet – I seemed so destined, back then, for motherhood.

As a teen, I had tried for a while to distance myself from my brother. After what had happened, I thought it safer. I thought that if we weren't so close, if I didn't love him so much, then maybe that would protect him. But distance only made me long for him more. Besides, by age three, like Jessie, Dylan had his own strong opinion on the matter. Sometimes, when homework was heavy, I had to turn him away, and that killed me. But my mother promised that so long as I gave him 20 minutes of focused attention each day, that would be enough to see us through the years of exams and routines and the making of our worlds. I clung to that instruction. 20 minutes.

In 20 minutes, we could play with his cars together – a variety of colours and shapes, carefully catalogued. I was the only one besides Dylan who knew their names, and which were the fastest and bravest, and most sacred to him. There was another game where I would lie on my parents' bed and pretend to be watching TV, and he would creep up behind me, climbing onto my back before I would suddenly leap up and jiggle and shake until he slipped giggling onto the waiting softness below. And if ever he was hurt, he would run to my lap, not my mother's, and we would put a napkin over our heads so that nobody but he and I could see his woe; he trusted me with this, with everything.

When I had commitments late at school, and lacked 20 spare minutes, I felt as if I was one of those parents, like Cassius's, who didn't really figure in their children's lives. The idea of this filled me with guilt. I knew I wasn't Dylan's mother, but I felt I had abandoned him nonetheless. And if he'd already gone to bed, then he truly had abandoned me. Because distance hadn't worked. Our bond was set. And nestling him into my neck was the crucial first step, the first ritual, the first part of everything I had to do that might see us both safely through the night.

Jessie slips her hand into mine.

"So, shall we go to the aquarium?" I ask her, pointing out the sail-like flags at its entrance. "Or find some rides?"

Jessie takes a moment to consider this. "If I choose one thing today, can we do the other thing another day?" she inquires.

I laugh. "Sure. If you'd like to."

"I would like to," she confirms. "Rides today, please."

Together, we walk down the pier, weaving around food sellers. With Jessie between us, there is an easiness to conversation. Not that we were awkward the previous night, but now that we have had time to think, now that our dynamic is more than muscle memory, there seems so much unsaid. I breathe deeply.

"Have you been here before?" I ask Cassius.

"I think so. That summer I was here with Mum, I think we came then, a group of us. Feels familiar. But only once if we did. Mum and I were staying in Malibu mostly."

"It's nice in Malibu," I say. "Is that where the clinic was?"

He pauses. "Yep."

There is a curt, strained tone to Cassius's answer, and I am overwhelmed by a sudden sense of stupidity. I have brought up his mother's illness, out of nowhere, when he has just lost his wife to the same disease. And specifically come to LA to escape such reminders. In the old days, I would have been tuned in to these things, but I don't know everything about him any more. I don't know if I am allowed still to probe, to challenge. I am not sure how softly to tread.

Fortunately, Jessie spots a ride she likes, and Cassius and I both make a big show of enthusiasm. It is essentially Cups and Saucers. He pays for her to go on, and she finds a glazed turtle, then the two of us stand watching, waving every time she completes the circle and passes us again. As she does so, the jingle of her giggle makes me laugh idiotically, and Cassius seems either amused or disturbed by this. I make myself rein it in, but still feel awkward, clumsy. Jessie passes us again.

"Well, she definitely likes it," I say to Cassius.

"She certainly does."

There is a pause.

"How was your night?" I ask him. "Are you jet-lagged?"

He has stopped looking at me and we both fix our sights on Jessie. "We woke pretty early. It's not too bad though." Another pause. "It'll be worse on the way home."

Another pause. Longer. Jessie passes us again. Cassius and I wave, but without her standing between us, it is as though the air has tightened, formalised. Should I ask him about Serena? Does he want to talk about it? We seem stuck suddenly with niceties.

"How long till you leave?" I say, clutching for padding.

But Cassius turns abruptly towards me. "Are you already trying to get rid of me?" He holds his chest in dramatic, mock hurt, but his green eyes are dancing as they explore mine. "Come on, it's not that awkward, is it?"

I laugh, awkwardly, but something starts to dissipate. "How long are you here for, I mean?"

Now, Cassius abandons the drama and pats a friendly hand on my back – warm, unaffected. It reminds me of this part of himself, this way he has always been – jazz hands one minute, sincerity the next. "I'm not actually sure," he answers. "I bought flexi tickets. I didn't really know, you know? They're booked for two weeks' time, but Jessie doesn't need to be in school yet, legally, and I thought after here, maybe we'd tour through America for a while. Our visas are good for six months."

"Oh, you should definitely tour a bit," I say gently, with what I hope is similar candour. "Do a road trip. Or the train is good. You can go up to San Francisco, and then take it all the way to New York. It's one of those old cross-country routes. But wait – what about your job? Do you… What do you…"

"What do I do?"

I laugh again, still a little awkwardly. "Sorry. Yes. It just, it feels crazy to be asking you that. You know? I'm talking to you and part of me feels like I know everything about you, and the other part of me knows that I know nothing about you, now. Are you still acting?"

"Yes, I'm still acting, thank you very much, Miss Big Time."

"Sorry. I didn't mean it like that." I am aware that despite Cassius's attempts at levity, I am apologising every few seconds. I do not want to be this way. It was never our dynamic. Not then, not with him, and it's certainly not who I am now. But suddenly I realise what is flustering me: it is not the time passed between us, it is not the absence of knowledge; it is the guilt. The guilt. It is that with every discovery about his life or confession about mine, I am reminded of the fact that I am the reason we both know so little. I separated us. I abandoned him. I left. And I am ashamed. Not only for cutting him out of my existence, but for succeeding in my own. Without him. For being so happy while he is so sad. "Of course you would be acting," I stumble. "Of course. What have you done lately?"

"*Lear* at the Palladium," he answers quickly. "And a BBC drama."

"Oh, wow. Seriously? I didn't know."

"Not seriously," he says, deadpan.

"Oh." I want to sympathise, or to joke, but I don't want to patronise. I hesitate.

"Mainly it's been corporate gigs," he volunteers into the silence. "And school workshops. I did have a couple of good years doing RSC, but then Jessie was born, and I decided not to tour, and it's been pretty dry since then. I'm not quite the new kid on the block any more you know."

Now we are on safer ground. "Are you actually going to claim male shelf life?" I ask, marshalling myself to join him in jest. "I should warn you that you are talking to a model of female empowerment here. You, my friend, are a white, straight, fully able 34-year-old male. You're OK."

Cassius laughs. "Glad to see you're still a raging feminist. Your parents would be proud."

"'Raging' feminist is probably not quite PC."

"Well, where's the fun in that?"

Where's the fun in that? It feels like something we have said to each other before. I am beginning to remember us, our way, to feel it again, and we stand there staring at each other. He is remembering too. I see the dance of it in his eyes.

* * *

"You're late," Miss Willis informed me, barely looking up from her script. "Hurry up, please."

From his seat on the stage, Cassius shot me a knowing glance, and I nodded, tucking a loose red tendril behind my ear. It was my play, written by me, so she couldn't dismiss me altogether, but she was clearly growing weary of my unreliability. All of the teachers were. Friends too. It seemed to get worse with every year that passed, and it was painful to disappoint them over and over, but I hadn't had any realistic hopes to the contrary. Rehearsals that final week started at 4 p.m. and ran till 7 p.m. Halfway through, we were given a break, and if Miss Willis really thought I'd be able to return on time at six, well, she didn't know me at all. Which she didn't.

"You have to stop it," whispered Cassius, who did, hissing into my ear a while later as we trekked out of the school's hall.

"Stop," I muttered under my breath. "And one, two. Stop. And three, four. Stop. And five, six."

"What?"

He had interrupted me, and now I needed to start again. I put my bag on the floor and pretended to be fumbling through it while I quickly repeated the numbers in my head. When I reached ten for the third time, I 'found' the book I'd been searching for. "Have you finished it yet?" I asked him.

We were studying *Pride and Prejudice* for GCSE. I'd read it the first time when I was 11, the summer before Cassius and I met.

"Don't deflect," he scolded. "I know what you're doing."

"So?" I shrugged.

"So I thought you were going to try not to."

"Yeah, well," I answered, linking my arm through his. "You know, where's the fun in that?"

"Hilarious," he said, squeezing my arm. "OK, sorry, but, you know, it's getting worse. People are going to notice."

"Not if you don't tell them."

"Your parents are definitely going to notice."

I shook my head. "It's been years, Cass, in some form or other. They haven't so far."

We had reached the door to the school car park, and he pushed it open. At the far side, I could see my father's cab.

"Am I coming back for dinner?" Cassius asked me, but quickly I shook my head.

"Nope. Shush."

"I thought I was coming back on Thursdays?"

I shook my head again. My father had pulled out of his parking space and started crawling towards us. Letting go of Cassius's arm, I balanced my toes on the edge of the kerb and slowly lifted them up and down, silently singing the words to a song from *Les Misérables*.

"Why not?" Cassius pressed, from half a step behind me. "And by the way, I see what you're doing. Why are you doing that?"

I ignored him.

"Lil." He stepped forward. "Come on, why are you doing that?"

Again, I didn't answer, still tilting up and down on the kerb. With my hand, I waved him away.

"Lil, you have to be rational. You are not that powerful," he goaded. Challenged.

I spun towards him. "If you must know, you didn't come back last Thursday because of your mum's whatever it was. And I stood like this, and did exactly this, and got in Dad's cab. And everything was fine. So. That's it."

"So now you have to do that every time? Do you know how illogical that is?"

I shook my head. "I wish I'd never told you anything," I spat at him.

"Lil!"

Quickly, I tried to start the song again, but there wasn't time, my father had almost reached us. A surge of blackness raced through my chest. An aerial vision of Dylan lying lifeless at the bottom of the stairs burst into my mind. Then another of his face raw and burnt. Heavily, I blinked the images away, pinching the skin at the top of my thigh, biting on my cheek, but they came again. Cassius's own face was angry, hurt.

"Thanks a lot," I growled, and without looking back, slammed the door to the car.

* * *

Gesturing now towards my truck, I say: "This is me."

We have walked far down the beach, stopping at Venice for Jessie to watch breakdancers show off their tricks, and tattoo artists display their flair on baked skin, and so that she can pick through fidget spinners and bracelets and nick-nacks she doesn't need. With Cassius's permission, I buy her a bag of popcorn.

"Remember how we used to sprinkle our popcorn with sweets?" I ask him.

"And chocolate." He nods. "Maltesers."

"Can I have chocolate too then?" says Jessie.

She is fighting, however, to stay awake and Cassius has decided it's time for a proper dinner back at the hotel. Both of us hover. There are adult things we wish to say.

"I don't suppose you can meet in the evening at all, while you're here?" I ask him.

Cassius looks down at Jessie. "Probably not."

The little girl hugs my leg, propping her tired body against it, and I reach out to stroke her hair. It is soft, and slightly sweaty. "Of course not, silly question."

It was a silly question. Jessie is Cassius's priority, and should be. Besides, it was only supposed to be a brief catching up. I am not trying to revive what I deliberately left behind.

"Actually—"

"No, it's fine," I tell him. "Really."

"I was going to say… if you come back to the hotel, I have a video monitor. We can be just downstairs, have dinner maybe? Just us."

I pause. Perhaps it's not a good idea. Perhaps this glimpse was all we were supposed to see. I can feel the memories already, pressing against me, scurrying to the surface, slipping on the sand. But. But. No. I am not the same person as I was when I cut him out. I am strong now. I can handle looking back.

I nod. "I'd love that."

"In a couple of hours then?"

"Oh," I say. "Tonight?" Suddenly, I remember Patrick. And drinks with Ria and Nola. "I'm meant to be meeting friends."

"Sure. Sure, no worries. Another night."

But I don't want to say goodnight.

It is not romance – he is a widower, and I am with Patrick – but it is not yet enough.

"Wait," I say. "Maybe I can do both. Early dinner with you, late drinks with them?"

Cassius tilts his head. "Look at you. Quite a social butterfly these days."

"And look at you," I return. "Mr Family."

"Almost," he reminds me. "Almost."

I shake my head. "Sorry."

"It's fine. I know what you mean. And it's true." He waves his arms in the air. Jazz hands. A magic trick. "Ironic, isn't it?"

I nod. Jessie presses against my leg and I reach down to give her a hug. "OK. Well, I'm here," I say, gesturing to my truck again. "Which way are you?"

"I'm wherever there's an Uber." Cassius shrugs.

"And I'm this way," volunteers Jessie, pointing directly at the sea.

* * *

From the driver's seat, my father raised a gently questioning eyebrow. Both of my parents had noticed changes in my demeanour, and as usual, my father attempted to talk to me with what had become standard timidity. I hated to see him so reduced – he, a master communicator, who from passengers great and small extracted chit-chat and political theories and confessions, with his own daughter now trod carefully. But I couldn't tell him, or explain.

"Alright there?" he asked softly, reaching over the gearstick to pat my hand.

Immediately, familiar tears sprang into my eyes.

The potential flood of them vexed my father's hands which he drummed restlessly against the steering wheel, wanting, I knew, to reach out and hug me. But he accepted my nod, my strained smile, and didn't push. "Mum kept Dylan up for you," he offered instead.

Now, I gifted a real smile to my father, who responded gleefully, as though he'd achieved some unheard-of miracle, and this filled me with even more guilt. I couldn't, however, focus on it then. Relief had rushed into the space where I'd been holding my breath. If I scooped Dylan up before bed, if I held him, and smelled him, and breathed him in, I would be fortified.

From what? For what?

I didn't know what to call it back then. The internet wasn't what it became. I only knew what it did to me, what it made me do; and what I had to stop myself doing to Dylan. Thoughts intruded, uninvited and unwelcome. Horrible, awful thoughts that I couldn't admit to anyone. Only Cassius. Because – what if they weren't manifestations of fear, of worry, or dreams, or things I'd seen in films, or any of the other explanations I'd tried to convince myself of? What if, instead, they were some kind of warped impulse, a perverted desire? What if I was a deeply evil person and these visions were things that I wanted?

In my conscious brain, I didn't want them. I would do anything to stop them from ever coming true. But that's what I feared – that they might somehow materialise anyway, that they would happen. That I would do something. When I wasn't myself.

Or that I would fail to stop something. Because that was my other theory – that the visions were warnings sent from a supernatural source. And in receiving the message, it was my job to act on it. I believed in those things. I felt there could quite possibly be greater forces at play.

In my visions, I would be throwing Dylan from the top of the stairs over the banister, or out of the window, and I would see his crumpled body lying lifeless on the floor. Or I would be smothering him with his old cellular blanket, until his arms stopped flailing. Or I would be squashing a pillow over his face. I would be prodding him again and again with the sharp blade of a kitchen knife. Or burning his cheek against a flame. I would be doing these things. To Dylan.

My Dylan.

I couldn't breathe when these thoughts intruded. I couldn't bear them. At first, I tried simply to close my eyes in the hopes that I could shut them out, block them from view, blink them away. But even if that worked for a second, they would return a moment later. If I walked past a potential weapon – which could be as innocuous as a skipping rope or a dressing-gown belt – the awful image of what I could do to him with that would force itself into my brain. And I didn't know if it was a forewarning or a premonition or a plan, these things that I might do without intention.

And I could do something. I had done something before. So it wasn't crazy. It was a reasonable fear.

Once, my mother took me to see a counsellor, a friend of hers in London. The room was bright and airy, flowers on the console, a jug of water and box of tissues on the coffee table between us. Books lined the shelves as though to avow the lady's credentials, and I believed them – here was my chance, my lifeline. This person would know how to make it all stop. Tentatively, I volunteered my fears – what if I harmed somebody, I ventured. Myself, or, well, my brother, for example. The woman nodded understandingly but went on to tell me only not to worry, that stress made these things worse, that the whole thing was quite common and generally harmless, that I would grow out of it. I decided not to explain about the visions – the less common, less harmless, less understandable thing.

Somehow, however, that night, miraculously, nothing happened. No visions, no incidents, nothing. A thrilling hope implanted itself. Perhaps the session had helped, after all. That evening, I tried to replicate the feat, and it seemed logical to me to exactly repeat everything that had occurred leading up to it. I began, as usual, with hugging Dylan – my pre-sleep dose of purity to stop me seeking it, seeking him, later on. The night before, at the end of our hug, I had kissed him on the forehead and handed him to my mother, feet first, his head passing to her left shoulder. Later, I had brushed my teeth while standing on the cracked tile in the bathroom. Then I had set out my obstacles in careful order. And in bed, I had said a silent prayer: *Please, God, please, please look after Dylan, please protect him, keep him safe*. I remembered these words and said them again, exactly. I did it all, again, exactly. And it worked. That night, it worked. I started to see how I could protect him.

On nights when it didn't work, when my lungs were flooded with the sensation of drowning, when something had gone wrong, it was clear to me that a new ritual was needed, an extra action. Like a sacrifice to the gods. I would add a new word or phrase to my prayer. I would incorporate something additional into my evening preparations. I would look for clues in the day. If there was a loose blanket on the floor, or a knife in the sink, I would pick them up and lock them away somewhere, saying a sequence of words as I did so: "Stop. One, two. Stop. Three, four..." I had ten seconds to accomplish the task. If I did, then it would stop the object from entering my mind later, it would keep it away from me. If I didn't, then it might become a prop, a weapon. I would have to start again, count again, from the beginning. Later, I found that this could apply to thoughts too. When an evil image intruded, if I said my 'Stop' sequence quickly enough, it could block it, for a little while at least, and for a few minutes I would feel relief, control. If somebody else happened to say 'stop', however, then it removed my power, and I would have to reclaim the word. I'd have to say the sequence three times without a breath. Under my breath.

Breath became difficult for me. Breathing freely. The

undertaking of it all was consuming. Sometimes it would interrupt me for hours at a time. Phrases. Rituals. Like any teen, there were things in my life that I wanted to do, wanted to achieve, goals I had; but none of them was as important as safeguarding my brother. Unable to focus on a conversation, I felt myself growing more introverted. It was frequently impossible to be on time. Often, I couldn't finish my homework. My grades began to suffer. Where I had been an A student, now I was middling. My parents concocted 'plans of action', involving colour-coded schedules and 'study time', but I couldn't stick to them. The only avenue in which I did manage to be productive was writing. At first, this was merely another tool with which to divert my brain, but I had started carrying a notepad, and as I walked around school, or sat waiting for the bus, or any other moment that I was alone and without another person's chatter to fixate on, I would scrawl down anything that came into my head. I would watch people and describe the way they walked, the specific lilt of their language, the tiny gestures with which they interacted. I obsessed over the detail, taking pleasure in the concentration required, the distraction. If there were no people, then I would channel my attention onto the landscape – the bluebells, the church, the old red telephone box on the high road that seemed now to house only flyers that nobody ever saw. I wrote a whole story about that phone box, inventing people to frequent it and bring it to life. The story won a place in the school magazine. So I began inventing more stories and found that there was a joy in fashioning worlds not like my own, from my own. As though here was a way I could control and constrain reality. Even if I couldn't control myself. When our drama teacher announced that our school production would use an original script written by one of our own, I had one ready.

Cassius was cast as the lead. The character was partially inspired by him, so it made sense, but I had nothing to do with the selection. He had remained the darling of the drama department and had taken every lead since we were 12.

There was something undeniably magnetic about him, but sometimes it felt as though it was less about his acting, and more to do with him, Cassius, and the magic of seeing this beautiful boy-man doing what was instructed, the instrument of a puppet master. In this case, me. The audience enjoyed him this way – blondeness and youth and vulnerability on display at their pleasure. When, during rehearsals, he spoke the words that I myself had written, there was something intoxicating about that for me too. I imagined, as I hadn't done in years, what it might be like, now, to kiss him. Since the last time, I hadn't kissed anybody else. Even Cassius's exploits hadn't seen rapid advancement, though he had girlfriends, who I didn't like. It was cliché, but there it was. He tended to go for that untouchable type – beautiful, brilliant, cold; his mother incarnate. I wasn't jealous. I didn't want to be with him. Although, I suppose, only that evening I'd imagined it again – a kiss; before I had snapped at him and shut my father's car door in his face.

Dinner eaten, Dylan hugged and put to bed, I sat at the small desk in my room, labouring over homework, knowing that I would never free enough mental space to get it done. It didn't even matter if I completed every ritual perfectly. Without Cassius's help, there would be no rest for me that night. But I had exploded at him. He had been trying to support me, and I had shut him down. He had every right to leave me to my fate.

Yet, suddenly, my phone beeped with a text message: Cassius. *Yes, you are a good person.*

A lump bulged in my throat. *Start again*, I messaged him. It was close, but not quite right.

K.

How do you know?

Because I know you.

Are you sure?

Yes.

Why?

Because you are a good person.
Night.
Night.
Night.
Night.
Night.
Night.
X
He didn't reply. He knew, after that kiss, not to reply.

* * *

My phone beeps with a message and I pull my truck over to look at it. I know who it will be from, and it is – Cassius. He has sent me the address of his hotel for us to meet at later. And then an X. And then, nothing.

CHAPTER 7

Nothing.

No footprints.

No threats written in blood.

No phone messages to allow one last whisper.

Everything wave-wiped clean.

CHAPTER 8

Two days after our argument, Cassius and I sat on his bed and made plans. Once the show was over, and after the end-of-year exams, we would pick a Saturday and take the train to the seaside. Cassius had never been to a British beach and we both needed a day out, we said, a day away, just us and an expanse of sea.

In the meantime, we ran lines. Cassius was feigning nerves about his performance the next day, but the real motive, I knew, was to distract me from myself. I bit my cheek and pinched at my thigh when he wasn't looking. Downstairs, his mother was in her office, her voice escaping every now and then in strident leaps across marbled tiles. Even years after the episode in her office, I dreaded seeing her, because ever since that day, she had enlisted me as her shroud. If a doorbell went, and Cassius or Mark asked later who it had been, she would turn to me across the room, always smiling, and say, "Oh, Lily saw, didn't you, Lily, just the postie." Or the dry cleaning. Or a Jehovah's Witness. As though I'd been part of her original sin, complicit in the lie, duty-bound to continue it. Which was true.

She'd seemed pleased to see me that evening when she opened the door: "We're going skiing at Christmas. I wondered if you'd like to join? Cassius would enjoy the company as I don't like a full day of ski, and for Mark, I think it's a working trip – he's bringing his secretary." She'd eyed me as she said this, a flash in her eyes – a warning, a justification, a plea?

"Have you met your dad's secretary?" I asked Cassius later.

He rolled his eyes and huffed. "She's about four years older than we are. It's pathetic."

"What do you mean?" I asked.

He looked at me. "Come on, Lil. It's so obvious."

My stomach clenched. Clearly, Cassius suspected his father of cheating. Did he know about his mother too? Did he know that I knew? "What?" I asked innocently.

"Don't stress about it," he said, picking up his phone. "Especially you – don't stress," he repeated emphatically. Then shrugged. "They don't."

But I should have. I should have asked more, dragged it out of him. I should have put him before my own guilt and, even, told him what I knew. Instead, limbs intertwined, I allowed him to distract us both. We lay on the bed, and felt the sweaty heat of bare legs, and threw pillows at each other, and ran lines, and planned a 'just us' day at the sea.

When I passed Mark on my way out that evening, an uncomfortable hotness crept up my throat, as though I'd just tasted something unpleasant. It made me blush again. And think of the way that—

Stop. One, two. Stop...

My mother declared the play a triumph. She hadn't quite realised, she told me, how mature my writing had become, how nuanced, how dark and yet how funny. Was I going to pursue that, she wondered. It hadn't occurred to me then, not properly. And Cassius was brilliant, she continued, alive with chatter from the front of my father's cab. Had I written that part for him?

My father too said he loved it. Though, he ventured, looking at me in the rear-view mirror, he wished that I would tell him about some of my ideas, some of the things I captured so fantastically on the page. He'd love to know them before seeing them on stage. Talk. Like we used to.

My mother shot him a look: *not now, not now*.

But he continued. Remember those long conversations we used to have?

My mother glanced at me apprehensively. She didn't want to ruin this night, this celebration. But of course, she felt it as much as he did. They missed me. They couldn't fathom me. They couldn't fix whatever was wrong with me. Even at the height of happiness, darkness hovered.

As my father spoke, I counted out time with my fingers beneath my bag. My left foot was turned at a 90-degree angle to my right, mirroring the position of my bed in relation to Dylan's. Tears threatened in my throat.

"We still talk," I argued.

I woke Dylan while my mother was paying the babysitter downstairs. He wriggled over in his bed and made room for me. Despite a bath, he smelled of home-made brownies, and washable paint.

"Was it brilliant?" he whispered.

"Brilliant," I whispered back. "There was a standing ovation."

"What's that?"

"I'll tell you in the morning."

He nodded sleepily, content in my success. Reaching up to my face, he plucked away the scrunchie that was as usual scraping back my curls and wrapped his finger within a tendril. "I knew it would be brilliant."

I smiled then and snuggled him until he fell back to sleep. Every 12 seconds, I pinched my thigh.

"She has cancer," Cassius answered.

We were at the allotments, pulling weeds for my father since rain had put pause to our plans for the sea. I had dared to ask him why his parents hadn't made the show. Not that it surprised either one of us really, but I figured I should ask, make sure he knew he deserved better.

I took off my gloves. "Oh my God. Cassius."

"It's OK."

"It's not OK. That's awful. That's… What kind of… I mean, when did you find out?"

As usual, he ran his hand through his hair, and shrugged. "Only just. It's containable, I think. They hope. So."

"Cass, I'm so sorry. Is there anything I can do?"

"Not really."

I hugged him and we stood like that for a moment, amidst the tomatoes, in the summer drizzle. Then, "Are you sure I can't help? I could, I don't know… Bring her some tomatoes?"

"There really isn't anything you can do." After fingering the vines for a moment, he turned back to me. "Except, well, maybe just, I dunno, help me sort things at school. I could do with not having extra work on. Mum wants to go to LA for the summer, she can do treatment there, it's better. But I can't be arsed with taking that stupid English with."

"I'm sure they'd exempt you," I said.

"Yeah, but it's for coursework."

"Still. You could ask. They must have some kind of allowance for things like that."

"Nah, they'll end up calling Mum and that'll stress her out. I don't want to add any stress."

It was unsettling to think of formidable Marianne as so fragile. It must have been worse for Cassius. "Well, what if I just do it for you then?" I offered.

"What? My English? No way. You've got your own to do."

"I don't mind. You know I like that stuff."

"Seriously?"

I smiled at him. "You do stuff for me all the time, Cass. And you should be with your mum."

"Wow." He looked at me. "Are you sure? I mean, only if you're sure. Thanks. Don't make it too Lilith-esque though."

I laughed. "Writing in different voices is my supreme skill.

Which you should know, having just acted one of them. D'you know, I was talking to my parents yesterday, and I think it might actually be what I want to do at uni, and afterwards. Writing in some way."

"Perfect," he grinned. "Once Mum's better, I'll get my parents to buy us a house in LA, and you'll write, and I'll act, and we'll be this perfect power couple who are not actually a couple, but everybody in Hollywood envies and tries to work out exactly what kind of relationship we actually have."

"What relationship do we have?" I asked him.

This time, his kiss lingered on my lips long after we'd parted. All afternoon I felt the tingle of it. Visions of us standing close weaved around me like the tomatoes. They burst into my brain, jostling with the darker pictures I was used to, distracting me from them. I could feel the heat of his hand at the bottom of my back, the warmth of his breath, the trace scent of chewing gum. At home, although Dylan was wanting to play, I steered my mother into the far corner of the room so that I could tell her.

"I was wondering when that might happen again." She touched me on the cheek. "Feel better about it this time?"

I nodded. "Much."

"So are you two dating now?"

I shook my head derisively. "Nobody says *dating* these days. Anyway, I don't know. It literally just happened."

"OK," said my mother, sensing my rapid withdrawal. "Well, I know you know what you're doing. And you know that we like Cassius."

"I don't like Cassius," interrupted Dylan suddenly. He had crept across the room and was standing directly behind me.

Smiling, I lifted him onto my hip, then continued to my mother: "We might go to the beach next weekend, if the weather's better. If that's OK?"

Dylan stuck out his tongue.

"Of course."

Now Dylan groaned. "You should take me to the beach. Not him. I don't like him."

My mother and I exchanged another smile.

"Oh really?" I said, throwing him onto the couch with a tickle. "Oh really?"

Later that afternoon, when we met up with friends at the cinema, Cassius and I sat together as usual. We didn't tell anybody what had passed between us, but we didn't hide it either. A few of the girls noticed our held hands, and whispered to each other without talking to me, but I had never felt an intimate part of that grouping anyway. We were friendly enough. We chatted. We partnered up for PE. But when there were only four to a table, or five across the back of a bus, I knew that I was the expendable one. It made sense. I didn't bring a lot to the pack. I wasn't funny or bold or any of the things I knew I could be, or had been once, and still was with Cassius. It was too dangerous to relax in this way with people who didn't know about all my rituals. It took concentration to maintain and hide the things I had to do. Besides, I had untameable curls, and untannable skin, and the other girls seemed not to be un-anything.

Cassius squeezed my hand. He was my 'in-group' anyway, the only one that I'd ever felt right at the centre of. The warmth of his hand pulsed through my veins, and that night, for the first time in months, sleep came softly.

A week later, however, school broke up for the summer, and long before the rain had a chance to clear, or we had a day to escape to the sea, Cassius left with his mother for LA.

CHAPTER 9

Uber is making a good trade. Miguel, in a white Toyota Prius, drops me outside of Cassius's hotel with 15 minutes to spare, triumphant over LA traffic. It is normal for me to be on time these days, but I don't like to be early, so I loiter outside, exchanging text messages with Jade, who is on a work trip to New Zealand but wants all the details of Cassius's reappearance, and begins to send me photo after hilarious photo of our final years at Sussex.

We had met our first morning there. She was unpacking boxes in the room opposite mine, and after tentative hellos through open doors, we discovered we were both studying philosophy. Unusually for me, I'd felt a quick connection with Jade. We had similar backgrounds – she was Hindu, not Jewish, but from a comparably non-religious, culture-appreciating, just-about-middle-class, close-knit family who called her equally as regularly as my parents, and nearly as often as Dylan.

Both Dylan and I ticked off the days that we would be apart – he on an actual chart that we'd made together; me, mentally only, in bed, each night casting an imaginary protective shroud around him, believing that I had the power to do this. We spoke every morning before Dylan went to school. Jade would often be sitting in my room at this point, helping me drink tea and burn toast, and she would stay silent while I chatted to him, while he detailed the triumphs and disasters of the previous day, while I made up a humorous tale for him, while we recited to each other our rhyme that ended every conversation between us and he didn't know was a ritual, for my benefit, not his. Jade, however, clocked on to it quickly.

"What happens if you don't end with 'Love you like a lucky duck, lucky lucky love you'?" she asked one morning as she bit into her slice of toast.

I laughed. "Nothing. Obviously. Dylan likes it."

She raised her eyebrow sceptically. "You know, my brother does a lot of stuff like that. He has OCD. It can be pretty tricky for him sometimes."

"Oh yeah?" I said nonchalantly. "What's OCD?"

It was the first time that anybody had named my compulsions for me. Or explained them. Or suggested that others did things like that too. And the impact of that revelation was immeasurable.

Jade and I talked. We talked. We talked. It made sense, she said, as though I wasn't a total oddity. It sounded familiar. For her brother, it had been a car accident that set things off. For others, she said, it could be nothing. She understood my trigger. We went online and she showed me a website that matter-of-factly listed all the symptoms of the condition, symptoms I had always believed were signs of my evil. She watched my head explode as I took this in. Still, when I told her about the things I'd done, the things all my rituals were meant to stop, the waves, the sea, she agreed to keep a key to my room, and, when I really needed it, on those nights when the compulsions were too out of control, the visions too dreadful, I persuaded her to lock me in.

* * *

"What?" demanded Cassius, when I told him about this that first Christmas break.

"My friend Jade. I've talked about her."

"Yeah, but she locks the door? That's a fire hazard," Cassius pointed out urgently.

"It's only sometimes. And she checks on me."

"She shouldn't do that. What if you need to get out?"

"How many fires have you encountered in your life?" I asked him.

"None."

"How many times would I have been better off locked in?"

"I get your point," Cassius retorted. "But a fire could kill you."

"So could the sea. It almost did once before, remember?"

He shook his head. "You need to be safe."

He'd grown his hair long again, almost like when we'd first met, although now he scooped it sometimes into a short ponytail. On his feet were boots, not trainers. He'd taken to wearing a leather jacket, though while we lay talking on his bed, this was strewn across a chair. His T-shirt had a crumpled, soft effect.

"Ah," I cooed, putting my hand on his cheek. "He cares."

"Of course I care," he said, playfully swiping away my hand.

"Ah," I teased again, cupping his face.

This time, when he touched my hands, he held them onto his skin. "I missed you," he told me.

"I missed you too."

* * *

Jade sends another photo – the two of us hanging off the Palace Pier – and both of us race to caption it. We could continue this for hours, and frequently do, but this time I text her goodbye when it is exactly eight.

Cassius is waiting in the lobby, a crackling baby monitor in his hand. The building is part of a strip mall in San Gabriel, more motel than hotel, which makes sense, I suppose, if Cassius doesn't know how long they will be staying. When I push through the door, however, I am struck by the dinginess of the décor, the simplicity of the facilities, the sign that instructs guests that the laundry room is in the basement and takes quarters. Never once, in the years in which I knew Cassius, would he have stayed in an establishment such as this. The 'restaurant' at which we are dining is a glorified café located in the lobby but also accessible from the beauty parlour next door. There is a slushy machine next to the counter, and a stand from which toiletries may be purchased.

"I know," says Cassius as we sit down. "Not the Ritz."

I shake my head and attempt convincing nonchalance. "It's fine."

He places the monitor on the table, checking the screen, then looks at me. "You can ask me."

"What?"

"Wow," he laughs. "Since when do you and I beat around the bush? You can ask me why I'm staying in a dump."

The waitress arrives at our table, and I shush him. But she isn't listening to us anyway. There is a television on above our heads, and she has one eye on *The Voice*.

"OK then, tell me," I say quietly, even after the waitress has taken our orders and moved away. "How come you're staying here?"

"I ran out of money," Cassius says bluntly.

I can't help but laugh at the obviousness of this response. But only for a half-second. "What do you mean?"

"Well, let's see. Turns out that my dad never quite landed that new job after the crash, and even though Mum was raking it in, still is by the way, she didn't feel like giving any of her dosh to her disappointing son. Spends it on her boyfriends. Fine, fair enough. I'm happy to make my own way. I don't want anything from her anyway. Thing is, my own way hasn't transpired to be such a lucrative way. Don't worry, I'm fine," he says, seeing my face contort. "We're fine. We just can't splash out on extravagant hotels for what might turn out to be multiple weeks of holiday."

"No, well, that's sensible," I say. There is a slightly weary look in Cassius's eye, but I am struck by how very little he has changed. Even after losing his wife, even after becoming a father himself, he is still bleeding fast the untended hurt of a boy pining for his parents. I wonder if we all carry our childhood scars so plainly. I have tried so hard to conceal mine. "It's fine here anyway," I insist. "When I was Jessie's age, we didn't even stay in motels, we used to camp."

"I know," says Cassius.

"Right."

Again, I feel the dichotomy in the dynamic: knowing everything, knowing nothing. There is a soft focus to it. Familiarity, but also the sense of being on trial, as though each of us is in the dock presenting our story, our new selves, and at any moment the other might jump up with damning evidence to the contrary. Something indisputable. The waitress returns with a beer for Cassius, and an iced tea for me.

"You still don't drink?" he asks me.

"No."

"Never?"

I shrug. "You know me."

Cassius looks at me intently. "Is it still… an issue then? Do you still…"

"We're really not beating around the bush," I laugh, a little uncomfortably. Then, "No, not in years."

"Wow," he says. "None of it? The other stuff too?"

"Yeah." We both pause for a moment, allowing this to wash over us – the disappearance of that part of myself that once defined so much of our relationship, the part, in fact, that began it. The part he held for me. "I'm sure I'd be fine to drink now actually," I hurry, emboldened a little by having articulated my transformation out loud, especially to Cassius, who knows the distance travelled. "I just… don't."

Cassius takes a sip of his beer. "Fair enough."

As our starters arrive – mine, clearly a microwaved soup – I glance at my watch. The evening is going fast. So far, we have talked about Jessie, and a little about Serena, though Cassius stiffens every time I mention her, and so I stop. But there is so much I still want to know. I am acutely aware that there is a time limit to this snatched reunion, Patrick is collecting me straight after BMXing, but we still have almost an hour.

I haven't yet told Patrick everything about Cassius. I've definitely mentioned him over the years. When we've spoken about our childhoods, I've painted him in nearly full colour – his friendship, his closeness with my family, his dreams being the ones that inspired my own. And when we embarked on the usual unpacking of first liaisons – kisses and more-than-kisses and first loves – Cassius was named again and again. So Patrick knows who Cassius is to me. Was to me. But he doesn't know what Cassius knows, about me. I haven't told him anything about what I was like then. I haven't told anybody here.

He has taken only slight offence to my blowing off dinner to reconnect with a boy from my past. In fact, he has not actually mentioned offence at all. But Patrick is not like Cassius, he doesn't volunteer his innermost, he doesn't exude vulnerability. Still, we have been together-not-together for almost four years now. Neither one of us has to speak to be heard.

"So," I say, returning my attention to Cassius and slurping a spoonful of soup, which turns out not to be bad. "The last 17 years. Where do we begin?"

"How about a game of join the dots?"

"Which dots?"

"Let's see." Cassius reaches for the tin box that is holding our table's condiments, then begins to lay them out between us. "Right. The ketchup is university." He places it next to his soup bowl. "We can skip to graduation if you want. And the mayo…" He pushes this all the way across the table to my elbow. "The mayo is you standing up on international television last year accepting an Emmy. Take me from one to the other."

"You heard about that?"

He cocks his head. “Lilith. Come on.”

I open my mouth to speak, but he interrupts me.

“If you are about to say sorry one more time, Lilith Fidel, please refrain,” he orders. “You left. It’s fine. I’m fine. I just want to hear about what you’ve been up to since. OK?”

“OK.”

“OK…” He gestures towards the condiments.

I laugh. “Fine. Well, shall I start with the ketchup? Or shall we dive straight into mustard?” I smirk now, placing the mustard down as though it is a game of chess. Cassius grins back. And so I tell him.

Or try to.

Because even though I do this all the time, on paper, in spoken form it’s more difficult to tell the stories of one’s soul. Without the tools of literary device, some things just come off sounding superficial, contrived.

Yet so much of that first year after university was unplanned and tied only to the wind. Tickets in a back pocket, passport in a bag, all I knew was that I wanted to live wildly. Freely. And with abandon, in a way I hadn’t since I was a young child. Like those days when I dragged my parents into the living room, and with a twang, would sing for them.

By the time I left university, I already had the scholarship from the film school in LA, and I knew that I would need a world about which to write. A world outside of my head. ‘Write what you know’, they tell you. So I deferred my offer, used the prize money from my Edinburgh Festival play on a ticket to Thailand, packed my notepad, and for the next 12 months adopted a policy of saying yes. Yes to the trek through a jungle. Yes to a boat ride to find hidden caves with two women as inexperienced in caving as me. Yes to the sudden flight to Vietnam with the professor of history I happened across in a slum. Yes to spending a week in his bed. Yes to sunrises on abandoned beaches. Yes to ‘bush food’ that I couldn’t determine. Yes to parties, to women, to men, to women and men. Yes to teaching English in Laos, to church work in Cambodia, to spending Yom Kippur on the roof of a hotel in Mexico with a group of similarly wandering Jews. Yes to five days herding goats on a mountain with no phone signal, sharing a hut with a boy who spoke no English but taught me how to whittle wood. Yes. Yes. Yes.

I was lucky in this foolish whimsy. Every few days I was able to call my parents, proud of my intrepidness, and Dylan, eager for stories, and report that I was unharmed. Nothing went wrong. And the almost-wrongs became the narratives from which my early scripts were grown. Just as I'd planned. It was stupid, of course. Had the Israeli boys not refused to lock the doors of the penthouse in Mexico, as they later told me the hotel owner had suggested, things might have turned out far differently. Had I jumped three inches shorter from the cliff in Thailand, I may have hit the rocks. Had I been bitten by a snake, or had my bungee cord failed, or had the sharks spotted me with my snorkel… But I was lucky. I lived. Even now, the pure fact of that remains exhilarating. It makes words come. Sometimes I still pull trinkets from that year, dusting them off for new exploration.

"But it's so unlike you," Cassius murmurs, finishing the last of his main – a steak the size of his head, and chips.

"Not any more," I tell him. "Once I stopped, you know, all that stuff, I was different."

"But how did you stop?" he asks me. "It was so consuming for you. It was uncontrollable. Don't you remember?"

My stomach grips suddenly with an old anxiousness, and I realise that I have not in fact allowed myself to remember for a long time. Not properly. It is as though there is a latent darkness around that part of my life, banished to shadow.

* * *

With Cassius away in LA, I spiralled. It was as though having had a brief taste of distracting, romantic gloriousness, my mind craved him like a drug in withdrawal. Night-times were out of control – barely a single one passed without some kind of incident – and in the day, intrusive thoughts were consuming. The energy it took to block them exhausted me. Most days, I found it difficult to get out of bed. When I would finally emerge around 12 p.m., Dylan would already be having his lunch, and by the time that was finished with, I'd have to get in a couple of hours on my various pieces of school coursework (and Cassius's), and because of all of the diverting visuals in my brain, instead of two hours it would take at least four, and by then, despite the long, light evenings, the creep of night-time would work its threats through my veins, so that even while I played with my brother, I couldn't stop imagining his limbs broken, his chest bleeding… all of the things that might befall him. Because of me. Zombie-like, I went through the motions. But I was unable to laugh. I was unable to cry. I was unable to do anything except search for new rituals that might bring even a few seconds of reassurance and relief. Inside my cheek grew a collection of painful ulcers. My thighs were permanently red.

Again, my mother offered a visit to the counsellor. But I knew now how useless her advice was and refused this time to go. In low voices, there floated words like 'depression', but that was only because my parents didn't know the thoughts that I tried intentionally to depress, to suppress, to trap within my head. Had they known those, they would have reached for other nouns: lunatic; psychopath.

When Cassius emailed to tell me that he'd tried marijuana at a party at somebody's beach house in Malibu, I replied that that was an incredibly stupid thing to do, especially when he, more than most, knew how fragile the mind could be. Why mess with brain cells, I demanded. Why screw with them?

He didn't answer. For two entire weeks, he didn't answer.

It's necessary to understand that things were different then. There wasn't FaceTime. We didn't have Skype. It cost a fortune to call internationally, and not even Cassius's mobile was up to it. At the beginning, I'd had expectations of long letters, Hughes and Plath style, flying across the internet between us. But it had felt wrong not to enquire first after his mother, and when he said he didn't want to talk about that, other admissions seemed to stifle too. Our notes were brief and uninteresting. By the marijuana email midsummer, it was hard to imagine that we were ever more to each other than we had always been. Everything. But nothing else.

A few days before he was due to arrive home, my father gave me a lift to the pink house so that I could post Cassius's English through the door (under the guise of specially collected magazines). Both cars were in the driveway, as expected, as I supposed they had been all summer, but, unexpectedly, there was music coming from inside the house. I'm not sure who I assumed would be there when I rang the doorbell – the cleaner perhaps, preparing for the homecoming; the gardener; a burglar. When Mark answered the door, I didn't know what to say.

"Oh," is what I uttered.

"Lily." He peered out of the doorway and waved to my father in his cab. "What brings you here?"

"Dropping something off for Cassius," I answered truthfully, handing Mark the bundle of papers I'd sealed in a large envelope. "Are you back then?"

"Back?"

"From LA?" I had assumed that they were all there, especially with Marianne not well.

"Oh. No. I stayed. But how's your summer been?"

"Is Marianne OK?" I garbled.

Mark squinted at me. "I think she's fine."

"That's a relief."

Mark said nothing then, only seemed to study my face. I shifted on the doorstep. It was a sweltering day, one of the last of that summer, and under his gaze I felt acutely aware of the shortness of my shorts, the flimsy cotton of my top. My skin was pale as usual, my redness piled high in a bun. I was glad, all of a sudden, that my own father was just behind me.

"I have to go."

He nodded pleasantly back. "Sure. Take care of yourself, Lily." He tapped the file. "I'll give this to Cassius."

"Thanks," I said. "See you soon."

Except that I didn't see him soon. When Cassius finally arrived home, he texted to thank me for the English, but made a series of excuses as to why he couldn't see me, why I couldn't pop round, even for an hour, before the start of school.

Perhaps it would always be this way when we kissed, I reasoned. One or other of us eternally unready or awkward, or having a change of heart. Perhaps we were only ever supposed to be friends. I could still feel his lips though. When I lay in bed at night, awake for hours, saying my prayers, constructing my obstacles, counting, and pinching, and tapping; between such rituals, between images of Dylan's face being smashed by a stray garden rock or a GCSE textbook (both locked away in the shed), between those things, I would think still of our snatched moments together. I would smell him. I would want him.

It was almost like one of my dreams, that desire. But not. Because my feelings didn't disappear with morning light, with fresh daytime air. They did wane. After a while they no longer crashed like icy waves upon me, but they never stopped truly, only ever in shadow.

* * *

There are still times when silhouettes crawl out of darkened spaces, and I have to catch myself. Not Cassius-shaped, not in a long time, but if I'm making mental to-do lists, for example. Because lists can turn to prayers. And prayers can turn to mantras. For this purpose, I keep a file on my laptop full of random typed thoughts. If they are deserving of action, then I transfer them to a Post-it stuck to the screen, where they will be seen and dealt with, but do not become something I need to hold within my head. If they are not, then I discharge them from my brain into digital storage. If they are crazy, if there is even the faintest suggestion of omniscience, the way I used to think, as though pinching my left leg could really control anything beyond the state of my skin, I type them out and then delete them immediately. It is a trick that my therapist in Sussex taught me: confront the thought; get it out of your brain; discard it. These moments rarely occur though. The file remains, but often months go by when nothing is typed at all.

"Don't you remember?"

"It's a long story," I tell Cassius.

And fortunately, there is not time to begin it, because all at once, walking through the restaurant door, is Patrick.

Wearing pale jeans, a rolled-up shirt and blazer, he has clearly showered since BMXing. And shaved. Prepared. He looks confident, and clean. When Cassius spots him, it is as though he already knows that this is Patrick, as though this is what he expected for me, this tall, dark, athletic American. He stands to shake hands, and Patrick reciprocates. I can see Patrick mentally adjusting the stories I have told him to insert this new, more accurate depiction. They exchange casual greetings, then Patrick pulls up a chair.

"Are you ready?" he says, kissing me on the cheek. Not cheek to cheek; lips to cheek. A statement. Cassius notices. In his presence, Patrick's accent seems suddenly more overtly American than I am usually aware of. And slightly loud. But he smells wonderful. I look over to Cassius, who raises his eyebrows at me, then coughs and picks up the baby monitor.

"Absolutely," Cassius says. "You should go. You've already changed your plans enough. Thanks for that," he adds, to Patrick.

"Not a problem." Patrick nods. "It's good to meet the infamous Cassius."

"Oh?" says Cassius.

But Patrick only grins. "I could kill for a slushy," he says, and gets up to order one at the counter. "Anyone else?"

Cassius and I both decline, and while Patrick is away from the table we say our goodbyes, making plans to meet again the following day.

"It's strange seeing you," I muse quietly.

"It's been stranger *not* seeing you," says Cassius. He holds my eye as he expresses this, and I feel myself blush slightly, the way I used to in front of his father.

Before I can say anything else, Patrick returns to the table with a bright blue slushy in his hand. "All paid," he announces. "Shall we make tracks?"

"You didn't have to do that," Cassius replies, reaching into his trousers for his wallet. "What do I owe you?"

"Please. It's my treat," Patrick insists. "It was nothing. Welcome to America."

Cassius looks to me, but I shrug. I had already planned to pay for dinner myself, and I smile at Patrick gratefully. Clearly, he had the same thought I had: that a man staying in such a grimy hotel could do with not having to fork out for a meal. Patrick is always generous to a fault. But as he smiles back, there is something else besides generosity in the corner of his mouth. It makes me slightly uncomfortable, as though Patrick is marking his territory, or displaying for Cassius the disparity in their wealth. 'It was nothing.' What did he mean by that? The gesture was nothing? Or the cost of the food was nothing, to him? Then again, I have never seen Patrick bitter about anything. He doesn't flaunt his wealth. And he is not normally competitive over me. I should not suspect it of him now. He holds out his hand, and I take it.

"Really good to meet you, buddy," Patrick tells Cassius with warm, unaffected friendliness. But Cassius has sensed something too – even after all these years I can detect it. I see it in the slight movement of his eyes, the tension in his neck, and I find myself thinking about it long after we have said goodbye, long after we have left the restaurant, long after he, and the run-down strip mall, have faded from sight.

When Patrick and I arrive at the bar on East 7th Street, Ria and Nola are already in full flow. We are in the Arts District, always buzzy, and the bar is teeming with enthusiastic clientele. From the ceiling hang neon-stained glass lanterns. An old-school garage track is pumping from the music system, and although she is sitting down, Nola's body seems to undulate to it. You can tell she is a dancer. She and Ria are gathered around a large sharing table with a few other people I recognise, actors mainly. As Patrick and I approach, they shift to accommodate us, and we squeeze in, Patrick's long legs bunched up. Somebody hands him a glass of champagne and I pour myself a water from the bottle on the table, then rest my hand tentatively on his arm.

In the car, we talked a little, but mainly about work. There is the chance to collaborate again on a new project, and Patrick wanted to know my thoughts. He also wanted to know if we could duck out early from the drinks to go back to mine. Amongst his friends, at a barbecue or on a hike or during a Thanksgiving game of football, he is the life of the party, but he doesn't enjoy this scene, and networks only when essential. I prefer more intimate gatherings too, but occasionally I crave the blast of music and hum of a crowd. Plus, I still value opportunities to say yes. As much as I can, I like to say yes to the young actors who sidle up to me, carefully building a conversation to lead to the Big Ask. The studio tells me frequently to stop giving free passes. But somebody said yes to me once, twice, many times. Much of my life is a gift bestowed. 'Because of your talent', Patrick reminds me. But also because of luck. Because the person reading a prize entry in my last year at Sussex happened to like my style. Because that prize had weight to it. Because I survived my foolish meanderings. Because I had people to believe in me. Because I didn't end up in a mental institution. Because, for years,

Cassius helped me to contain my nightmares, and, while awake, to dream.

"Did you like Cassius?" I whisper to Patrick.

Patrick looks at me. "Sure."

"What does 'sure' mean?"

"It means 'sure'." He smiles.

"So no then?"

"No. No means no. *Sure*ly you know that?"

I shake my head, irritatingly amused. "You are enough to drive anybody nuts," I tell him.

"Well, thank you." He wiggles his eyebrows.

From across the table, Ria shouts over to me. "So? How was the old flame?"

"He's not a flame," I correct her.

"He most definitely was a flame," Patrick responds. "Now extinguished, you'll be happy to know. My light still burns."

Ria laughs. So does Nola. "You don't like this man?" she says to Patrick. It is the first communication she has had with Patrick beyond hello. I barely even know her myself, and I am struck by her forthrightness. Perhaps it is a Spanish thing. Although, I suppose, I am often this way too.

"No, I'm only joking, he was fine," laughs Patrick. "He was nice," he tells me. "Honestly. I'm glad you managed to catch up."

"I think we may do something tomorrow too, actually," I inform him. "If you want to join?"

There is the tiniest pause before Patrick answers. "Maybe," he says. "Maybe. Sure."

We don't stay long. After my day with Cassius and Jessie, I feel windswept and exhausted, and Patrick makes frequent eye gestures towards his watch. I'm glad, however, that we came. Nola is an interesting addition to our circle. She tells stories about growing up in Spain, and about losing toenails from dancing, and how once she was in a company where every time the male lead lifted her, he moved his hand about beneath her skirt until one day she grabbed his finger and snapped it backwards as she was landing. This begins a conversation, first about the peculiar, forced physicality in both the worlds of dance and film, "I don't like it," decrees Nola. "I don't like to be grabbed at." And then about the feminist movement in the industry. Depending on the company, people speak now about this with either true passion, or overdone sincerity, or parody, or fatigue. Nola seems at ease with the whole gamut, a continuum she dances through on delicate points. Everything she says seems to be a dance, a rhythmic journey, each of her sentences ending with a punch as though she is vogueing to the beat. And never misses. I regret leaving my notepad at home. I want to write her. She is the dictionary definition of 'flaming red'. Before Patrick and I leave, Nola and I exchange numbers. She says she'll be at yoga on Thursday.

In the car, I lean my head against the window. It feels much later than it is, and I can't help but yawn. It has been confronting to see Cassius again. Just the sight of him makes me feel known, protected, but I am exhausted by the emotional overload in a way I haven't been for years.

"You seem a bit off," Patrick says as we near my house.

"Just tired," I breathe. "Aren't you? I still have to call my parents too."

He nods. "I'll do the talking then. Make their day."

Affectionately, I turn my head from the window to look at him. He is not being arrogant. He adores my parents, and they love him right back. So does Dylan. The two of them spent many days playing golf together last time Dylan was here, and recently Patrick helped Dylan with his final dissertation. Dylan has just graduated from the University of the Arts in London with a degree in art and graphic design. He has an incredible talent, fusing all sorts of different schools and mediums that I do not know enough about. Patrick does though. His father is a Brazilian-born artist, his mother a California-sprung cellist. Neither one ever reaped great financial reward from their talents – sparking Patrick's resolute decision to actually make money from art – but they nevertheless imbued their son with a vast store of knowledge, and appreciation, and curiosity.

"Is Dylan home too?" Patrick asks now.

"Yeah. He's there till January."

In January, Dylan will move to Germany where he has landed a job at a top branding agency. I cannot allow myself to think of how my family-oriented parents will feel when both their children are living abroad. Or how alone Dylan himself will be, how many dangers could befall him. He is so young. And potentially as foolish as me. These are the thoughts that often come to me in the pauses of life, the quiet moments, like now; but I force myself to shrug them off. They are concerns I should not be listing. Fears I cannot control.

"I think he's home anyway," I tell Patrick. "I haven't actually spoken to Dylan for a few days."

Patrick pulls into the driveway to park. "Let's call now then." He consults his watch. "They'll be drinking their breakfast tea."

Despite my tiredness, I laugh. "Coffee. My dad will definitely be on coffee. When will you believe me that English people do not just sit around all day sipping tea?"

"Well, when will you let me stay over, so I can be sure you're not secretly having tea parties in the middle of the night?"

Unintentionally, my face drops. "I wouldn't be," I stutter.

Patrick observes me oddly. "Yeah. I know," he says. "Although now, you look so defensive that I think maybe you are. You're having midnight tea parties, aren't you?"

I force a laugh and open the door to the car, unsettled by my own unease. The taste of it is unfamiliar, or long forgotten. Dredged up. Seeing my skateboard ramp, however, I shake it off. "Coming in?" I ask him.

Now Patrick turns off the engine and joins me as we walk towards the front door. "After the call," he whispers in my ear, "can we play Boggle?"

I am not sure if he means the board game, or a romp under the sheets, and I smile broadly, my disquiet immediately dissipating. I love Patrick for this. For his humour. For his affection. For not pressing the past, but embracing our present together. For learning what I need, and what I love, and also what I cannot give. For not demanding more from me than Boggle.

CHAPTER 10

There was always the sense that Cassius and I were fated for each other. Even my mother thought so, responding to blips in our friendship with calm interest, as though instead of there ever being danger of lasting fracture, we were two squabbling siblings compelled to make up. This isn't the first time she has helped to choreograph a reunion. Over FaceTime, she played it down since she loves Patrick too, but I know she is thrilled that we are reconnecting. She always cared for Cassius. And trusted him with me.

* * *

That term, after his summer in LA, we entered into the world with a new seriousness. This was GCSE year. Our first chance to determine our futures; our last chance not to screw it up. Such pressure both suited and overwhelmed me. It was useful not to have a second to allow my mind to wander, yet thoughts continued to intrude, and everything took an age. My parents began watching the time at which the lights in my room were switched off, and remarked in the morning about my darkened eyes, my pallid complexion, the wound tightness that had come over me. My mother talked about stress-coping strategies. She made me take walks. And then, she invited over Cassius.

She'd opted for a Friday night, when there wasn't the

pressure of homework, but when Cassius and I could still catch the bus from school together. Of course, it wasn't the first time we'd seen each other. Already five weeks into term, even if we'd been trying, which we later agreed that we weren't, we would have been unable to avoid each other at school, but this was the first expanse of time since before the summer that we'd spent alone. That term, as well as courting the drama crowd, Cassius had leapt across circles again, joining the clique who slipped out of school during lunchtime to smoke joints in the park. We shared English and science lessons that year, and in the afternoons, after lunch, Cassius would balance a textbook on his desk in front of him, closing his eyes with his head on his hands. It maddened me to see his flippancy with life, with his brain, and how easily he drifted to sleep. It maddened me also that the teachers overlooked it. He must have told them, I reasoned, about his mother. Or else his boy-man charm was still working its magnetism. Despite my disdain for his choices, it was still working on me.

"So." He smiled as we settled into a pair of seats halfway down the bus. "Hi."

"Hi," I replied, half rolling my eyes, half shaking my head, already smiling.

"How are things?" he sang, his voice tilting with playful politeness. He was wearing a khaki bomber jacket on top of his uniform. The back of his hair had been razored, the front only a little longer, though he still ran his hand through it as though he had tresses to caress. A pale scalp peeked through the stubble, as Dylan's had been when he was first born. He looked vulnerable.

I joked along. "Not bad, thanks. How are things with you?"

"Yeah, good, good, very well, thanks."

We stopped, holding each other's stare. Then Cassius gave an exaggerated grin, and a cheesy thumbs up.

"What happened?" I asked him.

Immediately, he pulled a wool beanie from his pocket and yanked it over his head. "Do we have to?"

"Fine. No. Let's continue to ignore things."

"Lil." Now he put his hand over mine, and a flash of electricity jolted me.

"You can't just do that," I said. "Do you even care how I've been?"

"Of course I care. Do you care?"

"How I've been?"

"How *I've* been."

"Are you serious, Cass?"

Cassius shrugged.

"You ignored my emails. And even so I've tried to see you."

"Well, congratulations, Miss American-Sized Morals." He said this petulantly, sour rimmed.

"That's not fair. All I'm saying is that *I've* tried to ask. Anyway, your dad told me your mum was OK now."

Now Cassius squinted his eyes at me, same as his father had done. "When did you see my dad?"

"He didn't tell you?"

"No."

"Just before you got home from LA. I dropped round the English. He was there. Why was he there?"

"Because now he's not," answered Cassius sullenly.

"What?"

"He's not," Cassius repeated.

"What are you talking about?"

Suddenly Cassius jumped up from his seat and, right in the aisle of the bus, stretched out his arms, waving jazz hands next to his face. "Ta-da!" he exclaimed, too loudly.

"What are you doing?"

"It's the big news!" he announced, still at too high a volume, though tuning his voice to a low register, imitating the voice-overs that announce wrestling matches, or new films. "It's the stupidly cliché event of the summer!"

"What are you talking about?" I muttered under my breath. "Can you please sit down?"

Finally, Cassius sat. "Come on, Lil. Naïve to the last.

With all the darkness in your head, you'd think you'd be a bit more savvy."

I raised my eyebrows.

"They've split up," he told me, spelling it out. "Dad's moved to a flat in London. Mum and I are maybe gonna sell. Why do you think I didn't want you coming to the house?"

"Oh. Cass." Without intending it, I felt a lump swelling in my throat, and I put my arms around him. The warmth of his body made the lump rise higher.

"I'm fine," he told me.

I pulled away. "Really?"

"Course. It's not like it came out of the blue."

"No." I touched his arm. "I guess not. Is your mum OK?"

"She's fine," Cassius answered. "I mean… Yes, thanks, she's OK now."

"And your dad?"

Cassius shrugged again. "Who knows?" Swinging his bag from the floor up onto the seat, Cassius started rifling through it. "Anyway, I'm trying not to think about it. I've been busy doing this." He had joined an actors' agency. In his bag was a black-and-white headshot. "I've already done a commercial," he told me.

"Wow. Seriously? For what?"

"Tesco." He smirked. "I had to walk past a chippy, and then a pizza takeaway, and then rush home for a good ole roast. I'm the face of family food. Ironic, isn't it?"

For a moment, I wasn't sure what to say. There was so much venom to his vim. But he was waiting. "We're having a roast tonight," I told him.

My mother lit the Shabbat candles. Cassius took pride in remembering the prayers and my father passed him the kiddush cup. We talked with more animation than I'd managed in a long time, and my parents couldn't stop smiling, plying both Cassius and me with questions about school, about our friends, about drama club, about all the things they had been wanting to know and had been too scared to ask me. I gave it to them now. While I could, while my mind allowed. I gave them the self I had been suppressing. For the first time in months, I heard the sound of my own laugh. I spoke quickly, as I had when I was younger, bursting with ideas. Cassius and I jousted playfully. And when I looked at him properly, his green eyes were shining, and I could see that he too had needed this: us, me, my family. He lapped it up with his nut roast and gravy, he dipped his challah in it and savoured it on his tongue.

Dylan, recently turned four, glanced at me many times throughout the meal, slowly making his way from his own seat onto my lap.

"Can you play with me after dinner?" he asked. "With that face." He pointed to my smile, and an abrupt pain kicked me in my chest, my heart tearing.

"Sure," I answered, smiling wider, pushing away a vision of his skull cracked and bloody, and instead, kissing him on a patch of beautiful, unmarked forehead.

When I glanced up, however, Cassius was rolling his eyes, looking surly again.

Later, he apologised. It was his dick talking, he confessed, making me wonder exactly what his dick was telling him, since we hadn't kissed, and weren't about to.

Even later, delivered home by my father, Cassius messaged me.

I loved this evening.

Me too.

I've missed you.

Me too.

You are a good person.

I sat up in bed. Over the past months I had constructed a replacement for this ritual, for him, but it had never made me feel as comfortable. *How do you know?* I texted.

After his final *X*, I lay my head on the pillow and began my mental routine. It took around 30 minutes now to get through everything, but I did it that night with a sense of hope.

* * *

In the morning, there is a string of texts from Cassius:

I loved our evening.
Great seeing you.
Lunch today?
X

CHAPTER 11

Jessie shmooshes herself into me. As my arms wrap around her, this is the word that comes to mind – shmooshing. It conjures memories of myself in my parents' arms, or Dylan in mine. Now that I think of it, I am not sure if the term is Yiddish, or English, or merely part of the Fidel family vocabulary, but it remains more apt than any other. Her body is heavy, in that warm, sweaty surrender specific to children, her back carving out a perfect pit in my stomach, her legs fitting seamlessly into my lap. Blonde curls tickle my nose. She laughs as Gabriella deepens her voice to become a dragon. Gabriella is the shop's owner. We are at my new favourite place. Over the years, I have passed it many times but never gone in, being, as it is, a children's bookshop. The walls are white and airy, the shelves blocked into cubbies with books turned front-out so that hands can reach and turn pages, and pictures can be seen. The pictures are important. I wonder sometimes why there are no pictures in most adult novels. Perhaps we reach an age where we'd rather imagine than be prescribed to; but I love looking at them. There are illustrators who, in one picture, with no words at all, capture everything it would take me a year to write. I stare at the facial expressions, at the tilt of a head, at the colours, at the wonder behind drawn eyes, and I want to applaud this depiction of childhood, detained in pen. Gabriella leads a story time twice a week.

Before the session begins, Jessie and I buy a few sweet treats from the shop's counter. They are not obnoxiously wrapped candies, but cookies and muffins that look home-made. We are tricked, I know, into this manufactured wholesomeness, but I don't care. We are sitting on cushions, reading stories, eating snacks, and shmooshing. At the end of the session, we buy books. Jessie keeps them at my house since she is there so often and there are no shelves in the motel room. We are up to 18. That represents nine sessions at the bookshop, nine afternoons of bliss. My assistant director, Will, cannot believe his luck in how much more work I am suddenly entrusting him to handle – though it is temporary, I warn him.

Instead of the car, we take my bike home. I have bought a child's seat that attaches to the back and Cassius trusts me to strap Jessie into. In just a matter of weeks, we have gone from not seeing each other for over a decade, to meeting practically every day, and to give him some needed time alone, I often carry on with just Jessie. I am trying to retain some distance from this little being, some armour, but I can't help adoring her. Frankly, she is impossible not to adore. And every day, Jessie makes me promise to see her again the following. I am sure always to ask Cassius's permission, of course, especially before introducing her to anything new – I still do not know the ins and outs of his parenting rules, or what Serena's might have been – but he liked the idea of the bike, and it is a simple ride back to my house. There is only a short strip of busy road, then the side street down to the promenade, and plain sailing from there until the pier where we dismount to say hello to Madge and deliver her cookies. I checked this diversion with Cassius too – this interaction with 'the homeless'. I think it is good for Jessie to see the vast difference between their modest abode, and what real deprivation looks like; but she is not my child. Cassius did not, however, express any reservation. In fact, more and more I find that he is happy for me to suggest what might be good or bad for her; he is new, I suppose, to parenting alone. This, I speculate sometimes, is why he found himself seeking me out in the first place, now, after all this time – a need to build his family; a memory of mine.

Because even during those darkest years – when I could see the exasperation of it on their faces, a weariness creeping into their voices – the solid presence of my parents never faltered. "Shall we sing? Something silly," my father would try in the car. My mother would dance madly around the kitchen, hoping the music could somehow trick me into my old, buoyant abandon. It was only Dylan, though, who could sometimes penetrate. With a hug, with a giggle, with a sweet-smelling head on my lap. I missed my parents desperately during this time. Close-quartered as we were, the loneliness seeped into me. But I could never bring myself to tell them about the increasing psychosis of my mind. I knew that they loved me, but if I was Dylan's parent, I would never let somebody like me anywhere near.

I couldn't risk that reaction. I couldn't tell.

I am not sure what Cassius does and does not want to tell me now. I don't know what he does while Jessie and I are out. If he wanted me to know, he would volunteer it, but I don't like to ask him how he is grieving for his wife.

When he and I are together, which is frequently, we focus on emotion rather than exploit. He tells me how he is feeling, how he is coping without Serena, how he senses that here, with me, he is slowly coming back to life. I ignore such allusions to our closeness. Not only because of Patrick, but also because I do not feel the same. Cassius's vulnerability reminds me of the boy he was, and the girl I was, and there is a wave-crashing familiarity to that, but we are no longer co-dependent. I do not need him the way I once did, the way he is describing now.

Even as teens, after his trip to LA, we were not quite as inseparable as before. He smoked, and I refused, and this swept us into different spaces. Still, I would listen while he talked about 'our ambitions', which for him seemed always so easy, so reachable, and so gladly intertwined. We were still going to Hollywood, he would inform me, laying out the future, glistening and bright. I needed only to get writing so that we could arrive with a bang. What would I write, he would ask, trying hard to get me to join in, to be bothered. Of course, the leading man would have to look like him.

Sometimes, if he noticed me muttering while we talked, or tapping, or biting my cheek, he would attempt to interrupt the ritual as though he could just shake it out of me. Once, he put his hands on my shoulders and did shake me. There was always the sense from Cassius that he wanted to save me, like he had all those years earlier, in the sea.

But I do not need him now, or Patrick, or my mother. I do not need anybody to save me, or jolt me, or hold my experiences most intimate, to know things I cannot say. Because, these days, I simply say them. It is easy to talk about the light-filled present.

The most frequent recipient of my current ruminations is Ria, and now often Nola too. Not because they are my closest friends, but because they are there, at the start of the day, while thoughts are still mulling. We update each other in the effortless manner possible with people you see regularly, forgoing the need to fill in and catch up. On yoga days, by the time I reach the TV studio and unpack my laptop, I am unburdened and centred. On running days, I leave my thoughts unsaid but dumped in the sand. Either way, my friends at work, and Patrick, receive me fresh. Cassius tries sometimes to delve deeper, beneath this airiness that is LA-born; but for the most part we are busy unpacking him.

Patrick has not complained about the amount of time I am spending with Cassius, but he doesn't like it. There are miniscule barbs beneath queries, and unusual attempts to book up my time in advance. Although he has always accepted that we are not 'a couple', we do not expect each other to strike up a romance with anybody else. "I'm not," I assure him when he asks, just once. "We're not. We're friends only. Besides, he's grieving." Patrick does not blindly accept this as a guarantee of Cassius's intentions, but he trusts me. He trusts me when Cassius and I take Jessie for walks at sunset, reminiscing about the days when we wheeled each other in barrows and stood in the tomato patch. He trusts me when we spend the afternoon at the beach and fall about hysterical over Cassius's attempts on my surfboard. He trusts me when we're buying churros at The Grove, and bunking afternoons off work like we once bunked lessons at school, reminding each other of those times, those feelings. He trusts me when Cassius and I catch each other's eye over the top of Jessie's head, and a glance lingers, a remembering. He trusts me.

I trust myself too. Cassius is my past; Patrick is my present. Nevertheless, Patrick prefers it when I am out only with Jessie.

When we reach the pier, I unstrap her from her seat, and hand her the bag of cookies. She has cottoned on to the fact that I intentionally buy too many, and today reminded me at the counter that Madge prefers the chocolate chip. At the alleyway, she skips happily over to announce this purchase.

"We got your favourite, but also we've got ones with black on top because we read today about a princess who wears black, and that's not very princessy, but she's an adventurous princess, and that's her disguise, so if you eat one, you might feel a bit royal too. Even though I know there aren't real princesses in America. And even though real princesses don't wear disguises. But they also don't wear frilly pink dresses, so go figure."

"Go figure," agrees Madge.

Madge's drawl is what I call deep-Californian. Not valley-girl, not Hollywood, but slow and rich and sun-baked. Jessie has inherited this highly American phrase from her. 'Go figure', she says now, to everything.

"Although maybe there *are* real princesses here in America," Madge continues. "Have you ever considered that? What if they're all in disguise too, like the one of yours who wears black? Maybe they wear bedraggled clothes even, like mine, and pretend to be poor so that you would never recognise them. Maybe they even pretend they need cookies." She raises her eyebrows knowingly, takes a chocolate chip, and Jessie stares at her in wonder.

I laugh. "Come on," I say to Jessie. "Your dad'll be back soon. What's the weather going to be tomorrow, Madge?"

"Sunny all morning," Madge pronounces. "In the afternoon, a little rain."

"Rain? Are you sure?" I ask her.

"Have I ever steered you wrong?" she says.

"You have not," I confirm. And as we say goodbye, again Madge smiles knowingly.

Cassius arrives while Jessie and I are preparing the salad. I have delegated the tearing of lettuce leaves to Jessie, and the selection of the bowl, and the pouring in of dressing. I am handling the knife. The quiche and potatoes are in the oven. I do not cook extravagantly, but I like at least a few meals a week to be home-made. Patrick and I are both foodies, and in LA there are endless places to eat. At the thought of Patrick, I wonder if I should have invited him to join us, but it is more comfortable without him. Like Patrick, Cassius has not actually voiced a dislike of the other man, but I sense it, and right now he is the one in need. The more time that Cassius and I spend together, the more apparent that need becomes to me, and the more guilty I feel for having abandoned him all those years ago. I want to be there for him this time, now that I am strong and have strength to spare.

As soon as the three of us sit down, I see that something is on Cassius's mind. He is fidgety, and impatient with Jessie. When she tries to tell him about Madge's princess theory, he only feigns interest, and asks none of the usual humour-tinted follow-ups he would ordinarily employ. When she tries to sit on his lap, he pushes her away. He doesn't do this hard, of course, there is no violence in him, only a whisper of not-wanting: death to a child. Cassius should know this, and as Jessie's face drops, I narrow my eyes at him. Ignoring me, he stabs at his quiche. For a while, I force my attentions to the food on my own plate, swallowing recriminations – she is, after all, his child – but when she has finished eating, I set her up with cartoons in the other room, and once the volume is up and the door closed, I turn to Cassius.

"OK. Spit it out. What's wrong?"

Cassius rolls his eyes. "Nothing."

"Tell me."

"Nothing's wrong. How could anything be wrong in paradise?"

I study him closely, still stabbing at the last morsels of his meal, distance and time somehow eroding; the two of us as raw with each other as ever. "Why do you say that with a sneer?"

"I didn't sneer."

"You did. It's like you think I've done something to make things, I don't know, not paradise. But you know, I'm not forcing you to stay in LA. It's been six weeks – leave if you don't like it. What happened to your road trip?"

He looks up at me. "Do you want me to leave?"

"That's not what I'm saying."

"But do you?"

"No."

In the old days, I might have thrown the question back at him – *do you want to go*? Challenging, goading, before confession. But I no longer feel the need to hide the truth of my sentiment. We are not romantically involved; it is not as though our relationship hangs on this sway of passion or power. I don't want him to leave, and he should know that. I would never have anticipated it, but I've loved having him in my life again. Besides, there is Jessie. I know that they have to leave sometime, I keep warning myself about it, but she pulls me in, just as Dylan used to. And I see her need. For me, for a maternal influence, I feel it. She needs somebody to shmoosh with. Cassius tries, but his family was never a tactile one.

For a full minute, we sit silently in my declaration.

"Well, I have to leave," he responds finally.

"What? Why?"

"I can't afford the motel," he answers. Then, with an unguarded desperation that reminds me of his ancient rendition of Toad, he rests his head in his hands, and through them, tells me: "Money's a lot more of an issue than I explained. I can't afford the road trip. I can't afford the motel. My savings were all eaten up by treatment for Serena; the drugs they said might help were new, not yet on the NHS, so we had to go private. And then there were the funeral costs, and we had a heavy mortgage, and then the flights here, and, well, there's nothing left. I can't even cover another night at the motel. I've been trying to find work here all day, I've been trying for weeks, but there's nothing. So we have to go home. There's a flight I can get us on tomorrow afternoon. I've checked out of the motel already. Our stuff's on your porch."

For a moment, I don't know what to say to him. I had no idea that things were that bad and my mind races, imagining how he must have been feeling – silently – all this time: water rising, air receding, a suffocating sense of being dragged under. But why did he hide it? It must have felt too humiliating. He must feel humiliated now.

Instinctively, I want to comfort him, to rest my hand on his arm, to intertwine our limbs like we used to, to make it OK. And to offer the obvious help – stay here, stay with me – surely the life buoy he is after. But, somewhere deep inside of me, waves are still crashing, ice is up to my knees, glass is piercing my feet. And when I speak, the words that come out are only: "Where will you stay?"

Immediately, Cassius's jaw tightens. He shakes his head and stands up from the kitchen island where we have been eating, then huffing, starts towards the lounge door. "You know what," he begins. Then stops. Then starts again. "You know what… You know what…"

"What?" I say. "What?"

He spins towards me. "You have no idea, do you? You have no idea what it's like to see you living my dream. *My* dream, that you stole from me. And trying to be fine about it, trying to be happy for you. Clearly, Lilith, clearly I was hoping we could stay the night with you. That we could trouble you for that. But don't worry. I'm sure Madge will have us."

"Cassius," I say.

But he is not listening. "You know, for somebody so apparently perceptive to human emotion, so says Hollywood, so says your Emmy awards, you ain't doing such a stellar job. Why are you so interminably naïve?"

"I'm not naïve," I say quietly.

Except perhaps I am, because I am slightly dumbstruck by the bitterness that has exploded from him. Then again, we have always argued like siblings, like almost siblings. Vicious on the turn of the wind. In his defence, his anger this time is not mislaid. I see that. More than that, I am sorry for him. Sorry I wasn't there before, sorry I let him down once, twice, sorry I am shrinking from his need now. This is not what I intended. I planned, this time, to make up for the past.

But he is asking me to break my rule. My one rule that I have clung to. The rule that keeps me free.

Except, freedom is not fear. Freedom is not weakness. I am supposed to be strong now. I am supposed to say yes.

"Sorry," I amend, finally, slowly. "Sorry. It was a stupid question. I didn't mean it like that. What I mean is, where do you *want* to stay? I can pay for the motel, or a hotel, is what I meant. Or of course you can stay here."

Patrick and I are standing at the end of the garden, in the rain. As ever, Madge was not wrong, except that she predicted a little rain, and it is pouring. Lightning has been criss-crossing the sky all morning, showing off, thunder clapping with increasing roar. My ramp has been flipped over. A hurricane is making its way in from the Pacific. Flights have been grounded.

"I just can't believe you let them stay here," says Patrick. "Honestly, I can't believe it. After everything you've always said. Separate hotel rooms. All these years. Separate houses. I mean, not that we would move in necessarily, but… I thought you had a rule."

"I do," I protest. "I do."

"So what happened to it?"

I look at Patrick, shoulders tense, jaw clenched, eyes blazing. "They had nowhere to go," I answer blandly.

I do not, however, feel bland. Not in the slightest.

It is not that I fear myself in the way I used to.

It is not that I still imagine myself a demon of the night.

It is not that I am consumed by spiralling obsession.

It is only that it has been so long.

So long since anybody slept near me, in my home.

And not just anybody; a child.

The night before, when Cassius brought in their bags, it was with a creeping nausea that I made up the guest room for the two of them to share. There are another two rooms spare, another three if you include my office, but it was too much for me to place Jessie alone. "That's alright just for the night, isn't it?" I asked Cassius, looking at him pointedly, hoping he would understand. He did, nodding, and agreeing that yes, it was much more comfortable for them to be together, in a strange place.

"It's not a strange place!" Jessie had argued, bouncing up the stairs, gleeful at the turn of events. "I want to sleep over in Lilith's bed!"

But both Cassius and I had rejected that quickly.

Instead, we made s'mores. We watched Disney. I braided Jessie's hair. And after she was asleep, Cassius and I stayed up with endless cups of tea, just as Patrick would have imagined, sipping slowly, letting the liquid stain the bottom of the mugs as though in so doing it might imprint for posterity this last snippet of time together. It was, after all, their last night in LA. One last night to reminisce and remember. One night of broken rules. One night to get through.

It took me a long time, however, to fall asleep. The urge to say a prayer or lock my door or just set up a couple of small obstacles invaded my thoughts. But I typed them into my laptop and deleted them immediately. Letting them go. Then I stood on my head, and balanced, and breathed.

In the morning, Jessie ran into my room to wake me. It was earlier than even I would usually rise, but the relief on seeing her unharmed was so fierce that I threw her into the air, and then shmooshed with her underneath the covers, and sang in the shower, with belt and twang. Making her a parting pancake breakfast, I felt a little sad, a little nostalgic already, but triumphant too. Victorious. Exultant. Because with their departure, my thoughts were already turning to Patrick, and to how first confused and then elated he would be when that afternoon, after dropping Cassius and Jessie to the airport, I would ask him to come over, and then invite him to stay over, the whole night, in my room, with me.

Then, however, came the rain.

"What's wrong with a hotel?" asks Patrick.

"Cassius can't afford it," I explain. "Turns out things are a bit dire financially."

"I mean, OK. I feel sorry for the guy. I really do, but—"

"And Jessie," I remind him. "Don't forget Jessie. 'Cos that's the main thing, really. She's lost her mother, and now they're on the move again, and she loves it here, she knows my house, and of course I want to help Cassius, but it's her I most feel for."

"You didn't even know this child six weeks ago," Patrick reminds me.

"But I do now. And she's a child, Patrick. To uproot her again, to make her pack up and move again, now…"

Patrick's jaw has marginally relaxed. "Geez, enough with the bleeding heart." He pauses. "It's for one more night, right?"

I nod. "So long as this storm moves on. There's another flight they can get on tomorrow."

"OK. OK, fine. Although, I still don't really get it, Lil. How could you break your rule after insisting for such a long time? How could you just suddenly drop it, for him?"

I attempt to take Patrick's hand, but he is not quite ready for this and manoeuvres it away. "The thing is, this has made me realise that the rule is unnecessary," I try, coaxingly. "I see now that I don't need it. That *we* don't need it."

"I don't know why we ever did," Patrick interrupts.

With another clap of thunder, I see his brow clouding again. Ignoring this, I continue cajolingly. "Actually, I was going to ask you today if you wanted to—"

"He knows why the rule is there, doesn't he?" Patrick cuts in again. "You told him. Right?"

I nod. "He knows."

"But you never told me."

"I will now," I promise. "And I never exactly *told* Cassius. He knows because he knows. Because he was there when I first needed it. But now, I see I don't."

"I wish I had the faintest clue what you're talking about."

There is rain dripping off Patrick's nose. His tall frame is hunched slightly. Instead of the afternoon of elation I'd been planning, like the weather, things between us feel dampened. My heart sinks a little in the puddles at my feet, but it is not his fault. I should not have expected unquestioning acceptance forever.

"Come inside," I entreat him now. "Let me explain."

And I do.

CHAPTER 12

The first time it happened, my feet were shredded with glass. Not that I even realised they were to start with. In the dark, I lifted and trod again, young pink flesh, groomed only by the occasional English oak, pierced now by sharp, indiscriminate shards. For what seemed like many minutes, I couldn't make sense of that feeling, and I remember flailing around with outstretched hands, as though the concrete touch of something, anything, would root me to this pain, to reality. But in truth, it was only seconds before my mother burst into the bathroom, switching on the lights like sudden sun, yanking me from that restless in-between.

"Oh my God," she gasped. "Lilith, stay still. Don't move. Are you awake?"

Now I was. Fully. And I took in the scene: we were in the upstairs bathroom, the window open its usual crack to let out persistent steam, the toilet lid dutifully down, the tub empty and soiled only slightly by the faint rim of bubbles. Everything else too was in its place, undisturbed. Except, of course, for the glass shelves that had once stood three-tiered above the sink and were now in thousands of pieces around my bare feet on the floor.

"Just… Just stay there, I'll lift you over." Mum ran out of the room to find a pair of shoes, while I took in the smashed perfume bottle of my mother's, and the cracked shaving bowl belonging to my father, and all three of our toothbrushes face down amid the litter by my toes. A moment later, my mother returned. "What on earth were you doing?"

"I'm not sure," I said.

My mother crunched over the puddle of glass and lifted me clear. "You don't remember?"

"I remember climbing," I muttered, an offering. "I think I thought… I thought the shelves were a ladder, and I was climbing at, at… I'm not sure. Maybe, you know, at the building site by the park. Or maybe… And then… I don't know."

Mum shook her head. "You were asleep." Carefully, she manoeuvred my legs through the bathroom door and then onto a towel she'd set out on my bed in the room next door. "You were asleep?"

I shrugged, and promptly burst into tears.

It wasn't the pain of the glass. It was something else, something unknowable and therefore uncontainable.

My mother's arms contained me. While I sobbed, she held me, and she bore witness for me – of my fear, of my relief – the same as she always had, holding in her head the history of me. For many minutes she clutched my small body, my head in her chest, my untameable red curls spilling blood-like over her, her murmurings of "It's alright, it's alright" working somehow, despite their fool's conviction, rubbing away at the gritty taste of darkness. By the time she leaned me back against my pillow, and kissed away final tears, I believed her.

"I was definitely climbing some kind of ladder," I declared now, more cheerfully, both of us determining to approach the episode as a glorious adventure, to be retold, and reconstructed, between us. This was always the way we handled my sleepwalking. Mum said that even as a baby I would babble and move around in my cot, but it wasn't until the age of five that the nightly sojourns around the house began. My parents grew used to me turning up downstairs while they were having dinner, or looming over them in the middle of the night. Mostly, it was amusing. To them. For my mother, with her psychology degree and books about everything, it was interesting too. She liked to talk to me the next day and find out what I could remember, what I had been *feeling*, that was the thing. But largely, I remembered nothing. Walked back to my bed while still in my stupor, I would wake up tucked neatly under the covers, safe and warm and oblivious, and enjoy the story of the night.

This story, too, would be retold. First though, it was necessary to inspect the fallout. Multiple glass fragments were wedged into the bottom of my feet – we lined them all up on a piece of bathroom tissue: a few large pieces that Mum immediately extracted; the rest, more complicated splinters for which she employed tweezers and the squeezing of flesh. I winced at the stubborn ones. In a number of places, blood trickled. For weeks afterwards, I was a patchwork of plasters, and I would flinch at the sudden eruption of a previously unnoticed shaving appearing unhurried from beneath my skin. I can still picture myself sitting barefoot on the sofa, or on a kitchen chair, or on my bed, running my fingertips up and down the soles of my feet, feeling for sharpness. For many months I did that. Aware that this time, something had been different, sliced open, spilled with my blood.

The second time, it was sand between my toes, but it felt like shards, piercing my skin, and the icy water lashed like blades at my knees.

Cassius's hand touched my arm. "Hey. Hey. Are you OK? Lily, right?"

I don't know how long I'd been standing there. When I'd woken, the darkness had hit first, wrapping so tightly that it squeezed my lungs and left me unsure whether my eyes were open or still closed. Through it, there was a cacophony of sensation. Without sight, without precursor, it takes a moment for the senses to distinguish things, to work out even simple circuits, like the difference between opposites: pain/pleasure; hot/cold; wet/dry; wakefulness/sleep. But his hand was warm, and my feet were numb, and he shone a torch first at me and then beneath his own face so that it lit in ghostly shadow.

"Your shoes are getting wet," I told him.

"What are you doing?"

He pulled slightly at my elbow, nudging me away from the waves, back up the beach. Clearly, he imagined that I had been about to throw myself into the sea. "It's not what it looks like," I attempted to laugh, gulping fear down my throat, fighting to control the shallow gasps of my breath. "I must've been asleep. I sleepwalk sometimes."

"You sleepwalked all the way out of your hotel and down to the beach?"

I shrugged, shivering, and looked around me, his torch and the moonlight making even more luminous my pale skin, and allowing the outline of nearby buildings to materialise. "We're staying in that house just up there. It's not far," I offered, as though it was no big deal, as though I didn't want to scream at the top of my lungs and run as fast as I could until I could collapse into my mother's arms.

"Still," he said.

In the distance, a military vehicle trundled by and instinctively I looked at my watch, which wasn't on my wrist. All I was wearing was the T-shirt I slept in, and I was suddenly acutely aware of the lack of cotton underneath.

"It's about one," he said.

At that time of night, my parents would definitely be in bed, not in the communal living room. They must not have heard me climbing out of my own bed, descending the stairs, opening the door, leaving. Abruptly, a cyclone of air flung itself up my throat. I'm not sure why. Something to do with the physicality of my disappearing, the potential of it, my absence, my presence here. It amassed inside me, pulsing. I turned away. My bony shoulders were shaking harder now – a mixture of repressed sobs and the cold – my breath still disappearing into the vortex; but in the dark, I hoped he wouldn't see.

"Are you OK?" he asked again.

I nodded.

"You must be freezing." He took off his jacket and draped it over my back, like the men in the movies. Then he placed a hand on top of it. I could feel the warmth of his body through denim, a sensation that was both comforting and awkward. I wasn't in the habit of physical contact with boys. I wasn't one of those girls who linked arms or sat on laps, not yet. But his hand felt anchoring, like it could weigh down tears. Standing there, neither of us spoke for a long time. In the silence, it occurred to me that I could have drowned by now. And that my parents would never have known what had happened. I would have been a missing child, my face on the front of newspapers. My mother would have given interviews to the press, and some people would have been certain that she was in fact behind it, to blame. And maybe one day my body would have turned up. Or it wouldn't.

"What are you doing here anyway?" I said finally as I turned back towards him, glad that my voice didn't crack.

"I'm staying at the Thalassa. It's just up the beach a bit. The one with the turquoise umbrellas."

"Oh." I nodded. "OK."

We both knew that that wasn't really what I had asked, but I didn't push further.

"I should go back." Carefully, I removed his jacket and held it out to him, standing in my T-shirt, my body curled in.

"You could give it back to me tomorrow," he said. "If you want. We could meet on the beach?"

"OK."

"If you want."

"OK," I repeated.

"Great." He smiled then. "About lunchtime." Even in the dark I could make out shiny, straight teeth. My own smile hid behind closed lips, new adult eruptions clustered in a jumble I had already been told would need braces. "Will you be OK getting back on your own?"

I nodded. "Will you?"

He smiled again. Open. Luminous. "My name's Cassius, by the way."

"I know." I pushed my arms through his jacket sleeves and held it closed around my T-shirt. For a moment, we both stood clumsily. "Thanks," I told him.

My parents were still asleep. I had closed the front door quietly, hoping that the landlady wouldn't wake and reprimand me for leaving it unsecured, and then I'd sat on the mat to brush sand from my feet. Still wet, I would have to run them under water for a proper clean, but caked thinly I had climbed the stairs to my parents' room. My mother was on her side, one arm tucked beneath her pillow, the other strewn casually across my father's chest. He lay on his back, either comfortable with this adornment, or oblivious to it. If I had decided to then, I could have crawled into the small space between them, I could have warmed my frozen limbs with their heat. They wouldn't have minded. Not being woken. And they wouldn't have been angry that I'd been out. They would have been worried, and upset, and asked a lot of questions.

I don't know why I didn't tell them.

I don't know why I stood there for minutes on end, shaking, freezing, watching them sleep.

Perhaps I preferred to breathe in their tranquillity than relive my fear. Perhaps I preferred to return to bed with thoughts of Cassius. Or perhaps it was something about knowing already that, even if I didn't tell them, I could talk to him. For the first time in my life, it was not my mother who had been my saviour, it was not my mother who had borne witness, an independent history was beginning. I was 11, on the cusp – perhaps there was something alluring about this.

After Cyprus, there wasn't anything extreme for a long time, and like so many childhood fears, during the day it receded in my mind. At night, however, I continued to wake in strange parts of the house, at strange hours, in the dark. And although at the start my parents walked me back, like the old days, I couldn't recreate that friendly obliviousness. Even when my father brought me hot milk, or my mother sat for an hour, talking me through my terror. Even with them both right there, tucking in the edges, it no longer felt quite safe under the covers. My legs felt icy. Waves lapped at my restless mind. So I figured I might as well stop shouting for my parents. Instead, when I woke, I forced myself to pause, to breathe, to let my eyes adjust, to reach for a light switch. With her expanding bump that was my brother, Mum needed her sleep. Besides, I no longer needed her to collect my experiences, to hold them all for me. I had Cassius. And I was maturing, growing up. That was enough.

Until Cassius's mother cheated on his dad.

And I saw. And didn't tell Cassius.

And didn't tell anyone.

And went to bed that night wracked with guilt and worry.

And everything changed.

The festering of fear was what did it. A slow serpent creep that coiled around my sanity. Twisting. Because what actually happened wasn't jump-out-of-your-skin scary. It hadn't whacked me over the head like a monster at the gate. What had it even been, really – a gentle arousal, a kiss from my mother, some hushed voices outside my door? But the story the following morning, the morning after I'd witnessed Marianne's affair, the story retold for me, carefully this time, not with the usual amusement; that was the beginning, the stately emergence of tangled thread, of dread, the last time I felt at peace.

This is what my mother told me:

In the night, she had woken. Dylan was six months old now and had been moved into his own room. Usually, he'd wake around 2 a.m., but it was three and he hadn't stirred, so my mother had crept in to check on him.

His cot had been empty.

Twist. That was the first. The bottom knot.

Of course, my mother had shouted for my father, who in a state of half-sleep had switched on the lights and run to my room with the sudden notion that whoever had stolen Dylan had also taken me.

And he was right, my bed was empty too.

The second twist. Harder.

Now my father, already hysterical, reached for the phone to call the police, but my mother steadied his hand. She was putting it together. "Wait," she told him.

They found me asleep on the sofa downstairs, a mug of hot milk next to me, buttered toast on my lap, the window open to a blast of January air. Dylan was asleep too, scooped silent in my arms.

Safe.
Fine.
You were looking after him, even in your sleep, see how much you love him.

But I had used a bread knife, and the stove. And walked downstairs. And lain on the sofa. And opened the window…

I could have thrown him out of it, left him to freeze. I could have burned him on the gas flame. I could have spilled hot liquid onto him. I could have squashed him against the cushions. I could have dropped him down the stairs. I could have smothered him in his blanket, or stuck the knife into his chest. I could have done anything.

Because here is what I remembered:

Waking up.

That's it.

Blankness, and blankness, and then waking up, prodded softly by my mother who lifted Dylan away. My neck was sweaty and wet with his dribble. I smelled deliciously of him, of purity. My father's arms under mine helped me sleepily back to bed, where the edges were tucked in, and I woke, like the old days, safe and secure.

Innocent. Oblivious.

Until my parents told me the story. They stirred milk into coffee as they talked, an attempt at flippancy, but they glanced anxiously over their cups towards me, and they spoke without their customary mirth. Before they had even finished talking, I burst into tears. And I said it out loud, what I was thinking, what we were all thinking: "What if I'd hurt him?"

"But you didn't hurt him," soothed my father.

"You would never hurt him," promised my mother. "You're like his second mummy, aren't you? Look, even in your sleep you were nurturing him."

"And even in your sleep, you've never done anything dangerous," said my father.

"What about the glass shelves?" I asked, not mentioning icy waves and shrapnel sand.

"That was years ago," he countered. "That was years ago."

But I saw a look pass between them. The final twist.

When I met Cassius later that day, I didn't even think about Marianne. Instead, I told him about Dylan.

"Shit," he said, the right response, getting it.

We were at his house again. I hadn't wanted to go there, but it was planned already, and thank goodness, Marianne was out. Cassius's father was back from his trip, though I hadn't seen him yet. Cassius had organised a movie marathon with a few of our drama-crowd friends and I'd arrived early to help. For once, we were in the living room. They called it a lounge, which for me conjured ideas of VIP waiting rooms or the lobbies of hotels too fancy for me, but in his house it seemed fitting. The sofas were deep and plumped, the windows tall and curved. A chandelier cast dimmable light across a vast glass coffee table, and a new flat-screen television stood proud in its bespoke surround. We were pouring popcorn and crisps into waiting bowls, scattering the tops with Maltesers and cola bottle sweets.

"Jesus," he said, putting down the popcorn pack. "That's scary. Remind me never to sleep next to you."

"Thanks a lot," I tried to laugh, but not convincingly.

He sat down. "Are you OK? Are you scared you might do something else?"

I plonked myself down next to him. "I can't control it," I confessed. "I can't control what I might do. And he's so little, so helpless. I just keep picturing all the things I could have done to him. How can I ever sleep again?"

"But you're not going to do anything bad," Cassius argued. "Because you're not bad. You're good. You, Lilith Fidel, have morals the size of America."

I focused on the popcorn as he said this, thinking of Marianne's breasts.

"So there's no reason that you would do anything bad, even in your sleep. Honestly, Lil, trust me. I know you better than anyone, and I can firmly say that even unconscious, there's no part of your brain that would let you hurt your brother."

"That's what my mum said," I responded. "But how can anyone really know?"

"She is a psychologist."

"She's a relationship counsellor," I corrected. "Which basically means she teaches husbands and wives how not to be despicable people." Again, I thought of his mother. "They don't really know anything about the unconscious brain."

"I say don't worry about it," Cassius insisted, returning to his task of pouring popcorn. "You always sleepwalk more when you're worried. You know that. So just… don't worry."

"Oh, easy as that."

Cassius grinned, raising his eyebrows irreverently. And for a moment, I did feel easier. But then he turned back towards me. "Wait. What were you so worried about last night to trigger it? Was it my DJing?"

Hurriedly, I laughed, resisting the growing heaviness pushing down on my shoulders. "See, you don't know everything about me."

And not noticing, he grinned again.

Only as soon as I'd said it, I wished that I hadn't. We teased. We goaded. But we confessed too. I shouldn't have dodged the opportunity. I should have grabbed the passing platform. Got off. Unloaded. Told him exactly why I had been worried, exactly what his mother had done. When his father walked into the room, I felt this doubly.

"Oh, right," said his father, seeing me. "I forgot you had friends over. Hi. How are you?" He reached out his hand towards me, smiling. "Mark."

I stood up to take his palm, instantly terrified that he knew about Marianne, and knew that I knew, and knew that I hadn't told. But his eyes were warm.

"And you?" he prompted me.

I wasn't sure if his not remembering my name was a joke – we had met at least ten times previously, and usually people remembered red, and height – but there was something about the touch of his hand that made me forget that, and forget my guilt, and, as I answered, blush.

In my periphery, I could see Cassius rolling his eyes. "Anything we can help you with?" he demanded of his father from the sofa.

Mark didn't answer, but now a flash of something less warm, less wholesome, traced his jaw.

After we'd heard his footsteps fade down the corridor, I turned to Cassius. "Why did you do that?"

"What?"

I pulled a face. "Prod him like that? You're always saying he's never here. But he was here. Were you, what, trying to get his attention?"

Cassius scowled at me. "Don't try to be your mother." He threw a piece of popcorn.

I removed it from my hair and ate it, studying him. Something was going on between him and his father, and I knew I should ask more. But it felt dangerous, and duplicitous, to talk about his parents. I hesitated.

"You don't know him." Cassius pointed the remote control at the TV. "You don't know what he's like," he added. And waited; but still I hesitated. Now Cassius turned and looked straight at me. But I said nothing. So he did. "Don't fall asleep while we're watching, OK? I don't want to be attacked if you sleepwalk."

Even as the words came out of his mouth, I saw him try to pull them back. He smiled weakly, softening the blow. But it was too late, my stomach twisted again. Cassius hadn't quite said it with malice, but he knew what that comment would do to me. We stopped talking. He threw another piece of popcorn. And another. But the lightness was lost, and with it, the chance for either of us to unburden ourselves of heavy things.

Still, I stayed at Cassius's as late as I could, avoiding the night.

The wind chime in the garden was hard to reach, especially in the dark, but the oak's footholds were familiar and welcoming. I used Sellotape to hang the chimes from the arch of my bedroom door. Around my bed, I scattered a mixture of collected shells and coral, many years' worth of them that I usually kept in a crocheted bag and occasionally took out to admire and order. In between, I placed the rain stick I displayed on my bookshelf, a stack of books, the tambourine I had acquired from a long-ago fair, and a few of Dylan's squeezy toys. Anything that might make noise. In bed, I tucked the duvet tight around myself, carefully placing my body on top of each side; and despite my dislike of sleeping in anything constricting, I wore as many bangles as I could fit on my wrist. They were the cheap plastic kind and dug into me when I lay on my side, but I was glad for sleep never to come. Earlier, my mother had said goodnight and dimmed my bedroom lights. Now, I turned them on again full blast, and although it was gone ten, I took out a book, and read. For hours I did this, or rather, I reread the same few lines of text, unable to concentrate on plot, until eventually I gave up and allowed myself to lie flat. There was no way, however, that I was going to close my eyes. Instead, I stared at the cracks in the ceiling, counted the dots on my wallpaper, recited poems in my head, did anything I could think of to occupy my unreliable mind. Around 2 a.m., I knew, Dylan would wake, and then my mother would take him into her bed. With her. Protected. I just had to stay up until then. I just had to wait.

It wasn't hard. Even if I'd tried, sleep wouldn't have come to me; my stomach was too tense, too twisted, my chest too tight. At some point, uncalled-for tears rolled down my cheeks and formed an uncomfortable wet patch on my pillow; all the better to keep me awake, I determined.

Yet I was so tired. From the shock of the morning, from the anxiety of the day, from carrying secrets, from my terror now.

I was so tired. So, so tired. So exhausted already.

But there were things to do.

In the early days, garrisoning my room was enough. I worked out a system, and each evening, after my parents were in bed, I set about constructing the obstacles I hoped would foil me in the night. I didn't tell them what I was doing. I feared they wouldn't let me near Dylan any more. They loved me, I knew that, but I remembered that flicker in their eyes.

It was hard, however, to hold the anxiety in my head alone. It was difficult too to stay up so late, night after night, waiting for Dylan to be protected. Soon, exhaustion took its toll. But of course, this was the beginning of a vicious cycle, I discovered later – sleep deprivation can trigger sleepwalking, while the fear of sleepwalking was what kept me awake.

After some months, our neighbours started reporting to my parents that they had seen me in the back garden, or on the front lawn, in the middle of the night. Once, I'd been digging in the flower bed. In the morning, there was mud on my feet and underneath my fingernails. I stared at the soil in horror. What had I been doing? Looking for treasure? Digging a grave? "What if she'd walked into the road?" I heard my father ask my mother. After that, they began to double-lock the doors, and set the alarm, and hide the keys to my father's cab. And to me, that was confirmation enough – my fears were real, and my parents were scared of me too. Anybody would be.

CHAPTER 13

Yet. I don't stop there. I tell Patrick everything. About what happened in Bristol. About my name, the curse of it. About the deal I made with myself to escape it. About the rule that set me free.

I have never before laid it all out like this, chronologically with linear progression. It is both draining and liberating, and when I finish, I experience again that intoxicating buoyancy I had back at Sussex when I was first unbound. It is as though cool air has rushed with the hurricane through my lungs, and into the storm I want to shout it: *Look at me, look at me soar, look at me fly*.

Patrick does not quite understand this seemingly bizarre uplift in my mood, but he does not laugh or belittle or dramatise the things I have disclosed. Not that I would ever have expected him to – the secrecy was never his shortcoming, but mine. Now, he is hurt that I hid such a lot from him. He says this, and I see an infinitesimal reduction of his frame. Still, he is happy that I have told him at last. He says this too. And he is curious about the sleepwalking. He has a friend, he says, with OCD.

"The strangest part to me, with him," Patrick wants to share, "is the idea that anybody can control anything. By, I don't know, turning on a switch, or washing hands, or whatever."

"Those are very clichéd examples," I tell him.

"But the principle," he insists. "How does anybody ever come to believe that they are that powerful? How did you?"

You are not that powerful. A simple truth. *You are not that powerful.* It is so clear now, so obvious, but as a teen, Cassius told me this too. And I didn't believe him.

"It's not logical." I shrug.

"It's fascinating," says Patrick. "And heavy." He takes my hand.

"And horrendous," chips in Cassius, entering the room suddenly with Jessie.

Patrick looks at Jessie hard. "Of course."

"You should have seen some of it back then, Pat. I can't say I miss it."

I exhale loudly. "Me neither." And lean against Patrick's arm. But Patrick lets go of my hand.

"Well." He stands up. "Good thing it's all handled now."

"Are you going?" I ask him. "Surely not now? In this weather?"

He hesitates, scanning between me and Cassius. And Jessie again.

"It's probably not something you can ever quite say is 'handled' completely though," Cassius interjects, nodding at Patrick, and then at me. "Right?"

Patrick hovers.

"I don't know," I say. "I do think it's handled. I mean, I haven't sleepwalked since I was at university, and I've barely thought about it in years. Until you arrived."

"Except for your rule," tests Patrick, glancing again at Jessie.

"Which is now redundant," I promise.

"Great!" says Cassius. "So we're OK here for a few more nights then?"

Patrick is putting on his coat, which is still wet from the rain, but he pauses now. "A few more?"

Cassius nods, then gestures at the coat. "You're not going,

are you? Sorry, Pat. I didn't mean to get in the way. Please don't go because of us."

Overtly now, Patrick regards Cassius. "It's Patrick," he tells him. "How long then, buddy?"

"Well, all flights are now grounded tomorrow," Cassius replies, waving his phone in evidence. "And after that, with the kind of tickets I have, I can't get us on another one till Tuesday. Do you mind, Lil? I'm really sorry." He says this to me but is looking at Patrick. "And honestly," he adds. "Pat, please stay, pretend we're not here."

"I already am, buddy." Patrick smiles.

Then Cassius smiles too, excessively.

There is an awkward pause.

Suddenly, however, Jessie throws herself between them. "More sleepovers!" she cheers, jumping onto my lap and hugging me around the neck.

"For you," Patrick says, bending his giant frame over her.

"For me *and* Daddy." She flaps him away. "But not you."

Cassius cannot suppress a laugh at this. Neither can I. Neither, in the end, can Patrick.

CHAPTER 14

Of course, we have had a sleepover before. My mind keeps flying to it.

Even then, it didn't feel like the first time. But it was.

Before that, even if we'd spent the evening together, even at 3 a.m., Cassius had always got up and dragged himself home. Since he'd passed his driver's test the previous autumn, he'd taken to arriving at our house late in the evening. His mother's boyfriend was living with them, and I had my usual demons, so we were both happy to pass the hours of the night. During these hours, we kissed sometimes. And occasionally did more than kiss. But then other times we didn't. There were no overriding rules governing this. The coming and going of his girlfriends made some difference, but not always. My state of stress was a factor. His buoyancy. When we were both full of theatre, our exploits were more frequent. Or if I'd had a good run of sleep. But in the main it simply became an extra ingredient to the language between us – spoken at whim. And nobody questioned us. My parents trusted Cassius. They trusted me. So I don't know if they thought that we slept together, which we didn't, but they knew that we would be responsible. And when Marianne planned three weeks in Tenerife, complete with the boyfriend, they agreed that this was not the best preparation for imminent exams.

I hadn't failed my GCSEs as badly as I'd feared. Without a full roster of A*s, I was no longer considering Oxbridge.

But only a couple of Bs had dusted my collection. Mentally, things were a little improved too. Cassius liked to analyse, particularly when he noticed a new behaviour – the way that my left foot had to step out before my right (because from my bed, left led to the wall, not to Dylan's room), or the way I always stood, then sat, then stood again before moving (an attempt to condition myself into hesitancy, into sitting back down) – and sometimes these observations lightened things, but often they annoyed me. At nearly six, Dylan had had a growth spurt and was virtually too big for me to lift. Of course, there remained plenty I could do to hurt him, but at least he was sturdier now. And if everybody just left me alone, just left me to handle it, just stopped asking me why I couldn't be on time or go to certain places, or interrupted me mid-mantra, then I was fine, I was fine.

That year, Cassius was in my English class only. His parents hadn't allowed him to choose drama. The expectation was that he would study economics at university, preferably at Oxford. Divided though they were, his parents were united on this. But by Easter, we had received our university offers, and decided on Bristol, together – he in rebellion, me in hope.

Only Dylan questioned the holiday study arrangement. "If somebody can sleep in Lilith's room, why can't it be me?" he moaned. He wrapped his arms around my waist as he said this, shining his melting eyes up at me. "Pleeease?" he begged. "You never let me. Pleease?"

But quickly, firmly, I refused, more firmly than I had ever spoken to him. And when I did, I felt his arms slacken, weaken, as though some fortifying fibre had been broken there. For weeks afterwards, I sensed a hurt, a pulling away.

Still, it felt good to fall asleep wrapped in somebody's arms.

Cassius's body was warm, his scent familiar. We both slept in shorts, he without a T-shirt. His chest had a spattering of hair, enough to tickle my cheek. I looped my leg across his, and he held me that way, one arm around my shoulders, the other holding my thigh. For the first time in years, it was as though somebody had walked me back to bed, and tucked me in, and I could be oblivious, contained. We whispered about the trip to the seaside that we had never taken, and how we would once exams were over. Just us. Although I still set out the obstacles in my room, not bothering to hide them from Cassius, on a number of evenings I found myself falling asleep before I could even finish my mantras. That had never happened before. And it was wonderful. Wonderful.

In the beginning.

For the first few nights at least, perhaps a week.

But then, of course, I walked.

Flesh pawing at wood. That was the first sensation. The dull numbness of semi-consciousness, like a tingling pins-and-needles limb. When my eyes adjusted, I saw that I had been batting at the kitchen cupboard, attempting to open its door, but reaching for the opposite side to where the handle was affixed. I had a sense that I had been somewhere else, or that I was still somewhere else. Yet here my body was.

"What are you doing?"

I turned. Cassius was sitting at the kitchen table behind me.

"Cassius."

"I knew you were awake now."

"What?"

"Your eyes did this weird extra-blink thing, and then I could just tell, that you'd woken up. It's so interesting."

I paused for a moment, trying to understand what he was telling me. On the table in front of him was a half-drunk glass of water. "How long have you been sitting there?"

"I dunno. You've been standing there a while."

A dark shiver shot through me. This had always been one of the things I'd hated most – the idea that I could be watched, seen, without seeing. "Why didn't you wake me?"

"I wanted to see what you'd do."

"It's not funny, you know."

"I know. I'm not laughing." His eyes, however, were glowing. "It's so totally weird. It's like you're awake, but you're somehow not quite, not quite, I don't know. There's something just slightly different. But you move around incredibly, considering that you're not actually cognisant. You were in the bedroom for a while, just wandering around. Then you went to the loo."

"You followed me to the loo?"

"No." He paused. "I waited outside."

"You stood outside the bathroom listening to me on the loo?"

"Only to check you were OK."

I raised my eyebrows at him.

"Anyway, then you walked all the way downstairs, absolutely fine, not bumping into anything. And then you came in here. And you've been trying to open that cupboard for a good five minutes."

"And you just watched me?" I asked him.

He shrugged, eyes still twinkling. "Sorry."

I sat down at the kitchen table and took a sip from his glass. The weather hadn't quite warmed up yet and in my shorts, without slippers, I was shivering. Then again, the weather may have had nothing to do with it. I wrapped my arms around my chest, reminded of the first time that Cassius and I had properly spoken, on the beach, in the sea. Whether or not Cassius was thinking the same thing, his face changed suddenly to one of remorse.

"Sorry," he repeated, stroking my arm. "I just really wanted to see what it was like. After all these years hearing about it. But, I mean, sorry. Next time I'll wake you."

"Or guide me back to bed. Get me safe," I said quietly. Then looked at him. "I just want everyone to be safe. From me."

"Lil, you're never going to do anything bad. You know that you would never—"

"It doesn't help, Cass," I interrupted him. "It doesn't help any more. Nothing does."

With that, I stood up from the table and took myself back to bed, where I left room for Cassius, but turned away from his space, his traitorous hope, tucking the covers in tight. A few minutes later, Cassius slid his body next to mine. His legs were cold. He put his arm over my waist, but I shrugged it off. I had nothing under control, after all. And Cassius couldn't save me. Nobody could save me from myself.

After that, it wasn't possible to concentrate on exam revision. A bleakness returned. There no longer seemed to be a point to any of it. Not to facts and arguments, not to talk, not even to bothering to dress or shower or eat lunch. None of it made a difference. None of it could rescue me from the trappings of my own mind. I became convinced that I was crazy. I wrote poems about it, then crumpled them up and threw them away in the sudden conviction that they might become evidence against me. My parents began whispering again. Behind my back, they spoke to Cassius. Dylan was even sent in. I accepted his hugs, his chatter, his small body curled up to mine, but not even he could drag me back into the light.

Nobody was surprised when I missed my grades for Bristol. Cassius would go without me. And without him, I would settle for Sussex, by the sea.

CHAPTER 15

Inevitably, a few nights turn into more. There is always a reason: no point leaving at the crack of dawn, better to wait for a more sensible flight time; a farmers' market that looks incredible and would be a shame to miss; a trip to Disneyland for Jessie, one last hurrah. In truth, it is me. I want them to stay. I want to stay up after a long day at the studio, talking with Cassius, feeling familiar in a way I had forgotten was possible. I want to wake up with Jessie's hands squidging my cheeks. I want this unit.

It is not him. It is not that I want him.

Patrick tolerates the delay but won't stay over while they're still here. I am longing for him to do so; I have wanted this for years. He does invite me to stay at his house; but it is always Cassius and Jessie's last day, or almost last day, or last Tuesday or Wednesday or… I make excuses.

Why do I make excuses? I'm not sure.

One morning, I get a call from Dylan. It is early, but he has been waiting for a reasonable hour. I have just finished my run.

"Tell them to go," he says, before hello.

"Hi, Dyl, nice to talk to you too," I laugh down the phone line. I am stretching on the front lawn. Jessie is at the kitchen window, waving. I wave back. Her hair is loose and not yet brushed. Cassius can only manage basic ponytails, so she waits for me. I do plaits: French, Dutch, singles, multiples. We have invested in coloured accessories.

"Patrick says they're never going to leave."

"Patrick *told* on me?"

"He didn't tell on you. We were chatting. He mentioned."

"Cass is going through a tough time," I say, more seriously. "I want to be there for him. He always was for me. You remember."

"No. I remember him being there for him," Dylan tells me.

"What?

"I never liked him."

"Dyl," I say.

"No. I never liked him."

Now I laugh gently. "Because he took me away from you."

"You're not being fair to Patrick," he presses. "Who I do like, by the way."

"Yes, Dyl, I get that. And by the way, I like Patrick too."

"You should tell him that."

"I do. All the time."

"Are you in love with Cassius?" Dylan asks bluntly.

I pause. Jessie is waving again. Cassius comes up behind her and holds up a hand. He makes a gesture for coffee. I give him a thumbs up.

"I'm not in love with him," I answer finally. "I love him, like a brother. Not like *you*," I add quickly. "But you know, like I've known him forever. I'm not in love with him."

"Good. You should tell Patrick that too."

I laugh. "Thank you for the advice."

"You're welcome."

"Now, can I please give you some advice about Germany?" I try. But suddenly Dylan has an urgent thing to do.

On the couch, it feels natural to interlink our limbs, but I don't. They have delayed for another day, but there are plans to book flights first thing in the morning. Real plans this time. Really. Jessie is in bed, and Cassius and I have ordered Chinese food. It is delivered by the son of the owner who I have known for years, and he gives me a free bag of prawn crackers. I have also ordered extra noodles, for Madge. When Cassius tries to open the box, I swipe him away.

"Just a little," he protests.

"No, they're for her, it's not nice."

"There you go again."

"What?"

"Morals the size of America."

I shake my head at him, enjoying the teasing, the goading; ignoring the latent memories this reference stirs.

For a while, we chat about his family, about mine, about Patrick, and Jessie. I tell him about the new idea I am working on. Time slips by with the ease of old meanderings. Distractions.

* * *

"You just need a distraction," Cassius used to declare, often.

But I would shake my head. "I'm going to fail."

"You are absolutely not going to fail. You're far too clever for that. But if you can't concentrate, you can't work. So we need to distract you."

"Distract me into focus?" I smiled.

"Exactly."

"And I'm the crazy one."

But I would let him, let him distract me with trivial things.

* * *

There is a finality, however, to our conversation now, a destination. And when at last we have picked through the remains of the Chinese food, we make it to where we've been heading.

"What are you going to do?" I ask him. "What do you *want* to do? Do you want to stay? I mean, do you want to properly live here? In LA?"

"I love LA," he answers slowly. "I always have. And I love being with you. And always have. But I don't know how that would operate realistically. I'd need a work visa. And a job."

"I could maybe help with that."

"Thank you. But also, we both know that Jessie and I can't stay with you forever. Patrick wouldn't be OK with that."

"No," I agree.

"And you care about what Patrick thinks," he continues.

"Yes."

"You love Patrick."

I pause. "Yes."

"And not me."

I notice suddenly that Cassius has moved closer to me. Our faces are almost touching, our limbs almost intertwined. I remember this. I remember this. I remember how this could be. Just an extra word, just an extra part to our vocabulary. My body pulses towards him. He smells intoxicating. But I put up my hand. Patrick trusts me. And I trust myself too. My conscious mind is in control, finally.

"I will always love you," I tell him, smiling so as not to make it uncomfortable. "But I have American morals."

These days, at least.

* * *

"Keep it," whispered Cassius.

He plunged the DVD deep into my bag and spun around to check that nobody was coming out of the shop behind us. It was the new Jim Carrey movie, just released. We were on the local high street, sandwiched between two boutiques that had opened the previous month. Bunting criss-crossed the road, hung early for the regatta. A busker was playing the violin. This was the exact kind of chic quaintness that had made Marlow a new commuter favourite. To their friends, my parents were no longer free spirits, but savvy property trailblazers.

The stationery shop from which we'd just emerged was one of those big multi-use ones selling everything from office supplies to sweets and DVDs. Cassius and I went there regularly to peruse the fiction charts and to add to his music collection. He wasn't DJing any more but liked to profess to eclectic taste. Although it was large, the cashiers worked on a regular rota and rarely changed. When we stood making our teenage pronouncements, they chipped in. They knew us. We knew them. That day's cashier was Verity.

"Cassius. I can't. No."

"You took it."

"I didn't take it. You put it in my bag."

"You saw me doing it."

I hadn't seen him, but Cassius's conviction made me question myself. It was down to physicality again, wasn't it? Presence? I'd stood there, next to him. The DVD was right there, in my bag.

"Why didn't you just buy it?" I demanded, glancing around and hugging my bag tight. "It's not like you can't afford to."

"Where's the fun in that?"

"Who are you?" I demanded. "It's not 'fun' to steal. I'm taking it back."

"Don't be stupid." Cassius led me by the arm a little further away. "Nobody saw. And look, it's a huge chain, it's not like we're stealing from Verity. I just thought, you know, everybody has to do something wrong once in their lives. And you won't smoke with me. So. You have to break the law just a bit."

"Why?" I demanded. "Why do I have to break the law? No, thanks."

"Lil, just let it sit for a minute. How would you even explain taking it back? Oops, sorry, I mistakenly slipped this into my bag?"

"No, I can tell them that my dumb friend thought it would be funny to take it."

I was whispering furtively, despite being too far away for anybody else to hear.

Cassius smirked. "You wouldn't dob me in."

"Oh really?"

"Really."

"Oh really?" I stared boldly at him now. He was right, there was a tiny bit of fun to it, though my heart raced with the sin.

"Let's just take it home, and think about it," Cassius coaxed. "And maybe watch it."

"There is no way that I'm watching it," I pronounced. "No way. And nor are you. We are not taking pleasure in this. Seriously, what if Verity gets in trouble? We should take it back."

"Don't take it back." Cassius hung his arm around my shoulder, guiding me yet further away. We were almost at the end of the road now, distance eroding my determination. "Let's just go back to yours and see how we feel tomorrow."

"Fine," I agreed at last. "But I'm going to return it in the morning. I'll say I had put it in my bag 'cos I was carrying too much, and then forgot to pay. Or something."

"Yeah," Cassius agreed. "Or something."

"I'm going to."

"OK."

"I am."

Except that after Cassius showed the film to my parents, and they thanked him and announced that yes, they'd love to watch it too, and said that actually it was even suitable for Dylan, we removed the plastic wrapping, and we slipped it into the DVD player, and we ate popcorn while we watched. And I did take pleasure.

Of course, later, I obsessed over the whole rigmarole. While I was trying to sleep, I thought about this instead of my usual rituals. When I was ploughing through homework, revising for a test the following day, the sin of it kept popping into my mind, and I had to concentrate hard on the words I was reading to avoid the gripping sensation of having done something so indisputably morally wrong.

You have turned me into a criminal, I messaged Cassius at last, two days later.

No answer.

Cassius.

No answer.

Oy. I can't stop thinking about it.

Finally: *You're welcome*, he replied.

I'm not thanking you.

You're welcome.

Huh?

For a couple of minutes he didn't reply again. Then: *Been thinking about anything else?*

All at once, it struck me. For the first time in many, many years, two entire days had passed without my imagining the horrific ways in which I might accidentally harm my brother.

Now it was me who didn't respond.

Well? Good distraction? Have I distracted you into focus?

He had. I had learned everything I needed for the test. I hadn't counted or muttered or said a mantra once.

Now, however, I did. Tenfold.

You did. I messaged him some minutes later, when I was finally able to pause.

See what I do for you?

I didn't reply, my fingers tapping against my leg, pinching my thigh. Hard. Harder.

Plus now you have a new story to write about.

Still I didn't answer.

If you write a screenplay, dibs on playing me.

Hello?

I forced myself to concentrate on the phone. *Just one problem*, I messaged back finally. *Now I know that I am actually not a good person. That I can do bad things.*

You are a good person, he messaged dutifully back.

But I turned my phone off and didn't allow myself the reply, the routine, the ceremony that gave me relief. I didn't deserve it. He was wrong. He had always been wrong. I was not a good person. I was capable of anything. And now he had proved it.

* * *

Not now.

Then.

Then.

This time, we don't need weeks or months to unwind the awkwardness between us.

We laugh it off and make plans. Good ones. He is staying. He needs work, and I can find him that – free passes are my thing. He needs a flat, but for now there is plenty of room in my house, and although Patrick won't be thrilled, he'll understand.

On the phone, Jade expresses reservation – "You guys were always so intense." But Ria welcomes the news. She likes Cassius. In fact, I think she really likes him. We have by now shared multiple lunches together and she's had her flirty face on. Nola has not yet met him in person, but she supports the concept. Nola, I am discovering, is all about concept. Ideas. The sensuousness of her dancer body is a misleading cover. She is not a carnal person at all. Nola's passion is cerebral. She thinks hard about everything and calculates carefully. She has an opinion always. On this, she affirms that letting Cassius stay is the right thing. And if Cassius does start work soon, she adds, she has a friend from Spain who is a nanny. Illegal, so cheap, but excellent. Employing her would be the right thing too.

I thank Nola, but it is difficult for me to imagine allowing anybody to spend extra time with Jessie. I still grab every moment I can.

Jessie tells me that she has seen her mother.

"Where?" I ask her. "In a dream?"

"No, by the beach."

I smile. "What was she doing there?"

"Just talking to me. And Daddy."

"What did she say to you?"

"She said that she loves me. And also that Daddy should kiss you."

"Oh really?"

Jessie nods and snuggles into me. We have moved her into her own room, separate from Cassius, and bought her a bed set depicting a midnight sky. I have just finished reading her a story and she is wrapped tight in stars. Cassius is downstairs reading the script for my show the following week. He has started giving me notes, sometimes excellent ones. I am reminded of our old fantasy, where we became a Hollywood power couple, who were not actually a couple. "She said it's OK," urges Jessie.

I squeeze Jessie closely. "You know your daddy still loves your mummy," I tell her.

"I know," says Jessie. "But she really said it's OK."

I squeeze her again. I can sense her longing. The same as Cassius's used to be. For a family unit. For love. "What did Mummy look like, at the beach?" I ask her.

"Just normal," she says.

"No wings?"

Jessie scrunches up her nose. "No. She looked like herself. She has peachy skin. And red hair."

I nod sadly. I have seen a picture of Serena. She was dark, with almost black eyes, and olive skin. Jessie is describing me. She is only three, and it has been almost four months now. I wonder if she can even remember her mother clearly. I wrap her even closer in my arms.

It is not that I want to replace Jessie's mother, I truly don't. But I like that she sees me as a mother figure, and I want to give her love. The love I kept at arm's length from Dylan. The love I would have bestowed on my own children, if I'd allowed myself to have any. The love I couldn't give Cassius when he was young and needed it.

Cassius says that Jessie talks about her mother with increasing muddle. Sometimes, he says, she tells him that she has seen her just that day. Sometimes she says that Serena is on holiday. Sometimes she remembers the hospital bed, and the hospice, and that her mother is in the ground. "I still don't correct her," he tells me. "I spoke to her counsellor again and she said not to. She said we have to let Jessie lead the process."

I nod, but also give Jessie a notepad and encourage her to draw. She doesn't yet have the dexterity for much more than stick figures, but we concentrate on emotions. "Draw the colour you're feeling," I tell her. This is a trick of my own mother's, resurfacing in my mind, but also, I know how important it is not to keep feelings inside.

Cassius and I explain the situation to the daycare we have signed Jessie up to. It is the best in the area, my friends assure me, with a long waiting list. At the interview, the manager tells me that there are at least ten children waiting for a spot, and also that she is a fan of my work. I ask her if she would like to come down to the set one day. And with that, Jessie is in. Cassius spends the first week 'settling' her, which means staying with Jessie for incrementally less time each morning, until on the Friday, she spends the entire day there alone. But Jessie doesn't need this slow introduction. She is gregarious and confident, like her father. Quickly, she charms everyone.

With chunks of his day now free, Cassius accepts the job I have offered him on set as an extra. To satisfy immigration – and thankfully I have an in on how to do this – he has also become an 'expert consultant' on various historical aspects of the show. I wish I could create a better acting role for him, but there are none available. It feels stifling to his talent to imprison him in such a small space, to see his face only fleetingly cross the screen; but all of the main parts are cast, and the season is meticulously plotted, there are no guest spots that will suit him. Unless I write one in. I think about this over the next few days and find a way I could do it – not a huge part, but one with lines, and the chance to show what he can do. That's all he needs. That's all so many people in this town need.

I spend an evening rewriting an upcoming *Moles* episode and send it to my assistant director, Will. It won't be filmed for another couple of months, but it's the only place it makes sense to insert a new male role. Will likes the change but questions the reason for it. When I explain, he reminds me about the network's warning about free passes. *He better be good*, he emails. I confirm that he is magnetic. I don't, however, tell Cassius about the part yet. It is a while away and things can change. Besides, I need first to sell the idea to Patrick. He thinks already that I am bending myself too much.

Unbent, we take a trip to a ranch just north of Santa Barbara. We are there with six other couples, celebrating the 40th birthday of a college friend of Patrick's. I have almost forgotten that I can do this – be spontaneous, go anywhere, that I am not in fact tied to the bedtime routines of a three-year-old. But extracting myself from it, even for the weekend, feels challenging. As I wave goodbye to Jessie at the front door, there is a torn feeling in my gut. It makes me think of Dylan, when I first left him for university. Soon, however, Patrick and I are roof-down in the truck, and far more quickly than I had anticipated, I am flying free.

We have a row of adjoining suites near the garden at the centre of the ranch. There are complimentary bikes parked outside of each our rooms, and that first evening, we cycle together all the way up to the lake where there is an extravagant barbecue, and a singing cowboy, and a hoedown where we are taught to square dance. A lot of alcohol is sprinkled into the night – wine and beer and cocktails. Patrick is not a heavy drinker, but he likes to participate. I am offered glass after glass, but as usual politely refuse. Until, towards the end of the night, when Patrick and I are laughing, and leaning against each other, it crosses my mind that there is no longer any real reason not to drink alcohol. It is habit only. Another redundant rule. And so I accept a half-measure of wine. After a single sip, I can feel it pumping through me. It seems to fuel my square dancing. This tickles me. And having never seen me this way, Patrick is amused too. At the end of the evening, we both wobble on our bikes.

It is the first time that Patrick and I have shared a room. Of course, we have shared a bed on countless occasions, but we have never fallen asleep together. Patrick watches me as I ready myself for the night, then moves over to make space under the covers. Despite the authentically Western décor that adds a slightly shabby feel to the accommodation, the bed is wide and sumptuous. There is an excess of pillows, and we toss a few onto the floor to make room for our bodies which seem to curl perfectly into each other. As my head rises and falls on Patrick's chest, I smell the freshness of a shower and cologne, the last tinges of beer and wine, the sweaty scent of a deep sleep. He is out long before I am, and alone with my thoughts, I savour this moment, this long-avoided, long-feared, long-desired collusion of flesh. I throw off the covers, no need in this heat, and let the soft sigh of it lull me to sleep.

In the morning, I wake to Patrick's lips upon mine. We have kissed a thousand times, but never like this. It is as though we are new lovers again. I giggle as our hands explore. I have missed this. I have missed him. I had not realised how much. As we take a hayride up to the river terrace for a buttermilk pancake breakfast, the birthday boy shoots Patrick meaningful looks. Patrick is clearly exuding something. I am too. We spend the morning riding horses and fishing in the lake. Later, we visit a local winery, and then don denim for a rodeo that we watch from bleachers, like a couple of high-school kids, hands intertwined. The following day is the official birthday lunch, set amid the beautiful gardens, catered by a private chef. It lasts all afternoon, and while the rest of the party retire to their rooms, Patrick and I spend that final evening walking back up to the lake where, except for a few lanterns, there is no light save for a spectacle of stars.

"I've missed having you to myself," says Patrick as we heave a kayak out of the water and sit opposite each other in it on the dock, knees touching.

"I have too." I do not wish to disrupt the romance, but I am still not quite used to California's poisonous creatures – spiders, and snakes, and scorpions – and use the torch on my phone to do a quick scan. Patrick rolls his eyes jokily, then reaches for my hands.

"Well, you know, we could always do this more often," he ventures, not blaming me, quite.

"I know." I agree. "We should. It's just hard to leave Jessie."

"You've gotten really attached to her."

"I have."

"To her, or to the idea of her?" he asks me.

"What do you mean?"

"Well, I know you don't want to have kids, but – well, maybe, *do* you want to have kids?"

A knot pulls at my stomach, a twist tugging, but only gently. Over the past few weeks, I have had this thought myself. Just fleetingly at first. Then for longer. I have been carefully holding it at arm's reach. "Maybe," I answer. "Maybe yes."

His face lights up. "Me too. So, maybe we could? You know? Have a kid of our own?"

Now I smile, broadly, a bubble of laughter pushing at my lungs. And suddenly, I find that I can't stop smiling. There is something about voicing this desire that has caught me off guard, something about saying it to Patrick. Something about the audacity of the very idea itself, the reality I never thought possible. "Maybe we could."

"Maybe we could also, I don't know, get married?" Patrick asks me now.

And before I know it, he has somehow snatched one of the stars from the showy display above our heads, and wrapped it onto a ring of gold that from bent knee he presents to me, and slips seamlessly onto my hand.

There is traffic on the Pacific Coast Highway. The longer we sit, the more nervous I grow about sharing the news with Cassius and Jessie. I don't want to rip the rug from under them. I don't want Cassius to feel I have abandoned him, again.

But he gives me a friendly hug. He shakes Patrick's hand.

Jessie has not really understood and thinks that Patrick will be moving in with all of us. "He can't have my room," she says to the group.

"That's OK," responds Patrick. "I think I'm going to share a room with Lilith."

Even to my ears this sounds incredible. More incredible, even, than everything else.

Jessie crosses her arms and sulks over to Cassius. "She'll be fine," says Cassius.

"Of course she will," says Patrick.

Much later, once parents have been called, and siblings and friends informed, once Patrick and I have kissed a dozen more times, and once Jessie is in bed, the three of us stay up toasting the engagement. We do this with actual alcohol, that I actually consume, more than one glass of it this time, until gradually I grow tipsy and tactile, and Cassius excuses himself so that Patrick and I can kiss more deeply. Before he leaves, I bestow upon Patrick a spare key to my front door, and there is yet more kissing at that.

Later that night, I stare for a long time at my finger, the diamond catching the shine from the hallway light that we leave on for Jessie. It is such a small thing really, a solo sliced rock, but somehow it casts brilliant colour into the night.

CHAPTER 16

As always, the darkness came in waves, tides, in and out, deeper, shallower, building, retreating, stripping the beach bare. Sussex offered a variety of water sports: surfing, windsurfing, sailing, scuba. Pamphlet-strewn tables at the Freshers' Fair jostled to promise the most, but I steered myself towards the drama society, the film society, despite the call of the sea. Most of the students in the drama group were aspiring actors, but with no interest in the spotlight myself, I manoeuvred into directorial roles – an assistant, a co-director, by the second year a director on my own. From such vantage, I was able to watch the others, scrambling in their rivalries. In my notepad, I wrote it all down, storing their characters like potted jam, a satisfying filling, saved for later. Some of these students were particularly mesmerising, their skills impressive, their faces beautiful. But none were quite like Cassius.

He said he was happy at Bristol. That first Christmas, we returned to Marlow with a great exhalation of breath. Although we'd spoken regularly throughout the term, we hadn't seen each other in the flesh since the summer, and there were questions that, without conferring, we had determined while apart not to ask. Now we discharged them.

He did not have a girlfriend. Nobody serious.

I did not have a boyfriend. Nobody at all.

He had tried a few new drugs, but no, was not addicted.

Yes, of course, I had sleepwalked.

* * *

So far, it had been nothing too terrifying, only within my bedroom, and only twice. The counsellor from all those years back had always said that I would grow out of it, and I had started to wonder if she might be right. I had learned by now that stress was a trigger, and the months leading up to my A levels had been awful. But over the summer, it had levelled out again, then diminished, and now an entire eight weeks had passed with only two incidents. Perhaps distance from Dylan had helped, or Jade, but whatever the cause, a foreign flutter of hope was stirring gently. And I shared it with Cassius.

That Christmas break, everything and nothing changed between us. It was like when we had first started kissing. Just a new word, a new tone, a new beat to our language.

He was always going to be my first.

CHAPTER 17

Cassius does not smile as he tells me. He knows what it means. He knows how I will react. He does not wish to be the bearer of this news. We are having breakfast. Patrick has already messaged me a *Morning fiancée* text. His ring shines on my hand.

"Are you sure?" I ask Cassius.

"I'm certain. I heard a noise, and I thought it was Jessie, so I hurried out of my room, and you were there, knocking on the banister."

"Knocking?"

"Like it was a door."

"And then what?"

"Then you turned around and walked straight past me and went back to bed."

"Did you follow me in?" I ask him.

He nods. "Just to check you were safe. Which you were. I know how this will make you feel, but seriously, Lil, I say don't worry. Total one-off. Not a biggie. Probably the champagne."

I nod carefully back at him. "Probably," I say.

"Definitely. Look, please don't worry. I just thought you'd want to know. I didn't want to keep it from you. But I'm not worried, even with Jessie here, you know, and you shouldn't be either. You should be happy! You're getting married!"

I smile at this reminder, but the effort to do so already feels laboured. It has been over 17 years since I last sleepwalked. 17 years. 17 years of growing stronger and bolder and fearless. Yet all at once it contracts to nothing. Because here I am again, just when I thought I had escaped. Steadying my breath, I try to balance, to calm, to make sense of Cassius's words – a one-off, just the champagne. But already I feel this to be wishful thinking, and a darkness creeps inside me. In that darkness, something old is awakening. Once again, a child is near me. And atop the smooth surface of gleaming Californian wood, sharp shards are piercing my flesh.

I tell Patrick. I tell Ria. I tell Nola. I tell my parents, and Dylan, and friends in LA, and Jade in London. I make an appointment to see a therapist and tell her too. This is my strategy, this time. Not to hide anything. Cassius encourages it – he doesn't want the responsibility, he says, he can't handle it again, of being the only person. To know, he clarifies. He will still be there for me, of course, he will always be there and always protect me, but he does not need to say what he has not said – that he is already the only person for Jessie, and there are limits to what can be carried alone. It is a sentiment I understand acutely. Old visions of his mother's breasts bounce into my mind. But in any case, I do not wish to bury the fear inside. I will not allow it that power any more. *Because I am not that powerful, I am not that powerful*, I tell myself, even as the urge strikes me to lock away kitchen knives. Of course, I am no longer worried about hurting Dylan. But if Patrick and I are to one day have a child of our own, I cannot let this take hold.

Also, there is Jessie.

"Definitely the alcohol," agrees Patrick, seemingly undaunted about what this might mean for our plans. "Anybody can have weird sleep after drinking too much. And you've gone from stone-cold sober, to drinks two nights the same week. One sleepwalk does not a relapse make."

My mother corroborates this. "It's fine. No need to panic. But it's good you're seeing a therapist. Make sure she knows your whole history. The sleepwalking is one thing. The OCD is something else. We can stay on top of them both if we don't let it spiral."

"The two are not even comparable," says my father. "This time you're talking about it, confronting it, so it has nothing on you. It was the inner turmoil that blew it up last time, I'm sure of it. You're an expressive person, Lilith, you need to express. So just keep talking. Trust me, you've already got this beat."

"You should ask them to go," says Dylan. "Not because you're going to do anything to the little girl. You aren't. And you never did, by the way. To me. But clearly having Cassius there is stirring it up again, so why stress yourself?"

"Wow," says Nola, when I explain the whole thing from the beginning. "This is intense. Very intense. Actually, I think that if it was me, I may feel a little afraid to be near the child too."

"But you can't kick Cassius out," says Ria.

My therapist is a 50-something-year-old woman named June with greying hair that she does not colour, and which sits on top of her head in wild frizz. I like her immediately. Patrick got her number from his friend with OCD, even though the OCD isn't my issue, yet. Still, the two were always linked, and it's good, we both agree, to be prepared.

"So if you want to be absolutely prepared, I can write you a prescription for a sleeping pill," says June. "It could knock out a cow. You will certainly not sleepwalk. But I think if we can steer away from medicating for now, that would be better. So how about we think about this practically?"

"Practically?"

"Yes. Clearly my telling you not to worry and that, yes, it probably was triggered by alcohol will not calm your anxiety. Correct?"

I nod.

"And anxiety is only going to create bigger problems for you, given your history. So what we need is to find some practical solutions to the sleepwalking, to your concerns about what you might do when sleeping."

"You're not going to just tell me not to worry about it?" I ask, incredulous.

"Of course not. It's not an irrational fear."

"That's what I always thought!" I exclaim. "That's the thing!"

"But it's not such a big disaster either," June calms. "What we need first, is a list of steps to take."

Lists.

"We will write them down, and then you will do them, and you don't need to think about them any further."

"Oh. OK."

June turns the page in her notebook and tears out a sheet. "One," she says, writing this down. "Move Jessie back into a room with her father, or better, into their own place."

"OK."

"Two – buy a tracking bracelet."

"What?"

"You can get them all over the place. Mainly, they're what paranoid parents put on their kids. But we use them also for elderly people with dementia. You can track your whereabouts on your phone, or get a friend to. So if you walk off somewhere in the night, we can find you."

"Wow," I say. "OK."

"Three – can we fit an alarm to your bedroom door?"

There are a number of further points that June continues to list. By the time we have finished, the page is full. June hands me the sheet and I look at it, skimming through the inventory. I am going to need a fair bit of time to set all of this up. I am also going to need an electrician, and a locksmith. It will certainly make me safer. It will make Jessie almost un-gettable. Cassius too. It will solve things. But it will make me feel like a demon again. And suddenly, looking at it like this, it all feels a little ridiculous. "Do you think that maybe it's overkill?" I ask, glancing back up from the list to June. "I mean, it was only once that I sleepwalked. And I didn't do anything unsafe. And it probably was the alcohol."

June smiles. "Well, thank goodness."

"Sorry?"

She reaches out and takes back the sheet of paper. "That was the response I was hoping for. You are quite right; it probably was the alcohol. You absolutely do not need to worry. You are not as disturbed as you imagine."

I grin sheepishly.

"It's a good idea to keep talking though," says June. "While you work through this. And I'll hold on to our list, just in case. But let's see first if it happens again."

As I drive to the studio, I breathe a sigh of relief. Of course it was an overreaction, a latent coil spring of fear. It is no wonder that Patrick wasn't bothered. Cassius isn't either, not about himself, or Jessie. Everybody thinks it was the alcohol, and in choosing to believe this too, I feel as though I am taking back my power. Besides, Patrick has said he will stay with me for a while, just to make sure. "What if I do something to you though?" I had asked him, but he merely laughed at that, and kissed me.

That morning, I do not even think about it during work. Cassius is not in today and my mind is clear. The table read goes well. It is as though every actor has perfectly understood my intention, and I marvel, as I have marvelled before, at the indescribable magic that transforms thoughts in my head, onto the page, and then into human action. As though I can but think a thing and make it manifest. Mulling this as I return to the studio after lunch, tension stirs for a moment in my stomach. But I rationalise that this kind of creation is carefully made, consciously, with toil and effort and a fully engaged brain; it is not accidental, or some nefarious magic of the night. Nevertheless, I send out a runner to buy me a tracking bracelet from Nordstrom. They are far easier to find than I had imagined, and since I don't need the especially simple ones for Alzheimer patients, there are a vast array of choices. I get one that tracks my steps too, my fitness, my heart rate. It is more of a watch than a bracelet, but thin and sleek. The runner chooses me a turquoise strap. Jessie will love it.

She does. I don't explain to her its purpose, or tell anybody else – I barely even acknowledge it to myself. I connect it to Patrick's phone, not mine, figuring that if I am lost, he will be the one to find me. But I don't tell him that I have done this, not yet, and he doesn't notice the new app among the many he already has. I know that it is a small return to concealment, to secrecy, but it is only a safety net, not needed.

To Jessie, I explain that the watch-bracelet thing shows me how much I'm exercising. We talk about the importance of exercise, and how lungs and muscles and hearts work. I let her wear it and she runs up and down the house counting her steps. Then faithfully returns it. When we are reading in bed, she fondles the device distractedly, flicking the end of the turquoise material back and forth. When I am carrying her, she takes to gripping the strap as though it is a safety belt. Sitting on my lap at the bookshop, she smooths the surface with the tip of her finger, and then wiggles her tiny thumb gently underneath so that it is nestled tightly between the rubber and my skin. She has found a way to feel held like this, looked after, contained.

I do not wish to be Jessie's mother, or to replace Serena, especially now that Patrick and I have plans of our own; but if Cassius asked me to be her godparent, I would not say no.

I do not sleepwalk again. Not for the entire week. Patrick is a light sleeper and promises that I have not stirred. Cassius hasn't heard any transgressions in the night. We move on. It was a one-off. A blip. The alcohol, after all.

Cassius doesn't do well with Patrick around so much. I can see his nerves triggered, the same way they used to be by his father. Patrick comes running with me, athletic and strong. Patrick calls him buddy. Patrick offers to find him a job at his company, raising money to make films. Without words, I hear Cassius's train of thought – he wants to be in the films, not raise money for them. The suggestion reaches his ears as an insult. He starts to compete with Patrick. Over me.

It strikes me that there shouldn't be a competition. Any romance between Cassius and me happened a lifetime ago. He has had girlfriends and lovers and been married since then. He and Patrick were never rivals. Still, it riles him that I have chosen Patrick. I can't think of a time that Cassius was not chosen first for anything, except by his parents, which is the core of things, I suppose. Remembering this, I feel desperately sorry for him, as I have always felt sorry, sad that this fundamental cornerstone is lacking, sad that it still fuels so much inside him. I contemplate recommending my therapist, but Cassius could not afford that, and the fact of this may only rub salt in the wound. He will not let me pay for anything. It is enough of an affront to him that he is not able to pay me rent, and he cooks dinner in an attempt to make up for it, taking offence when Patrick orders in, trying to help. Patrick does not stop trying. When he makes an effort with Jessie, however, Cassius dislikes this. He dislikes it more when Patrick does not, and more still when Jessie starts asking Patrick to play with her. Slowly, the two of them are developing a bond, and Cassius hates this more than anything, but right now he has no patience for such games himself. In the shadow of our joyfulness, he is distracted and stressed. He doesn't want to be beholden to anybody but has little choice. Patrick hides behind the curtain, and the armchair, and outside in the back of the shed. Jessie looks for him for ages. She hides for ages too, Patrick teaches her how, quiet as a mouse, more still than I ever could have been as a child, usually beneath the covers of my bed.

At the end of the month, there is a party after work to celebrate the birthday of one of the show's stars, Joella. The party is in a trendy restaurant/club. Joella's agent will be there, and her manager, and A-list actors, and industry big shots. We've known each other for years and she has invited me to bring a few friends. "You know what, I'm going to be out every night next week in New York. Why don't I stay home with Jessie?" Patrick volunteers. And then to Cassius: "And you take an evening off, buddy? Go to the party with Lilith?"

I nod surreptitiously at Patrick. We have discussed this in advance. Patrick is no longer threatened by Cassius, and we can both see him flailing. We are looking for ways to cheer him, to lift him. The quicker we can get him back on his feet, the quicker he can get his own place – which is Patrick's ultimate aim. The sooner he is strong again, happy, I can feel absolved of blame – which is mine.

Cassius wears a pink shirt that brings out his tan, and splashes himself with a scent that for some reason makes me think of the Italian Riviera. I have invited Ria and Nola too – Ria, because she is always looking for opportunities to make contacts; Nola, because she is still new. It is hard in LA sometimes to find real friendships. Everybody is nice, but few mean it. As Cassius and I enter the party, I spot the two of them already inside. Ria is wearing a short white dress that sets off her complexion and looks fabulous. Nola is more understated in black trousers and matching top that wrap her like second skin, and with an air of not even trying, she pulses sexuality across the room. Her red hair is luminous, and the sight of it makes me swish my own. When they notice us approaching, Ria jumps up from her bar stool, hugging first me and then Cassius. Her greeting is so warm and enveloping that it is hard not to feel lifted, but in the background, I notice Nola taking Cassius in. This is the first time they have actually met, though she has heard all about him. I have wondered in fact about encouraging the two of them together – both new, both cerebral, both bold in their opinion. And she's so very his type – beautiful and brilliant, yet somehow razor-edged. But Ria is so patently interested in Cassius already. And I am a little apprehensive anyway about what Nola might say to him in his struggling state – she has a tendency towards the inappropriate, a propensity to make the fragile shrivel. I have forgotten, however, that Cassius is not fragile. Not socially at least. He can handle himself at a party. And when I glance around a few moments after arriving, I notice him already talking to a group just behind us, flitting, as usual, seamlessly fitting in.

While he is chatting, I sweep Ria away to introduce her to a casting director she has been desperate to be seen by. Then I leave them to it and mill around the party, showing my face. It is not my gathering, so I don't have hosting duties, but there is a certain obligation, I have discovered, that comes with being a decision maker, an opportunity provider. I don't wish to be like some of the people I had to deal with in my early days – egotistic and aloof, mixing only with their chosen elite, daring you to try to talk to them, to bring something interesting enough to interrupt them with, as though you must offer a momentous contribution simply to be deemed worthy of speech. I want to be accessible, amenable, nice. With Cassius here, however, I am struck by how different this is to the way in which I operated as a teen, when I clung to corners and rituals, or to him. The distance between these two expressions of self fills me with a pleasing sense of triumph, and I wonder if Cassius will notice this change in me, or comment on it. When I look over to him, however, he seems oblivious. He too is working the room, magnetising everybody. A few times we nod to each other over bobbing heads, checking in, but he doesn't need me. Instead, I begin to feel a residual sense of needing him. Not to buoy me up, or protect me, or want me. But to place me first. It is like when we were 12 and he kissed a girl from Morocco. I didn't want him for myself, I just didn't want her to have him either. This is probably how he feels now about Patrick. I wish Patrick was here.

Across the room, I see Cassius locked in intense conversation with Nola. She is gesticulating with what, from where I am standing, seems almost like anger, but what is probably

Spanish passion. Later, he stands with Ria. Their conversation seems more comfortable. Her arm is around his waist. He leans down to whisper into her ear. They dance closely.

I am not sure how long I watch them. At some point, a young director sidles up to me and starts a conversation, and I let Cassius slip from my sight, wondering why this feels difficult, forced, trying not to let it show.

Later, in the taxi, Cassius and I are finally alone. "What were you and Nola talking about?" I ask him casually.

"When?"

Next to me, Cassius is buzzing in a way he often used to be, but I had forgotten – eyes ablaze, fired by confidence, in himself, in the way the world responds to him.

"I don't know when. You guys were talking, and it looked intense."

"Nola seems like an intense person," replies Cassius.

He pats my leg good-naturedly, and closes his eyes, resting his head on my shoulder. I push him off.

"True. But what was she saying to you?"

Now Cassius sits up properly and adjusts his attention. His voice comes out more earnest. "Just asking about Serena mostly."

"Oh no, sorry. Was that OK? Nola does like to probe."

"It's fine," he says. "It was fine."

"Good."

"Oh, and she asked me about your sleepwalking," he adds abruptly. "About how I feel having Jessie near you."

"Really?" Now it is me who is unexpectedly earnest. I have barely thought about this for weeks, but clearly she has. She has thought of me, darkly. And suddenly I feel dark, demonic. I find my voice sticking in my throat. "Why did she bring that up?" I ask uncertainly. "So, what, she thinks you shouldn't let Jessie sleep near me?"

"She said she'd be cautious."

"Wow." For a moment, I say nothing more than this. I am not sure how to respond. I feel hurt by Nola's interference, betrayed. But I know that I shouldn't; Nola has said as much to my face. "Do *you* feel you should be cautious?" I ask him.

Cassius cocks his head with bemusement. "Have I ever?"

I smile weakly, but for the next few moments we sit without talking. After a while, Cassius pats my leg. "Don't overanalyse," he tells me firmly. "I didn't mean to remind you of all that. It's not been an issue, has it?"

I shake my head, take a breath. Smile a little more fully.

"And Nola wasn't being unkind," he continues. "She likes you."

"Ria likes you," I tell him.

By the time we arrive home, I have almost managed to lift myself. We take pains to enter quietly and find Patrick asleep on the couch. Jessie is in bed. My bed.

"We were just drawing and chatting," Patrick explains when we nudge him awake. "And then she suddenly jumped up and said she wanted to hide from me, so we played hide-and-seek. But I took too long to find her, I'm afraid, and she fell asleep under your covers. I thought I might wake her if I tried to carry her to her own bed. I did make a breathing hole though."

Face still alight from the evening, Cassius laughs. "I'll move her," he says. Unless…" He turns to me. "Sorry, it's your bedroom. Do you want to do it?"

"She's your daughter," I say.

Cassius laughs again. "You want to, don't you? Go on, she'll be happy to see you."

"OK," I tell him.

Jessie doesn't, however, wake. She is a heavy sleeper. With heels removed and tracksuit donned, I scoop her up silently, and snuggle her sweaty mass into my neck, breathing her in. There is no other feeling like this. It is impossible to substitute. Adults may choose to embrace each other, even to sleep together, to amalgamate their bodies through the night. But they do not surrender their weight into your chest, they do not breathe with that soft, sweet release, they do not curl and cling, monkey-like, extracting sensations most primal.

I want to be a mother.

It is a truth I have denied myself for so long that it strikes me now with the weight of stored-up years. The force of it presses into my chest, my frame shaking slightly. As I lower Jessie into her bed, I worry that this may wake her, and I try, my first instinct, to swallow the emotion away. But Jessie doesn't wake. And even after she is safely tucked in, I don't swallow. I don't. Because who cares what Nola thinks? Patrick is not concerned about my sleepwalking. And I am not concerned either. I am strong now, in control, and different from before. There is no reason that we cannot have a child.

Skipping back down the stairs, I feel light in the epiphany of this, lifted, scooped up. I am no longer even thinking about the party, or Cassius's lack of need for me, or Nola's judgement. When I reach the lounge, I spring into Patrick's arms.

But, "I think I'm going to split," declares Patrick. "If it's OK with you? I'm going to head back to my place for a few nights."

"Oh," I say. I am surprised by this. We haven't seen each other all evening, and he is going to New York soon. "Sure. But how come?"

"Just need to sort a few things there before the trip. And you're fine now, right?"

"Right."

"You sure?"

I nod but notice Patrick and Cassius glancing at each other. Less sure?

"OK." Now Patrick pats Cassius on the shoulder, and gives me a hug, lingering as our lips meet. Then he leaves.

Cassius picks up the TV remote and settles immediately into Patrick's spot on the sofa. By the window, I wait until Patrick's car has pulled away. Then I turn to Cassius.

"What did you say to him?"

Cassius looks up. "Nothing."

He doesn't look at me. For a good many seconds he ignores the glower of my gaze and continues to watch TV, a stubborn sibling. Eventually, however, he pauses the programme and gets up to go to the kitchen. I follow him. At the fridge, he pours himself a glass of water. Then sits at the island. Waiting. The expression on his face lands somewhere between guilt and amusement.

"Tell me," I say.

He shrugs. "Nothing. Really."

"Cass."

Cassius sighs, putting down his glass of water. "OK, look," he begins. "I just told him that you might have been a bit put out by what Nola said to me about letting Jessie sleep here, near you, and suggested that maybe we need to prove to you that everything's fine. Before Patrick goes to New York next week. So you don't build it up and worry about him leaving. And he doesn't feel he needs to stay."

"I wasn't worried," I retort. "And I don't need you messing in our relationship."

Cassius looks slightly hurt by this. Or at least affronted. "Sorry," he says. "I was trying to help."

"I don't need you to help."

"You were getting anxious, Lil, come on, I know you. I was trying to protect you from spiralling."

"You don't need to protect me. You don't. Not any more."

Cassius stares at me for a moment. "Fine. I won't say anything to him again."

"Good."

"Good."

We sit facing each other on the bar stools. For a while. In silence. I don't want to argue with Cassius, I don't want to undo the night's boost to his mood, but I am infuriated. Just moments ago, I had been so light in my epiphany, and now his interference has clouded things.

"Come on, Lil," he tries. "I was trying to do good."

"Were you?" I demand. "Or was it that Nola made *you*

unsure? Made you want to test out whether I *would* actually sleepwalk if Patrick wasn't there to stop me? Made you worried?"

He rolls his eyes. "Come on, of course not."

"What about Patrick? Did Patrick want to test things?"

Without meaning to, I feel myself holding my breath for this answer, but Cassius delivers it quickly.

"Of course not."

His face is sincere as he talks, and I let this sit. "Fine then," I say eventually.

Now Cassius leans towards me. "Fine… you forgive me? Fine… you *were* worried, it's a good idea? Fine… I was right?"

He was not right. But, as always, he was only trying to protect me.

"Well?"

It's not a bad idea, I suppose, to test things on my own before Patrick has to go. If we are really going to be parents, then it's not a terrible suggestion to test it all properly. Besides, I do feel strong right now. There is nothing to fear.

"Well?" asks Cassius again.

Still a little irritated, I roll my eyes, but when he asks me a third time, with jazz hands, I allow myself to smile.

And then, I keep smiling. Because the next day, and the following, and the one after that, I sleep soundly, and quickly, and without anxiety at all. And even with Nola's apprehensions in my head, and without Patrick next to me, I do not sleepwalk. And Jessie is fine. And then Patrick leaves for a two-week trip to New York.

CHAPTER 18

Jade agreed to come on the trip with me.

She had recently broken up with her boyfriend Craig – a third-year scientist who took every opportunity to belittle the arts and had no idea that he had become a starring role in mine. There was a New Writing Festival on campus, and I'd submitted a short screenplay, my first one. Occasionally, I was struck with the sudden fear that Craig might recognise himself in it, and take offence, but Jade pointed out: "What is art if it doesn't offend or inspire? You have to move people. Not that Craig would get that." She said this with her usual deadpan innocence – unassuming yet discerning, forthright but without malice. It was impossible not to like her. Five weeks after the break-up, she thought a weekend in Bristol just the ticket.

We hired a car. My job was to stack it with petrol-station snacks (I also visualised force fields and clear roads and did everything else necessary to keep us from crashing); Jade's job was the music. She brought her entire 100-strong collection of CDs. The sleeping arrangements had already been planned. I was to squeeze into Cassius's single bed, and Jade would sleep on the couch in the communal living area. Cassius shared a house in the university residential village with five other male students, so we came prepared: Jade with a clean pillow and duvet, both of us with flip-flops for the shared showers, and earplugs. We were anticipating a Saturday afternoon hanging out with Cassius's friends, a party Saturday night, and a fried breakfast somewhere 'Bristol-y' the next morning, before making the almost four-hour drive back to the sea. We both had an essay due on Monday, but we'd crammed the previous week, so there were only a couple of final paragraphs to knock out, fuelled by tea and chocolate, on Sunday night. It was all planned.

Not part of our plans was Cassius calling 20 minutes before we pulled in, instructing us to divert, reroute, head straight past the university accommodation and all the way to the Marriott. We had rooms, he said. And a spa treatment. And lunch. And hotel slippers.

We didn't know how to greet each other. Despite the goings-on between us at Christmas, we had not officially declared ourselves a couple. We both understood that for the next few years, we couldn't be together properly even if we wanted to. Besides, we were just us. 'Us', however, usually operated behind bedroom doors, not as a public exhibition. When we offered awkward, friendly hugs, Jade remarked: "I mean, that's not exactly Austen." Then she took herself off to the loo so that we could kiss properly.

"Why the hotel?" I shouted to Cassius, much later, over the blare of garage music. The party was in a shared house in Clifton, the top floor of an old building that was only partially rented by students. The late-20-somethings on the ground floor had begun the evening with giddy attempts to remain modish, but by now had threatened to call the police. Jade was in the corner chatting with a boy she'd met on the stairs. Cassius was stoned out of his mind, head in my lap on the sofa. I had refused all offers of drugs, and alcohol, and lips, and was ready to go.

"Wanted to spoil you," Cassius mumbled, patting my knee, then kissing it.

"You didn't need to waste your money. I mean, I know we don't have quite the same budgets, but still. You're a student! What do your friends think?"

"Haven't told them," he replied. "Why would I? I only care about you."

I rolled my eyes in mock exasperation and stroked his cheek. With his face pressed against me, I was reminded of that first summer when he lay, just a boy, against the sand. He had seemed so beautiful and vulnerable to me then. He did still.

"I've always only cared about you," he told me.

Without turning his head, he ran his hand through his hair. I wondered if he realised how often he made this habitual gesture. I had always determined it a mark of either vanity or awkwardness, but now I wondered if he caressed himself so much because his parents had never done it for him. I moved my hand from his cheek and placed it gently on his head. In return, he lifted his face and reached for my hair. As usual it was tied back, but he caught hold of a loose tendril in what seemed to be an attempt at affection, clumsily yanking me downwards. I prised the hair out of his fingers.

"Don't hurt me then!" I teased. Then, "I care about you too."

Next to us, a couple of girls sat down, laughing loudly. Cassius waved at them, and they waved back, and he waved again, more wildly, before closing his eyes and abruptly nodding off. The girls laughed again.

"How do you know Cassius?" I asked them.

"Who's Cassius?" one of them replied. "Oh God, it's not his party, is it? We came with friends."

"This is Cassius," I assured them, pointing to the dead weight on my lap.

"Oh," the girl laughed further, wobbling slightly as she stood. "More drinkies," she slurred to her friend.

While Cassius slept, I repeated almost the exact same dialogue with three other groups of students. One offered me an array of jelly shots; another held a platter of 'special' brownies. As usual, I declined, but sober amidst such unravelling, it was hard to start conversations, and I started to feel irritated. I'd wanted to meet Cassius's friends, to see which version of himself he'd decided to be here, in this new incarnation, without me. When he opened his eyes, I prodded him: "Cass, introduce me to some of your people."

Blearily, Cassius's eyes swept around the party, but they were far too glazed. "Can we go?" he asked suddenly.

Nodding gladly, I glanced around for Jade, finding her still talking to Stairs-Boy.

"Um, I think Jade might not be ready," I told Cassius. "Shall we give her another half an hour? I'd really like to meet some of your uni friends anyway."

But Cassius shook his head. "I just want to go. I've had enough of it all."

"Enough of what?" Ordinarily, this was Cassius's ideal scene. It was me who liked to duck out early.

"Of everything," he said. "Besides, it's probably the last time I'm gonna stay in a fancy hotel, so let's make the most of it."

"What do you mean?" I asked him. "What's happened?"

"Oh, you know, nothing. Just my parents have been lying to me for the past six months. But then they've been lying all my life. So."

I heaved Cassius up to sitting and looked at him straight on. "What are you talking about?"

"Like you don't know," he hissed with sudden venom.

Guilt gripped my stomach as, for the first time in a long time, I was reminded of the afternoon when I walked in on Marianne, and my complicity since. Her breasts bobbed now in front of me. "Don't know what?" I skirted.

"Haven't your parents told you about the house?"

I shook my head.

"It was in the *Marlow Gazette*," he said. "It's sold." He proclaimed this last revelation with a flourish of jazz hands, as though he was punctuating a magic trick. "It's sold, and my dad's moved out of his flat to a dingy one in the suburbs somewhere. Apparently, he lost his job months ago. You know, banking crash and all that. Forgot to tell me about it."

"Oh no. I had no idea. What about your mum?"

"She's OK. She's still working. But it's not enough, just her, is it? Not compared to before."

"OK," I soothed, reaching for the silver lining. "So it's not so bad."

"Not so bad? Goodbye to the only things I've ever liked about my life – holidays and restaurants and, I don't know, stuff. Doesn't matter to you, does it? 'Cos you have family. You can be all noble. What have I got?"

"Cass, you're not destitute." I attempted to calm him. "Your dad'll find something else soon. He's bound to, knowing him. And anyway, give it a couple of years and we'll be working properly ourselves."

I already had a part-time job in a bookshop, but I didn't mention this to Cassius. It wasn't Hollywood, the dream we still talked of together, but I feathered my dream with a buffer. Not Cassius. For him it was all or nothing. In fact, it was just all.

"I'm not sure an actor's salary is going to pay for things like hotel rooms," Cassius sniped. "Not to start with anyway."

"I didn't ask you to get the hotel," I argued. "I was happy in your dorm."

He shook his head. "What do you mean 'knowing my dad' anyway?"

I squinted my eyes at him, not understanding where the conversation was heading. "I mean – he's successful, he's charming, he'll be fine. What are you getting at?"

"What are *you* getting at?" he parried. "What do you mean 'charming'?"

"Cassius, seriously?" I demanded. "How stoned are you?"

He didn't answer. Wouldn't. I should have let him do an upper when somebody had offered earlier. I knew he did them when I wasn't there, but he knew I'd freak at anything stronger than weed. Or maybe it was marijuana. I wasn't really sure of the difference. Or if there was one.

"Cass," I pressed.

It was at this moment, however, that Jade strolled over to the sofa and bent down to speak into my ear. Stairs-Boy was loitering by the door, waiting.

"Yeah, so, this guy thinks we're hooking up, even though I've told him we're not," Jade shouted into my eardrum over the continuing din. "I've been signalling at you for the past ten minutes to save me."

"Sorry," I said, squeezing her hand. "Didn't realise." Then I nodded towards Cassius. "We've been having a bit of a chat."

"Eek," she said, frowning with exaggerated apprehension.

But, "D'you want to go?" Cassius slurred suddenly into Jade's face, leaning clumsily between us.

Jade's expression immediately changed to enthusiasm. "Yes!" She took his hand.

I responded more slowly, irritation with Cassius lingering, but I didn't say anything to him. Likewise, he said nothing to me. Jade corralled us. "Onwards!" she declared, after we had hoisted Cassius up, but a second later, Cassius's feet slipped, and we all toppled sideways. Jade burst into hysterics. Cassius did too. But I felt myself fuming, and wet, having landed in something sticky. What was Cassius doing? I'd driven all this way to see him, I'd dragged my friend along, and all he could do was get stoned and pass out, and then take out his petty frustrations on me. Unfairly. Because OK, yes, his parents were crappy, and it was unsettling having to move house; but he had no idea how blessed his life still was. Not only financially, but mentally too, and culturally. He was privileged. Utterly privileged. Charmed. For somebody so perceptive to emotion, he was blinkered to the world. And I was tired of it. While Jade laughed as we pulled him again to standing, I remained silent. When he swerved into me, I pushed him away with a wordless roll of my eyes. He too said nothing. Until at the door, we paused so that Jade could speak to Stairs-Boy.

"Really sorry," she explained – kindly, apologetically. "But I have to go, my friends need help."

"They can manage," the boy slurred, attempting to put his hand around Jade's waist.

Seeming to sober a little at this, Cassius raised his eyebrows and stood straighter, but Jade quite capably peeled the boy's palm away. "Maybe. But there's also that tiny matter of my having told you 17 times that it's not going to happen." The boy's face dropped. "So nice to meet you though!" Jade enthused. And then she waved, leaving the boy dumbfounded, and flitted with us away. Despite her bluntness, as usual it was impossible to draw even an ounce of malice from her tone. And at the exact same time, halfway down the stairs, both Cassius and I caught each other's eye, and despite ourselves, we started to laugh.

Later, Jade asleep in the adjoining room, Cassius and I in bed, the effects of the weed lessened, and he turned to me: "Sorry about before. It's not you. I'm just kind of spiralling. I don't know who I am, without the house and everything. And I feel like I've been lied to my whole life, you know? It's not just this job thing with Dad. Neither of them ever do what they say. They lie constantly. The money was the only thing about them that was ever real, that I could ever count on. Supposedly, they split up over this one affair of Dad's, but I'm sure he'd had others before that, and I bet Mum knew. And, I don't know, I think maybe Mum was up to something too."

I turned my face away from his, laying it on his chest, my stomach tight. "Why do you think that?"

"I don't know. It's just something I kind of… feel. Did you see anything, ever?"

Keeping my face turned away, I said nothing, and like an icy wave, a rush of shame washed over me. What a hypocrite I had been, reproaching him for a fleeting burst of anger, while for years I had hidden a momentous betrayal. Silently, I reached up to stroke his chest.

"I always wished we were like your family, you know?" he said. "Just… nice. And real."

"I know that," I told him.

"You're lucky," he said.

"I know." I paused, biting the inside of my cheek. "Charmed."

"You are though."

"I know."

Neither of us said anything then, but slowly, beneath my cheek, I felt his breath quickening a little. "About the hotel," he started finally. "Lil, I just… I knew you'd expect… I didn't want to tell you that… I…"

"It's OK, Cass, I get it," I told him. And he stopped, inhaling a few times as though to speak again, but then not, both of us wrapped in the stillness.

This was our comfortable. Him holding me, me holding him. Containing each other.

"At least you've never lied to me," he said eventually.

I had of course set out obstacles, but in unfamiliar places it was difficult to predict my route, and somehow, without tripping over anything, I had made it out of the room, into the lift, and down to the hotel lobby. Thank goodness I was wearing full pyjamas, though the doorman who grabbed my shoulders half a second before I stepped out into the road didn't seem much assured by that.

"Oy! Oy!"

He was shouting in my face when I came to. His own cheeks were red, as though he'd been slapped, the rest of his face a pasty hue. In the lights from the hotel and passing cars, his eyes startled.

"Sorry," was the first word that came to mind.

"What are you playing at?" The man was bellowing, flustered. "Didn't you see the lorry? Or did you? Are you trying to kill yourself?"

That had been Cassius's thought too, all those years ago, on the beach, in the sea. "Sorry," I muttered again, shivering now, like I did then. "Sorry. I was… You won't believe me."

“Try me,” the man said, slowly letting go of my shoulders, though watching carefully as though he might have to jump in at any moment to stop me from leaping again to my death. Somewhere in his mid-40s, his voice was squeakier than I would have guessed from looking at him, perhaps scared into soprano.

“I was asleep,” I said directly. “I sleepwalk.”

“Shit.” The man blinked multiple times as he took this in. “Shit. You mean you were about to sleepwalk in front of a lorry? Are you OK? You’re awake now, right?”

My stomach twisted as I heard him say it again. The words thudded. I had been about to walk in front of a lorry. “I’m fine.” I nodded. “I’m fine. Sorry.”

Now, however, his eyes were alight. “Good thing I followed my hunch there! I don’t normally follow residents out of the hotel, see. I stay by the door. But I saw you there, in your PJs, and I thought, no, that’s not normal, is it? And then you stood there for a while by the road. And then that lorry came over the roundabout, and I just saw you going, and I moved. Quick. Good thing I did. What a thing. That’s a story then. Happened to you before, has it?”

I nodded again, still shivering. “I don’t suppose you can give me another room key so I don’t wake up my friend?”

“Course. Course,” he said, leaping into action as he ushered me through the revolving door and called out to the check-in clerk in the lobby. “Room… what was it now?”

“Twenty-three,” I muttered.

“Twenty-three! We’ve had a little case of sleepwalking! Can you believe it?”

There was nobody but the clerk about, but I wished he would do all this less noisily. I understood his need – to talk about what he’d witnessed, to share it, relive it, have his role acknowledged. But I felt my body curling inwards. Reaching for my undone hair, I tucked it beneath my shirt. All I wanted to do was get somewhere where I could be alone, where I could concentrate, where I could go through my mantras, and my rituals, and keep doing them, doing them, doing them, until I felt relief.

Except, there never could be relief, I realised suddenly, devastatingly. Not really. Because it wasn't even about Dylan any more. He was at home in Marlow, safely away from me. But *I* wasn't away from me. And never could be. And anybody unlucky enough to be within my reach was in danger too. Upstairs, Cassius had been asleep right next to me. Jade had been in the adjoining room. These were the two people in the world who knew most, who were armed best. Yet neither of them had stirred, neither of them had stopped me. I could have slit their throats with the knife by the fruit bowl. I could have burned them with the water from the in-room kettle. I could have whacked them over the head with the iron. What had I been doing daring to sleep so near to others? How had it got away from me? It had been better. It had been better. For months it had been so much better. But I'd become too flippant. I'd thought I was growing out of it. I'd thought there was hope.

Back in the room, I slunk into bed next to Cassius, but I didn't sleep again. Round and round in my mind it went – the fact that there was no escape. Because, look, it wasn't only stress that set me off; it was sin. It was me. I had sinned when I hadn't told Cassius about his mother the first time. I had sinned when I'd stolen Dylan from his bed. I had sinned when I'd not returned the film to the stationery shop. And I had sinned again now, still not telling my best friend the secret that his manipulative mother had made me keep. I did it for him of course, for Cassius, so as not to hurt him further, or so I told myself. But there I went again, because that wasn't true. It was only a lie I told myself to make it easier not to hit him with the hard reality. I was a liar, just like his parents. I had lied again. Another sin.

But then Lilith, it turned out, was the original sinner.

Back in Sussex days later, restless like the nearby sea, I sat next to Jade and learned this. That term, our final of the first year, we had begun a new module on feminist philosophy. So far, it had mainly examined discrimination, and political equality, but suddenly, pushing its way through my melancholy, the voice of the professor was talking about the bible, and rabbinical legend, and Adam and Eve. And Lilith.

"'Lilith' means 'ghost'. Or 'night monster'," she said.

In those days I still went by the name of Lily, so in the lecture hall, it was only Jade who knew my real name. As 'Lilith' was mentioned, I felt her head turn towards me, though I tried not to show my shock. Even in front of my trusted friend, it felt foolish to be so unversed in the roots of my own appellation and I couldn't understand why I hadn't investigated my name before. Simply on faith, I supposed. I had trusted my parents' description of female strength, that this is what they had wanted for me. But 'night monster'. Clearly, there was more.

According to legend, the professor elucidated, Lilith had been Adam's little-known first wife, made by God at the same time as him, like him, from the earth. Because she was equal to Adam, however, she didn't want to be ruled by him. She wouldn't obey him, or lie beneath him. They quarrelled, and eventually she left. When God sent angels to bring her back, they found her bearing children all on her own. And when Lilith refused to return, in punishment, God caused 100 of her children to die each day. Lilith remained free, but it came at the cost of motherhood. Meanwhile, disgruntled by the nuisance of a disobedient wife, Adam spoke to God, who created for him a second wife, this time made from Adam's own rib, a part of him, less than him, who he could rightly rule. Thus, Eve became the first accepted wife, the first real woman.

The discussion turned then to the way in which this story, this genesis, informed every idea of partnership and womanhood that followed, how compliance was etched into our very earliest understandings of what it was to be 'good'.

"But what about Lilith?" I found myself suddenly interrupting, my hand raised before I could stop it.

I was sitting near the back as usual, my notepad at the ready. I had never yet raised my hand at university. The professor squinted at me across the hall. "Lilith became lost from the paradigm. What the discourse evolved into…" She attempted to redirect. "What became important—"

"But was there any more to her story?" I pressed. "To Lilith?"

The professor paused again. Adjusted. "Well, legend told that Lilith was so furious with the way she'd been treated that she began to kill the newborn babies of other families. In some communities, parents would invoke the names of God's angels – Senoy, Sansenoy, and Semangelof – to prevent her from snatching their babies from their beds. Which, in fact, is pertinent to one of the issues we're talking about in this series, and to current debates about…"

She continued.

But I was no longer listening.

I couldn't breathe.

The professor's voice droned on outside of me. Inside, dizziness swirled. *Lilith took babies from their beds.* Took babies. Just as I had taken Dylan. I felt the colour drain from my face. *Killer. Night monster.* Against whom angels were needed. In my notepad, I wrote down their names: Senoy, Sansenoy, Semangelof.

On her own pad, Jade hastily scribbled a note and pushed it towards me: *Total feminist badass. That's the take-home.*

She nodded at me encouragingly.

I shook my head.

Jade again: *Disrupter. Real woman.*

But I closed my eyes. Jade knew. She had heard. We had both heard it. I, Lilith, had been cursed from birth. It was my destiny. I had always been, and was always meant to be, a child-stealing demon of the night.

CHAPTER 19

"Don't freak out," says Cassius.

I am lying flat against my pillow. His hand is on my shoulder, the lights in my room have been switched on to a dim brightness, he is hovering over me. My arm feels heavy. I look down. Blonde curls are tumbling across my chest.

"Don't freak out," Cassius says again.

Immediately, I want to be sick. I want to scream. I want to run fast along the beach. It is 20-odd years ago and I am back. Back at the beginning. But I don't freak out. Instead, because she is sleeping, I whisper: "What happened?"

It is a stupid question. A stupid, useless question. I am not naïve. I am not.

"I don't know," says Cassius, knowing. "I woke up a few minutes ago, and went to check on Jessie, and she wasn't in her bed. So I looked here."

"Oh my God," I say.

"Wait."

"Oh my God."

"Wait. Maybe she crept in to you," Cassius suggests. "You know she's been wanting to sleep in here. Maybe she came in on her own."

"We know that didn't happen," I say. There are tears in my eyes. My throat is constricted. I wish Patrick was here.

"In the morning, we'll ask her," Cassius insists, reaching out his hands to lift her up. I shift my body slightly to let him, and Jessie tumbles sleepily into his arms. Oblivious. Pausing, Cassius looks at me, but I can't quite work out whether it is to convey pity, or horror, or concern. "Just for now," he repeats. "Don't freak out."

"Will you sleep in with her?"

He nods. "Sure."

"Don't leave her."

"I won't."

"I'm sorry," I tell him.

"She's fine," he says. "Lil, she's fine. It's OK."

They slip noiselessly out of the room. I hear the door to her bedroom swing open. I hear his footsteps padding across wood. I hear the faint creak of her bed as he lays her down and climbs in next to her and, probably, tucks in the sheets.

Later, I hear a dog barking. I hear a distant crashing of what must be wind but feels like icy waves.

I hear the growing hum of morning traffic. I hear a nearby car starting its engine.

I hear Jessie's voice singing across the hall.

I hear feet on the stairs, the TV going on, the coffee machine starting.

I hear everything beginning, and arising, and ending at once.

CHAPTER 20

My computer is covered in Post-its. I try to discharge things quickly, but my mind feels littered. It has only been three days since I sleepwalked with Jessie, but it feels as though years have passed, backwards, unwinding my strength. On my morning run, I tread heavily, as though if I stamp my feet hard enough, I can shed my fears and leave them stuck there, shoe-shaped in the sand. But there is no escape from myself. That was always the problem with the darkness residing within. I would never do it, but I feel that I understand why some people cut their arms to pieces, shredding their flesh – it is a way to let what is inside, out. And to punish. I have not yet harmed anybody, but already I loathe myself a little. For endangering Jessie. For troubling Cassius. For sabotaging my own dreams. For doing this again.

I cannot bring myself to tell Patrick. It is not that I think he'll take back his proposal – although he did make it right after my agreeing to have a baby together. But it is not that. It is not him at all. It is the idea of the baby, of the child, our child, that's the thing. What if my sleepwalking changes things for Patrick, makes him not want to risk it? How could anybody knowingly subject an infant to a dangerous parent? Surely Patrick couldn't. I couldn't. That's why years ago I took the decision never to have one.

And yet.

Now.

Now I can no longer deny myself. These weeks with Jessie have done it. Ruined it. Reminded me. I was always maternal, my mother told me so all the time growing up, and I felt it, knew it, pretended otherwise. It has been years since I have desired anything this way. Since I have adored anything this way. Since I have felt like this. It is time to say yes, this time to myself. I cannot risk Patrick not being on board. I need only to get a handle on things.

Get a grip.

This time I am sure I will be able.

By the time Patrick returns from New York, I'll have it under control.

As I head breathless up the alleyway from the beach, Madge stops me. She is leaning against her ribbon-flecked trolley, her legs still zipped inside her sleeping bag, but she extends an arm and beckons me over. Crouching before her, I notice how thin she is looking, and I regret not having remembered my usual note. For the millionth time, I wish that she would let me do something to help her properly. But I will pop back later, I decide, with a meal of some sort. Meanwhile, Madge scrutinises my face. She does this with the expertise of a practised mother, detecting, and I wonder, as I have wondered many times before, what happened between herself and her own daughter, what could have dislodged that bond. Wrinkled in excess by the outdoors, it is impossible to know Madge's age, but I suspect she is only a couple of decades older than I am, and I wonder if perhaps she has parents of her own still, if she is still somebody's child. She sucks in her cheeks.

"You doing alright there, sweetheart?"

A bubble rises up in my chest, but I nod. Pat her arm. Thank her. I'm fine. I'll be fine.

"Well, good," she says. And, "You take care of yourself." And, "Whatever's going on, sweetheart, you got it."

I nod again, and this time tentatively believe her. Madge

may not possess a crystal ball, but she has never been wrong yet.

"And bring that gorgeous girl to see me," she instructs. "Soon. The weather's going to be fabulous."

When I arrive home, Cassius is with Jessie in the kitchen, making toast. She has taken to the American classic – peanut butter and jelly, although it's jam really, and I can't bring myself to call it otherwise. She likes it spread to the very edges, with a gloop of jam left undispersed in the middle, and is trying to explain this to her father. He rolls his eyes and offers me the knife. As I take it, there is a momentary flash in my mind suggesting its use as a weapon, but the thought doesn't linger. I will type it into my laptop and discard it. I'm fine. I'm fine.

Patrick will be in New York for nearly another week, but Cassius has promised that when he returns, he won't say anything about the sleepwalking. "I'm sorry," I have told him, again and again over the past three days, for burdening him with such a secret, again. But he understands.

"It's my job," he replies. "It's always been my job to protect you. Don't make me unemployed. Again." Besides, he agrees that it is better not to tell until things are handled. He eyes me now, however, over the kitchen island, searching, I imagine, for clues of breakdown. And each night since it happened, he has sat up, waiting.

I have sleepwalked on every one of those nights, observed by him. Downstairs to get a drink. Scraping the wall in the corner of my room. The third night I just stood in the middle of the upstairs hallway, "As if you were waiting for a bus," Cassius told me.

Listening to Cassius's accounts each morning, I feel blind, dumb. Powerless. I try unsuccessfully to laugh at the humorous flourishes, as I used to when my parents gave their reports, but instead I receive the news grim-faced. As always, I don't remember any of it. It is as though somebody alien is inhabiting my body, or else it is the old me, the young, troubled me, clawing back into existence. As though in order to acknowledge my supressed desire for a child, I also have to acknowledge her. Or run from her. Run far and fast.

A thought occurs to me – have I really not sleepwalked in years? Perhaps I have. Perhaps there was simply nobody living with me to attest to my madness.

"It's not madness," says Cassius over Saturday lunch a couple of days later. We have picked up our favourite bagels and juices from the deli on the corner, and he has brewed coffee. Jessie is in the living room. "And actually, it's progress. Every night, you've sleepwalked at almost the exact same time, around midnight. So all we need is for me to wait up until you walk, make sure you get safely back to bed, and then that's it, no problem."

"You can't stay up every night."

"It's not that late."

"I can't ask you to do that."

"You're not asking," Cassius insists. "I'm offering. I told you, it's my job. Plus, don't you think I'm glad to finally be able to do something to help? After all… this."

Through the open door, his eyes sweep the living room. Jessie is colouring at the small table I have purchased for her. Her legs are bare and swing contentedly. On her feet are a pair of cat slippers we found together in the mini-mall. In her hair are pigtails I have braided. I hope that these small gestures have helped her, made her feel secure. And him. But lately I've felt more of a threat than a saviour. Really, it is him saving me. Again.

"You know that I appreciate you looking out for me," I tell him. "I've always appreciated it. I'm not sure if I ever actually told you that. But I always have. I never even needed to ask you."

"I know you do." He nods. "I always knew."

We sit silently for a moment, then from the next room, Jessie giggles. Cassius smiles breezily, but I remember something. "Jessie told me she saw Serena again yesterday," I tell him abruptly. "She said this time it was at the park."

"We did go to the park," Cassius mulls. "And she was quiet there."

"She said that her mother told you to hurry up."

"Hurry up?"

"That's what she said. What do you think she's imagining?"

"I've no idea," says Cassius. "Maybe to hurry up and come back here? To you? You know she loves us all being together."

"Maybe. Or maybe – to hurry up and go home?" I ask him. "Do you think she misses her life in England?"

Cassius looks at Jessie as he considers this, then shakes his head. "Serena's parents live abroad," he says. "Mine are typically absent. She has no cousins or aunts or uncles. She hadn't made close friends yet at nursery. We had a small flat on a nothing street. No beach. And it rained. A lot. I wouldn't say she misses much."

I find myself feeling relieved by this. "So long as you're sure all this imagining isn't her trying to express a need. Is the therapist certain we shouldn't be addressing it more directly?"

He nods. "She was very clear. But I'm keeping watch," he assures me. "On both of you." He pats my arm then the way he used to, and I place my palm on top of it.

"Are you sure you don't mind staying up?" I ask him. "Just till Patrick's back?"

"I don't mind."

"What am I going to do once he *is* back though?"

Cassius purses his lips, and shrugs. "It might stop," he offers. "Or didn't your therapist suggest some kind of pill?"

The problem is, in my mind, sleeping pills are akin to any drug in that they mess with brain cells, or, at least, they mess with consciousness, control.

Without them, however, I have no control either. And this is the thought that plagues me – at the studio when I'm trying to concentrate on a scene, later when I'm writing, down the phone line to Patrick, at night as I lie trying to sleep.

Cassius is right, the sleepwalking might simply stop. It might.

But it might not.

I might get a handle on it, or I might not.

I might walk, or I might not.

I might, or might not, stab somebody with a left-out knife.

I should tell Patrick already. Not wait. I know it. That was my plan this time: tell people, no more secrets. So I should tell him. I should do it soon. And I will. A quick rip of the plaster, nearly pain-free. He would gladly take over from Cassius, he would watch me just as closely, do anything to help. But…

"Last time I saw June, she didn't really want to medicate," I tell Cassius when he presses me about pills again, a couple of days later, the day before Patrick is due to return. "She said the sleeping pills are super strong. But also, I don't want to become reliant on them. I mean, I couldn't long-term, could I? If Patrick and I do have a baby, I won't be able to look after it if I'm knocked out all night."

Cassius pauses. "Maybe nights can be Patrick's domain?"

I raise my eyebrows. "He'd need boobs."

"Who needs boobs?" pipes up Jessie suddenly from across the room.

I hadn't realised that she was listening. "Nobody," I laugh, trying not to tap my leg as I do so, trying not to bite the inside of my cheek. "Nobody. What are you drawing?"

Jessie is always drawing now, constantly, almost as attached to her notepad as I am to mine. She holds her picture up to show me and I examine it as though it is a true work of art. In essence, it is a mass of colours, one on top of the other – she is, after all, only three – but there are a few circles dotted around the page, and looking more carefully, I notice that one of the circles has red lines on the top of it, with what I can see are supposed to be arms and legs sticking out from the sides. It is a person. With red hair. She has drawn me.

I scoop her up. And breathe her in. "Shall we go see Madge?" I ask her.

Jessie squeals and wriggles down so that she can run to the wooden chest which used to hold spare cushions but is now where we keep her bucket and spade, a turquoise set we bought on the beachfront. I stand up to follow her, but Cassius stays my arm.

"Why don't you just try the pills temporarily?" he suggests. "Not long-term, just to break the cycle. That's all you need, I'm sure of it. Just to get back to normal. I don't want to see you spiral again, Lil. I can't watch it."

There is a ferocity to Cassius's eyes, a pleading, and I understand it. It is the same reason that he is here, living in my house. We are not destined for romance, but our pain is symbiotic. Our happiness too. It always has been.

"Mummy might be at the beach today," says Jessie.

That evening, I finally have an appointment with June. I have been trying to see her all week, but this was her first available slot. Patrick will be back the next day, so I waste no time. I tell her what I have not even told Cassius – that as well as the sleepwalking, I have started to envisage Jessie getting hurt because of it, in the same way that I used to imagine something awful befalling Dylan.

"Do you mean you are picturing yourself doing something to her?" June asks me bluntly.

I fiddle with the turquoise strap around my wrist. "Yes. I suppose so. But by accident, in my sleep."

"Yes or no?"

"Yes."

"Well, then we need to confront that," she tells me. "That is the fear we need to lean into. Don't try to run from it."

I have been running daily. Even on yoga days.

"I got a bit weird with the door latch yesterday too," I confess all of a sudden.

"You mean you had a compulsion?" June wants me to name these things. To say them.

"Yes. I guess. At first I was just checking the latch, practically, you know. Then it suddenly came to me that if I locked and unlocked it three times, then Jessie, who's three years old, would be safe."

"But you know that the compulsion has no power to keep anybody safe," says June slowly.

"I know."

"It's just a way to relieve your anxiety."

"I know."

"So we need to find another way to handle that anxiety, which has clearly been triggered by the sleepwalking," she says. "You're lucky actually, in that there is a very specific trigger for you. I mean it's an overarching one about control, of course. That's something we need to discuss much more deeply. But it's triggered by the sleepwalking."

"Control?"

"Most of my patients aren't able to pinpoint something so specific, so with them we have to focus very much more on the feelings causing the compulsions," June continues. "Which of course you and I must do together also, long-term. But for now, to immediately relieve your anxiety, which will reduce the obsessions, which in turn of course will stop the compulsions, we need to address the sleepwalking."

"Easy," I say sarcastically.

She frowns at me over the top of her glasses. "But it is easy," she says. "It's very tangible. Now to start with, there are a lot of things that I'm sure you know which may help reduce the incidents. Going to bed on time, no alcohol, deep breathing—"

"They don't work," I interrupt her.

"Well, they are not bulletproof," she agrees.

"They do nothing."

June pauses. "I see you are wearing the bracelet."

I stop fiddling. "Yes."

"OK. So how about we set up some other measures to reassure you…" She squints at me. "In case deep breathing doesn't work?" She smiles and I humour her with a half-smile in return. "What about the alarm on your door? Or moving the child and her father out?"

"I've decided to have a baby," I tell her.

"Ah." June shifts in her chair and writes this information down on her pad. "For that we will definitely need some longer-term work. I suspect that the force of that decision, the weight of responsibility you anticipate in caring for a child, in protecting that child, the pressure you feel to do that, I suspect that has a great deal to do with these new episodes, and always did, with your brother. Possibly it's to do with the expectations in your family culture about how precious children are, how precious you all were to each other. And you, you see, you with that vivid imagination."

"I don't understand," I interrupt.

June waves her hand. "We'll come to this. We'll come to this. For now, we only… Well, let me ask you – what would make you feel relaxed? To know you're not going to do harm to Jessie in the night, that she is safe? Or to know you won't sleepwalk at all?"

"To know I won't sleepwalk," I answer immediately. "And that nobody will see me sleepwalk."

"Like your fiancé?" she asks.

I hesitate. "Yes."

She writes this down too.

"So, the sleeping pill?"

I nod.

June pulls out a fresh pad to write me a prescription, but she doesn't fill it in immediately. "This is for short-term use," she stipulates.

"OK."

"They can lead to some fuzziness, reduced awareness, memory loss."

"OK."

"And they can become addictive. I'll give you enough for ten days, to see if we can interrupt this cycle. But we must work on the emotional issues around this."

"OK."

"OK." June looks at me hard. Eventually, she writes the prescription. When she hands it to me, however, it comes with a caution. "It's a lapse. Not a relapse," she stipulates. "Your OCD, I mean. I don't want you to go away thinking that this is necessary for it, or that the obsessions are back. They're not. They're specific and temporary. And the pills are specific and temporary too, for the sleepwalking. We are merely shortcutting the anxiety while we work on some longer-term adjustments. OK?"

"OK." OK. OK. OK. I nod again, and take the prescription, and book in for another appointment the following week.

The pill practically melts on my tongue. It tastes like those chemical sweeteners that are supposed to replace sugar. And something else. A memory is stirred of licking envelopes – glue, perhaps, or paper? I am lying in bed. On my nightstand is a glass of water, and on the floor a bucket – the leaflet that came with the pills has advised me that nausea is a possibility. I check my clock – it has been 13 minutes. I have never taken anything stronger than paracetamol and Cassius has been recruited to stand by my bedroom door, just in case. In case of what, I don't know, but I feel the need for a safety net. I have asked him to protect me, this last time. Cassius watches dutifully from the door. A few seconds later he raises his eyebrows as though in question – are you OK, am I OK, are you…?

It is the last thing that I recall. In the morning, I feel marginally groggy, as though I've been on a flight and had to adjust a couple of hours, though nothing like long haul. It was normal sleep, almost, only without a journey, without the dream-infused meanderings of the night-time mind. Or night-time legs and arms and other moving parts, which is the point. It was like drifting to sleep normally, except there was a heaviness around the head, a closing of a blind. So actually, more like something between slipping to sleep and sudden, bludgeoning oblivion.

Cassius confirms to me at breakfast that the pill worked. He waited up, but I didn't move from my bed.

I go for a run and let this permeate, let it pump through my veins. Already, I feel more concentrated than I have done in days. More balanced than in weeks. Madge beams at me when I reach her alley and pats me on the arm knowingly, as though she can already see the change in me and believes her intervention to have been the crucial thing. But go figure, she tells me, glancing out towards the sea, a storm is brewing.

At lunch, Patrick appears at the studio straight from the airport. We hug fiercely, as though we have been apart for months. The engagement seems to have intensified things between us in ways I never expected, commitment to forever somehow working its way into our bones. When I see him now, visions of our future slip themselves around our present – silver hair, and fuddy-duddy pyjamas, and hands intermingled through triumphs and tears. When we touch, our arms wrap around each other more ardently.

And suddenly, without premeditation, I tell him. In his arms, feeling forever, I find that I can't not.

But I say it flippantly, and don't confess everything – not about taking Jessie as I once took Dylan and might take our own child. I say only that I sleepwalked again while he was away. That it did happen, after all. Then, "I'm taking some sleeping pills," I mention casually. "Just for a week or so. Just to get back on an even keel."

And, trusting me, trusting my lightness, my balance, this version of me that he knows, he replies with equal breeziness: "Great." And, "Shall we order Chinese?" And, "Has Cassius found a place yet?"

CHAPTER 21

Cassius himself asks Patrick to babysit Jessie so that he can tell me. Days ago, I caught sight of a brochure for an apartment building in Arlington, and I know this dinner is a cushion for the long-awaited news: he and Jessie are moving out. Over Thai noodles, I receive the news with all the jubilation, for him, and trepidation, for me, that necessitated a private dinner. Private because he wants to thank me, he tells Patrick. Private because of the sleepwalking, he confirms to me.

Patrick still doesn't know the whole story, but it is this: since he has been back from New York, whenever he stays over, I take a pill, and the sleepwalking stops. On nights when he doesn't stay, I resist the shortcut to sanity and, sometimes, I walk. The incidents are unpredictable. They come without apparent trigger and with no obvious pattern to them, so each night, just in case, Cassius has been waiting up. What will I do without him to keep me safe, he presses now. He knows I have only three pills left.

June is working with me on 'deeper causes', and to my relief, the intrusive thoughts at least have tapered off; but they are not gone completely. Sometimes I get visions of suffocating Jessie with a pillow, or throwing her down the stairs, just like I used to with Dylan. Why do I still imagine these things? Why? I know that I am supposed to detach, to regard these intrusions as external to myself, but where then does that darkness come from? June has introduced me to hypnosis. She is optimistic, she says. She doesn't, however, have all the information. She thinks I have taken the pills as directed. She thinks that with a straight run of ten nights' undisturbed sleep, we have successfully interrupted the sleepwalking. She doesn't realise that there is a rational reason for my continued anxiety – that despite years and miles and therapy and pills, I am still a demon of the night.

I should tell her. I know it. I know it. But she won't give me more pills. She was absolutely clear that they were a one-off circuit breaker. She won't prescribe them again. And then, she'll make me tell Patrick.

I can't tell Patrick. Not yet. Not until I have it under control.

I could buy some pills at the pharmacy – everybody in LA is on something and nobody would bat an eye. But the over-the-counter variety are not as strong as the prescription ones, and when I look them up online, some of their potential side effects include sleepwalking. I don't want those. I don't want those. I need the ones that could knock out the cow.

Once Cassius and Jessie leave, there will be less urgency. I calm myself with this. If Jessie is no longer in my house, across the hall, there will be no immediate threat of hurting her. And then I'll have time to work with June properly – two years, a year at least, depending on when the wedding is and how quickly we fall pregnant. I wonder why it is that people say '*fall* pregnant', as though it is associated either with accident – a trip, a tumble – or descent. A descent from grace, a plunging, a sinning, like Adam and Eve from the Garden of Eden, like Lilith who came before. Girl plummeting into base, elemental womanhood.

Am I plummeting?

Once Jessie has gone, I won't worry as much about sleepwalking. So perhaps it will simply stop. Like it did before.

Once Jessie has gone, there will be no opportunity to hurt her unknowingly. So perhaps the visions will stop too.

Once Jessie has gone, none of it will seem so treacherous.

So perhaps I'll be able to make light of things, and confide in Patrick.

Then again, once Jessie has gone, she'll be gone.

And Cassius will be gone with her.

I raise my glass of water, which you are not supposed to toast with, and clink glasses with Cassius. "I'll be fine," I say. "You don't need to protect me. Really. Congratulations. So many congratulations, Cass. I'll miss you though."

And her. I'll miss her.

She is not my child, but she is Dylan reincarnated. She is Cassius reincarnated. She is my past, and the future I disallowed myself. And want. Want. And am terrified I will never have.

The following afternoon, Jessie and I take my bike and cycle to the bookshop. After the stories are read, we choose a new book, and select our cupcakes, which we eat on the way to the beach. Madge thanks us for hers and, while we chat, I see her absorbing Jessie's enthusiasm, her vitality and youth. It is such a pleasure to unfold the world for this child, to tell her things, to watch them dance through her eyes. It is a way to remember newness and freshness, to glimpse again that brilliance. I see it in Madge's eyes, this glimpsing. I feel it in my own. Is it why, I wonder, we ache for children? To summon back the purity we never knew we had? Must we forever claw at the locked gates of paradise?

While Jessie unpacks a series of shells from her bucket, earnestly lining them up in preference order for Madge to inspect, Madge tells her about the molluscs and other tiny creatures from which shells derive. For a moment, my mind wanders, as it is wandering more and more often, and I recall my own childhood collection, the beaches on which I gathered shells with my parents, their ultimate usefulness in impeding my passage from bed. I am not sure how long I am distracted by this remembering, but at some point I notice Madge casting a surveying eye upon me, then reaching out and squeezing my hand, and I shake myself back into cheerfulness. Meanwhile, Madge explains to Jessie how the living organism dies, but the protective shell remains. Like when a person dies, she says meaningfully, but their spirit lasts, protecting the people they love. Except you can't see a spirit. Or touch it. But still it's there. Jessie nods, wide-eyed. She asks Madge if she has a spirit-shell protecting her. "Well, the shells move all day long," Madge replies to Jessie. "The ocean moves them up and down the beach. So even when the shells are there, you can't always quite grab hold of them. Go figure." She muses, a little sadly.

Jessie looks up at her. "Go figure."

"This time of day though," continues Madge, "the best selection of shells is right over there."

Immediately, Jessie's face lights up, and then she leaps up, hurtling towards the indicated patch of shore. It is a wide beach here, an expansive, stretched-out piece of sand. There seem miles between paving and water. But Jessie's shoes are off, and sand is flying behind her, never mind about burnt toes. I squeeze Madge's arm, I mouth thanks, then I throw off my own sandals, and run fast toward the sea.

We sit with our feet in the water, the waves lapping against our toes, burying them beneath the sodden grains, our shells encased in turquoise. Jessie is between my legs and leans back against my chest. She reaches out and fiddles with the strap on my wrist. Her thumb wriggles underneath it. In a recent development, she has grown out of her afternoon nap, but she closes her eyes now and her body feels heavy. I stroke her temple, I lift hair out of her eyes, I brush sand from her arm.

"I love you," she whispers suddenly, eyes still closed. "I don't want to move out of your house."

"I love you too," I say. "And we'll see each other all the time."

"But Mummy doesn't cuddle me."

I squeeze her. And squeeze her again. "She would if she could."

"Then why doesn't she?"

Her face is turned towards mine.

"I guess," I say carefully. "I guess sometimes you just can't quite hold on to some things. Like Madge was saying. Like the shells in the sea."

Jessie doesn't seem convinced, but she snuggles further into me, her hand still lodged beneath my strap. "Anyway, you're cuddly," she murmurs.

I don't reply. I am afraid that if I do, I won't be able to let her go. As I must. As I had to with Dylan. As I never want to have to again.

What I want is to stay wrapped up with Jessie forever. But our feet are sinking deeper beneath strengthening waves that pile sand upon us. The tide is coming in. A storm brewing, just as Madge predicted. It is necessary to move. It is necessary to sort things.

I will. I will.

Despite crashing water, I will, this time. I will find my balance. And then there will be nothing to fear. Nothing to hide. And Patrick and I can have a child of our own, a baby of our own, to love, and to keep, and to never let go.

CHAPTER 22

It was Jade who called my parents. Almost three weeks had passed since I'd picked up the phone to them, or to Dylan, or to Cassius. I had missed the deadline for two essays, failed to turn up to lectures, dropped out of the drama group, and was barely eating. Jade still had my key, so she let herself in and out of my room and forced me to drink tea; but she'd reached her limit. "It's your parents, or the university administration," she threatened. I handed her my phone.

My mother swept into the room smelling of fresh air, and Dylan. "Lilith, you look awful." She yanked open the curtains, then sat directly next to me on the bed in which I was curled. "What's wrong? Tell me. What on earth is going on?"

I couldn't answer. So many years had passed without me telling the whole truth that it felt impossible to do so now, as though my mother would think I was making it all up. I should have fed her more than titbits. I should have let her hold me, hold my history. I should have let her see. Now she would never understand.

My mother pulled the duvet off of me. "Lilith, you're stick thin."

I shrugged, and reached for the cover, tucking it firmly back around my legs.

"You can't go on like this. You need to eat."

"She has toast," Jade offered from the doorway. "A few bites here and there."

"But why?" my mother urged. "Why would you not eat? What's got into your head?"

I didn't answer because I didn't know. Perhaps I was trying to erase my presence, expunge my body, obliterate the physical fact of my being. The danger of it. But thoughts hadn't filtered that way. I simply couldn't eat. Couldn't carry on. Couldn't do anything. At my silence, frustration clouded my mother's face. I saw it saturate her brow. "Senoy, Sansenoy, Semangelof," I whispered under my breath.

"What?"

I didn't want her to hear, it was meant to be a personal prayer, but if I said it inaudibly, it didn't count. "Senoy, Sansenoy, Semangelof."

"What? What are you saying?" She turned to Jade. "What is she saying?"

"It's the names of the angels invoked to protect people from Lilith," Jade explained. "The biblical Lilith." She shot me an apologetic look but moved further into the room. "She thinks she was cursed to be a night monster. Because of her name. She's been sleepwalking loads. Every night. So now she's barely sleeping. Except during the day. And the compulsions are out of control. And now, this."

"What compulsions?" Under the covers, my mother grasped at my hands.

"Her OCD," said Jade.

I turned over. "Senoy, Sansenoy, Semangelof."

"OCD?" My mother shook my shoulders gently, attempting to get me to turn back over. I wouldn't. "Lilith. You have OCD? Lilith?"

"Sorry," Jade offered. "I thought you must know."

"Clearly, I should have," my mother pronounced. "Lilith, can you please look at me?"

I shook my head.

"How long has this been going on? Well, you need to come

home. There are treatments for OCD. There's a lot we can do, a lot even I can help you with, now that I know. Why… Why did I not know?"

Still not turning, I shook my head. Quietly, Jade left the room. There was silence.

Then, "You must be so exhausted," my mother said gently. Carefully. "The effort of hiding it from us. For how long? Was it always…" She paused. "I'm so sorry, darling. I'm so sorry. You must be so, so exhausted."

Without meaning to, I started to cry, and whether or not she intended to, my mother did as well, both of us sobbing. Then, slipping her arms beneath my skinny frame, she scooped me up to her chest, like she had done when I was very small, like the night that I climbed the bathroom shelves, and she burrowed her face into my messy, unwashed hair, and she breathed me in, as I had once breathed in Dylan, and she held me, and she held me, and she held me.

For many minutes we remained this way. In the distance, there passed the sounds of laughing students, of irritated car horns, of music pumped too loud. Birdsong meandered past the open window. An early spring breeze knocked the blind against its frame. A muted moment hung itself around us. Until finally, after a long time, my mother pulled slightly back. "You need to let me look after you," she told me.

Now, however, I yanked myself away. "I can't come home."

"Why not?"

"I can't be near Dylan."

"What? Why?"

"It's not the OCD, Mum. It's the sleepwalking. I can't control it, even with the compulsions. I could never control it. You know that I stole him once."

"You didn't steal him, you—"

"I took him from his bed. I could have done anything. I could still do anything."

"Lilith. I can't believe you're still thinking about that. It was so long ago. Is this what it's been? All these years? Why didn't you tell me?"

I shrugged.

"Lilith, you would never do anything to hurt your brother."

"You don't know that," I said, breaking down again. "You don't know that. That's the problem. Nobody knows. Nobody knows what I'm capable of. I can't be around him. I can't be around anyone. I did it right next to Cassius and Jade just last month. I nearly… I nearly…"

By now I was hysterical, screaming. And my mother was crying again too.

"What?" my mother asked. "What?"

But I couldn't finish. I couldn't reveal how close I'd come to death.

"Fine," my mother sniffed eventually, putting out her hands to placate me. "Fine. Fine. You don't need to be around Dylan. You don't have to come home. But you need something. You can't go on like this. If you want to be on your own, be on your own, but darling, talk to somebody. Talk to somebody. Somebody professional. Even if it's not me, OK, I wish it was, but then somebody else who can help. OK?"

I shrugged.

"OK?"

Hesitantly, I nodded.

"And you need to eat, Lilith. And sleep. And smile. Smile, darling. I don't care about anything else; I just want you to be happy."

Weakly, I attempted a smile.

"No, not for me, for you," my mother clarified. "I don't need you to act happy. I want you to *be* happy. How can I help you to be happy?"

Again, I shrugged.

"Shall I call Cassius?"

I shook my head.

"Do you want Dad to come?"

Another shake.

"Are you sure you don't want to see Dylan?"

But I shook my head again. And now she did too. She looked defeated. Desolate.

"I don't know what to say. What to do. To help you. I only want… I only want…" She paused. "Never mind."

"What?" I asked. "You want what?"

But she only shook her head. "When you have children. When you have children, you'll understand."

"Understand what?" I pressed again.

But she shook her head again. "When you're a mother, you'll know."

Except, I didn't have to be a mother.

The word serpent slunk around my head.

Mother.

People presumed it. People sleepwalked into it. Even my own – feminist – mother expected it. Just like Adam, and Eve, and God. Even I had. I had imagined it, wanted it, thought about it countless times. But I shouldn't have. I shouldn't. I shouldn't ever think about being a mother. Because Lilith's babies die. Because Lilith takes babies from their bed. Because Lilith is a demonic female. A pariah. A woman alone.

Abruptly, I sat up in bed.

My mother looked at me curiously, wondering perhaps at the sudden wildness in my eyes, the energy in my emaciated frame, and I blinked in the light as though the curtains had only just that instant been drawn. A great weight seemed to have lifted from my soul, and it was with unprecedented lightness that I found myself reaching out to squeeze my mother's hand. Maybe it was naïve, stupid even. But I felt suddenly so hopeful, and I couldn't believe I hadn't considered it earlier: that presumption was only… presumption. Only an idea. Only nothing.

I didn't have to become a mother. I didn't have to marry.

If I never had a child, I would never have to protect it from myself.

If I never had a partner, I would never have to protect them either.

If I lived a life 'other', a life alone, a life away from the people I might hurt…

Well then, I could be free.

CHAPTER 23

The lease will be theirs in ten days. Cassius is already packing. Patrick is thrilled. Jessie and I spend every moment together we can. At work, I am balancing *Moles* with development meetings for the new show, but I ring-fence the hours before she goes to bed. One afternoon, Patrick lets himself in while I am still at work and surprises us all with a picnic, but mostly he busies himself elsewhere. He still prefers to sleep at his own house while Cassius and Jessie are there, and says he doesn't mind giving us this last burst together. I think he sees it now for what it is – a friendship, a pretence at family perhaps, but no longer steeped for him in threat. Because we all three of us understand clearly now – Cassius and I were not, after all, destined for anything more than this.

One evening, Cassius and I let Jessie stay up with us for takeout and a movie. Another time we put her early to bed and reminisce about our youth – the school plays, and our parents, and the way our eyes locked that day at the airport in Paphos. Moments. Crossroads. These conversations always take place in the evening, late, on the cusp of night. And afterwards, on each one of those nights, Cassius waits up, letting me save my last remaining pills. He waits up, and then he reports back: a jaunt in the kitchen, a trip into the garden. One morning he shows me the knife that I took out to butter some toast. He leaves it there on the counter for me to see, the crumbs and smeared butter attesting to my unconscious hunger, and at once I think of the old tale of Hansel and Gretel. Because, just as theirs did, these crumbs lead me back – back, back, back to Dylan and the night I stole him. Cassius must see the horror on my face because that is when he suggests that I write down these episodes to tell June – perhaps there is a pattern to them, he says hopefully, perhaps if we record them, we will see it. He is trying to find ways to protect me once he is gone. Still. Despite my historic abandonment of him, he cannot leave me unprotected. For the hundredth time, guilt overwhelms me. But it is a good idea, almost the same as my Post-its, a way to detach and dismiss, and deal with. Together, Cassius and I are building each other up, letting each other go, finally. He remarks that it was always this way for him, gearing up to leave my family, to go back to his. He was always steeling himself for it.

But then, two nights before he is due to leave, my family is once again upon him. Because the doorbell rings, and there is Dylan.

CHAPTER 24

On the doorstep behind my brother, Patrick, who I have not seen in three days, is laughing. They have conspired together to surprise me. At six foot four, I can no longer scoop Dylan into my arms, but I throw myself into his. It has been eight months since I saw him last. There is a slight smell about him of sweat and aeroplane, but also of home. I pull back to take in his face, more exposed somehow than on FaceTime, screened by distance and glass, and he smiles with the knowingness we have always shared. My mother was right – 20 minutes a day was enough; even with an ocean between us, our bond remains impenetrable. We hug again, and then I drag him inside where there is a gasp from Cassius who hasn't seen Dylan since he was six. There follows a great deal of telling and retelling of the secrecy involved to get him here, a dash to whip up some food, and so much laughter that Jessie is woken from her sleep and appears in her nightie in the kitchen.

"Well, hi there," says Dylan, the first to notice her. "I'm guessing you're Jessie?"

Jessie nods, and slinks herself against the cupboards around the room until she reaches my leg, which she promptly hides behind. In the daytime, she may be gregarious and confident, but now it is night.

"It's OK," Cassius tells her, moving down to her level and speaking close to her ear. "This is Lilith's little brother, Dylan."

Jessie eyes Dylan circumspectly and reaches her arms up

to me to be lifted. Carefully, she looks from my face to his. Then she whispers in my ear. "He doesn't look little."

I don't mean to, but I cannot help but laugh at this. "He's not little because he's grown up now," I explain. "But he's a lot younger than me, so he's still little, to me."

"When I first met Dylan, he was even littler than you," Cassius adds to Jessie.

"Do you remember what you did when you first held him?" I say.

"No? What? Not something awful, I hope."

I shake my head. "No. It was nice. You laughed. You just laughed, like it was the best thing ever."

"Did you?" Dylan asks. Then laughs himself. "Well, I guess that's understandable."

But Cassius is quieter. "I did think it was the best thing ever," he says. "You know, having a sibling. Having a family like that." He pauses for a moment and allows the vulnerability of that confession the space it deserves. Sensitivity and hurt, as always, on his shirtsleeve. Then he shakes himself and looks down at Jessie. "And now I've got you," he declares. "Which is even better. Sorry." He winks at Dylan.

Dylan shrugs, continuing the joke and speaking to Jessie. "So, you've taken my spot, have you?"

It takes a whole day after this for Jessie to warm to Dylan. She seems to have enshrined it in her head that he thinks she has taken something, stolen something from him, and she behaves with distant indignation. It would be difficult, however, for even the most determined of three-year-olds to resist my brother's charm, which comes packed with jokes and silly faces and a youthful energy for games, many of which I taught him. And gentleness. And insight. He is my father and mother melded into six-foot splendour. Cassius sees this too. More than a few times, he comments on how like my father Dylan is, so it doesn't surprise me that he takes to accompanying us everywhere.

It is partially because of Cassius's constant presence, and partially because Dylan is Dylan, that I end up telling my brother about the persisting sleepwalking. That first night that he arrived, Cassius and I had had a hurried, hushed conversation about what to do now that Dylan was in the house – should I take one of my precious pills, being saved for when Cassius was gone, or risk it. In the end, Cassius had volunteered a third option: to maintain his night watch, delaying his and Jessie's departure until Dylan had left. Eagerly, I'd jumped at that offer, a latent desire to shield my brother from worry, and from me. But a few days later, when Cassius is quietly relaying to me my latest sleepwalk – horrifically, to the door of Jessie's room – Dylan overhears us.

We are all in the queue for the Urth Café at the time, minus Patrick who's coaching football. Dylan has always loved the Urth Café – graduating from the watermelon smoothie as a kid to the green tea boba – and it is tradition for us to breakfast there together at least once each visit. This is, however, Jessie's first outing, and stationed happily on Dylan's hip, she is listening to him describe the vast array of smoothie flavours, when Cassius takes the opportunity to whisper to me the secrets of the previous night.

"I thought the sleepwalking had stopped," Dylan interrupts suddenly, leaning between us.

"Oy, stop eavesdropping, you," I scold him jokily.

"Then stop pretending things are fine. I knew they weren't."

"What are you talking about?" asks Jessie.

In front of her, we dance around the topic, Dylan accepting the unspoken caution in my eyes. But later, that evening, before Patrick arrives to take Dylan and me to dinner, the three of us sit on the couch downstairs, and Cassius explains to Dylan what he has seen.

"But I don't want Patrick to see," I hurry. "I mean, he knows a bit. He knows I've had a few incidents. But not some of the recent stuff. And I don't want him to worry."

"He won't worry, he'll help," Dylan objects immediately.

"Dyl, you don't understand all of it," I tell him. "Patrick may not worry now, but in the future, if we have kids of our own—"

"You're going to have kids?" Dylan interjects. "I thought you didn't want any? Wow. That's a big change."

"Yes. It is. And it's recent. I haven't even mentioned it to Mum or Dad yet. But so, you see, now that's on the cards, I don't want him to worry about me being around a baby. You know, in the night."

"He wouldn't."

"He might. It would be in his mind. How could it not?"

"But you've been around Jessie."

"Only because Cass has been staying up. Keeping watch."

"I'll keep watch," volunteers Dylan.

"You don't need to," Cassius assures. "Honestly, I'm used to it now. And Jessie's my daughter. We're the imposters here. I'm happy to do it."

"But I want to see," declares Dylan. Firmly. He looks at me. "This is the reason you moved out of home, right? When I was still a kid? OK, so I want to see why."

There is a slight resentment to the way in which Dylan speaks these words. I have never detected this in him before. But then it has never occurred to me that he would hold me in contempt for leaving him. I had always realised that he would miss me, that he might be upset, but not that he would blame me. At the time, Jade had counselled that it was normal for older siblings to move out, to move away, to move on – besides, I had to – but of course Dylan and I were never just siblings, and I had known that. Our relationship occupied the space between sibling and mother-son. I wonder now if he'd also noticed my drawing away when he was younger, if he'd felt my attempts to create distance, safety. If he'd heard my mutterings to Cassius behind closed bedroom doors, or seen my descent into myself, and felt shut out. Rejected. Even as an adult, I've never quite explained it to him – how debilitating it all became. I hadn't wanted him to blame himself for my trauma, to take on any of the responsibility that, after all, was not his to bear. But, I consider now, perhaps that has led him to begrudge, to blame. Perhaps that's why he wanted Cassius and Jessie to move out of my home. Perhaps they represent for him what he has been denied. Perhaps he really does feel that Jessie has stolen something. And wants it back from her.

"Some nights there's nothing to see," Cassius cautions.

"And some nights there's what?" Dylan presses, holding his hand up to stop Cassius from interjecting again. "What do you do, exactly?"

Cassius and I both try to describe it. We try to explain. We tell him about the night that Cassius found Jessie in my bed.

"But you were just cuddling her, right?" Dylan asks.

"Yes."

"OK." He pauses. "I don't get it."

"It's the not knowing," I state plainly. "That's always been the thing. Not knowing if I will just cuddle her. Or do something else."

He nods, taking this in. "OK," he says again. "I still want to see."

For the following seven nights, Dylan waits up and Cassius goes to bed. Now that Cassius's move has been 'delayed', Patrick grows impatient and stays over too, but I decide not to take a sleeping pill. With Dylan waiting for me, I know I won't do anything harmful, and I feel I owe it to him to let him see.

But I don't walk.

I don't walk.

And I don't walk.

All week, even on the night of the storm Madge predicted, I sleep solidly, Dylan retreating to bed around 2 a.m., well after the hour of my usual wanderings.

Slowly, the relief of this is filling me with an unexpected exuberance. Because perhaps it is over. Perhaps Dylan's arrival has done what the pills didn't – broken the cycle. I am not sleepwalking. I am not sleepwalking. It has been seven days and I am not sleepwalking. My mind dares to imagine it. A week is a pattern. A week is a lifetime. In a week, God made the entire world, including Lilith.

I feel almost like the old Lilith. The old new Lilith, that is.

I spin Jessie in the air during mad dance sessions before her bath.

I run with Patrick, and Dylan who is faster than us both.

I surf, lending Dylan my old board.

We skate together, he having learnt as a teen, here, with me.

At work, I feel myself daring and commanding and reaching for boundaries to break in a way that I haven't in months.

At yoga, I exhale. I exhale. And realise that I have been holding my breath. Both Nola and Ria remark on how lifted I seem.

"Are you taking a new supplement?" asks Ria, wanting the Amazon link.

"It's your brother," decrees Nola, not a question.

They both ask for updates on Cassius. Nola asks also about Jessie. "She is OK? You're not sleepwalking now?" she wants to know. And I gleefully respond with the truth.

Now that he is no longer so worried for me, Dylan plans a trip to San Francisco. We decide to gather our friends for a proper night out to see him off. Patrick hires a space at our favourite bar on La Cienega, and we all agree to dress to the nines. Even Cassius is coming, having asked a worker from Jessie's daycare to babysit. Secretly, I arrange for a huge cake to be brought out towards the end of the evening in my brother's honour. There is a need, I feel, to celebrate – his visit, his graduation, his new job in Germany, the way his presence has liberated me. Thinking about that, I am struck by the strangeness of the way in which things have come full circle. Once – small, vulnerable – Dylan was the cause of my anxiety. Now he has saved me from it. I watch him emerge from his room in a black shirt and slim-fit jeans, and he looks every inch the man he has become. Tears choke me slightly on seeing him, as if I am his mother sending him off to prom. But it isn't quite the same as that. It is not the nostalgia of seeing a child grown that arrests me. More, sadness at having missed such chunks of the growing. I can't do that again. I will not do that again. I hug him hard, and he lets me.

We all travel to the bar together. Waiting already are a number of Patrick's friends – a close-knit crew of three from his college days, a couple of guys he works with, and a few others he has collected over the years and I know well. On my side, there is also a ragtag assembly – both men and women whom I have met at different times, in various guises, and have come to care for and count on. Then there are those couples who Patrick and I have evolved with together. It has been a while since either of us have thrown a party and as I stand just inside the door, the sight of everybody there, for us, halts me for a moment. I have been so busy lately with old fears that I had forgotten this – this proof of life, my life, here, this testament to how far I have come. It is rejuvenating to see it, to feel it, to receive it. Wrapping my friends around me, I move further into the room and look for Dylan who has already disappeared. He is familiar with some of these people already. Nobody has known him as long as Cassius, but there are a few who met him first when he was only just double digits, and they share now in my wonder at his height, at his deep voice, at the absurdity of his having a real job, in Germany. Dylan, however, is not next to me to accept their marvel and admiration, because Patrick, it seems, has already immersed him in his fold. When he emerges a while later, he is grinning from ear to ear. "Meet my best man," says Patrick, hugging Dylan around the neck, his friends cheering in the background, and Dylan claps him on the back in reciprocation, and smiles first at me, and then, a little oddly, at Cassius. I am not sure what is behind that smile, it is defiant almost, a heckle, and it makes me glance towards Cassius myself.

He is standing, in typical fashion, illuminating the space

around him. Ria is a little way off and I notice her gazing every few seconds in his direction. She clearly likes him still and I wonder if perhaps, one day, when he's ready, they might pursue things. I am glad to observe in myself that I am not put out by the idea of that. I am ready for it. For now, however, Cassius is locked in intense conversation with Nola. The two of them always seem to be discussing something weighty. It is Nola's way, of course, all passion and conviction, I have seen both men and women mesmerised by it; but this time Cassius seems frustrated, or indignant, or upset. He keeps throwing his hands in the air as if defending himself, and then bowing his head and listening, while Nola gesticulates wildly. Perhaps she is warning him again to be careful around me, to protect Jessie. I still don't begrudge her for this. Not quite. It is not an irrational fear. But it doesn't feel good to know that this is how she thinks of me. In the end, Cassius turns around and notices me looking. *Everything OK?* my eyes communicate. He nods quickly, then rolls his own eyes upwards in silent aggravation. From across the room, I reciprocate with a mock frown, a wagged finger: *be nice*. And Cassius shakes his head in exaggerated agony before air-kissing Nola on the cheek and moving to where Ria has a glass of something more welcoming waiting for him.

Sometime later, Dylan and I are seated together at the bar. Perspiration trails across his brow, and he orders a bottle of water. As he drinks it, I find myself remembering all the times over the years that we have sat together – him in his highchair, then hiding beneath a napkin on my lap, then later looking up at me from across the table, hanging off my every word. As though it is necessary for physicality to verify these memories, I reach out and touch his arm. My Dylan. My Dylan. His shirtsleeves are rolled up and his skin is warm. His presence here with me feels more visceral, somehow, than on previous visits. Because then, there was a sepia quality to it, almost as though he was a photo I could admire, and then re-box and compartmentalise. This time is different. I used to think that

I'd remade myself in California entirely, but I hadn't; I had only left part of myself behind. And finally, I feel the two parts coexisting, merging. And – it's OK. I'm OK.

I try – suddenly, eagerly – to explain all this to Dylan, but I don't articulate it properly. He hears only me saying something about how good it is to see him, and likewise to have reconnected with Cassius.

"I don't know about Cassius," Dylan responds unceremoniously.

He is a little drunk, and I am not sure what he means. The veins in his neck pulsate as he almost drains his water, and again I am in awe of time's magic. It doesn't hit you this way when you're with somebody daily. Sometimes you need distance to see.

"I wasn't ever a fan," he continues, his words slurring slightly. "You know. But I was only a kid, and the rest of you loved him. So."

"So?"

"So I don't think he's good for you. Even before I got here, I could tell… I could sense from you… It's bloody aggravating to see him getting between you and Patrick."

I furrow my brow. "He's not."

Dylan shoots me a look of scepticism, an expression he has learnt from me, though alcohol tinges its intensity.

"We've just got engaged," I insist. "Did Patrick say something?"

But Dylan shakes his head. "Patrick aside, Cassius doesn't do you any good. Don't you think it's a bit telling that, after all this time, you become friends again, and you're suddenly having all these issues? Cassius is only good for Cassius."

I can't help but feel amused by Dylan's overprotectiveness, our roles reversed, but I try to give his worry weight. "Cassius was always there for me," I tell him gently. "We may have been through tough stuff as teens, but he always tried to help."

"Maybe his 'help' isn't what you need."

A defensive determination shoots from Dylan's eyes and

I see now how fervent he is about this, inebriated or not. He wants to move my opinion, convince me of Cassius's flaws, so I listen, as he has always listened to me. As I do so, however, I hear something else tracing his tone. Not only determination, not only care, but another, malice-made timbre. And although I'm not sure if he even realises it himself, suddenly, I don't think that Dylan's concern is about my well-being at all. Nor do I think it has anything to do with Patrick. I think it is the little brother in him, not wanting Cassius – and Jessie – to take me away. Like he has already done once, perhaps, in Dylan's eyes, when we were all young.

I smile again and squeeze Dylan's arm. "It's stopped now anyway, the sleepwalking. Thanks to you."

Dylan shrugs. "Well, I'm glad about that. But I wish you'd asked me to start with. Or Patrick. You should tell your fiancé this stuff, you know, not Cassius."

"But Cassius already knows, already knew, I mean," I explain, and then pause. Because actually, Dylan is right, about that at least. Patrick does deserve to know. "I will tell him," I promise. "Soon. Now it's under control, I definitely will."

"Good," he says, then slowly takes another sip of his water. When he has finished, he raises a comically high eyebrow. "I saw bloody Cassius a few weeks ago, by the way."

"You saw him? Where? He's been here."

"I don't mean I *saw* him. I saw him. In a photo."

"Oh yeah?"

"Yeah. I went to an exhibition at the University of the West of England."

"Very cultured of you," I say. "Where's that again?"

"In Bristol. You know, it's the one you go to if you don't get the grades for actual Bristol. But good for art."

"OK," I laugh.

"Anyway, in one of the rooms, there was a bunch of old work up on the walls – paintings, photographs, a collection from previous students."

"Right."

"They were really good. Not that that's relevant, but actually…" His eyes begin to sparkle. "If you're ever in the area, you should try to see this one—"

"Dyl," I interrupt. "The point?"

"Geez, impatient much?" His tone has returned now to the joviality that for the past few minutes has been lacking. "The point, dear sister, is that I saw Cassius in one of the photographs. I can't get away from him! His blooming mug staring up from centre stage, as usual, showing off."

"Showing off?"

"Come on, he *is* always showing off."

I smirk, not agreeing, not denying, picturing jazz hands. "What was the photo of then? Some kind of joint uni theatre production?"

"No, I don't think so. Just UWE. Isn't that where he went?"

"No. Bristol."

Dylan shrugs. "I dunno then. I just know he's bloody everywhere I go. When's he actually leaving your house?"

I roll my eyes in mock scorn at this gripe, and take another sip of my own water, but the coldness of it seems suddenly to freeze inside my chest. Why was Cassius in a UWE photo? My mind flies back, years back, to the party that he took me to when I visited him in Bristol, the party where I had wanted to meet his friends but didn't. Then I think of the hotel room from which I sleepwalked, that was not university accommodation. I shake my head. Something had always felt off about that weekend. But Cassius wouldn't have lied, not about something so big. The photo must have been from a joint production, or something.

Again, my mind trawls over that night and tries to picture Cassius, but as usual, I had been so wrapped up in my own life that I'd barely noticed his. Was he OK that weekend? I remember his parents were getting divorced around that time, and his dad had lost his job. The details are foggy, and it hurts my head to dig for them, but I suddenly feel certain that he'd been trying to tell me something. And I'd missed it. What had I missed?

"Seriously though," continues Dylan. "If I feel like I can't escape him, how do you think Patrick feels?"

What had Cassius been feeling? What had he wanted to say? I hadn't listened. I hadn't even thought about it, about him. Instead, I'd gone back to Sussex and unravelled. And in my unravelling, and then reweaving, I'd cut him out of my life. Just like that. Without checking in, without making sure; consumed only by my own remaking. As though we were but strangers, passing in an airport lounge.

"I totally let him down," I breathe, putting down my water.

Dylan lowers his own bottle and searches my eyes. "Don't start spiralling," he says earnestly. "I was half-joking. Patrick will understand."

"Not Patrick," I reply. "Cassius. I totally let him down. But… I'm not going to this time." As I say this, I glance across the room, and there Cassius is, laughing loudly, happily, lightly. I smile. "I haven't yet. And I won't."

For a moment, Dylan holds my eyes, and I turn my smile to him. But then suddenly he pushes back his bar stool and shoves his water away from him. The stool falls over. "That's what you take from my spotting Cassius in some photo?"

I am bewildered. Why is Dylan so angry? "Dyl—" I laugh.

"No, seriously, bloody Cassius. No questions to me about the rest of the exhibition, or what I thought of it, or why I feel like I can't escape him. Why maybe I could've done with seeing a bit of you here without him. No worrying about how Patrick feels. It's just always about Cassius. Cassius. Cassius."

"Dylan—"

"Or Jessie. She figures sometimes. But then she's an extension of him."

"Dyl," I say again. I have never seen him this incensed. I have also never seen him drunk.

"Bugger that then," he says, still slightly slurring, and signals to the bartender. "I'm switching back to tequila."

There is something unsettling about Dylan's anger, something pent up and locked deep, but it is also devastatingly comic to witness this novel display of wrath, especially in public. As he orders his drink, I can't help smiling. And then laughing. My little brother – enraged.

Hearing my laughter, Dylan continues to shake his head at me, intent on his fury, but slowly, slowly, a grin emerges. And then an old, familiar chuckle. My Dylan. Old enough to be exasperated. Old enough to swear. Old enough to order tequila. And now we both giggle at each other.

When our laughter finally dissipates, he tries in vain to refocus his eyes, to regain a serious composure, but in the end he gives up and rests his head on my shoulder. "What am I annoyed about again?" he asks me.

There is no time, however, for either of us to unpack it. Or for me to joke about the pointlessness of all those years I tried not to swear around him. Because this is the moment that the surprise cake is suddenly brought out, and both Cassius and Patrick gather round and push Dylan forward, and Dylan kisses me on the cheek, and our friends clap for him, for me, for us, and all at once, I feel even more glad than I did earlier, even more lifted up – elevated, intoxicated, surrounded by warmth and support and purpose. Because I realise that Patrick and I haven't yet had an engagement party, but this is as good as one, and my brother is here for it, and he is grown and safe, and Jessie is safe, and the sleepwalking is over, and the obsessions are all but gone, and next month we are shooting the episode of *Moles* that might finally put Cassius on the map, and that will help him, that will help him, he will be OK, and I have done this, I have made this life, and only this morning Madge told me that the weather this week will be beautiful.

Then, Dylan leaves for San Francisco.

And Cassius and Jessie have one more night with me before they finally take up the lease for the new apartment.

And so that afternoon we take Jessie out for lunch, and

then to see a movie, her very first, and she watches it from my lap, her thumb tucked beneath the turquoise strap of the bracelet I no longer need.

And Cassius lets me put her to bed, and I read her a fairy tale in which all of the gender roles have been reversed, and we talk about the silliness of love at first sight, like eyes meeting across a baggage reclaim. Because that's not how life works really. Only sometimes.

And she tells me again that she loves me. And I say the same to her.

And she says that she thinks tomorrow, perhaps she will see her mother.

And I brush past this and promise to take her at the weekend to see Madge.

And agree that, yes, we can take her a cupcake, we can take her two, and we can look in the water for more shells.

And yes, of course I'll come to see her at the new apartment.

And she strokes my hair. Red, she muses.

And her eyelids grow heavy.

And Cassius signals to me from where he has been watching us at the door.

And I kiss her on the forehead.

And I creep from her room.

And Cassius and I stay up for hours talking and talking and talking and talking.

And finally, we go to bed.

And in the morning, there is dirt on my feet.

CHAPTER 25

And she is gone.

CHAPTER 26

Afterwards, these are the minutes that will pass through my head again and again. The obliviousness of them. The self-deception.

It is still early. I am dressed for yoga, brewing a coffee, staring out of the window and considering the perfect blue of the sky. Cassius has asked me to drive him and Jessie to the new place, but I'll be back from yoga long before then. He's planning to rent a car himself this weekend. Finally. In this city, I don't know how he's waited so long, but he insisted that he didn't want to have to rely on help with the repayments. I am thinking about how maybe he'll at least let me buy Jessie a really good car seat, and how I should approach that with him, when I hear him moving about upstairs – the floorboards to his room creaking, then the door to his bathroom shutting, the flush of the loo. A few minutes later his feet pad again, this time across the landing, and then the door to Jessie's room groans on its hinges. I imagine her waking sleepily, lifting her arms to him. Anticipating their arrival downstairs, I add another scoop of coffee into the French press and pop a few slices of bread into the toaster.

When Cassius appears in the kitchen a minute later, still in his sleeping shorts and a T-shirt, he gives a thumbs up to the coffee, and then peers into the next room. "Where is she?" he asks, doubling back and looking through the side window into the garden. "Not colouring?"

"She hasn't been down yet," I reply casually. "Not since I've been up. Isn't she in bed?"

"No," says Cassius. "No. I thought she'd come down here with you."

I haven't realised yet. I will reprimand myself later, but I haven't realised. After all those weeks of obsessive worry, I don't even guess.

Together, we start calling her name. "Jessie, Jessie, Jessie." But we are breezy. *Where is that monkey hiding?* We carry on this way for a good minute. And it is only then, it is only then, when she still doesn't answer, it is only now, that it hits us. Though even for a minute or two longer, we pretend otherwise, as though there is deliverance in denial. During those minutes, we shout up the stairs, into the garden, out of the front door to the street, acting as though she has, aged three, just popped outside alone for the first time in her life, reached the latch, gone for a walk, and any second she'll waltz back into the kitchen. When, after a number of minutes more, she doesn't, our outward calm begins to waver. We still don't speak it, our growing fear, we still pass each other with half-smiles on our faces, as though this is merely the routine work of tracking down a three-year-old; but we tear around the house now with the speed of Olympians, ripping open curtains with more force than is necessary, yanking frantically at cupboard doors, checking inside the washing machine and the oven and anywhere we can think of that she might have crawled into and got stuck. At some point, Cassius remembers her love of hide-and-seek with Patrick, how he taught her to hide so well, quiet as a mouse, and so he checks all of her favourite places, even the garden shed. Twice he checks it. Three times. Until, eventually, neither of us can pretend any longer, and we reunite at the kitchen island. Cassius's eyes are wild. I am struggling not to cry. Still, neither of us want to say it. But we must.

"Did you stay up?"

Cassius doesn't look at me.

"Last night," I press. "After we went to bed. Did you stay up to watch for me?"

Slowly, still not raising his eyes, Cassius shakes his head. His jaw flickers with tension. "I'd drunk a lot of wine," he explains. "And I thought you were fine now. And it was already past midnight."

His words are like a grenade. My tears explode around them. They are loud, uncontainable, as though they are coming from my throat. I start gasping for air. Choking on nothing. I look to Cassius, who is staring right at me now, observing my plight with what can only be described as disgust. And of course I don't blame him. I don't know what I expect from him. Not to look after me. Not to protect me. But I don't know what to do.

"Where is she?" I whisper.

Now, a switch seems to flick in Cassius, and he stands up straighter. "Stop. Just stop, Lil," he says, wrestling back a vestige of control. "Don't start spiralling. You might not have done anything. We both know that Jessie didn't want to leave here, so maybe she, I don't know, maybe she ran off."

"She wouldn't," I say. "She couldn't. She can't even reach the locks on the doors."

"Then maybe she's just hiding somewhere," Cassius insists, fooling nobody. "She must be hiding. You know she can hide for ages now. Jessie!" he shouts again. "Jessie!"

I put my hand on his arm, but he recoils from me. We both notice this, and Cassius averts his eyes. "Let's check my room," I volunteer. "In case I took her in there." And still without looking at me, he nods. Of course, I know that she is not in my room. I am dressed and have already drawn my curtains, made my bed, I would have noticed her. But together we climb the stairs, and when we open the door, Cassius spots a faint trail of wet sand on the white rug next to my bed. It is not obvious, but it is there. When we fling back the covers, I discern more granules within the sheets. And when we both look down to my bare feet, together we see the remnants of dirt between my toes. They are tiny grains, barely noticeable, not sharp like glass, but nonetheless piercing – to my heart if not my flesh.

Now that we know what we are looking for, we easily find clumps of sodden sand throughout the house – on the mat by the back door, in the hallway, on the stairs. *The trail is like a murder scene*, I think to myself, and then will that thought away, because what if it is, what if it is, what if I have done something terrible? I am staring directly at my worst fear and have no way of knowing anything. Slowly, I sink down to a crouching position on the floor. My stomach is contracting so hard that I can't breathe. There is a pain in my heart, an actual pain, as though it is breaking, or dying, or crushing itself beneath unforgiving waves.

Waves.

Sand.

We know where to look.

As this thought crosses my mind, Cassius says it out loud: "The sand, the beach." Together, we throw on our shoes and run to the front door. We are about to jump into my car when I recall that usually when I take Jessie to the beach, we cycle, or walk, so that we can cut down the alley and see Madge. I remember how much Jessie loves Madge, 'Bring me that gorgeous girl', and I think that if there was any rationale to my sleepwalking, if my mother was right all those years ago and even in my sleep I was myself, my awake self, nurturing and protective, then maybe I simply tried to take Jessie somewhere that she loves.

"Madge," I tell Cassius.

He nods, and we start running towards the beach – my route, my run, my anchor to sanity. Except that this time, we are not jogging but really running, sprinting for our lives. I have a crazy hope that even if Jessie isn't with Madge, then perhaps Madge saw me with her in the night, perhaps she can tell me where we went. Perhaps she knows what I have done.

People look at us as we pass them. It is still too early for the morning crush of LA traffic, but Cassius and I tear across roads regardless of the few cars that are there, on their way to places or events that seem suddenly mindless and irrelevant. Cyclists and skaters and runners move out of our way and turn to look behind as we move past, our wake of terror almost tangible, tainting their paradise. Cassius is still in his sleeping shorts. I am dressed more appropriately, but my eyes are fierce. With every step, thoughts career through my head – have I left Jessie somewhere? If I left her at the beach, would she try to find her way home? Would she try to find Madge? Would she try to swim into the sea? She cannot swim yet. What if I took her into the sea? What if I carried her there? What if I stood in icy water like I did so many years ago, but without Cassius there to find me? To stop me? What if I stood there, with her in my arms, and then, let go? A vision of this muscles its way into my brain. I am in my night clothes, her hair is loose, she is screaming; my eyes are blank. Is this real? Did I do this? I shake my head. I am moving so fast that the sideways movement dizzies me and I almost trip, but I cannot bear to hold such thoughts in my mind. Thoughts that may be worse, or better, than the truth. Is it the truth? What have I done? WHAT HAVE I DONE?

Without thinking, I hit myself on the top of my head. Surely, the memory has to exist somewhere. I try to force myself to remember it. I know that I went upstairs, that I brushed my teeth, and washed, and got into bed, and although it was late, I read for a while, and then edited a page of script, and then lay down and turned out the light… And then woke up. There is nothing. Nothing. Between the two, only darkness. Again, I shake my head, and this time I do fall. Cassius helps me up. There is blood on my knees, and my hands are grazed, but we do not stop. We are nearly there. We cross the road, and there is Madge's alley, and there is Madge's trolley, and there, in front of it, is Madge.

From a distance, Cassius and I both call out to her, but she doesn't wave back. She is facing towards the ocean, leaning against one of her ribboned sacks, slumped forwards a little, her sleeping bag pulled high to her head. It is unlike her to sleep during the day but perhaps that means she was up in the night. Hopefully, I dash forwards, calling her name again. Cassius lags a little behind, but a few seconds later, he catches up to me, where I have stopped, a foot away from Madge's body, which, it turns out, is not sleeping, but unconscious, a gash across her forehead, a train of blood dried against her sun-worn cheeks.

It is only for a few seconds that I am paralysed. After that, although my mind is still consumed by Jessie, I am also propelled into action for Madge. The two of them coalesce messily in my mind, as though there is a thread to be untangled there. Meanwhile, my phone is out, and I am calling for an ambulance. I am feeling for Madge's pulse, which is still beating. I am watching for her breath, still warm. I say her name again and again, I touch her hand, and try to lay her more comfortably, but there is no response. Cassius stands rigid, staring at the blood. Removing my thin yoga jacket, I take my wallet from its pocket and slip the material underneath her head, then I throw the wallet to Cassius. "Get her some water," I instruct. "Get a lot so we can clean the cut."

Cassius, however, doesn't move. He takes out his own phone.

"Cassius." I wave my hand in front of his face. "Cassius."

Finally, he blinks. "Jessie," he says.

I look down at Madge, then back at him. "I know."

"We can't wait," he says. "I can't stop. It's too long."

I nod. "I know."

"I'm going to call the police."

I nod again.

Eyes locked, neither of us speak. In the California air between us, questions lurk. Thread tangles.

"Do you think…" he begins, but then stops himself. "Do you think…"

"Do I think I did this to Madge?" I demand, suddenly angry, although not at him. "Do I think I took Jessie and then assaulted Madge? I have no idea. I have no idea. I have no fucking idea."

"I'm sorry," Cassius hurries, placing his hand on my arm. Now it is me who recoils from him. "I just… I just… I just need to find Jessie."

Every time he says her name, my heart hurts. He is stabbing me with it. Glass shards. Did I stab Jessie? Did I attack Madge?

He moves slightly away from me and lifts his phone to his ear. Now that we have paused, I don't know why we haven't called the police already. Forcing myself to breathe, I turn back towards Madge, whose unmoving body folds into the mess of bags and paving and blood, but who is at least here, in front of me. A runner jogs by but doesn't stop. A man on a Segway weaves past us. For a long time I stare at Madge, unable to move, unable to blink. "The paramedics are on their way. They'll call the police too," I say to her. "I'm so sorry, Madge. We'll tell them. We'll tell them what happened."

"We don't know what happened," Cassius interjects, returning to my side. His face looks harried, his hands clenching and unclenching. "What are you planning on saying?"

"That I took Jessie. That maybe I hurt Madge too."

Now Cassius looks at me frantically. "Lil, they'll arrest you."

The thud of this hits me hard. Again, I am finding it difficult to breathe.

"We don't even know if it's true."

"Of course we know." It takes all of the air in my lungs to spit out these words, but I hold Cassius's eyes as I say them, searching him desperately for a sign of doubt, for uncertainty, for the slightest trace of belief that it wasn't, in fact, me who stole his child. But the truth is obvious. "What did the police say?" I ask, shaking my head free of Cassius's silent confirmation.

His face contorts in anguish. "They're sending a car to the

house. I told them we left the back door open. And they're going to search the beach. And they're checking all the nearby CCTV. She's not officially a 'missing person' yet, but they're going to get her photo to all their teams and put her on some kind of alert system."

I nod. "Good. Good. That's good. And we'll keep looking too. And… what did they say about me?"

Suddenly, from the road at the top of the alley, we hear the sirens of the ambulance.

Cassius shakes his head. "I didn't tell them, Lil. Not that bit," he says. "And don't you say anything to the paramedics either," he warns me. "Not yet."

It is still barely possible to squeeze sound from my throat, but, "We have to," I whisper.

"No." Cassius looks at me darkly. "If they arrest you, we'll lose her, Lil, I know it. If anyone can figure out where she is, it'll be you. Something will trigger a memory. Something will occur to you. It has to. Please, I need you here. They're looking for her already, they're doing everything they can, but if they take you, we'll lose her. We'll lose her. We'll lose her for good."

The paramedics are out of their vehicle now and hurrying towards us.

"Lil," Cassius urges, sensing my dissent. "Lil, please, look at me. I know you. I know you. You have morals the size of America, remember. And I know that means you want to confess. But I also know that you won't have hurt her. You won't. You'll have tucked her up somewhere thinking it's her bed, or you'll have built her a sand fort and hidden her in it. She's here somewhere. She is. I know it. We just have to get to her before something happens. Please. Please. If they take you away, we'll never find her. She's probably nearby. You just have to remember. She's probably here on the beach."

As he says this, our eyes turn towards the sand, and, just a few metres away, toppled onto its side, we simultaneously spot it – Jessie's bucket. Turquoise. Unmistakeable.

Instinctively, I move to run towards it, but Cassius's hand shoots out to steady me. He squeezes my arm. "Stay with Madge," he whispers urgently. "Deal with that. Get them to check CCTV here."

I open my mouth to speak, but the paramedics are nearly upon us now, and he hushes me again.

"She's here," he promises, pointing again to the flash of turquoise. "She's here. I know it. I'm going to find her."

And he goes. Dashing with his promise. Running towards the bucket. Hurtling into the sand.

The minutes that follow are surreal in their stasis. It feels wrong to stand there, not running with Cassius, and though my feet don't move, my mind races, my eyes darting again and again towards the beach. Has he found her? Is she there? Has it all been but a fleeting nightmare?

The paramedics are asking me questions now about Madge and, somehow, I manage to explain that I know her. Somehow, I describe how I was out looking for Jessie, and how I came to find her. Their interest piques at that – could the homeless woman have kidnapped the little girl, should they inform the police? But I brush this away. No, no. The police already know Jessie is missing. What happened to Madge is something else. Yet still the tangling. I recall for them the details I can offer – Madge's name, where she is from, the fact that she has a daughter. With this last piece of information, I look again to the sand, but Cassius has slipped out of sight, beyond the bucket – is he with his daughter? Has he found her? I glance to my phone – he hasn't called. The paramedics gesture to my phone too and ask for my number, ask if they can list me as Madge's in-case-of-emergency contact. I nod at that, and ask about the police, ask about CCTV, will they search it, but I do not ask to accompany Madge to hospital, because I can't, I can't, I can't stretch my stillness that far, I need to move now, to get back to Cassius, get back to searching for Jessie. My feet shuffle restlessly. The paramedics will not let me ride in the ambulance anyway, they inform me, pre-empting the unasked question, I will have to meet her there. Nodding again, hurriedly, duplicitously, I wish that I could. I don't want Madge to be alone – lovely, hurt Madge, who might have been hurt by me. The thought of that swarms into my brain and I feel as though I'm going to be sick. Could I really have hurt her? I wish I knew. I wish I could know. I wish I could stay with her and protect her, and apologise to her. But I wish to find Jessie more. If only the paramedics would stop talking now. If only somebody else could go to the hospital in my stead.

And then, strangely, just as I am thinking this, wishing it, almost as though my mind can conjure and control, at the bottom of the alleyway, not on the path but trudging through the sand, there is Patrick.

For a moment, the sight of Patrick there, here, actually walking along the beach that he will never ordinarily set foot on, throws me off-kilter. Part of me wants to launch myself into his arms, to break down in them, to tell him everything; but I feel my mind momentarily turning to this new puzzle – the puzzle of his presence. Patrick looks equally disturbed to see me. "What are you doing here?" I ask him.

Very slowly, Patrick recovers himself. He shakes his floppy dark locks free from sand and gradually moves towards me. A salty smell surrounds him, and a mixture somehow of chill and heat. "Don't you have yoga this morning? It's not your running day."

"What are you doing here?" I repeat.

Now he kisses me on the cheek. "You caught me."

My stomach clenches, though I am not sure why. "What have I caught you doing?" I glance towards the sea. I cannot see Cassius. There is no sign of Jessie. Only Patrick. Why is Patrick here? A wetsuit is rolled down to his waist. He looks like a seasoned beach bum. Handsome, but suddenly, unknown.

Clearly reluctant to answer, Patrick cocks his head.

"Patrick."

He sighs. Shifts his weight. Then finally he opens his

mouth to speak. But before he is able, one of the paramedics behind us moves to help lift Madge, and abruptly, Patrick spots her. "Oh Jesus. Is that Madge?"

Now, a fresh urgency grips me – *Madge, Jessie*. I need to go. I need to look for Jessie.

"Will you go with her?" I ask, my eyes darting again toward the sand, my feet moving, my arms tugging Patrick up the alley.

"I…" The paramedics are loading Madge into the waiting ambulance. Patrick hesitates. "I… I hardly know her, Lil."

"Please. I don't want her to be alone."

"Then why don't you go?"

"I can't. I, I lost something. On the beach."

Why am I not telling him? Why wasn't it the first thing I said? I should tell him. Of course I should tell him. And this is the moment to do it.

But if I haven't been able to tell him about the sleepwalking, how in hell will I tell him this? That I have stolen a child. That I might have killed her. I do not even pretend to be capable of it. Instead, I avert my eyes and look again towards the sea. "I have to look for it," I mumble.

And I do. I have to look. I can't stand still much longer.

"What did you lose?" Patrick scans the shore. *Tell him. Tell him.* "Is that Cassius?"

It is Cassius! He has reappeared on the stretch in front of us and is beckoning me towards him. Why is he beckoning? Perhaps he has found her. Perhaps she is OK. Perhaps everything is OK! "Yes," I answer quickly. "Yes. He's helping me look."

"Have you ever heard the phrase 'needle in a haystack'?" Patrick teases gently, gesturing at the expanse of beach. "What did you lose anyway? What's so important?"

"I… I…"

All of a sudden, Patrick's presence is maddening me. I just want this conversation to be over, for him to go, for him to let *me* go. Boosted by hope that Jessie has been found, my mind kicks into action, and surreptitiously, I wriggle my finger out of the engagement ring that he gave me weeks earlier. I hold up my bare hand. His face falls. "Oh."

"Please go with Madge," I urge, the doors to the ambulance closing, the driver giving me a wave. "Please. I have the hospital details. I'll come as soon as I find the ring. I'll find it," I add.

Patrick looks at me. "Can't Cassius go with her?"

"He won't be as practical as you. And there's… Jessie… to think of." As her name leaves my lips, I wince, just a little.

Patrick looks at me again, hard. "Where is Jessie?"

Perhaps I am imagining the way his eyes bore into me when he asks this, or perhaps any whisper of her feels now like the whole world. I am no longer able to delineate real from imagined. Perhaps I never could. I wave my hand. "She's somewhere round here. But Madge – they're taking her now. Please, Patrick. Please do this for me. I'll join you as soon as I can."

Patrick still doesn't take his eyes off me. "I'll have to change first. I'm soaking wet."

"That's fine, that's fine, just be quick." I nod. "Wait. Why *are* you wet? Why are you at the beach?"

But now Patrick shakes his head. "Am I being quick, or am I standing here explaining?"

I pause. He's right. Yet, his not answering feels like the last straw, the last thing my sanity can take. Nothing makes sense any more. Not Jessie, not Madge, and now not even Patrick. I thought things were different now. I thought I understood.

"You OK?" he says, reaching for my hand, studying my face.

I want to tell him. With a pulsing longing, I so very want to tell him. I want him to say it'll be OK, and help me figure it out. 'Go figure', said Madge. *Go figure.*

But the ambulance is pulling away.

From the beach, Cassius is still beckoning me. *Why is he*

beckoning me? Hope leaps again across my chest. Hope, and also fear. *What has he found?*

Patrick is waiting.

I nod. "I'll join you soon. I'll join you. Thank you."

So Patrick turns. And goes. Quickly, as I have asked. He doesn't press me about the ring. I don't tell him about Jessie. And I don't demand to know why he was there, suddenly, on the sand.

But Jessie's bucket bears no clues. Cassius has not found her. And any footsteps there might once have been have long ago been scattered away by morning runners like me. Cassius no longer seems as confident as he was minutes earlier. His face has fallen, his skin deathly pale. He and I use the bucket as a marker for where it's possible that Jessie entered the water, but the ocean laps against the shore with all the inevitability of forever, a clear, opaque, sleeping abyss, keeping secrets, crashing and crashing again. For a number of minutes, we run along the waterline calling her name, looking first out into the horizon, then down to the sand as though she might be stuck there half-buried, a limb or wisp of curl escaping. Perhaps she is buried there, perhaps she is. An image flies into my head of the two of us digging in the dark. Is it a memory? Is it real? Real or not, once it is there, I can't stop my mind from thinking it, from seeing it again and again. But we do not, in the sand, see Jessie, and after a while, Cassius and I realise that we are wasting time. What are we doing? We will not find her like this. Yet we seem unable to stop. We kick into lumps of sand. We stride out into the waves and kick these too. We peer abruptly into patches of water.

Until, "Cassius," I cry at last, standing knee-deep. "Cassius, stop, stop. It's useless."

Cassius is in tears now too, sobbing, heaving. Not the contrived tears I have seen him summon on stage, but raw, elemental, like a wounded animal letting out a death wail. Striding through the icy water, he pulls me to him, his head in my neck, and I wrap my arms around his shaking frame. For a moment we stand there like this, this way that we have stood before, frozen together, though this time I am comforting him. Protecting him. From myself. It feels like forever for words to formulate, as though in speaking them, we will have to acknowledge what has happened, we will have to say it out loud – she is gone. She is gone. We are not going to find her. But the waves beat out passing seconds against our legs. And the seconds matter. The minutes matter. Isn't that what they say when a child goes missing? You have only hours. You have to act fast. We have to tell the police the full story. Now.

"Cassius—" I begin finally.

But he clasps me tighter against him. He squashes his face into my shoulder, and his words come gasped through cotton and shallow breaths: "I can't," he says. "I. Can't."

"I'll do it then. I'll tell them," I soothe.

"No. She. I. I. I can't lose you too."

Although I know it isn't his intention, this confirmation of my guilt sticks like sand in my throat. Not only my guilt, but the consequence of it. I will be arrested, he assumes. I will be taken. Like I took her. For how long? Forever? It is wrong, but for the first time, I feel paralysed by this thought. By my own extinction, as well as hers. I loved her. I love her. I didn't mean to hurt her, I didn't mean it, I didn't mean any of this.

"We just have to keep looking," Cassius declares abruptly, pulling away, shaking himself free of my arms.

I cannot articulate what I want to say.

"Lilith."

I cannot articulate what we need to do.

"Lilith, come on."

It is as though everything is upside down and what I feel to be right might not be. Because what I think is 'right' – confessing – will hurt me for sure. And if Cassius is right, then it will hurt him too.

"We have to keep looking," he implores me.

Yes. That is right.

"It's our best hope," he says.

I don't know. Maybe.

"You wouldn't have hurt her. You wouldn't have."

I cannot speak, still. So I nod.

"You'll think of something, you'll remember something. You will. I know you. You will. Won't you?"

I nod again, hesitantly.

Cassius shakes me slightly. Shaking me out of it. "Lilith. Lilith."

I meet his eyes.

"Lilith, we're wasting time. Come on, please, think. Think of the places the police won't. Come on. Where to next?"

"I… I…" I can't. I can't. I don't trust myself.

"Lilith!" Cassius screams at me, his voice high, manic. "Please. Please. Wake up! Stop thinking about yourself! I can't deal with your self-obsession. I can't do it any more. Confessing to the police is not going to help Jessie. Confessing is the easy route, it's your way out, it's the way to leave, to cut and run, just like you always do. But I need you here. This time, I need you to do the hard thing, I need you to stay. The police are already doing everything they can, you know that. I already called to tell them about the bucket. So they know everything we know. Except for the sleepwalking. But if there's anything you could tell them about that, that would help, you'd have told me already. Right? So all they'll do is ask loads of questions, and we'll waste time explaining." He shakes me again. Shakes me. "We're wasting time now. Lilith, say something. Come on. I need you. Jessie needs you. Focus, just focus, just try. For once, try. Think of something."

Slowly, I reach for the words. "OK," I agree, quietly, hearing my voice outside of myself. "OK," I say again, placing my hand on his heaving chest. "OK. OK. Venice."

Together, we pace rapidly up to Venice, searching every stall we pass, every shop, every café. When she isn't there, we run to Muscle Beach where Jessie likes to play on the pull-up bars and hang upside down from the trapeze rings. I have the sudden idea that asleep, I could have mistaken Madge's alley, and so we criss-cross every alleyway that links the beach to the road. Then we hunt through the pier, under every popcorn stand, behind every ride, in every room of the aquarium, even though at night it would have been shut. The police call Cassius with an update and ask him to come in to the station to make a full statement. It is a short distance from the beach, and while he is gone, I keep searching. Every few minutes I circle back to the spot we have agreed to meet, hoping for news, but when Cassius finally returns, he reports that they have found nothing. They are, however, following some potential leads, and asked Cassius if we were aware that the car outside my house was unlocked. They have already searched it, they told Cassius, and found nothing there, but perhaps, she could have been hiding in it earlier. We race. It had not occurred to us that I could have driven somewhere. Now, the possibilities are endless. Frantically, we start visiting each of Jessie's favourite drive-to spots – cafés, the bookshop, the playground. Before entering each one, there is a surge of anticipation in my chest and I imagine myself coming upon her – smiling, laughing, arms lifting for me; but every time, hope is followed by a consuming devastation, by fresh panic, by unfathomable fear. Cassius and I don't need to speak to absorb this from each other. We don't need to move our lips to taste evil. By evening, our bodies are full of it, close to collapse, weighted with dread, yet we tear through the house again, upturning cushions and wardrobes and baskets full of laundry. Even though we have done this already. Even though the police have too. There seems something impossible about the fact of her absence. The house is here, so it must contain her. We are here, so we must find her. The alternative is too dreadful and renders us too entirely without power. We listen, quiet as mice. We look in places that are far too small for her to fit. We look in spots we have previously combed. We look and we look and we look and we look. But still, she is gone.

When at last we pause again, it is growing dark outside. Cassius sinks onto the couch, and I lower myself uneasily next to him. Both of us perch on the edge, poised to stand again, as though if we were to lean back, to sit comfortably, we would be betraying Jessie.

A great stillness sweeps over us, stillness where there should be childish laughter, and the smell of crayons or paint.

"It's time," I say finally. "It's time. We have to tell the police about me."

But Cassius shakes his head.

"Cassius," I plead. "This isn't like shoplifting. This is your daughter."

Gently, I touch his arm, but all at once Cassius rounds on me with unexpected fury, throwing my hand away. "I know it's my daughter!" he screams. "Don't you think I know?"

"Sorry," I reply, searching his eyes. "Sorry. Sorry. I am so sorry. I just… We have to tell them."

"What difference will it make?" Cassius growls. "It's been too long. We've waited too long. You should have confessed straight away."

"But… Cass, that's not fair," I exclaim. "I wanted to tell them this morning! I wanted to. I said we should."

"Then why didn't you?"

"Because you told me not to."

"Because I was scared. Because I wasn't thinking straight. Because I wanted to protect you, I always bloody protect you. Because I truly didn't think you would have hurt her. Because… I trusted you."

"Trust-*ed*?"

"You've fucking taken my child, Lilith. My child. My daughter. My… My…"

For the millionth time that day, I break into hysterical sobs. "I'm sorry," I gasp. "I'm sorry!"

Cassius looks at me with disgust. And rage. And venom. It is as though my own grief is an insult to his. Desperately, I try to calm myself.

"Look," I say finally, forcing a deep breath. "If we tell them now, they can still—"

"If we tell them now, they'll ask why we didn't earlier. And we'll look guilty. We'll look like we did something to her. Both of us."

I take another breath. "But, if I did, if I did do it…"

"Of course you did it," Cassius spits at me suddenly. "It's what you've known you would do since you were a kid."

"Cassius!"

"Well, it's true, isn't it? You know it. I know it. We both always knew it."

"Then why did you come here?" I yell at him suddenly. "Why the hell did you bring her here? Why did you bring her into my house? Near me? This is why I left. This is exactly why I left. Why I made my life alone, away from you, away from Dylan, away from anybody I could hurt. Why did you do this to me? Everything was fine before. Everything was fine."

"For you," he sneers.

I look at him. "Well, not any more."

For what feels like a long time, we remain locked in confrontation. Resentment and blame bubbles beneath his eyes. I accept the weight of it but throw it back at him also. The sin may be mine, but he has been the serpent, or Eve. He placed the apple in my hands. Not so obedient, after all. I didn't want this. I tried to banish myself, like my namesake.

"Can't you just fucking remember something?" he snarls suddenly, with renewed fury. And now my rage explodes too.

"No!" I scream. "No, Cassius! That's the point! That's always been the point! I have no idea what happens when I'm asleep!"

"Can't you just try?"

"Are you serious? You think I haven't tried?"

"You could try to—"

"I've tried! I've tried! I've tried!"

Suddenly, my hysteria seems to dislodge something in

him. Visibly, a force rushes out of his chest, and he sinks downwards, backwards, into the folds of the couch. For a long time, he holds his head in his hands, before finally looking back up. "I just… I just…" Now, tears envelop him. They clasp at his breath. And without thinking, I reach for him again. "I just want her back," he sobs, shaking against me. "I just want Jessie back. I can't believe she's gone. I thought, I really thought you'd remember something." He shakes his head. "I don't know what to do. I don't know what to do. I don't know how I'll even live without her."

I don't know what to do either. And I don't know what to say to him. We sit, entwined, quiet, unmoving, save for the silent shake of his desolation. There is nothing to divert us from this. Nobody to pull us apart. The person who should be shmooshing between us is the reason we are braced as we are. The only other person who might intrude is Patrick.

Patrick.

I haven't thought of him all day, but suddenly I remember that Patrick went to the hospital with Madge… who may have seen Jessie! I was supposed to meet Patrick there. I can't believe this didn't occur to me earlier. Untangling myself from Cassius's arms, I take out my phone, which I've been too frantic to look at all day. There are 27 missed calls and a string of text messages, all from Patrick asking where I am – first with genial inquiry, then irritation, then increasing urgency, and finally concern.

I reach for Cassius's hand. "Madge," I tell him. "Madge. Patrick's been calling. Maybe Madge has woken up. Maybe she'll know something."

Like an unbidden dawn, a flash of hope skips across Cassius's brow.

"Maybe she'll have seen me with Jessie," I encourage. "Or maybe I was there, with Jessie, and then somebody else took her from me, and that same person attacked Madge."

Cassius looks at me sceptically as I make this last suggestion. He no longer believes in my harmlessness, but I choose for now not to unpack this. "It's possible," he concedes eventually. "It is possible."

"It is," I agree, latching on. "It is. Let me call Patrick. Maybe Madge is awake."

Suddenly, however, as the screen to my phone comes to life, I remember something else. Or rather, I notice something else – my collection of phone apps, and all at once I recall the app I installed on Patrick's phone that tracks my bracelet. My bracelet! I had forgotten it completely. Hope rushes into my lungs. We have two leads now. "Cass!" I breathe. "My bracelet!"

"What about it?" he says. "Come on, call Patrick."

"No, listen – my bracelet is a tracking device. I installed an app months ago onto Patrick's phone. It should tell us where I've been."

"What?" says Cassius, barely able to speak. "What?"

"I bought it ages ago in case I wandered off somewhere. But I've never used it so…"

"I thought it was just a fitness thing."

"Well, that's what I told Jessie, but no."

"Oh my God," says Cassius. Then he gathers himself. "Is it only on Patrick's phone? Didn't you put it on yours?"

"No. I thought what was the point in tracking myself?" I explain. "I figured wherever I am, well, I'm there. But maybe Patrick might need to find me."

"Did you tell him about it?"

"No. I mean, not yet. I was going to."

Cassius looks at me queryingly. "Effective," he can't resist pointing out sarcastically. Then, "Well, come on. Call him. Tell him to come round. Fast. Let's find out."

I nod and press Patrick's name in my phone, but as soon as I do so, Cassius and I both hear a ringing. It is Patrick's cell. He is here.

At once, Cassius and I look up, and Patrick walks into the room from the hallway where he has entered. He is holding up his phone.

"How long have you been here?" asks Cassius, before hello.

"What are you doing here?" I ask him.

"What are *you* doing here?" he rebuts unpleasantly. "What happened to meeting me at the hospital?"

Quickly, I stand up and go to him, hoping that my face is not as puffy and tear-streaked as it feels. "I'm so sorry."

"She's your friend."

"I know."

"Where were you?"

I look over to Cassius, who shrugs – the decision is mine. I hesitate. I want to tell Patrick. I want to tell him, but he will never trust me again. He will never want to have a baby with me. He will… "We got caught up," I answer slowly.

"Caught up? Sitting on the couch with Cassius?"

"We only just got back. We've been looking all day."

Now Patrick studies me carefully, then glances between me and Cassius, then around the room where shelves and drawers and cupboard doors are all disturbed. "Well? Did you find it?"

I hold up my hand. It is complete with engagement ring, as it always was. "Found it," I manage to utter. "Thank goodness."

"Where was it?"

Somehow, I conjure a half-smile, but the lies feel worse and worse; I am regretting them, all of them, already. How can any future be built upon this? I should have just told him at the beach. I should have trusted him and told him. But now it is too late. "Ridiculously, on the kitchen floor," I say. "I might get it adjusted slightly."

Patrick opens his mouth to speak, but then frowns and considers things again. "So you found the ring, but you didn't come to the hospital?"

"We only just found it," I explain, my stomach clenching. "Just now. That's why I was calling. To tell you, and to find out how things were there. I'm so sorry I didn't come. Or answer your calls. How is she?"

"You only just found it?"

"How long were you standing there before Lil called?" interjects Cassius.

Patrick is still holding his phone and I see Cassius looking at it, trying to think of a way to get hold of it to find the tracking app.

"I just arrived," Patrick answers coolly. Then pointedly, to Cassius: "Where's Jessie?"

I shoot Cassius a worried look, but with an unbelievable display of outward calm, and what must have taken all of his acting skill, Cassius replies: "In bed. We were just about to order takeout. Would you like to join?"

Patrick hesitates. I am not off the hook, I know, but I can see that he doesn't have the energy to continue the fight, at least not in front of Cassius. "Sure," he exhales. "Whatever. I'm starving." Wearily, he opens his phone to look for the number of a takeout, but seeing my chance, I lift the phone out of his hand.

"I'll order. My treat," I say, pushing him gently towards the couch. "I'm so sorry about today. You sit and do nothing for a minute." Overtly taking out my own phone, I subtly pass Patrick's off to Cassius. While it is unlocked, he should be able to find the app. "Sushi? Your usual?" I ask.

Half-heartedly, Patrick nods, and it is with clear exhaustion that he reaches for the TV remote. Meanwhile, Cassius moves quietly with Patrick's phone off the couch and out of the room.

"Wait," I say to Patrick as the television flashes on. "Can you tell me about Madge?"

Now, a hint of agitation darts back into his eyes. "I've been trying to tell you all day, Lilith."

"I know. I'm sorry," I say, sitting beside him. "But please tell me now. Is she awake? Is she OK? Can she talk? Does she know what happened?"

With a sigh, Patrick tilts his head. He knows how much I care about Madge, and with what is clearly preparation for bad news, he mutes the TV and places his hand on my knee.

"She's still unconscious. The doctors aren't sure, actually, if she's going to make it."

"Oh my God."

In that moment, all the hope of the previous minutes seems to sink inside me. I have been so absorbed by Jessie that I have barely been thinking about Madge, who might be my victim too. Sensing Patrick studying me, I try to steady myself, but—

"Look. Would you rather ditch dinner and check in on her?" he offers.

I nod. "Sorry."

He stands up.

"Did the police come to see her?"

"Yep."

"Does anybody know what happened?"

"No. They're checking footage, but nothing yet."

"Poor Madge," I say.

"Poor Madge."

"Poor Madge," echoes Cassius, returning suddenly, and shaking his head at me from across the room. I am not sure what that shake means. Did the app work? Has it told him something awful? I squint my eyes at him.

"Let me just go to the bathroom, then I'll drive you there on my way home," says Patrick. "But I'm not staying."

"Of course not." I nod gratefully. "You've done more than enough."

Despite my worry, there is no time to ruminate further about Madge, because as soon as Patrick has left the room, Cassius throws his phone to me, and Jessie surges back to the fore. "It's not there," he says. "There's no app."

"No! Are you sure? There must be," I protest. "I installed it myself."

"Maybe Patrick saw the app and deleted it." Cassius shrugs. "I've searched. It's definitely not there."

The phone has locked now, but I know Patrick's passcode and quickly type it in, scrolling through the pages of apps. "It has to be," I insist. "It has to be." But there is nothing. And in a minute, Patrick will return. "Maybe if I download it now onto my own phone, it will still show me past data," I suggest, grasping at straws.

"Do you think?" says Cassius, fervour or faith flashing again into his eyes. "Yes. That could be possible. Maybe it's stored in the cloud or something."

Nodding, I find the name of the app and begin to download it. One last grain of hope has risen inside me. Everything's on the cloud these days, isn't it? The information must be there. Even if it doesn't tell us where Jessie is, it must hold some clues. But before it finishes downloading, we hear Patrick's footsteps in the hall.

"Here, give me your phone. I'll do it," whispers Cassius.

I stuff both my phone and the bracelet into Cassius's hands, and as Patrick reappears in the doorway, he slips into the kitchen to pair the devices. I want to go with him. I need to know. I cannot leave this way. But…

"Ready?" Patrick says, looking for his phone. I hand it to him.

Then I nod. And I pray. I pray that the data is there. I pray that it tells us something. I pray that my prayers have power, that my mind really can conjure.

As slowly as possible, I fetch my jacket. As slowly as possible, I locate my shoes.

"Come on, Lil," Patrick hurries me. "It's been a long day."

"Sorry." I nod. But still I make two more unnecessary visits into the lounge, first for my 'keys', then for my 'wallet'. Finally, we leave the house, but when Patrick and I are almost at the car, I can bear the not-knowing no longer. Telling Patrick the truth – this part of it at least – that I don't have my phone, I dash back towards the house. But long before I reach it, Cassius's face at the window reveals the answer.

"No old data," he confirms, handing me my phone and the bracelet across the kitchen island. "I don't think you'd paired the devices properly. Works now though."

"No."

It can't be true. It can't. It can't.

I begin to sob.

I wait for Cassius to break down too.

But in those intervening minutes, something in his mood has altered – maybe it was seeing Patrick, or seeing me with Patrick, or the reality of a dead end. Either way, his eyes have steeled, and he shakes his head firmly. "Not now," he instructs. "You can't break now. You have to go and see Madge."

He is right. She is our last hope. With difficulty, I gather myself. "What are you going to do?" I ask through subdued tears. "Will you stay here?"

"I'm going to look once more at the beach," he says. "I'll give you an hour to talk to Madge. See if she knows anything. Then I'll call, and if Madge can't help… I guess… I guess…"

I nod.

"I guess I'll go back to the police, and… I'll tell them. About you. I'll have to."

I nod again. It is the right thing to do. It is the right thing to do. I know it is. And a certain relief floods through me. Maybe it will give the police something to go on, a new strategy for their search. And at least I'll be able to tell Patrick the truth, the rest of it. Besides, I want to be held accountable, I want to be punished, I want something to hit me hard enough to knock out of my brain the tilt of Jessie's smile and the warmth of her body and the visions of her being swept away by the waves.

Yet – the weight of Cassius's decision folds over me too. How could it not? When I talk to Patrick, I will be telling him that I am likely a murderer. And when the police talk to me, the delay in confession will make me look more guilty. Despite all my years of running, all my breaking of chains, these moments, now, will be my last moments free.

As I turn towards the door, Cassius's eyes soften a little, and he hugs me – a familiar hug, full of protection, and apology, and knowing. And shoring up. For now. For a few moments more. Until he can plaster over my sins no longer. "I'll call you," he promises. And hugs me again.

Through the window, I see Patrick watching.

Without her sleeping bag and her trolley and her arsenal of plastic bags, Madge looks thin, and old. Though weathered, her skin seems less leathery than waffled, like a delicate piece of tissue paper that has been crumpled up to make a craft flower and then flattened out again. Just last week, I made flowers like that with Jessie. The gash on Madge's head has been stitched with dark thread that juts out like barbed wire, and a bruise creeps downwards from underneath the bandages, but her breath is steady, her eyes are closed.

The doctors have been through her belongings and have found a small book with a handful of names and numbers in it. Many others have been crossed out, scribbled through with such force that the writing beneath is no longer visible. But by means of calling all of the numbers, they think they have established Madge's full name – Margaret Vannay – and somebody has found a number for her daughter. A woman from Santa Barbara is on her way.

As the nurse is explaining this, I find myself checking my phone a number of times in case there is news from Cassius. The nurse scowls at me, surprised, I assume, by my apparent rudeness, or flippancy, or lack of care for Madge. She doesn't know, of course. She doesn't know why I cannot concentrate, but still she is right. Whatever happens now, next, to Jessie, or to me, I owe this moment to Madge.

She doesn't have her own room, but there are only two other patients here, both old, both asleep. Softly, I sit beside Madge's bed and hold her hand to my cheek. The touch of her skin feels like the holy hand of a priest, or so I imagine, having myself only experienced occasional murmurings of rabbis in a language I don't understand. Or perhaps hers is, after all, the hand of royalty, a princess in disguise. Whatever the reason, somehow, Madge's flesh anchors me, a mixed blessing, both fixing me to the ground and dragging me beneath it. "I'm so sorry," I tell her, as I have said again and again today, but not yet to her. Then I force myself to look at her bloodied face. "What have I done?" I whisper.

"What?" Patrick is hovering behind me.

I shake my head. "She's so hurt. Who would have done this?"

"It's terrible," Patrick agrees, but even as he is speaking, he moves towards the door. Understandably – he has been holding vigil all day. "I'm grabbing a coffee before I go," he says. "Want one?"

I nod. I am not hungry, but my body feels faint. I haven't eaten since breakfast. Since those ignorant moments before. Nor has Cassius, I mull. Has he stopped for food by the beach? Is that why he hasn't called? Has he allowed himself to pause? Or is he at the police station already? It has almost been an hour. Soon, I may be able to eat only what I am given. "And something to eat, please," I say.

Patrick goes off to find the canteen, or a vending machine, while I remain with Madge, and now that nobody is listening, I speak more freely. "I'm so sorry," I tell her again. "I'm so sorry." And I keep saying this. Over and over, to her, to Jessie, to Cassius, to Patrick, to myself, to everybody whose world I am destroying. I am, after all, a destroyer. Lilith. The demon. The demon. The demon of the night.

I don't even notice at first, when Madge's hand strokes the side of my face.

"Madge?"

Her eyes aren't properly open, not properly, but at the edges, they flicker. Her hand is not strong enough to grip mine, but her fingers are moving, working against my skin. When she tries to speak, her voice croaks in her throat.

"Wait, I'll get a doctor," I tell her, and I stand up, moving swiftly towards the door. Madge, however, coughs beseechingly, and when I turn back, she motions for me to stop, to sit back down, to listen.

When eventually she tries to speak again, this time, words form. “Your friend,” she rasps. “Your friend. He was there.”

“Yes.” I nod. “Patrick has been sitting with you all day. I’m so sorry I couldn’t come sooner.”

She shakes her head. “He was there,” she says. “He…”

But then her voice fails, and her eyes flicker again.

“Let me get the doctor,” I insist, and this time do not let her deter me from dashing from the room. Too many times today I have been dissuaded from acting. Dissuaded from doing the right thing. The doctor will stabilise her, I tell myself as Madge rasps behind me. The doctor will help her speak, help her recover, help her reveal what she knows.

When the doctor and I return, however, Patrick is back sitting by her, and Madge is already sleeping again.

CHAPTER 27

Cassius and I lie curled towards each other in Jessie's bed. It smells of her. There is a picture book open on the floor that we bought together. A new pack of hair bobbles has spilled off her bedside table and litters the carpet like spring flowers in the old allotment. In the corner is a jar for collecting butterflies – a promise I had made to her. And broken. Same as the promise I had made to myself. Not to be a danger. Not to ever allow myself to be a danger.

I don't know when Cassius crawled under the sheets next to me. After leaving the hospital, I walked again for many hours – first, everywhere I could think of that Jessie might be, and then just anywhere that my legs took me, blindly wandering in the dark. All the time, I waited for my phone to ring, for Cassius to tell me that it was done, that the police wanted me. At one point, I even stood outside the precinct with the intention of turning myself in, but in the end, I couldn't bring myself to do it. Cassius had said he would call, so perhaps there was a reason for the delay, perhaps he had already found her. I knew of course that this couldn't be true, not really, but it is easier to hope for the impossible than accept the abyss. Eventually, I decided to go home, to wait there for the inevitable. As I reached my road, I half-expected police officers to be stationed at my door, or for TV cameras to be camped outside, waiting for a glimpse of the night-time murderer, the Hollywood star, fallen. But the house was dark as I entered. Cassius was not back. And nor, of course, was Jessie. I called her name one last time, just in case. Then in the shadowed void of silence, I crept upstairs, and fell onto her bed, and somehow, at some point, must have drifted into slumber.

But I have been awake now for the past hour, watching Cassius's breathing, wondering how it is that I am still here, still free, and remembering all the other times we have positioned ourselves in such close proximity, connected by horror or grief or longing or love. Symbiotic. I cannot bear to wake him, to witness that awful moment when sleep-edged nightmare registers as reality. When life crashes into blissful oblivion.

Finally, however, he opens his eyes.

I see the truth filter across his brow. He winces. So do I. My heart hurts, actually hurts – with Jessie's absence, with what I have done, to her, to him. And my head pulses. It feels tight, pounding, pushing against my skull, as though it is caged already.

"Has she been found?" I whisper as his eyes find mine.

He shakes his head.

"Did you tell them?"

Cassius sits up a little, his blonde-grey hair messy against the pillow, his face turned towards traitorous Californian sun.

"Cass?"

He doesn't answer. His eyes are blank as they gaze out of the window, blurry, as though all of the light has been snatched from them, and now there are only pale, insipid traces of what used to be. This is my handiwork. Again, there is pain in my chest.

"Cass," I press.

Slowly, he drags his face to look at mine. "I couldn't."

"What?"

"I couldn't do it. I went there, to the station. I stood there for hours, hours; but I couldn't go in. I couldn't do it to you."

"What?"

Cassius's eyes are still trance-like, his voice devoid of life. "I've thought about it and thought about it. Over and over. But it's already been too long, Lilith. It's been too long. What are the chances of finding her? Really? Honestly? Especially when we know that you took her to the… That she's probably already…"

"Say it," I tell him.

"That she's dead."

As he utters these words, he winces again, and clutches his stomach, and then abruptly vomits over the bed. I run for a bin, but it is just this one almost dry retch. After we have removed the sheets, we sit back on Jessie's bed, facing each other.

"We don't know that she's dead, Cass. We don't. If we tell the police I was involved, maybe they can… They can…"

"They can what? What can they do? Extract the answer from your brain? No. They'll ask me why I didn't report it sooner. Question *me*, that's what they'll do. They always question the father. Assume things. Drag me in front of news cameras. I mean, it sounds crazy, doesn't it? Sleepwalking? But of course people who know you will corroborate, and when they do, once the police understand, well, it will have taken days already and then… I just… I can't… I just… I should have stayed up, stayed awake, waited for you to walk. I should have protected you. And her. I just, just… I'm not letting you go to prison. Not when it won't do any good."

"Cass—"

"No. You were right. I shouldn't have brought her here. We should never have come. I knew the danger, but I was out of options, and so I convinced you into it. It's my fault. It's all my fault. I can't have more things be my fault. Besides, it's… I know that… She's…"

Breath catches in his throat, and he pauses, reaching slowly into the pocket of the jacket he is still wearing. From it, he pulls out his phone, and silently selects an image before carefully handing it to me. Barely a second passes before the phone falls from my hand. Cassius picks it up and tries again to show me, but I can't look, I can't look, I can't even glance at it, for I have already seen: it is a photograph of Jessie's nightie, muddied, sodden, but the cheerful face of Winnie the Pooh still plastered across the front. I recognise it at once as what she had been wearing that night. I remember distinctly, because she'd chosen it from the drawer while balancing on one leg. Pain shoots from my heart through my lungs, and a sound I have never heard before rushes out of my throat. I double over, clutching the side of the bed.

"The police found it early this morning," whispers Cassius. "Under the pier. They called me to identify it."

"Oh my God," I gasp. "Oh my God, oh my God, oh my God."

"Look," says Cassius. "If I believed there was even the tiniest chance that the police would find her, alive, that they could actually find her, that she might be OK, I would do it, I would turn you in. Sorry, but I would. But they won't find her, Lilith. You know it. You know it. And I… I can feel it." He puts his hand to his chest. "I can feel it. She's gone."

"No," I say. "No."

"Yes." There is a long pause, silence slithering between us. I don't know what to say. There is nothing left to say. When Cassius finally manages to continue, that nothingness infuses him too. It is as though something has evaporated, left his eyes, left his soul. "The perverse thing is," he begins. "The thing is, without her… I mean, it's madness, 'cos it's you who… It's you who has… But I… I need you. I need you. Serena's gone. Jessie's gone. I have nobody else. I can't lose you too."

With the spectre of the nightie still reaching across the space between us, I can barely talk, but I make myself. "Cassius, do you realise what you are doing?" I ask him slowly. "And what you're asking me to do?"

He says nothing.

"You are not reporting the kidnap and potential murder of your daughter."

"Don't say that." He grimaces, covering his ears with his hands.

"And you are asking me to hide the fact that it was me. That we both know it was me. That I've… killed her."

"Don't say that," he pleads again.

I don't want to say it. I don't want to think it. "But it's what you've just told me yourself," I protest. "It's the truth. We have to confront it."

He shakes his head. "What good will it do?"

The sunlight is streaming through the window, casting deceitful speckles of brightness across the room. A blue sky streaks like fresh paint through the glass. Paradise pushes against us.

"We need to tell the truth."

He shakes his head again. "What good did the truth ever do?"

"What do you mean?" I say.

"You haven't always told it. Neither of us have."

I look at him, confused.

"I know you knew about my mother."

For a moment, I don't comprehend, I don't understand what he's talking about, until of course I do, and the words are like a bullet. The secret that I harboured for so many years, to protect him, the secret that almost drove me to insanity – he knew, all along. "I was trying to protect you," I say softly.

"Exactly." He nods.

"No, this is different."

"Even if you don't go to prison," he argues. "Even if there's some legal out, some sleepwalking defence, your life will be ruined. Your career will be over. Your friends will disown you, and Patrick. And how do you think your family will cope? Don't you think they'll blame themselves for never taking your fear seriously enough? Dylan will. Dylan won't cope with it."

"Don't talk about Dylan."

"And it won't even bring her back. That's the thing. It won't bring back Jessie. All it will do is leave me with nobody. No parents. No wife. No friends. No daughter. No life. No money."

"I'll give you money."

He stops. Looks at me. With disgust.

"It won't bring her back."

I take a breath. "Cass, we cannot keep this a secret. Even if we don't tell anybody that it was me, people will twig. I've told everybody about the sleepwalking. Patrick knows I've been scared of hurting Jessie. Ria knows, Nola knows, June knows. As soon as they find out she's missing, don't you think one of them will put it together?"

Slowly, painfully, with eyes closed as though to avoid witnessing his own proposition, Cassius answers me: "Not if we don't tell them she's gone."

I am not sure if I have heard him right. Or understood him right. "What?" I say. "What?"

As he looks at me, tears leak out of his eyes, and as he speaks, even his own mouth curls away from him. "There's nobody to notice," he whispers.

Cold air crawls across my skin.

But Cassius continues. "Nobody at home is expecting Jessie back. She has no family around. She's not at school. She's not registered anywhere, except the daycare, who wouldn't think anything of it if I took her out. There are the people here – your friends, and Patrick. And Dylan. But if I was to leave, if I leave this area, there's nobody. There's nobody who would know a thing."

As he speaks, I cannot help but physically recoil from him, and I stand up from the bed. "Cassius, you can't be serious," I whisper. "Do you hear yourself? Do you hear what you're saying?"

"It's the only way," he says. "It's the only way not to destroy us both." He stands up too and follows me across the room. "Jessie loved you, Lilith."

At the mention of Jessie's name, I take a huge intake of air. And suddenly can't breathe. I stand there gasping, and Cassius rubs his hand on my back. The feel of his touch disgusts me. Like him, I want to be sick.

"And... I still love you, too. I always have."

I put up my hands and push him away. "How can you possibly love me after what I've done?"

It takes a long time for him to answer. His eyes darken. As though he is summoning the devil. Or an angel. Or both. Then he speaks, plainly: "I have nobody else to love."

The rawness of these words works its way into my throat and, for a moment, stifles my objection. He is right. Because I have taken everything.

Now, tears push themselves again down Cassius's cheeks. He doesn't bother to wipe them. He moves back to the bed and puts up his own hand to prevent me from following him, but I force my fingers onto his arm. Despite his pain, I need him to hear me. I need him to feel my touch, to feel the mass of what he is suggesting, to feel this reality while there is still time to change it, to challenge it. Because this is what we do. This is how we have always induced each other to face life. Challenge. Goad. Shore up. Confess.

"You can't give up on Jessie, not yet," I say. "It's only been a day. If we tell the police about me, you never know, they could get a new lead, they could still find her."

"Stop it, Lilith!" Cassius screams suddenly. "Stop it! Stop it! Stop it!" With sudden violence he throws my hands off him and wraps his own around his ears. "I'm trying so hard to do the right thing by you. To... But I can't listen to you say that again! We're not going to find Jessie. We're not. It's been two nights, Lilith. Two nights, and a day. And look!" He holds up his phone, the damning image glaring out at me. "We already know what happened. You took her. You took her. Drowned her probably. You've done what was always your destiny. She's never going to be found!"

"Then how can you be standing here protecting me?" I scream back at him. "If that's what you think, how can you still care about me? I don't. I don't care about me. I *should* go to prison. I should have my life destroyed. If I've hurt a child, Cassius… If I've hurt Jessie… Jessie… How can you even… How can I… I've… I've…"

I cannot speak any more. When I close my eyes, all I can see is her smile and her blondeness. In her room, I can still smell her, and feel the soft warmth of her arms around my neck, her whispers of 'I love you'. I cannot breathe. I cannot breathe. My lungs are full of her, and I cannot breathe.

For a number of minutes, Cassius doesn't say anything, and nor do I. Until finally, he speaks again, this time quietly, through gritted teeth.

"Will your guilt be eased in prison?"

I shrug. "Maybe. It's what I deserve."

"Well, I deserve something too. I've lost everything, so I deserve something. Don't I? I deserve to have you."

He turns from me then, and strides heavily out of Jessie's room. Along the corridor, I hear him opening and closing cupboards, treading in and out of the bathroom, pulling on a pair of trainers, then a few moments later, he is thumping down the stairs and leaving the house through the back door, towards the beach. Through the window, I watch him go. He is running. Running. Running away from me. Running towards her. To search again, for her, his daughter, even though she is dead.

He runs. And he runs.

And in the Californian sunshine, I am swallowed by the dark.

CHAPTER 28

I am seeing things.

Everywhere I go, I am seeing things. Not as in visions, not obsessive thoughts that stride unwanted into my head, but real apparitions that I could touch, if they weren't so fleeting.

Then again, I am fleeting myself. Flying. Moving constantly. Searching endlessly. Same as, but never alongside of, Cassius.

Four days have passed, and Madge is still in hospital, still floating in and out of a consciousness that never lasts long enough, though I try to be there, to catch it, to catch the last clue there might be. In her alley, a new homeless woman has taken up her stoop. One morning, I spotted her from a distance and sprinted forward, deliriously certain that Madge had returned, but the woman had no idea who I was and took offence to my hand on her shoulder, to my enquiries as to her name. She had no interest in the weather.

The beach is filled with little girls with blonde hair. They giggle and splash in the waves. Some of them line up shells picked out from buckets. But none of them are her. Not even when I creep up slowly and catch them off guard, for fear they may otherwise dissipate, a vision unhinged. They do not like me grabbing their shoulders this way. There have been tears. And angry parents.

In Urth Café, I am sure I see Dylan. There is a man at a table near the back, sucking boba through a straw. He has

Dylan's erect posture, his open smile, and that unguarded surety as he leans across the table to speak to a small child whose legs are swinging back and forth against the seat, feet bearing what I am sure are turquoise trainers. Shielded by a throng of other customers clamouring for their takeaway coffees and juices and superfood smoothies, I cannot see the face of the child, but I shove my way through, I push towards the vision of my brother – unmistakeable. I hear his voice – English, Marlovian, his. I hear her giggle. I call out. Only by the time I make it, both the man and the child are gone, and it is silly, because Dylan is still in San Francisco. And Jessie has been gone for 113 hours. Maybe more. And when I ask, nobody else in the restaurant noticed the colour of the child's shoes.

I have not heard from Dylan. He has gone off-grid, though my parents message me often for updates. He was going camping, they tell me, but is there really no signal in the hills? Can I please let them know when he checks in? He hasn't checked in, but I cannot worry about him for now. I have spent too much of my life doing that, looking in the wrong direction. He will be back in a few days. And Jessie will still be gone.

I call in sick to work, letting Will handle things. I cannot pretend the confidence necessary to command a room. I can barely command myself. Some days, I sit by the window while the sky turns dark and cannot summon the impetus even to switch on the light. One morning, it strikes me that I could have taken Jessie to the studio. I have all the keys for the lot. I pull a beanie over my head, and shield my face with a scarf, and appear in the studio while the actors are rehearsing. Then I search all of the small spaces. There is a fridge in my office in which she could fit. There is a trapdoor beneath one of the stages. I have worn Cassius's clothes so as not to be recognised, but I feel eyes upon me. Later, I sense the questioning that was within them, the examination soaring into my skull – who is this loon, who is this psychotic woman, who is this demon – and I ponder their faces, their judgement.

Did they recognise me? Did they know? Their features blur in my brain, and suddenly I am not sure if I have even been to the lot at all. Did I imagine it? Did I imagine everything? Night has fallen by then, but I take a flashlight, and duck under the fence, so that I can search my office again.

Meanwhile, Patrick asks to see me. I have not answered his calls since we parted ways at the hospital. I don't know what to say to him. I cannot lie, but I cannot tell the truth. Besides, Cassius's words spiral through my head: 'I deserve to have you.' I don't know what he meant by this. To have me to lean on? To have me as his? I would do it. I would cast Patrick off. I would give Cassius anything he asked for, including myself. But Patrick has texted me to meet him at our lunch place, and Cassius tells me I have to go.

Despite his declaration of love, Cassius barely speaks to me. Most days, he breaks his silence only to ask me for updates, or inform me of the communications he's had with the police, or to tell me to stay away from him. And I do, I barely see him. He spends every day out of the house, sleeping for only a few snatched hours of the night. Although he is certain that Jessie is dead, he cannot stop searching for her. Or perhaps he cannot bear her absence. I wonder sometimes if he leaves only to avoid having to be near me. When he and I pass in the kitchen, he glares in silence, repulsion dripping from his eyes. He cannot, however, eschew me altogether, because even when he returns in the small hours of the morning, I am there, at the island. I spend much of the night in the kitchen now, unable to sleep, biting my cheek, collecting ulcers. I am not surprised by this and do not fight it. I accept it as a way to survive, because it is hard enough even in the daytime not to scream, or sob, or throw myself off the Colorado Street Bridge. In many ways, it is like being a teenager again in that I cannot escape, I cannot escape from myself. Except this time it is worse, because no therapist or parent or friend or lover can tell me that I haven't done anything, that I am imagining it, obsessing. This time my sin is clear. It is done. Some nights,

Cassius suddenly breaks from form and wants to talk, or rather shout, at me. He demands to know what I have done, for me to find the memory. He spits this at me, screams, rails, cries on me. Pleads for comfort. Pleads for Jessie. Pleads to the gods. But not even Senoy, Sansenoy, and Semangelof can help with this one. The angels have failed. It is too late even for them. Still, while Cassius crumbles, he will not allow it of me. I owe him that, he says. I owe him.

When Patrick and I meet, I can feel his eyes working me over, as though hunting for clues, trying to prove something, some point upon which he has already decided. I am wearing tracksuit bottoms and a T-shirt. I have hidden my usually wild locks in a bun, and despite the warm weather, wrapped an oversized scarf around my neck to breathe into, as though by taking the edge off the freshness of air, I can blunt the sharpness of life too. On my face, there is no make-up but vast sunglasses that cover the entire width of my head. Underneath them, my eyes are puffy.

"What's going on?" asks Patrick.

We are both sipping on coffees. Avocado toast is on its way. The pretence of normalcy sickens me. "What do you mean?"

"You look awful."

I shrug. "Thanks."

"That's not what I mean. What's going on with you?"

I shrug again. Shake my head. Sip my coffee. "Nothing."

Only now do I notice that Patrick too is not his usual self. His own eyes look tired, anxious. His shirt has a stain on the sleeve. He is not smiling.

"What's going on with you?" I return.

"Well, it's nice to be asked."

"What?"

"It's nice to be noticed."

"Huh?"

"Where have you been?" he says. "Where the fuck have you been all week? It's like you've checked out of our relationship and forgotten to tell me. You're just wrapped up in Cassius."

"I haven't even been with Cassius," I reply honestly.

Patrick flaps his hand. "And Jessie."

There is something about the way Patrick intones Jessie's name that makes me uneasy, almost as if it's a test, and it crosses my mind that perhaps he was listening to mine and Cassius's conversation the other night, after all. Perhaps he had been there longer than we thought. Perhaps he heard everything. Maybe he has been waiting, since then, for me to tell him the truth. But if he knows about Jessie, why hasn't he asked me about it? And if he knows, why hasn't he told the police? And if he knows, why is he sitting here with the murderer? I shake my head. "I've not been with her either." It hurts to talk about Jessie. It hurts so much. To think about her, to pretend. How can I even be sitting here, not looking for her? My chest hurts. My heart hurts.

"Well then, where on earth have you been?"

Again, I shrug.

"I don't like being out of the loop, Lil."

"What loop? What are you talking about?"

"You and Cassius keep having your little secrets, and being 'caught up'. Is there something you're not telling me?"

"No." I say this quickly. Too quickly.

"Are you sure?"

Again, there is something about the way Patrick is looking at me that makes this feel like a test, and I am struck by the sudden conviction that he does know. He knows. He knows what I have done and is merely waiting for me to confess it. Is he wearing a wire? Has he already told somebody? Are police on their way? Or here? "What do you think you know?" I ask innocently, my chest tight with trapped air.

Patrick narrows his eyes, dark, opaque, giving nothing away, and now another thought suddenly enters my mind. It is a crazy thought, a crazy idea, but, I think, I think it is possible, and I allow my mind to follow it… What if it was

Patrick who took Jessie? What if that is why he knows she is gone? He has a key to my house. In fact, he is the only person outside of myself and Cassius (and Dylan currently, but he is in San Francisco) who does have one. And he knows the codes to the alarm, and he knows where Jessie's room is, and which floorboards creak. And he was at the beach that morning. Why was he at the beach? Madge said something about seeing my friend and I thought she'd meant at the hospital, but perhaps she'd meant there, in the alley, by the sand. Maybe it was Patrick who took Jessie, out of spite, out of hatred for Cassius, out of a desire to see them both gone. What did I know about him really? Yes, we'd been dating for years, but it wasn't like Cassius who I'd known since childhood. Patrick could have done anything in his past and I would never know. He could have been anyone. He could be anyone. How can you really know?

"Look, you don't have to tell me everything," Patrick says now, soothingly, shifting gear, laying his hand on mine. It is almost as though he can hear my mind whirring, as though he knows he has to rein things back. "But we're supposed to be getting married. We're supposed to be a team. I know something's wrong, and you're keeping it from me. Why can't you trust me?"

"What were you doing at the beach?" I ask abruptly.

"What?"

"The other day. When Madge was hurt. Why were you at the beach? You hate the beach. You're scared of the beach."

"Lilith, I'm trying to express something important to you here, about us. I'm trying to tell you how I feel. Which, as you know, is hard for me."

"You don't want me to keep things from you," I say, emboldened. "I get it. I feel the same. So tell me – why were you at the beach?"

"I can't get married to somebody who doesn't trust me."

"Likewise."

"So tell me what's going on."

"Tell me why you were at the beach."

Angrily, Patrick pushes his plate across the table. "God, Lilith. Why are you pushing this? Why are you fixated on it? For you. For you, that's why. I've been learning to surf, as a wedding present to you. I've been seeing June, working on expressing 'feelings'. And working through my fear of the ocean. It was supposed to be a surprise."

I have never seen Patrick so livid. "Oh," I say slowly.

"Oh? Oh?"

I shrug once again, unhelpfully.

"Now you tell me," he demands. Warns. "Tell me. Right now. Right now. Something's going on with you and Cassius, I know it is. So tell me. Tell me."

But I can't. I can't. I have promised Cassius. I owe him.

I don't want to lose Patrick.

But if I tell Patrick, I will lose him anyway.

I don't want that.

And I don't want to lose my life. Everything I have worked for.

As I sit there, the weight of this comes into sharp focus. Thinking for even a second about my own misfortune feels depraved, evil; but for the first time, I force myself to consider it. And to consider the secret, the possibility of living with it, of living with what I have done. Almost immediately, I feel my shoulders hunch lower in my seat. It is heavy, the burden of hidden sin.

"Tell me," Patrick probes again, and for a second, his face softens, the fine lines around his brow dissolving. I can feel the pull from within him – he wants to help me, he wants me to be OK, he knows that I am not. But then I see another thought cross his mind – self-preservation perhaps – and again, his eyes blaze. "Tell me now."

I hesitate. Then, "Nothing's going on," I promise.

For a moment more, Patrick lets the echo of my lie occupy the space between us, then pointedly, he puts down his coffee, as though the taste of it has turned bitter. The look he gives me now is an expression I have never seen from him before – something between deep hurt and bewildered disgust. The sharpness of it seems to cut at my throat. My breath feels short and razor-tipped. The ring he gave me sits weightily on my finger. Patrick sees my turmoil. He sees it, and he waits. But I cannot tell him. I cannot. And finally, shaking his head, he stands up, and walks away.

CHAPTER 29

I dream of her.

I dream at the kitchen island. I dream in my bed. I dream while I am sitting in the waves, my clothes soaked by a slow, encroaching tide.

She is laughing. She is sobbing. She is shrieking my name.

Patrick watches me. I see his car in the alleyway. I see it on my road.

Dylan speeds past on a bike, a child strapped to the back – her? Him? Is it me cycling?

Cassius vomits again. It splatters over me. Sticks to me. I wade into the waves, but it will not wash off. I try to silence the world beneath the water, but the current keeps pushing me up. He said he deserves to have me, and it is true. I am ensnared by his unravelling. It was me who pulled the threads.

I wake up. It is light. And it is dark. And she is still gone.

CHAPTER 30

Cassius has stopped looking.

He spends an entire day in bed. Then another. Not eating. Not talking. Not doing anything but staring blankly in the dark.

I examine my own dark, the recesses of my stupid fortress mind. I try hypnosis, meditation, free writing. Visions crawl out of small spaces. In most of them, Jessie is screaming, and I am striding into the sea. In some, I am digging with her in the sand beneath the pier. But as always, I do not know if these pictures are real, or imagined, or if my mind is powerful enough to conjure, or likewise conceal. One day, I pay a fortune teller down at Venice Beach to tell me, *tell me* – but she says only that she sees a great darkness. And I could have told her that myself.

Dragging himself finally into the lit kitchen, Cassius instructs me to stop. "You need to act normal," he says. "You're spiralling. You need to learn how to control this. So do I."

I say nothing. It has been days since he has spoken to me. Days since he has spoken to anyone at all, except for the police who have no leads, nothing. He staggers now, weakly, over to the counter and makes himself a coffee and a slice of toast. He avoids the peanut butter and jelly, still readied on the shelf above. He sits at the kitchen island opposite me.

"I'm leaving."

Now I answer. "What?"

"I have to. I didn't think I could go anywhere without finding her, but it's harder to stay. I thought it would be better for me to be here, with you. But it's not. It's worse. I can't be near you. I can't look at you." As he says this, he forces himself to meet my eyes, but even across the island, I can feel the sting this sends through him, and he looks away. "Besides, Dylan will be back soon. If I'm going to disappear, I need to do it now."

"I understand," I say. I want to ask him, again, about telling the police about me, but every time I try, it only worsens his suffering. And if I am honest, I only ask it now to relieve mine. I do not know what I would do if he actually agreed to it. It has been far too long. We would both be jailed for sure. "Are you going to the apartment?"

He shakes his head. "I can't stay in LA. It's too painful. And the daycare has called. And other people will start noticing. I have to leave."

I nod. A thought opens up – once he leaves, I am released. Not from the concealment, but from the burden of continuing, the burden of being, of living with what I have done. He said he needed me, and that I owed him, and he is right, I owe him a thousand times over, I owe him more than I will ever be able to repay, I owe him his daughter. But once he has gone, my existence will no longer be necessary. "When?"

"As soon as possible. Before I go mad."

"Where will you go?"

"I don't know. Away. I'll just take a train somewhere."

"That makes sense," I say quietly.

But, "I have to go," he declares again, as though I have disagreed with him. "I have to. I have to. I have to."

"OK, Cass. OK, I get it."

"But I can't," he hisses, looking at me hard, the words clearly repulsing him. "I can't get away from you, because I can't afford to go. So now, I have to sit here, and ask you…"

We go to the bank together. Cassius opens a new account and I transfer funds into it. It takes a few days to arrange. He has asked for a million dollars. A million dollars for a new life.

"A million for a child," I spit at myself – a dagger, a knife, a twist in the flesh. Replacing despair, I am filled now with hatred only, loathing for myself, and it spews out of me. I am a volcano spitting ash. I am determined to burn everything.

I give Cassius seven million dollars. Aside from the asset of my house, it is everything I have. I will not need it. A conviction is growing inside me, lashing like icy waves, and I will not need it. Even if I have a change of heart and remain, even if cowardice gets the better of me, at the very least I will sell the house and downsize. This will be my punishment. If Cassius will not destroy me, then I will do it for him. I have already begun. Patrick has not phoned. I have ignored calls from my parents. I haven't been to work. Or out for a run. So easy, it is, to spark ruin.

If I live, then I will live in a small way. I will be like one of those mad, reclusive artists who emerge only to give the world the gift of their talent. I will write a new show, a dark show, a true show. But I will deny myself everything else. Perhaps I will stop eating.

Or perhaps I will disappear.

"Act normal," says Cassius again. "You owe me that."

He has booked a train ticket for lunchtime. He is heading north, he says, but doesn't know where because he doesn't really care. He will simply keep going until he finds a town that feels right, somewhere it feels possible to exist in for a while. He'll tell the police where he is, just in case, he says, just in case, but he doesn't need to say again what he thinks about that – there is a searing deadness in his eyes. Eventually, he will have to return to England, or at least leave the States when his visa runs out, but for now he wants only to be. To be. To exist. Unlike his daughter. He has stopped saying Jessie's name and I cannot bear to. Cassius asks me, however, to pack up her things. These he wants to take with him, or rather, cannot endure leaving them behind, in the house of the murderer. I call myself this, not him, but it is what he is thinking.

In a holdall I once used to trek the Baja Peninsula, I fold Jessie's skirts and T-shirts, and colourfully dotted leggings, her frilled socks with cherries on the trim, her jumper with the sequinned ice cream that she'd decided was flavoured strawberry, the hat I gave her, her toys, her books. I cannot find her turquoise trainers. As I caress her things, the sensation of her sitting on my lap, reading, shmooshing, is visceral and raw. It throbs in the space on my body where she should be leaning. I lean forwards, as if she is there. Did she rest her face in my neck when I carried her out of her bed? Did she flop trustingly over my shoulder as I lifted her onto my bike, or into my car, or held her in my arms? Did she protest when I dropped her into the waves? Was she awake? Did she see? Did she know what I was doing? Did she call my name? Did she beseech me? Claw onto my skin? Beg me to stop? To hold on to her? To hold on?

My bracelet catches on the zip of the holdall, and I look down at it, the strap loose from where Jessie liked to imprint her thumb underneath. How ill-thought-through that protection had been. I had considered only the need to track myself if missing, not to retrace the journey of where I might have been. Between sharp, painful breaths, I remove the useless bracelet from my wrist and place it in the bag between the other items that Jessie will never see or use again. Then I zip up the bag and rest it silently outside of Cassius's room. He still cannot look at me. He loves me, he said. He wants to protect me, he said. But he hates me too. We are leaving for the train station at 11 a.m. Until then, I am supposed to act normal. *Do that at least.* Whatever normal is supposed to be.

Ria has saved a space for my mat next to hers. As usual, she is bubbling over with enthusiasm and bombards me with news: the casting director I introduced her to a while back has finally called her in; she has three auditions that afternoon; she has met a man in an acting class who is three years younger than she is, but who she thinks she could really like, except that she also likes Cassius, and has messaged him a few times and been hoping he would call – do I think he is ever going to call? Also, where have I been?

It is the first time I have seen any of my friends since it happened. The distraction of her words is like a tonic, but a toxin too. They rock me between strange, surreal, everydayness, and the poison of carrying on. Yet my performance of normality is breathtaking, even to myself. I wonder if all actors feel the kind of pollution that I do now, the waste product of their skilful deceit. I smile apologetically. "Cassius is leaving."

Now that I have interrupted Ria's flood of words, she takes a breath, and prompted to do the same, I inhale slowly. It is, I realise, the first time I have breathed properly in days. Deeply, not snatching from the shallows. In my lungs, I hold the air and let the oxygen transfer, feeling the life force of it. Then I close my eyes and cross my legs, steadying myself, searching for balance.

"Oh. Like, permanently?" Ria interrupts. "Is he going back to the UK? I thought he was staying here?"

"Plans changed," I answer. "I'm sure he would have called you otherwise."

"Oh. Shit. Shame."

I nod, but do not open my eyes. I have released the breath and take another: longer, calmer.

"When's he going?"

"Today."

"Wow. OK. Tell him bye then, I guess."

"I will."

"I guess Nola will miss him too."

"Where is Nola?" I ask.

"Got me. Unreliable foreigners." Ria winks.

"Like me?"

She squeezes my arm. "Not like you."

Except that, of course, I am the most unreliable of all. "Senoy, Sansenoy, and Semangelof," I whisper through my inhale, realising as I do so that there is no point to belated prayer.

"Huh?"

I open one eye. "Go for acting-class-man," I confirm. "Where's he from?"

"The Valley," she laughs.

Her laugh resonates in my head. I don't deserve it. I don't deserve to hear laughter, joy. I don't deserve the air in my lungs. I don't think I can do it – continue this act, not even for Cassius. "Perfect," I say.

The instructor enters the room, and the class begins – with another breath. I bring my attention to it. To the in and the out. To the now. To the what is. But quickly, this reminds me of what isn't. What would it be like to be an isn't?

I shake myself. I cannot fall apart. Not now. Not yet. I try again, start again, breathe again. I have done this before; I can build from the ashes. By the time I am standing on my head, I even, almost, feel the possibility of it. Instead of channelling darkness and longing for banishment, for Lilith's destiny, I find myself, for a moment, actually imagining it – the possibility that somehow, slowly, someday, it may be conceivable to return to 'normal', to re-enter the gates of paradise. Then, however, my headstand wobbles, and the thought falls away from me. Because how can I possibly countenance such a thing? How can I ever stop atoning for what I have done? I may be a monster, but I can't do that.

At the end of the class, we breathe zen-like again. Or rather, now, I pretend to. Mine are focused furies of air, directed, controlled. I must do this more – concentrate on the things I can control. Control. The crux of everything. I need to control myself. Protect the world from myself. Make myself smaller. Invisible.

Or not there at all.

Ria air-kisses me goodbye. "You OK?" she asks thoughtfully. "You seem a little out of whack. Things OK with Patrick?"

I squeeze her arm. "You are one of the good ones, Ria. I want you to know that," I tell her.

"Thanks," she says. "You are too. But – are you sure you're OK?"

Are you OK? Are you OK? My old friend Jade flashes suddenly into my mind. And my parents. And Dylan. And Cassius. All the people who have stood at the edge in front of me, rescued me from the brink. Or tried to.

"I'm fine." I nod. "I'm fine," I breathe. Balance. Control.

And I do have to be. For now. Because Cassius needs me to be. For now.

Dylan needs me to be OK too. He needs that. And so do my parents. They need me. And if Madge ever wakes up, she may need me to help with bills or rehab or just living. And Patrick – Patrick has just staked his future on me, he needs me. And the team at *Moles* needs me, everybody whose salaries are paid for by the creations begun in my mind. That I control. And don't control. And can't control.

Ria waves goodbye.

And must control.

I am losing control.

It is all a sham. I cannot balance. I cannot break through the dark. Even for others, I cannot give everything that is needed.

Then again, nobody needs me really. It is only a necessary way to see the world, otherwise we would all jump off a cliff at the very first thought of oblivion. This is not the first time I have considered it. Only the most recent. It is a viable option. It is not an irrational thing.

I don't deserve better anyway.

I don't deserve even a fleeting, yogic intake of air. Because Jessie is not taking in air. I don't think. I don't know, but I don't think. And so, nor must I.

I can control that.

I will control that.

Except for now, Cassius needs me to drive him to the train station. For that, I must exist. And so I will. For now. For this moment. For this day. For this is a promise I have made, and even demons keep promises sometimes. It is how you learn to count on their evil. It is how destiny is foretold.

CHAPTER 31

Patrick's car is in my driveway. The engine is running, and Patrick's hands rest on the steering wheel, ready to move. He is wearing sunglasses, so I can't see his eyes, but I sense him watching me as I pull up, turn off my own engine, and step out into the California sun. I stand on the driveway, waiting. Upstairs, there is a flicker of curtain. I glance up at it, then retrain my gaze to Patrick. He opens his window but doesn't get out.

"I rang," he says finally, from the car.

"I was at yoga."

"Your yoga finished two hours ago. Ria called. She's worried about you."

I shrug, not offering an explanation of where I have been, thinking only of the sensation of the sand between my toes, the shells piercing my skin, the shock of ice hitting my waist. Did she feel the cold that way? What did she feel?

"You weren't at work."

I shrug again.

"Cassius not in?" Patrick presses.

Another shrug.

"That's it?"

"What?"

"That's all I get from you?"

This time I don't shrug, but I say nothing.

Slowly, Patricks takes off his sunglasses. "Lilith, all you

have to do is tell me," he says emphatically. "Tell me, and I'll be here for you. I mean for God's sake, look – I'm here."

As he speaks, pain surges against my chest, and tears push themselves upwards, but I choke them down. I want to reach for him, I want to reach for him, he is right there. But I plant my feet into the cement.

Patrick shakes his head. "You're OK?" he asks defeatedly. "You're OK?"

I cannot answer, but again, I shrug.

CHAPTER 32

By the time Patrick's car has disappeared from my road, Cassius is waiting for me in the kitchen. He has not been out of tracksuit bottoms in many days, but now a crisp shirt is tucked into pale denim, a pair of loafers on his feet. With his tanned complexion, he could almost be straight from the Riviera. When he runs his hand through his hair, I am struck by a flash of our youth, of Cassius always appearing and disappearing like this, in a whirl of energy and elegance, and fresh scent. But he has forever been good at embodying personas not his own. Beneath his sunglasses, his eyes are red around the rims, his cheeks mottled. His feet shift uneasily. Another man I have destroyed. For a moment, we only stare at one another from across the kitchen island. There has always been too much to say between us, and too little. We have always shared too much, and too little. We have always loved too much, and too little.

"Are you ready?" I ask him.

Cassius looks to the bags at his feet – a single suitcase for him, plus the holdall I packed with Jessie's belongings. He nods.

"We still have some time before your train," I say. "But we can go now, if you want to?"

He nods again.

"Cassius."

He says nothing. But even if he will not speak, he can hear.

"Cassius," I persist. "Cassius. I'm sorry. I am so, so sorry. I need you to know that."

Now, Cassius begins to heave uncontrollably, as though all that careful dressing has been taping his pain to his skin, but at last it is seeping through cotton. Exploding through it. And although I know I am no longer the right person to comfort him, I move around the island and try to embrace him. With two hands, he fobs me away.

In silence, we load up the car. I have a sense of us being observed, observed in our estrangement, but when I glance around, I can see no one. Jessie's old booster is still plugged into the back seat, but neither of us look at it. If we don't look, then it could almost be that she is asleep in the back. Or that we are asleep. That this was one big dream. Though sleep has never been as benevolent as that for me.

As we drive, he still won't talk. I reach for the radio, but he turns it off. Moving through the LA traffic, I feel as though he wants to say something, one more thing, but he can't. Until finally, when I have parked, I turn to him. "Just tell me," I demand, as Patrick demanded of me. "Before you leave and regret it. Whatever it is. Just say it."

He shakes his head. He is angry. Afresh. "Why are you going along with it?" he asks suddenly.

"What?"

"Why are you just acting normal, just doing what I say?"

"Because…" I am bewildered. I am not sure what he is getting at. "Because you've asked me to," I tell him. "Because I don't know what else to do. Don't you want me to?"

"I do want you to. But you don't."

"No."

"Then why are you?"

I shake my head, still not understanding. Does he want me to disagree with him? Has he been waiting for me to tell the police myself, to turn myself in, because he is unable to do it? Does he blame me for allowing him to protect me? Am I the only one who can do the right thing? Me with my American-sized morals. "Shall I tell the police?" I ask him.

"No." He glowers at me fiercely. "I don't want that guilt. That's your burden to bear."

I nod. Accept this. "Then… what?"

"I don't know," he says. And then he starts crying again.

Of course he doesn't know. How can he know anything right now? How can he even be thinking and breathing and moving? I lean over the gearstick, and this time he allows me to touch him, to stroke his back, to pull him towards me. I wish we could go back, back to a time when our union felt so bolstering and familiar. Back to a moment when the biggest question between us was whether our closeness was more than it should be. Fleetingly, I feel again that sense of someone watching, and wonder what Patrick would think if he saw us locked together like this now, but we are only clasping so tightly because we are about to be torn apart. Torn more apart. More than I've torn us already.

"I always wanted to be part of your family," Cassius whispers between sobs. "I always wanted that, what you had, what you still have. Family."

"And now I've stolen yours."

He shakes his head. "I wanted to have – you. I've always loved – you, is what I mean."

"I love you too," I tell him.

But now Cassius pulls slightly away from me and averts his eyes. "I will never get over what's happened," he says mournfully. "Never. But I don't blame you for it. You need to know that." And then, although we are still early for his train, he opens the car door, and gets out, and pulls the bags from the boot. And after everything, leaves without saying goodbye.

Through the fogging glass of my car window, I watch as Cassius crosses the car park and enters the arched whiteness of Union Station, melting into the masses.

As he does so, a fresh nervousness gathers in my stomach.

It is happening. Once I have driven away, then it is truly over. He will be gone.

And I will be too.

Or not. I could do as he's asked. I could pretend to everybody that they have both simply moved on, him and Jessie. It could be easy. So easy. Nobody would doubt me. Nobody would check. He is right, there is nobody to notice. And I could do it.

Except that, I cannot do it. I have known this deep down for days. I cannot carry this sin. One way or another, my life, as it is, must end.

I will give him time to leave. To get away. To distance himself from here. But then there are only two choices: confession and captivity by turning myself in; or extinction of my own making.

The nervousness grows. I cannot seem to drive it away. Or drive away. The engine is running, but I cannot move.

Because if I do, if I let him go, then there are not two choices really. I am fooling myself. There is only one, the one I have been nurturing, growing, plotting. Once Cassius leaves, if I confess, there is no way he will not be implicated. How would he explain his departure? How would he explain his silence? I cannot do that to him. I cannot take his life as well as his daughter's. So, either I stop him from leaving, I stop him and confess now, while his actions are still explainable. Or I end it all. I carry the secret to a watery grave. The choice is not between paradise and hell; Eden or the wastelands. The choice is only between existence and oblivion.

Do I mean it? Oblivion? Am I really capable of this? Physicality is everything, isn't it? What happens when that is gone? Absence.

Absence.

Absence forever.

My hand hovers over the gears.

Then over my seat belt.

Then slowly it moves to the door handle.

I already know I will regret it. When I am trapped behind bars and no longer have the means to absent myself from anything. I will regret it too when my career is in ruins, when I am remembered only by this. And when Patrick marries somebody else. And when my parents and Dylan are sobbing on the phone. I will regret it as I already regret everything. But I cannot do anything else. There is something inside me that will not be snuffed out. There always has been. It pulled me out of the night. It dragged me across an ocean. Besides, I can still feel Jessie's arms around me.

There is something about Union Station that conjures relics of civilisation. Not that it was built so long ago, nothing in America is that old, but there is a gentility about the sweeping arches and the marble floors and the vast waiting area, as though here would pass not only people, but history. If it were any other day, I would be reaching for my notepad, jotting down descriptions of faces, watching the way people sit, and mill, and greet each other. In the past, I have come here to do exactly that, with nowhere to go myself, just to sit, and watch, and steal snippets of life.

Having stolen an actual life, however, today I ignore the throng, and search for only one head among the story-soaked multitudes.

Cassius is not in the waiting area.

He is not in the queues for tickets.

He is not having shoes shined or buying a crêpe.

I begin to check train platforms, peering over barriers. I do not know where he is going, but he told me that his train leaves at 11.30 a.m. Affixed to one of the walls is a great departure board and I scan it hastily. There is a train for Chicago on the half-hour. That must be it. Rushing to the designated platform, I contemplate what I will say to him when I find him, if I find him: that I can't do it, that I must let him down again, that I am sorry. I am so sorry, I am so, so sorry. I am used to running fast, but I can barely breathe.

By the time I find the correct gate, the train is already pulling in. I don't have a ticket so am not allowed to pass through the arched entrance, but I ignore the disdainful looks of the patrolling official and lean as far as I can over the barrier. There is a hub of travellers. A group of high-school students who look like some kind of cheer squad or sports team, rowdy in their camaraderie, are blocking my view. There is a young woman in a wheelchair, for whom a ramp is being adjusted. There is a group of typically Californian tech-heads – jeans and T-shirts and laptops. And then, then, amongst the mob, I notice somebody else – a woman, with luminous red hair, her body curvaceous and undulating. It is Nola. For a moment my heart leaps with the excitement of familiarity, and serendipity. My instinct is to shout out, to wave hello. But before I can, she turns her face to the side, and she smiles, and when I follow her gaze, smiling back at her is an unmistakeable head of grey-blonde: Cassius. He bends his body towards hers, he lowers his head, and then, then they kiss. They kiss. They kiss. Cassius and Nola. Cassius and Nola? Kiss. As though they are lovers. Deep, passionate. Familiar. Protracted. Until, from behind Cassius's frame, creeping out from the light denim of his legs, there is another flash of blonde, and also turquoise, and pink-cheeked laughter, and Jessie springs between them.

Jessie!

For the millionth time that week, I cannot breathe. I cannot compute and I cannot breathe.

Jessie. Alive.

But where did he find her?

Cassius scoops the girl up as though unsurprised by her presence, and now my mind starts racing. Jessie is alive. And Nola is with them. And they are leaving. Together.

With seven million of my dollars.

"Cassius!" I yell across the platform. "Cassius!" I still can't quite put it together; I still don't understand. But I scream for him anyway.

Cassius looks up but doesn't at first see me. He glances

around shiftily, as though watching for a security guard, as though caught shoplifting, but he doesn't find my eyes. Instead, he mutters something to Nola, who looks around too, searching, checking, but through the hub of boarding passengers, she cannot make me out either. The doors of the train will be closing in a moment, and she tugs Cassius's arm to get on. But the people are thinning out now, and so I shout again, louder this time, louder, and finally, Jessie is the one who sees me.

"Lilith!" She wriggles out of her father's arms, throwing herself towards me. She screams in delight. "Lilith! Lilith! Lilith!"

My heart soars. My head is still adjusting, and my feet are not moving, but my heart soars. "Jessie." I open my arms for her, but I am still trapped behind the barrier, and the guard who has been watching me pre-empts my attempt to climb over it. He is talking to me now, asking for my ticket. "Jessie!" I shout again.

From behind her, Cassius, who has now seen me, is moving up the platform. Nola is dragging their bags onto the train and gesturing to him in frenzy. She has seen me too. "Come on!" she screams at Cassius, her Spanish twang rising over the American bustle. "Come on, it's leaving! Cassius, grab her. Jessie, come back right now!"

But Jessie is fixated on me, her face full of excitement. "We're going on a trip!" she gabbles loudly from halfway down the platform. "Mummy's coming too!"

Mummy. Mummy. Nola?

"Will you come with us?"

The stick figures, the red hair – like me. *Mummy is on holiday. Mummy was at the beach. Mummy told Daddy to kiss you.* I shake my head in bewilderment, but keep my arms outstretched towards hers, willing her to reach them.

Behind, Cassius is nearly upon her. Nola is calling her name, and also shouting for Cassius, and the whistle sounds to mark the closing of the train doors. The guard continues to block my path, but slowly his head is turning, an interest growing in the shouting three-year-old flying towards me. Others watch too. Like me, they are trying to figure it out. One lady on the platform hovers, unsure whether or not to intercept. Who is this child meant to be with? What is going on? She manoeuvres herself hesitantly between Cassius and Jessie – the grown man chasing the little girl. I try to move, to get to Jessie, but I cannot. I cannot reach her. I cannot free myself from the guard's outstretched arms. Cassius circumvents the woman who has still not decided whether or not to stop him. I try again to reason with the guard to let me through, *let me through*, but he stands firm. And I am trapped. I am trapped. I am always trapped by something.

Untrapped, however, suddenly, appearing from nowhere and with American athleticism hurdling the barrier is – Patrick.

Patrick.

I have no idea what he is doing here, or what he has seen, but I shout to him: "Stop him! Patrick, stop Cassius!"

"Cassius!" screams Nola, even louder, spotting Patrick too. "Cassius, the train!"

Now, Cassius glances backwards and Nola gestures at him wildly. *Get on. Get on.* He spins again to look at Jessie, only a few feet away from him. He sees Patrick, sprinting towards them. He freezes. And then he looks at me. Just for a moment, he looks straight at me. Into my eyes that once knew everything.

"I'm sorry," he mouths. Once. Silently.

And then he turns on his heels, and leaves his chattering daughter skipping still towards me, and jumps onto the train half a second before the doors shut.

Patrick stops still on the platform. He turns towards me and lifts up his hands. Clearly, he doesn't understand what has happened, and nor do I. I do not even understand where Patrick came from or why he helped. But for now, it doesn't matter, because there is only one thing that does: Jessie is here. Jessie is here. Alive. And left. With me.

Unlike us, she doesn't stop. She is the only one amongst us still moving, still smiling. She skips into my waiting arms, and the feeling of that is like nothing else – relief, and release, and surrender, and love so deep I want to cry. But Jessie giggles. She giggles. Oblivious of the departing train. Oblivious of the past weeks of hell. Oblivious of the parents who have abandoned her, who have gone, without their daughter. Without even a word.

There will be words though, I realise, even as we are hugging. Soon. Very soon. In just a moment, Jessie will notice. She will want her parents. She will want to understand. She will ask me all sorts of questions I cannot yet fathom. How will I answer? My mind flies ahead – weeks, months, years. She will want to know things I will never be able to explain to her. Perhaps it will not even be me that she is asking. Perhaps she won't know me then. But right now, right now, today, it will be me she looks to, it will be me, because in just a moment she will pull back from our embrace and ask me the first, necessary, impossible question – where are her parents?

Except…

That question is not, in fact, impossible.

That question, I realise slowly, is actually OK.

Because that question I can answer.

The train may already be moving. It may be too late to board, or get off, to reach for a passing platform. But I know exactly where Cassius and Nola are going. Or will do soon.

There is a turquoise bracelet in Jessie's bag. On the train. In Nola's hands. And there is an app on my phone that Cassius himself installed. And there is an interested guard standing next to me.

CHAPTER 33

We meet at a hotel – Cassius, Nola, Patrick, Dylan and me. Neutral ground.

It is two days after the train commotion. Two days after their arrest in the Fullerton hotel they'd ducked into to evade detection – tracked down, at last, by my bracelet. Two days since things were decided.

It was Patrick's suggestion. He was with me when the call from the police came and listened in to what they told me: Cassius's jumbled, hurried defence – that he had arranged to leave Jessie with me; that it had been planned, organised; that we'd all simply got confused at the station. I was confused. The local precinct didn't seem to know anything about Jessie having gone missing, and quickly I rowed this conversation back. Because of course. None of it had been real. Except in my head, except in the excruciating delusion Cassius had created for me. The police would think I was crazy. For the moment, Cassius and Nola were being remanded in Fullerton, and Jessie was home with us, but now the officers had some questions for me. They were on their way.

"We can't let them take her," Patrick had proclaimed immediately. "We can't leave her to be raised by Cassius and Nola. What kind of sick parents could use their child like they have? How could he have staged her death? How could they both have left her? How could he have done what he did to you? What kind of life will she have with people like that?"

"We won't let them take her," I'd said. "We'll just tell the police what really happened. I'll explain it all."

"It's hard to explain," Patrick had warned.

By now, I'd confessed it to him, all of it, all of what I knew, trying to piece the parts together, trying not to let Jessie hear. She was in bed now, and Patrick had said that he understood – my fear, my dilemma, my desire to tell the truth, in the end. But in his tone there lingered a wrath-wrapped wound, and he was right; there was a danger I would not be believed. After all my deceit, all the lies I told Patrick, it was amazing to me that even he believed such a tale, but then that was Patrick. At last I saw this fully – the way he had refused to believe that I was OK, the way he had known me well enough to see that I wasn't, the worry that had made him follow Cassius and me to the station, even when I'd given him so many reasons to no longer care.

"Besides, the truth could make Jessie's situation worse," he'd cautioned, caring again.

"What do you mean?"

"Well, she'll be taken into care, won't she? If the police think she's been deserted by her parents, they won't just leave her here. Cassius and Nola will be jailed for abandonment, or for fraud once you explain about the money, and you're not her relation, or her guardian, are you? So she'll be put in care, and who knows what that will be like? The kids I coach don't always come out of that so well."

The weight of this thought had pressed against my lungs.

"Then," he'd continued, "at some point, Cassius and Nola will get out, and Jessie will be sent back to them. And on it will go. She'll be used and abandoned and let down, and put in and out of care. I've seen it so many times before."

"But then what?" I'd asked him.

"Well… You could let them go."

"Let them go? What do you mean?"

"I mean, you could not prosecute. You could corroborate Cassius's story. And you could let him go, with Nola, and with the money, like he was doing. And we could keep Jessie."

"We?"

We hadn't broached this yet: his hurt; my lies.

"I hope there'll be a 'we'," he'd answered solemnly. "But no, you're right, for now, this is a choice for you. You have to choose for you."

And so, I'd chosen. Quickly, because it had to be quick. Because my mother wasn't there to ask, and I couldn't consult Cassius. Quickly, because the police were arriving soon, and I had to either challenge Cassius's defence or not. Because I had to chase my seven million or not. Because I had to tell the truth or not. Quickly, without internal analysis, or obsession or meticulous planning. Quickly, I had to trust myself. Or not. And so I'd chosen. I'd chosen Jessie.

My body shook as I did so, confusion and panic and self-doubt still upon me – could I be a mother? Was it right for her? Would a child be safe? But I chose to take the leap, to start fresh, to believe that was possible. I didn't care about the money. It sounds crass, naïve, privileged, but I knew I didn't need it. I could always write a new show, make more. That part of myself was no leap at all, that part of myself never wanted to be snuffed out, that part I have always trusted.

Patrick and Dylan flank me at the table. We are in the lobby of a hotel on the beachfront where LA elites meet for working breakfasts and tourists lounge by the pool. Cassius chose the location, a last taste of Hollywood. Sour, I hope. Jessie is back at daycare, not yet aware of the turn her life is taking. She skipped in happily this morning, eager to see the carers and friends she had missed, but when I dropped her off, a mild panic entered my lungs.

"Perhaps we shouldn't leave her," I'd whispered to Patrick.

But he'd squeezed my hand. "She has to feel secure and do the things that feel normal."

He was right, and I'd nodded. Still, I'd instructed the staff not to allow anybody else to collect her, only to release her to me.

There'd been some questioning glances at that request. "Not her father?" one of them had clarified.

But I'd been firm. "No. Not him."

Not him.

I cannot quite swallow Cassius's deception. I cannot yet untangle the sticky mess of it or feel the ways in which it will continue to bind. I can only think again and again of the history of him – hurt and floppy-haired, lying in the sand; hot and insistent, lips against mine; raw on stage; then slipping from me in a fog of adolescence and substances unknown. My everything, once. The person I trusted more than any other, pulling me from icy waves. How could he have done this? Not him.

Not him.

Patrick and Dylan sit tall, their backs braced to convey full stature. All of our eyes are trained towards the door, waiting for Cassius and Nola to enter. My heart races, my palms are wet. Dylan pats my arm. I half-expect him to produce a napkin for the two of us to hide beneath.

"I knew he was up to something, I knew it," Dylan had decried when he returned from San Francisco to the tumbling shock of it all. "That's why you never sleepwalked when I was waiting up. He was making it up the whole time."

Despite the magnitude of Cassius's dishonesty, only when Dylan spoke these words had it occurred to me that this might be true. Before that, I had thought the lie was only that I'd taken Jessie, it hadn't entered my mind that there might have been no sleepwalking at all. I want to ask Cassius this before he leaves. I need to know. After all those weeks of anxiety, I need to know the extent of my unravelling. Of course, there are other things to discuss too – he must give me legal guardianship of Jessie, we must make plans for his and Nola's future contact with her – but we have agreed most of this already on the phone. It is only this last thing, this truth, that I will demand of him fresh, today.

And all the other truths too.

I realise this abruptly, but yes, I need them. I need to know the exact point at which the things I believed became fantasy. As I sit between my brother and my fiancé, my mind flies to all of the *un*truths I have now discovered: that Cassius knew about his mother's affairs, that his wife never died. Did he ever go to Bristol? Was there ever anything real between us? Was it all a fiction?

Through polished glass, I see a taxi pulling up and Cassius and Nola step onto the hotel's perfect paving. Nola is clad sharply in a tight-fitting dress, attired for battle. Cassius, behind sunglasses, puts his arm around her waist. Together, they saunter towards the lobby, Cassius casually palming a dollar into the hand of the doorman. Already, they are playing the part of a happy, wealthy couple, and they do it so convincingly. So easily. Cassius is, as ever, magnetic. "Here we go," breathes Patrick. And I should be steeling myself too, I should be angry and resolved and ready for combat. But suddenly, watching Cassius stride in, a debilitating panic rushes through my gut. Because all at once it occurs to me that he might not only be playing a part, he might be playing *us*, again. He might be acting, still. Lying, still. What if he has no intention of keeping our agreement? What if he has squirrelled the money away somewhere untraceable, and has told the police another lie? That I am trying to kidnap his daughter, perhaps? What if the police are already here, in the hotel, waiting? Waiting for me. I have just told the daycare staff not to release Jessie to her father – what will that look like? Frantically, I glance around the lobby, searching for anybody who might be an official undercover, but Patrick takes my hand. "You are ready for this," he whispers, not understanding my concern. "Don't let him rattle you. You were always stronger than him." And then, before I can explain, Cassius and Nola reach our table.

"Hi," says Cassius.

Despite everything that Patrick, Dylan and I have been

going over for the past two days, despite all the things that have incensed and hurt us, despite the tears from my mother down the phone, and all that we want to say, all that we have practised saying – none of us reply. There is something about the fact of Cassius, his presence, sitting there, in the same body we have known, the same face, the same person, that casts everything he has done as, somehow, unbelievable. He is still him. He is Cassius. But who is that really? I no longer feel that I know. Again, my eyes scan the room.

Meanwhile, Nola perches proud next to him. For once, she has little to say. Not hello, not an attempt to explain, or justify. Not an apology. Her mouth is set in stony defiance, like Cassius's mother. She will not be judged for her mendacity, for her duplicity, for her abandonment – her clear disdain for motherhood. I can see this in her face without her even speaking – the indignation, as though to judge her is to condemn her simply for not putting motherhood first, as though all she has done is shun an outmoded maternal stereotype, as though she is the feminist, the first woman, the first wife, and we the misogynists trying to cage her.

Cassius wears it differently. He runs his hand through his hair. He takes deep, fortifying breaths. His eyes dart uneasily between ours, and then around the lobby. This unnerves me again – who is he searching for, are the police here? Finally, his eyes settle on mine.

"Are the police here?" he asks me.

I am taken aback. The police? He thinks *I've* called the police? Here we are, symbiotic still, our distrust entwining where our limbs once did. But why? Why does he think I would call the police, now, after corroborating his story? What does he think I'm trying to do? Entrap him, perhaps. Catch him red-handed, making the trade – seven million for his daughter. Or maybe the question is a challenge, a trick – he *has* arranged for the police to be here and asks me now only to see if I've realised it yet, if I've cottoned on to his ploy, his triumph. My chest tightens. I search for the goading in his voice. Surely this is it. Because this is what we have always done to each other. Teased. Goaded. Challenged.

I respond the only way I can. "I don't know. Have you called them?" As I say this, my eyes continue to dart as apprehensively as his, but there is a venom to my tone, more than I knew I had. I am goading him now, or so it sounds.

"Why would I do that?" he retorts.

Challenge. Goad.

What's next? Confession?

Patrick and Dylan look to me. They have caught on now to my fear, my worry, but they shake their heads. No. I must not reveal it. If he hasn't plotted this already, then I must not give him ammunition. Ideas.

"Why would you do any of this, Cassius?" I reply quietly.

Now, Cassius runs his hand through his hair again. Years and endless moments flash before me. The men at my side are physically restraining themselves from lurching across the table and yanking that well-fondled hair off his head, but the agreement was to let me handle things. Cassius ignores their daggers and fixes his gaze on mine. There is remorse within it. He knows. He knows that I know – the way his parents treated him, the worse way he is treating Jessie, what that means.

And he has no answer. Nothing real. Nothing good enough.

"I couldn't find work," he tries. "We were broke – you know I'm no good broke. And I saw you accepting your award. I knew you could afford it."

"But why not just ask me for help?" I say. "I would have helped."

"Like you helped before?"

Nola leans in. "You ghosted him, darling. You were a cold, selfish bitch. What did you expect him to do?"

Cassius throws Nola a warning glance, and she sits back, but he doesn't correct her. Instead, he looks at me defiantly. "I do deserve some reward, Lilith. I made you who you are. I kept you together." Nola nods him on – they have practised saying things too – and emboldened, Cassius raises his voice. "And you… You stole my dream."

Now, Dylan scoffs, unable to contain himself any longer. "Lilith made her own life, you leech. She didn't need you. She deserves everything she built. If you had an ounce of nobility in you, you'd return the money and be glad you're not in jail."

At this, Nola smiles sardonically, and I put my hand on Dylan's arm. Dylan is blinded by his own goodness, but there is no chance of Cassius exchanging the money for our silence. That was never going to be the deal. It is the money, for Jessie.

"What about Jessie?" I ask him.

At the mention of her name, a sadness seeps into Cassius's frame. Despite everything he has done, he loves her, I know this, she is the family he always wanted, and for a moment I hesitate. Am I doing the right thing? Should she not remain with him? In the silence, I glance around. And Cassius glances around too. Both of our eyes darting. Again, my breath catches in my chest. I am still not sure if he has something planned. They have promised they will leave Jessie, but I am waiting for somebody to jump out and tell me it's not over, the nightmare is not over, and that she will disappear. And so may I. Biting my cheek, I wonder if I will ever be able to trust or relax again. Still, I force myself to breathe deeply, to breathe, to breathe. To wait for his answer.

Finally, it is Nola who speaks: "She wasn't planned, you know. I was very young. And she's our daughter, of course, but… We think she will do better with you."

Cassius looks at Nola uncomfortably but doesn't contradict her. I wait, that old trick of my mother's, silence sometimes the best response, a way to exact more. It works as always, and eventually, Cassius looks back to me.

"I love her," he says. "We love her. We do want her."

Truth? Lies? I test him.

"Return the money then, and you can take her," I say. "I won't tell the police what you've done. I won't tell them anything. We'll let you go." As I speak, I feel Patrick's body tensing. But I have to know. I have to know if I am sinning. I cannot live with another sin. "I know you love her, Cassius. I know you want a family. And I won't stand in your way, I promise, so long as you return my money. It's your choice. Choose."

And so he does.

Now, I allow Patrick to take over. There is a document he's had prepared assigning legal guardianship of Jessie to me. There will be further steps needed, and the presence of a lawyer, but this is the start. Cassius hands the bundle to Nola who slips it into her bag. Next, Patrick runs through the agreement, printed in black-and-white: they are to leave California, they are not to visit without warning, they are not to see Jessie unaccompanied, but they are encouraged to stay in touch. Communication should go through Patrick.

Once the business is done, Nola stands up and Cassius follows, but I lift my hand to stay him. As I do this, again Cassius glances around the lobby, and I see how afraid he remains that he will be intercepted. Finally, my own anxiety recedes. Cassius has the money, he has what he wants, he is not plotting more. But I hope he will always feel a little like this – watched, observed, seen without seeing. Like walking in one's sleep. "The truth," I say to him now, simply. "Before you go, tell me the truth. Tell me all of it. Tell me what you did."

That truth, it turns out, was that Cassius had manufactured everything. Dylan was right – I had never started sleepwalking again at all. They were stories only, that Cassius had sowed meticulously, carefully, remembering the past, remembering our childhoods, my sojourns at night, the useful blankness that plagued me afterwards. He had invented the left-out knife. He had planted the sand. He had encouraged me to tell everybody, proof of his fiction. He had watched me spiral – and cared, he said, and hated it, he said, but needed it. Needed it. So he had met with Nola. He had used Jessie. He had contrived it all. A slow, drip-fed lie. A stunning performance. His finest.

And he was sorry.

He says this, finally, once, as we part. *"I'm sorry, Lil."*

A truth, I think, though I no longer believe him.

"Did you go to Bristol?" I ask him abruptly. "Were you ever at Bristol university? Or were you at UWE?"

Cassius's face clouds, surprised, not expecting this. "How did you know?"

But I only shake my head, glancing at Dylan. "It wouldn't have mattered."

"I know."

"Then why?"

"I don't know."

"So many lies," I say.

He nods. "I lied about my mother too. You might as well know. She never had cancer. We spent the summer here in LA because she and Dad were fighting."

It takes me a moment to process this. It is so long ago, so irrelevant now. So trivial compared to what has just occurred. And yet, I had felt so sorry for Cassius back then. Sorry for Marianne, even. I'd done his homework for him, and worried about him, and waited for him. And worried about my own parents and their lack of immortality. It had had an impact. "Why didn't you just tell me about your parents?" I ask.

"I don't know. It was hard."

I nod. "But it was me."

"Some things," he says, "are still better unsaid."

I don't agree. Nothing has ever been better when I've kept the truth inside. Nothing has ever been better wrapped tight in deception. I have not been better. I have not been well at all.

"I wrote you a part on *Moles*," I whisper, leaning in. "A good one. It's filming next month. Such a shame you won't be able to make it. I've always believed in your talent, you know. I've always believed in you."

At once, Cassius's face falls. Regret filters across it. Now he is really sorry. He hovers. But there is no turning back, he knows this. And he lowers his head. Vulnerable. Beaten. Raw.

It is ridiculous, but I want to comfort him. Closure, perhaps, one final time. I lean in again, not whispering this time, but looking him hard in the eyes, catching the vigour of them, just as they were across the baggage reclaim all those years ago. And earnestly, I give him the last help I can. "I will love Jessie," I tell him. "I will love her. She will be safe, and she will be loved."

Now, Cassius coughs, stifling tears. But behind him, Nola calls his name – the doorman has a taxi waiting, she is ready.

Cassius lifts his head. He returns his sunglasses to his face. He runs his hand through his hair. "I know that, Lil," he says softly. "I know that. You have morals the size of America." And with jazz hands, he smiles.

CHAPTER 34

June tells me that it will take time.

Time, for the nightmares to stop.

Time, for the panic attacks to subside.

Time, for Patrick to trust me again.

Time, for Jessie to adjust.

Time, for us all to move on.

It has been eight months now. Cassius and Nola have not been in touch, though frequently my mind drifts into imaginings of ways and places they might reappear. I still cannot believe that any of it happened. I cannot believe that Cassius would trade Jessie, that he would choose the money. I cannot believe that he who longed for family, or said he did, was in the end more lured by the lifestyle he lost, the wealth his own parents spoiled him with, literally, and then snatched away.

"So what do you believe?" June asks me.

I am still trying to sort my beliefs from the fiction. It is so difficult to unravel. All those days of believing I had killed a child. All those weeks of anxiety about sleepwalking again. All those returning tricks of the mind, obsessions threatening, compulsions creeping in, reminders of a darkness I'd thought was far behind.

"I believe he is sorry," I tell June.

"You give him too much credit," she replies, a rare meandering from neutrality.

Jessie asks less and less about her father. Nola seems almost forgotten, although I know that is unlikely. Perhaps Jessie senses my apprehension, perhaps she sees my fear, perhaps she knows how much I both do and do not wish to replace her mother. I have determined to tell her only good things. When Nola and Cassius came to say goodbye to her, and to sign the papers transferring guardianship, they explained that they were having to travel, for a long time, and that it was better for her to stay put with me. They didn't say that they would be back, and she hadn't asked this of them. She had nodded, and hugged them, and hadn't seemed to mind at first. We had our routine, our things that we liked to do together, and she benefited from tuned-in adults at daycare, and Patrick taking an extra interest, and then the summer holidays and a trip to England where she saw Dylan again and met my parents who almost suffocated her with love, and she began to piece together a chain of people who she viewed as her tribe, her family, that essential thing. I am at the fore of that. I am her person, her everything, the one who holds her history, the one whose arms she runs to, whose name she calls, whose bed she sleeps in.

I had to let her sleep with me. She was scared, and she was three. I was scared too, but I was older. An adult. Who no longer sleepwalked, I reminded myself again and again. Who hadn't for years. Who had to get over it.

I repeat this to myself every day. *Get over it. You do not need to fear yourself. You are capable of protecting a child. You do not sleepwalk. You are not out of control.*

"Ah, control," says June, often. "That is what we need to get to."

I am working on it. With June. With Patrick too.

"You are not that powerful," Patrick likes to joke, when

he sees me jotting down a Post-it. "Even if you keep it in your head, you can't make it happen." He grins. "Go on, try. Think: *Patrick is going to make me breakfast. Patrick is going to make me breakfast. Patrick is going to make me breakfast.* Anything? See, unfortunately you cannot control the world."

I laugh. But I put many of my thoughts onto paper and I do make them happen. On the screen. I am working on another new show. It has already been picked up by the network. There is a little girl in it. She is adopted. I watch Jessie carefully.

Sometimes these days, there are moments when she will go quiet, or seem angry – determinedly, inexplicably angry – and there is nothing I can do to pull her out of it. She is talking to a therapist too, a recommendation of June's. We are all aware that we must be attuned to hidden hurts, to what those can do. While I wait for Jessie outside her therapist's office, I read up on psychology. My mother is visiting, and helping – we talk for a long time about child development, about traumas, about me, and her, and Jessie. My mother adores Jessie, and the feeling is mutual. She says perhaps she and my father will think about splitting their time between California and England. Now that Dylan is flying the nest, perhaps it is time for them to be intrepid again. I hope they will. I am ready for it, ready for the return of people from my childhood. Ready for this third incarnation of myself. Of Lilith. Who does not, after all, have to abandon motherhood in order to be free. I think about this often – the false fight between the maternal and the independent self, Eve versus Lilith, the lessons of my long-ago professor. And I feel the two states coalescing now, dancing in a way I'd never imagined, carving out a new condition, stronger than their parts. I wear my hair loose again, with a lip of red.

Jessie would love for my parents to move here too. She hasn't yet met Jade, but she's coming for Christmas. Her favourite person to see, however, is Madge.

Madge doesn't live on her alley any more. She tells Jessie it is because her palace is finally finished, and when we see her next, she is wearing clean clothes, and she has brushed her hair, and she seems more regal than ever. She confesses to me, however, that the alley is frightening to her now. Even with her back to the wall, she hadn't seen her assailant. Although she had seen Cassius, planting Jessie's bucket on the beach, minutes beforehand. He had come over to speak to her when she called out, he had joked and parried, and held court seamlessly. "But anyway," she told me, "my daughter has reappeared, and she wants me to live with her. Go figure." She still hasn't told me what happened with her daughter, what broke them, what mended things. But Madge lives now in Santa Barbara. Jessie and I drive up there every few weeks, with shells and cupcakes.

On the journey home, Jessie sleeps in the back. Sometimes Patrick is with us, and we fight over who gets to transfer her to her bed. He likes the warmth of her arms around him. He doesn't say this, but I see him breathing her in, and he looks at me differently when he returns downstairs. I know what he is imagining, because it is what I imagine too – our own children, our future. We still need time, time, but I believe we will get there.

"I believe I'll get there," I tell June, who nods an affirmation.

Although, I am learning, I don't even need her affirmation. Because I am awake now, not sleepwalking.

Awake, I choose things with purpose.

Awake, I write, and make my imaginings real.

Awake, even in the dark, there is a warm body next to me, tucked safe beneath covers, defying the demons, knocking on Eden.

And in the light of paradise: I skate. I surf. I balance. I run forwards.

Sometimes, I still stop at the pier and look out at it all. Sometimes I kick off my shoes and stride into the icy water. Sometimes I close my eyes and stand there: allowing the waves to whip to my knees; recalling frozen memory – Cassius pulling me from another sea, saving me, hurting me, saving me again; remembering how maternal I felt for Dylan as a child, and feared harming him, and feared myself; recalling the warmth of my parents' house, the smell of the allotments, the pull of the stage, the gift of my notepad; letting the visions come, allowing them, all of them, the innocence, the bleakness, the gasp for freedom, the journey of it; letting it all wash with the waves over me, through me, off me; feeling the sun on my face; feeling the sand between my toes; feeling the sway of the water, and of the world. Of presence. Of being. Feeling the wonder of being. Of being there. Here. Now.

ACKNOWLEDGEMENTS

The premise for this book was sparked by a memory from my childhood, and the fear it induced. Thankfully, unlike for Lilith, that emotion didn't become chronic or debilitating. But I would like to thank those people close to me who shared their personal insights into OCD and other aspects of mental health. Their knowledge and experience greatly informed this story.

I would also like to thank those who read early versions of the manuscript and gave such valuable feedback – Geraldine Wayne, Zeb Wayne, Olivia Wayne (there's a Wayne theme here), Naomi Gryn, Anna Seymour, and Rachel Rushbrook. I am indebted to my agent Eve White, and to the Legend Press team, particularly my wonderful editor Cari Rosen whose careful readings and suggestions have made this a much better book. Also to Ross Dickinson for his enormously appreciated pedantry.

Finally, thank you to my husband James, and to my family – Jeff, Geraldine, Anna-Marie, Zeb, Joab, Damian and Olivia, as well as the extended Wayne and Kattan tribe – for their continued love and support. Most especially, as ever, my children – Audrey, Alice and Elijah – who inspire me every day.